Katherine Johnson was born in Brisbane, Australia, in 1971. She has a Bachelor of Arts (Journalism) and holds an honours degree in marine science. Katherine now lives in Tasmania with her husband and two children, and has worked as a science journalist for a government marine research agency. Her non-fiction articles have been published internationally.

Pescador's Wake, which won a HarperCollins Varuna Award for Manuscript Development in 2007, is her first novel.

Pescador's Wake

Katherine Johnson

FOURTH ESTATE • *London, New York, Sydney* and *Auckland*

Fourth Estate
An imprint of HarperCollins*Publishers*

First published in Australia in 2009
by HarperCollins*Publishers* Australia Pty Limited
ABN 36 009 913 517
www.harpercollins.com.au

HarperCollins*Publishers*
25 Ryde Road, Pymble, Sydney, NSW 2073, Australia
31 View Road, Glenfield, Auckland 0627, New Zealand
1–A, Hamilton House, Connaught Place, New Delhi – 110 001, India
77–85 Fulham Palace Road, London, W6 8JB, United Kingdom
2 Bloor Street East, 20th floor, Toronto, Ontario M4W 1A8, Canada
10 East 53rd Street, New York NY 10022, USA

National Library of Australia Cataloguing-in-Publication data:

Johnson, Katherine Jane, 1971–
  Pescador's wake : a novel / Katherine Johnson.
  ISBN: 978 0 7322 8826 6 (pbk.)
A823.4

Cover design by Darren Holt, HarperCollins Design Studio
Cover images: woman © JupiterImages Corporation; wheelhouse and sea scene by
Austral Fisheries; paint texture by shutterstock.com/Joerg Hausmann
Author photograph © Lea Crosswell
Internal design by Agave
Patagonian toothfish illustration © Peter Gouldthorpe
Typeset in 11/18 Minion Pro by Kirbyjones
Printed and bound in Australia by Griffin Press
70gsm Bulky Book Ivory used by HarperCollins*Publishers* is a natural, recyclable
product made from wood grown in sustainable forests. The manufacturing processes
conform to the environmental regulations in the country of origin, Finland.

5 4 3 2 1   09 10 11 12

For Craig, L and C

Tasmania
Explore the possibilities

This novel was assisted through Arts Tasmania by the Minister for Tourism, Arts and the Environment.

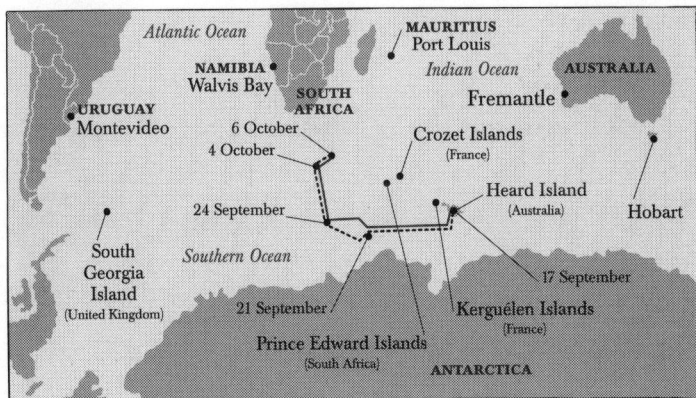

Atlantic Ocean

MAURITIUS
Port Louis

NAMIBIA
Walvis Bay

Indian Ocean

AUSTRALIA

SOUTH
AFRICA

Fremantle

URUGUAY
Montevideo

6 October

4 October

Crozet Islands
(France)

24 September

Heard Island
(Australia)

Hobart

South
Georgia
Island
(United Kingdom)

Southern Ocean

17 September

21 September

Kerguélen Islands
(France)

Prince Edward Islands
(South Africa)

ANTARCTICA

————— Route of the *Australis*

----------- Route of the *Pescador*

Nautical Miles

0   2000

2000

Kilometres

'Beyond 40 degrees south there is no law ...
Beyond 50 degrees south there is no God.'

A MARINER'S SAYING

And now the STORM-BLAST came, and he
Was tyrannous and strong:
He struck with his o'ertaking wings,
And chased us south along.

With sloping masts and dipping prow,
As who pursued with yell and blow
Still treads the shadow of his foe,
And forward bends his head,
The ship drove fast, loud roared the blast,
And southward aye we fled.

And now there came both mist and snow,
And it grew wondrous cold:
And ice, mast-high, came floating by,
As green as emerald.

FROM *THE RIME OF THE ANCIENT MARINER*,
SAMUEL TAYLOR COLERIDGE

LOGBOOK OF EDUARDO RODRÍGUEZ TORRES, FIRST MATE, *PESCADOR*

∽

It's broad daylight as I stand on deck, but there is no sunlight two thousand metres beneath the sea where our hooks prowl in the dark.

I am a fisherman, but I know little of this other world — the abyss. No one does. It is the largest and least known environment on Earth. I've heard that it's so dark at the bottom of the sea that life must make its own light. It must survive the enormous weight of water above it, and be prepared for near-starvation.

I saw a documentary before this trip, footage taken by men in a submersible and shown for the first time on television. It made me want to write, not fish, to glimpse this other world. To proclaim its magnificence, not plunder its depths. Perhaps even to begin my book … Out of the blackness, bizarre torches shone from the heads of angler fish, and bands of flickering cilia radiated rainbows of light down the outsides of jewel squid and jellyfish. Tiny beacons adorned hatchet fish in patterns that disguised their shape, fooling predators. Flashes of phosphorescence created nocturnal firestorms. The oversized, needle-sharp teeth of viper fish held fiercely onto meals that came by only rarely, and gulper eels with distendable stomachs swallowed prey larger than themselves. Giant sea spiders patrolled the seafloor alongside armoured isopods that resembled military tanks.

I close my eyes, blocking out the sun, and try to picture this alien realm at the outer limits of man's reach, where our longlines rob the Southern Ocean — the sea's last great wilderness — of its last hidden treasure.

A Patagonian toothfish — the size of a german shepherd dog — rests, ripe with eggs, on the fine mud of the deep sea's floor. She lies in a groove carved into the seabed by deep ocean currents. If you could see her, you would wonder why her vanishing species attracts such high prices in the best restaurants of New York and Tokyo; why we fishermen have risked our lives in leaking pirate fleets, traversing the planet's wildest seas, to arrive here at the ends of the earth in pursuit of such an unlikely prize.

She is ugly. Her gross underbite and black lips, pierced with hooks from earlier failed fishing attempts, hide teeth that feast on inky squid. Eyes perch atop a flattish head, gazing upwards, for the entire world is above you when you inhabit the base of the ocean. But it is what lies beneath her dark grey leather that is so determinedly sought: her thick, white, firm flesh that, no matter how it is cooked, is always moist, always sweet.

The toothfish ascends now, chasing the scent of squid.

There is more food than usual today. An endless procession of baited hooks drops from above.

Through her skin, she senses an unfamiliar, distant thrum — our engine working overhead — but she is more interested in the vibrations she has detected at a closer range. An ambush predator, she darts forward at five metres per second before fastening her jaws around her prey. The frozen squid catches in her throat. She rams ahead only to be drawn back. She shoots forward again but the hook has taken. She fights, but without effect.

Along the mainline there are countless shorter lines, each with a hook five centimetres long; fifteen thousand hooks in total. The large female — the largest fish in the school; at thirty-five years of age a grandmother many times over — is in good company. Thousands more toothfish hang like macabre jewels from a thread of necklace. They are hauled up and onto the deck as the line is wound in. Hooks are cut. Fish are skidded along wet metal and down to the factory deck for immediate processing. The large female is brought up and out of the water. She glimpses dark faces and bad weather.

We are not supposed to be here.

~

CARLOS
The *Pescador*
17 September 2002

Carlos Sánchez Rocha looks up from the radar and out to sea, first through binoculars and then with naked eyes. It always makes him nervous, the calm before the storm. Petrels are feeding on the surface, diving and harpooning slender fish with infinite precision. White clouds are reflected on the sides of waves. From the weather faxes, the Uruguayan fishing master knows that in a few hours all of this will change.

He calls out to his crew in Spanish over the ship's intercom. 'Now! Bring the line in now. There's another front coming. We could lose the lot.' His deep voice crackles in the air above the deck, large and certain, like a god sending messages on the wind to his men.

His first mate raises an arm in acknowledgment, and the crew begins the long task of winching the fish in. With any luck, the approaching storm will keep patrol vessels away. Carlos watches as the fish are dragged aboard through a gap in the midship rails. He has risked too much to lose this catch to bad weather.

Taped to the wheelhouse wall, on top of peeling paint that has lost its grip after too many voyages to sea, are two photographs. His wife and his daughter. He takes the pictures off the wall and a shiver passes through his body, as if he has touched the Antarctic continent itself. He sometimes feels that he loves his family too much. They make him vulnerable. More so than any storm the Southern Ocean can throw at him. He reminds himself that he is fishing for them. For their future.

In the first photograph, Julia is looking directly at the camera. Carlos finds himself smiling back at the woman he fell in love with when they were just teenagers, almost a decade ago. He wishes he could contact her, but knows he must be patient. The satellite call could be traced.

He studies the picture. Julia is wearing her favourite dress — white cotton with a red floral print. The fine straps have fallen from her shoulders and her smooth brown hair, bleached gold from the summer sun, shimmers in the half-light of a wooden building, perhaps a boatshed. He didn't ask his wife who took the photograph but whoever it was must have known her well. She has that particular warm glint in her eyes that she reserves for only a few. Carlos remembers finding the picture tucked away under a sea of unpaid bills, the day before this fishing trip. It was with a letter Julia was sending to her parents, but he managed to convince her that he needed the photograph more. 'They'll be seeing you sooner than I will. It's only fair,' he said as he stroked her hair and kissed her mouth, missing her before he even left port. He fed the picture between the heavy pages of his logbook, not giving her the chance to argue.

Carlos looks at the other photograph. It was taken at their daughter's fifth birthday, just a couple of months ago. María has her mother's wide smile and dark, almond eyes. He and Julia are on either side of their daughter, kissing her face and being pushed apart by her smile. His forearm is protectively across his wife's swollen belly. They're a handsome trio, soon to become four.

He pulls his woollen beanie further down over his forehead, just as Julia did when she kissed him and said goodbye at Montevideo Harbour five weeks ago. She had stayed up late the night before, knitting the hat after seeing the old one stiff and frail from salt.

'*Te quiero*, Carlos Sánchez,' she said before he boarded the *Pescador*, her lips brushing warmly against his freshly shaven face. Carlos remembers the gentle weight of her hands then running across the bulk of his chest and down his arms made strong from a life of fishing.

'I love you too,' he replied, gripping her fingers and then finally letting go.

'Be careful,' she called out as he walked up the gangway. 'We want you back.'

Carlos touches the photograph through well-worn gloves before looking back out to the frozen deck and his crew. The ocean would make even the largest of men feel small, he thinks. His father and grandfather braved the sea in boats a fraction of this size. But it was different then. They fished close to the coast with nets, catching just enough to supply the local markets. This is the Southern Ocean, the wildest mass of water on the planet.

He scratches his jaw, itchy from a new beard caked with salt. Beneath the stubble, his skin is dark from years of exposure to the sun. His lips are full, but cracked from the weather, and his thick, black hair is pulled into a short, rugged ponytail, which protrudes from under the hand-knitted beanie and sits over the hood of his polar fleece. A small silver stud pierces his earlobe, just visible below the woollen hat.

Carlos returns his attention to the radar and scans for patrol boats. In these rich waters off the subantarctic islands — all of them owned by other nations — there's always a risk they'll be caught. He calculates the *Pescador* is one hundred and fifty nautical miles from Heard Island, squarely within Australian territorial waters. Fishing here in broad daylight is brazen, but he knows it will shorten the trip by a couple of weeks. The alternative was to try to locate the toothfish clustered around Southern Ocean seamounts — those submerged deep-sea volcanoes whose surrounding waters are rich in upwelled nutrients — or, despite Uruguay being a signatory to the Convention for the Conservation of Antarctic Marine Living Resources, to head south into the perils of the ice. How much easier if they could still catch toothfish along the continental slopes off Patagonia, where the species was commercially discovered only in recent decades, but those grounds offer a fraction of their original bounty. If they can just get this last line in without being spotted, they can leave the Southern Ocean in their wake and begin the four-week journey home via Mauritius, where they will unload the catch.

He thinks of the *Sevilla*, another in *Señor* Migiliaro's lucrative fleet of ten, and of the decision her master took to head south to the pack ice. In his last radio call, the master had boasted of massive catches. Carlos had overheard the call, boldly broadcast to the *Sevilla*'s sister ship but audible to all boats in the area. Then there was silence. Perhaps the *Sevilla* had been overloaded, or had hit a rogue wave, or struck an iceberg. Whatever the reason, Carlos knows there will be no search beyond the sister-ship's futile efforts. The authorities won't even be alerted. Not even the families of the thirty-five men on board will be told that their husbands and sons won't be coming home. Migiliaro will keep that news quiet until the last of his fleet has unloaded — until his catch is safely on its way to market and out of his hands. He'll show surprise when the *Sevilla* fails to dock, and issue a statement of sympathy to the families of the missing.

The Spanish owner has plenty more rusting hulks — most of them registered in countries other than his own — to throw at the Southern Ocean. The Uruguayan-flagged *Pescador*, too, is dispensable. If he's caught fishing here illegally, Carlos knows he'll be on his own. Migiliaro will have covered his tracks. His mobile phone will be disconnected, his company address a dead-end. He will ensure that his middlemen, the ones whose names and companies appear on most of the paperwork, will take the fall for him. They will be compensated for their silence. Paid to say Migiliaro had nothing to do with any of this. Like his lost vessel, it will seem that the real owner has simply fallen off the face of the earth. Carlos looks through the wheelhouse window and out to sea. It's time to go home.

He watches as his first mate, Eduardo Rodríguez Torres (a large 'E' painted in black on the back of his orange sea jacket), leaves the deck and climbs the external stairs to the wheelhouse, five metres above where the crew is bringing in the ten-kilometre length of line. Carlos reads his watch. It's noon. By the time the last fish is brought on deck, it will be dark and the storm will be upon them. He urges the boat forward with just enough force to retrieve the line without breaking it.

'We're a few days short of two hundred tonnes,' Eduardo announces, pulling open the wheelhouse door. 'We should stay longer; fill her up completely. No patrol boat's going to be risking their balls this far south with a storm coming.'

'What does that say about us?' Carlos says, laughing. He knows that Eduardo's bravado — his eagerness to pillage these waters — is purely a means to an end. Once they own their own boat, the rules will change.

Carlos senses the subtle changes in the weather, viscerally reading signs that those unaccustomed to the sea would miss.

It is as if the seawater and looming atmosphere are communing with the water and air of his own body. The birds, too, have felt the shift and are starting to leave the building seas for the shelter of the island. Carlos raises his binoculars and scans the ocean for the dark line of water that will signal the edge of the front. It can't be far away.

'Come on, where's your spirit of adventure?' Eduardo persists, slapping Carlos on the back.

'You'll never change will you, *mi amigo*?' A smile folds dry salt deeper into the folds at the corners of Carlos's eyes. Eduardo has always been the one to take the greatest risks, he thinks. As a boy in La Paloma, Carlos remembers him climbing a fence to steal a bike, which he then hid under old nets in his father's boatshed. Eduardo boasted that he rode the bike on the beach at night, flaunting his crime under the sleeping nose of the bike's wealthy owner, who lived on the waterfront. Carlos, always the moderating influence, recalls now how he took it upon himself to secretly return the prize, rescuing his oldest friend from himself.

'Why not get it while we can? We're on a hot spot here,' Eduardo urges. 'And the fish are bigger than the ones Migiliaro's other boats are catching around Crozet and Kerguélen. Just one more day and we won't have to try our luck further south.'

'We've done well enough,' Carlos says, watching his men reel in the excellent catch. He turns his face towards

Antarctica, losing his smile in the distance. He thinks again of the *Sevilla* and the frozen corpses separated from their families forever. 'Migiliaro has already lost one boat. He'd rather we come home with the fish we have on board than have the lot seized because we stayed too long and got caught.'

'To hell with him. If we catch another day's worth here and don't record it, we can sell that too without that bastard ever knowing. We'll be that much closer to getting our own boat and quota. No more illegal shit.' Eduardo pauses at the sight of Carlos's fixed expression.

'Twenty unrecorded tonnes is enough. I'm not risking more. If we're inspected in Mauritius, how long do you think it'll take them to figure out that what's in the log doesn't match what we've got on board?'

'They'd turn a blind eye for a small fee.' Eduardo rubs his fingers together to indicate the bribe.

'Let's just get home.' Carlos shifts his focus back to the photograph of Julia.

Eduardo's eyes, too, linger on the picture.

'You'll thank me when you're back with Virginia, a Pilsen in one hand and a steak I've cooked for you over the *parilla* in the other,' Carlos says, returning Eduardo's earlier slap on the back. It lands heavily on the first mate's shoulder. They've been friends for too long to argue.

Eduardo surrenders a long sigh.

'You know I always value your opinion,' Carlos says, the good-humoured gleam returning to his sideways glance.

'You're just getting old and conservative, but our wives will thank you for heading home now.' Eduardo counts to three, using his fingers, feigning stupidity. 'Carlos, Julia, Virginia … It looks like I'm outnumbered.' He winks and leaves to join the crew.

Carlos again checks the radar and sees another boat enter the field. '¡*Vete al infierno!*' He moves the *Pescador* slowly along the longline while he tracks the course of the new arrival. Perhaps it's just the fishing boat they saw earlier. He watches as toothfish pile, one after the other, onto deck. They are, without a doubt, the largest specimens they've caught so far — plucked from the pit of a world he can barely imagine. 'Freeze the biggest one whole!' Carlos tells the crew over the loudspeaker. 'The owner wants a trophy for his palace wall.' He pictures Eduardo rolling his eyes in response. One of the crew sends the largest toothfish down a chute to the factory deck. Carlos sees him, hands cupped around his mouth, relay the order to the men below.

A black-browed albatross is landed next. Having fallen prey to the baited hooks, the bird has drowned beneath the waves. Eduardo slams his hand against the rail and Carlos knows, from the accompanying flick of the first mate's head, that he is swearing. '¡*Maldito!*' he'd be saying. According to the first mate, it is the male albatross that goes to sea to fish while the female waits at home on the nest. They have one partner for life, Eduardo told him, and Carlos imagines this bird's sole companion waiting now in vain for his return.

Carlos hates to catch seabirds too, but it's a price they pay for longlining hurriedly in daylight like this. He has heard the Australian boats are banned from using longlines here and instead use deep-sea trawls, avoiding the curse of killing an albatross. He watches Eduardo remove the hook expertly and throw the drowned bird to the hungry sea. If the *Pescador* was theirs, they'd do it all differently.

Carlos studies the radar. The other vessel has maintained its course and is headed straight for them. His guts reel. 'Cut the line,' he barks over the loudspeaker. 'We have company.'

He sees Eduardo look up and locate the vessel on the horizon to the north. The first mate shakes his head but follows the instruction, leaning over the rails as the dark shadows of fish on the surface are dragged down by the weight of those below. A wasted catch; a sunken treasure — the five-tonne load spiralling towards the abyss, the fish starving and dying on the discarded hooks. Carlos regards the radar and the approaching vessel. What choice did he have? Another two lines had been set five nautical miles to the east, anchored to the seabed and marked with a GPS buoy. They'd been lucky to retrieve both of those before being spotted. Eduardo will forgive him in time.

With the wind chill, it's minus seventeen degrees Celsius

outside, and ice has formed on the rails. Carlos drives forward the engine control, while half his crew, fifteen men, clean off the decks and stow the gear. The boat surges faster now, heading south towards high seas and the front. The remaining crew has already moved to the factory deck to process and freeze the catch.

The VHF radio crackles and a voice floods the wheelhouse. '*Pescador, Pescador, Pescador,* this is the Australian civil patrol vessel *Australis, Australis.* Do you copy?'

Carlos doesn't reply. If need be, he can claim that communications were down. He strikes the instrument table with his fist. They were so close to getting away with this. So close to heading home. He maintains his southerly course and sees Eduardo making his way back up to the wheelhouse.

The first mate heaves open the door and feeds himself inside. He tears off dripping gloves and unzips his wet-weather jacket exposing a face turned stiff from the cold and the effort of concealing his fear.

The radio starts up again. '*Pescador, Pescador,* this is the *Australis.* You're fishing in Australian territorial waters without authority and we order you to proceed to Fremantle, Western Australia. I repeat, your operations are illegal; proceed to Fremantle.'

'They know our vessel,' Eduardo says, visibly surprised. 'They're too far away to see the name.'

Carlos nods. 'That fishing boat we saw yesterday must have told them we were here. *¡Maldito!*'

'We should have covered our name.'

'And admit guilt?'

'Guilt's only a problem if we're caught.' Eduardo looks away, squinting in the direction of the patrol boat just visible off to port. 'And they'd still have to prove it's their fish we have on board.' He pauses, his expression hardening. 'How far will we take this?'

Carlos lifts the binoculars to his face. There's a line of unlit water only a nautical mile ahead — the front. Dark clouds are amassing above them. Soon the sea will be the same deep metallic colour as the skin of the oily fish being processed below. In minutes they'll be caught between the upward thrust of angry waves and the downward force of a sky unleashing its frozen rain.

'We'll run south until we're free of the government boat,' Carlos says, studying the chart and avoiding Eduardo's eyes, trying to suppress the surge of panic rising in his chest and into his throat. His mouth is acid dry. After a decade of fishing, this is his first trip south and his first time breaking the law. Migiliaro had made it clear that if they were spotted fishing illegally, they must ignore all calls to stop. They must flee, into the ice if necessary. Under maritime law, any high-seas chase must be continuous for a vessel to be successfully prosecuted. Above all, the owner had said, he must not be contacted. If the *Pescador* escapes, Carlos was promised he would be handsomely rewarded. If not, he, alone, would sink — one way or another. 'They won't follow us in this weather and, once the chase is broken, we can't be charged.' He knows they have no choice. If they go to Australia as instructed, they'll be made an example of. They'll lose the catch and the boat, and be fined the value of every fish they have ever caught in their lives. 'Julia's having the baby in a few months,' he continues quietly, almost to himself. 'We have to go home.' He grips the wheel hard, trying to keep his emotions from clouding his judgment as he reads an updated electronic weather chart. The isobars are piling up behind the front.

The Australian master speaks again. '*Pescador, Pescador, Pescador*, you have breached Australia's Fisheries Act and the United Nation's International Law of the Sea by fishing without permission in these waters. We will pursue you. Do you understand?'

'They won't, Look at those clouds. They wouldn't dare,' Carlos says, finally looking his first mate and best friend in the eye. '¡*Vete al infierno!*' he shouts at the vessel on the horizon and hammers the *Pescador* towards the storm.

DAVE
The *Australis*
17 September 2002

'Stupid bloody selfish bastard.' The Australian master spits more saliva than words. Dave Bates doesn't usually wear his heart on his sleeve, but he is angry. The illegal vessel is forcing a chase and threatening his crew. Still, he observes his orders to follow the boat — for now.

The *Pescador*, waving a Uruguayan flag from the stern, is ploughing through the large seas, heading due south. Every now and then, she disappears like a toy behind a wave.

It's September, the maximum extent of pack ice, and while most icebergs will be frozen into the pack, Dave knows he can't rely on it. He keeps his eyes on the radar, and on the seas in front of him. From the number of birds feasting in the *Pescador*'s wake, it's clear the illegals have discarded fish scraps — valuable evidence — from the processing. But he hasn't got time to trawl for that now. Soon it will be dark for twelve hours. He uses the arm of his fleece to wipe a film of nervous sweat from his forehead and upper lip. Harry Perdman, his first mate, hands him a covered mug of coffee, and Dave takes a sip, burning his lips.

'Sorry, mate. Should've warned you,' Harry apologises, behind a careworn smile.

'Least of my worries, Harry.'

Dave's thick, freckled fingers, tug at the red-grey beard forming on his chin. He thinks of Margie, his wife, teasing him every time he returns home from sea: 'If you'd just shave off that atrocious beard, you'd look a decade younger.' But he knows that if she were here now she wouldn't be joking. She'd be spitting chips.

He broke his promise to her the moment he embarked on this chase. The 'hot pursuit', as it's legally known, is his first and, with any luck, will be his last. Since throwing in the towel on his own fishing career, he's been skippering the *Australis* for six months each year on behalf of the Australian Maritime Safety Authority. His main job has been to ensure that vessels don't pose a pollution threat to Australian waters, with the occasional search-and-rescue mission just to keep him on his toes. The last few weeks, however, had been a whole new ball game. The *Australis* had been chartered by Customs and the Australian Fisheries Management Authority to act as a deterrent to illegal fishers. He was to report sightings of suspected illegal fishing activities around Heard and McDonald Islands, three thousand nautical miles southwest of his home in Tasmania. The only contact with foreign boats, he'd been assured, would be a radio call, informing them of their crime. He'd promised Margie he'd stick to his brief. 'Don't go playing cowboys,' she had said. 'You're not the bloody navy.' But what was he supposed to do when the

Fisheries Minister moved the goalposts on him? The naval frigate that was on standby to help out had been called to Timor, leaving just him and the illegal boat and the water between them.

Harry answers a call from the Maritime Operations branch of the Australian Customs Service and hands the phone to Dave.

'It's Roger Wentworth,' Harry says.

Dave silently swears. 'Dave Bates here, Roger.'

'G'day David. I take it our illegals haven't responded.'

'Did you really expect they would?' Dave asks, studying the radar and the illegal boat's plotted course. He continues before Wentworth can answer. 'It looks like they're heading southwest. Further into the weather. We've just crossed a front into a low-pressure system and, to give you an idea, I reckon the seas are building to fifteen metres.'

'That's big then?'

Dave shakes his head in dismay. He imagines Wentworth phoning from a comfortable Canberra office, perhaps doodling a picture on an otherwise blank notepad. Busy work. 'What level of that government office block are you on there, Roger?'

'The fifth …'

'Well imagine being on the street below and having a wave as high as your office hurtling towards you like there's no tomorrow. And then throw in eighty-knot winds!' A large wave strikes the boat side on. 'Shit!'

Dave drops the phone's receiver and switches off the autopilot to use the wheel, the manual helm. He heads the boat directly into the weather.

'Jesus! Harry, take the wheel, mate.' Dave hands over control of the boat and hauls the phone back up by its cord. 'Okay, Roger. I'm back. Bit hard to chat and steer in these conditions.'

'Okay, okay …' Wentworth placates.

'It's not bloody okay. You clearly have no frigging idea.' Dave reads the instruments and watches the boat's speed slow momentarily on the ascent of a wave. He swears again as the *Australis* accelerates off the back of the wall of water. 'Look, in many ways this is a typical Southern Ocean storm. What's not typical, though, is that we're less than twenty-four hours from the pack ice, which I can tell you right now I'm keeping the hell away from.' Dave's words are forced out as the boat hits the bottom of a trough. 'And I'm not keen to rub shoulders with an iceberg down here, either, if it's all the same to you.'

'You're into icebergs already?'

'Anytime now.'

'Well, mate, just keep on top of the illegals for as long as you can.'

Dave cringes at Wentworth's attempt at sounding blokey and familiar. Who does he think he's fooling? But Wentworth perseveres, oblivious. 'They can't keep going south forever. By the way, I've done a search on the boat. *Pescador* means fishermen. No surprises there. Still can't track down the owner though —'

'No surprises there, either.'

'No, well, I'd bet my bottom dollar he's not from Uruguay. But he can't hide behind the bloody flag state forever. Uruguay might be happy to register foreign vessels and then turn a blind eye to their illegal activities, but it doesn't mean we have to let them get away with poaching in our waters. We'll flush them out. And your boat's got a clear advantage. It turns out that while the *Pescador* was built in Vigo, just like ours, *she's* not ice-strengthened.'

'And that's supposed to make me feel better?'

Roger is silent for a moment. 'I'm under instructions from the Customs Minister to not let this one go. And I gather the Fisheries Minister is pretty adamant too.

'Apparently.' He recalls his conversation — just hours ago — with a staffer at the fisheries management authority. Dave had made the call as soon as he sighted the *Pescador* moving slowly, as if bringing in a longline, within Australian waters. The staffer had phoned back with the Minister's answer inside ten minutes: 'Chase them. Don't let them out of your sights.' The Australian master feels the breath of both politicians — two departments — down his neck.

'Well, I know I'm not telling you anything you don't already know, but it's vital under the International Law of the

Sea that the chase is "hot and continuous", to use the lingo. If you break it, we'll have Buckley's of prosecuting this boat. That means keeping the *Pescador* in your sights, or at the very least on your radar. You need to be in constant contact with those bastards. We're setting a precedent here. You could be making history. We need to send a message to all the other illegals out there once and for all.'

'We'll do what we can, but I'm not going to endanger my crew. If things begin to get dicey, I'll have to pull out, or just shadow the buggers from further north. End of story. It's on my head if something goes wrong down here, not yours or either of the flaming Minister's. If they were here right now, I reckon they'd be wishing they were in brown trousers. And it's not exactly blowing my frock up, either!'

Dave hangs up the phone and inspects the weather chart. The centre of the intense low is spiralling just south of them. 'This is madness,' he mutters to Harry. In another month he'll be handing over the reins of the *Australis* to the alternate master and crew and can get back to renovating the latest investment property that he and Margie have bought. Right now he knows what he'd rather be doing.

'Yep, those government types'd be the first to duck for cover in a storm half this size,' Harry says, as he concentrates hard on the seas. At fifty, Harry is as good a seaman as they come. 'The only storms they know about are the storms in their teacups the politicians blow up for them.'

Jack Everett — who they all call Cactus in honour of his prickly personality — enters the wheelhouse and Harry briefs him on Wentworth's satellite call. 'If we know where they're headed, why don't we just arrange for an armed ship to board 'em there?' Cactus asks. 'Why the hell do we have to chase 'em?'

'Once they're in another country's waters, they're off the hook,' Dave says, registering Harry's smirk at the pun. 'It's Law of the Sea stuff, Cactus. You know the deal.' But Dave suspects Cactus has kept his knowledge of international law to a bare minimum. He's a seaman, not a bureaucrat.

'Christ knows what we're s'posed to do when we catch up with the bastards. *We* can't bloody board! What sort of mugs does Canberra think we are? The illegals'll 'ave guns. You can count on it.'

It's the sort of rise Dave has come to expect from Cactus, but the lack of a plan for apprehending the *Pescador* is on the master's mind, too. 'We'll just have to hope for armed assistance if it comes to that.'

'What a bloody joke! We could chase 'em from 'ere to kingdom come, and still not nab 'em. And there'll be another ten boats fishin' out there right now, changin' their fuckin' flag state whenever the hell it suits 'em.' Cactus flattens the palm of his hand across his eyes and presses his fingers and thumb into his temples. 'I've 'ad enough of this bullshit. I'm grabbing some shut-eye, *if* I can manage to stay in me bunk. No doubt you'll want me at the helm later tonight.'

Dave nods and Cactus leaves with an exasperated flick of his hand.

'I'll sit this one out with you,' Harry says. 'Till she blows over a bit.'

Dave gives an appreciative nod and the men fall into a companionable silence. Dave finds himself thinking of Roger Wentworth, who he met briefly last year at a border protection workshop in Hobart. He pictures him regarding the world through his fashionable square-rimmed glasses from the fifth floor of the Australian Customs building. He knows the pen-pusher won't be able to fathom a wave that high. He imagines Wentworth sitting down in a rush of vertigo and taking a sip of herbal tea. But then how could he expect this man to understand what it is like to both love and fear something in the same instant? Wentworth has probably never even been to sea. At sea. No doubt he has only ever seen fishing vessels in port, where they loom like monsters, forty metres long and ten metres high above the water. Out here, it's a different matter. They're almost invisible.

Dave loses the *Pescador* behind a wave. It's uncanny, he thinks, that the two boats — the *Australis* and the *Pescador* — are, in effect, siblings, born of the same Spanish port. Fate has reunited the vessels, both painted red and white, for their toughest journey yet. The *Australis*, he knows, while slow for her size, is at least up to the conditions. The *Pescador*, according to Wentworth, was not built for this.

Dave pictures the chase from the air, and sees the boats as small bath toys knocking about in a foaming tub. He imagines a giant child, like a dispassionate god, creating enormous waves with clumsy hands. The child laughs as the twin boats pitch and roll, silent against the force of the sea, leading each other deeper into trouble.

JULIA
Montevideo, Uruguay
20 September 2002

Julia Pereira de Sánchez stirs a large pot of *ensopado*, leaning over to breathe in the stew's meaty warmth. She looks out through the kitchen window at the solid wall of apartments on the other side of the street. Their square hulls swim in a sea of people and traffic, blocking her view completely. There's no horizon — barely a sky — here on the outskirts of Montevideo's crumbling old town, the Ciudad Vieja. She thinks of Carlos and doubts if their worlds, at this instant, could be further apart. How she would love to trade her claustrophobia for the emptiness of the ocean. In a second she would swap the solidity of concrete, of buildings planted in the ground, for a sea of space.

She watches the cars and buses haul people along her street, taking them either north in the direction of the harbour and the Puerto de Montevideo, only a few minutes' walk from her ground-floor apartment, or east towards the Plaza Independencia, the hub of the city, which separates the old from the brand-spanking new. As she stirs the stew, Julia thinks how much Carlos would enjoy the meal. She hasn't heard from her husband since he made a satellite call from international waters south of Australia over a week ago, and suspects his lack of contact means that he is now fishing illegally off one of the subantarctic islands. She hopes that's all it is.

Julia stretches back, placing her hands in the small of her back and arching against them. With her growing abdomen, standing up for any length of time is a physical challenge. The baby and the fluid around it have tipped her centre of gravity so far forward that she is certain it's only a matter of time before she performs a spectacular belly flop. She can still see her toes, just, but is alarmed at the transformation of her feet. It's as though the extra weight has forced them outward, splayed them wide like a frog's. She thinks of her mother's feet, spread sideways like this, and how the small leather boots she left behind last time she visited still carry the bulging shape of her bunions in loyal memory of their owner. When she tried the boots on last week, Julia was comforted to think that she was, in a sense, slipping inside her mother's skin. She has worn the shoes, which are a perfect fit, every long day since.

With the back of her hand, Julia brushes damp strands of fine, dark hair from her forehead. The steam from the cooking adds to the cramped confines of the apartment, and she lifts her long-sleeved shirt away from where it is sticking to her stretched skin. She goes to change into something cooler and catches sight of herself — ballooning, half naked — in the mirror behind the bedroom door. She stands side-on and is relieved to see that, apart from her enlarged abdomen, she is still slim. She sweeps a hand over her belly and a tiny elbow, or a fist or foot, beats against her drum-like middle, before rolling across her like an internal wave. It makes her laugh, and she gives the baby inside a little nudge with her own hand to say hello.

She puts on a white T-shirt of Carlos's and returns to the kitchen, where the pot is spitting with all the fury of an abandoned wife. The meal is starting to burn, and she quickly gives it another stir with the wooden spoon. With her finger, she collects a sample and decides that she has caught it just in time. The stew will serve María and her well for the next couple of days. How much easier it is to be able to cook again, she thinks, without the sickly cloud of nausea that plagued the early months of the pregnancy. She couldn't have even considered making *ensopado* then without ending up face-down over the toilet. On the calendar she has recorded each day of this pregnancy. Today marks twenty-five-and-a-half weeks, well past the risk of early miscarriage; still not quite out of the woods.

María skips out of her bedroom and into the small kitchen. 'I'm hungry,' she whines, reaching up onto the counter for a carrot stick.

'Well, this will be ready soon, sweetheart. What have you been up to in there?'

'Just drawing,' María says, opening the fridge.

'Can I see?' Julia asks, trying to distract her daughter from snacking before her meal.

'Not yet, I haven't finished.' María shuts the fridge and absconds to her bedroom with an apple.

At least it's healthy, Julia concedes, deciding that she hasn't got the energy to make a fuss. She tosses the last few ingredients into the stew and reaches for her phone book. She finds *Señor* Migiliaro's mobile number, which Carlos wrote inside the front cover for her, and dials it. It's typical, she thinks, that there are no other contact details for the Spanish owner. If one of his boats gets caught fishing illegally, the coward can disappear in a flash like a rat up a drain pipe. No address, no contact number, no accountability. All of the benefits, none of the risk.

'*Hola*,' Migiliaro answers. Julia has only spoken with him once before but recognises his voice: cold and dismissive, as though he is in a hurry to get somewhere and doesn't want to be bothered.

'*Buenos tardes, Señor Migiliaro*. This is Julia Pereira de Sánchez, Carlos's wife … Carlos Sánchez from the *Pescador*.'

'*Si*.'

'I haven't heard from Carlos for a while, and just wanted to know if everything is all right.' Julia resents the way this man makes her feel nervous, and small. The way he risks men's lives for profit, without a second thought.

'As far as I know. *Si*.'

'Well, when did you last hear from him?'

'About a week ago.'

'Me too,' Julia says, her anxiety building. 'Is that unusual?'

'Not necessarily.'

María bursts back into the kitchen, grinning and waving her completed drawing in the air, her half-eaten apple clamped between her teeth. Julia holds her hand up, motioning her to wait.

'Well … can't you reach him somehow? I can't get through.'

'I'll get one of the other boats to make contact. Call me in a day or two and I'll let you know.'

María takes the apple from her mouth and flaps the picture noisily in front of her mother's face. '*Mamá*, look it's *Papá* fishing!' she whoops, jumping up and down and ignoring Julia's finger forming a 'shhhh' across her lips.

Julia hears the clunk of Migiliaro ending the phone call. She returns the handset to the wall and shouts: 'That was important! I said to wait. It was about *Papá*!'

'What about *Papá*? Is he all right? Can I talk to him?' María appears instantly worried and Julia is overcome by guilt and a desire to protect her daughter from the panic that is invading her own body.

'I'm sure he's fine. But we can't talk to him right now. His phone isn't working.' Julia reaches out to hug María but her daughter pulls away, all apple-breathed and huffy tears, withholding her affection with the power of a five-year-old who knows when their mother needs their love. 'Can you show me that picture now?'

María casts her drawing aside in a storm of anger and Julia watches it land face-up at her feet. The drawing is of a large red ship, not a bad representation of the *Pescador*, which is riding high on waves three times its height. There is a person with a sad face in the wheelhouse. It makes Julia shiver. Beneath the boat, María has drawn a school of fish and a broken line. There is no one on deck.

'It's very clever, *mi quierida*,' Julia says.

'The line broke. The fish got away. *Papá* has to stay away longer.'

'*Papá* will be home soon.'

'No he won't!' María stamps her foot and runs back to her room, leaving Julia, Carlos and the boat at sea together in the kitchen.

Julia slides the drawing face-down into a kitchen drawer and wipes tears from her face. She hopes this trip is worth it. She stirs the stew for another few minutes before testing that the carrot is cooked through, and then spoons out two modest helpings. With Uruguay's skyrocketing inflation, grocery bills are getting harder to meet. If Carlos does well this time, it will make all the difference.

'Dinner's ready,' she calls out. 'If you come right away, there should be time for a walk down to the harbour afterwards.'

María is smiling when she reappears, seemingly having already forgotten about their altercation, and eats hungrily. Julia wishes she had the same appetite. After the call to Migiliaro, she feels sick to her stomach.

It's a five-minute walk to the Puerto de Montevideo, which is stacked high with large, foreign-owned factory ships that form a floating extension to the city. The piers are awash with poorly dressed, desperate-looking crews from China and Russia. All the local fishermen, and there aren't many left, have been pushed up-river. They nestle together alongside refugees who have fled rural poverty only to co-habit in *conventillos*, the crumbling houses of the old city. Julia watches as another factory ship heavy with its cargo of stolen fish steams along the Río de la Plata. Beyond it, on the opposite shores of the harbour, is Argentina.

Julia recognises a former neighbour, a fisherman from the days when locals caught *Brótola* and *Pescadilla* inshore off Montevideo in boats they owned themselves. He was a friend of Carlos's father, and one of generations of coastal families who earned their living this way until the factory boats flooded the market with their mega catches and forced them out of the industry.

María races ahead to the old man and he greets her warmly. 'Look at the size of you, *mi chica*! You're a little Sánchez, there's no doubt about it.'

'*Hola,* Rubén,' Julia says as she takes his proffered hand and joins him on the bench. The old man frowns at the big ships with a mixture of fascination and distaste. María takes a piece of bread from a plastic bag that he has been dipping into, and skips off to feed some gulls clustered around a stinking slurry of discarded bait.

'How is young Carlos?' he asks. 'Master of one of these monsters now, I hear.'

'I'm afraid so. A Spanish-owned boat: the *Pescador*.'

Rubén raises an eyebrow.

'I haven't heard from him for a few days, but I'm sure everything is fine. They're a long way south.' Julia looks closely for his reaction, hoping for reassurance.

'*Sí*. It's not easy these days, either.' The old man gazes out towards the mouth of the harbour where the Río de la Plata yawns brown water, heavy with fields washed away by the ploughing of soil and felling of forests, into the Atlantic Ocean. 'I couldn't tell you the number of times I passed through that river mouth. But then, we would set off in the morning and be home in time for dinner.' He takes a pipe from his coat and lights it. 'Your Carlos is away for much longer.'

Julia agrees with a resigned dip of her head, and Rubén blows a thin stream of smoke into the coming night before speaking again. 'He was always determined to make a success of himself. I warned him to take another trade, but fishing was in his blood. You can't help that. He teamed up with another young fellow, didn't he?'

'*Si*. Eduardo Rodríguez.'

'Rodríguez. Of course. His father is still fishing at La Paloma.'

Julia nods again. '*Si*.' She thinks of the beach town, just a couple of hours' drive north of Montevideo, where she first met Eduardo and Carlos, and laments to herself its countless changes. With the exception of Eduardo's father's boatshed, which is still cradled steadfastly in the lap of the dunes, there are few reminders of its fishing hey-day.

'Well, good luck to him.' Rubén removes his hat and scratches his wiry, white hair. He draws another breath through his pipe and exhales, mixing tobacco smoke with the smell of fish and fuel in the evening air.

'He's away a bit then, your Carlos?' Rubén asks, his eyes on the fullness under Julia's coat.

'*Si*,' Julia says, stifling tears. Old people always make her feel emotional. Perhaps it's because they are not afraid to say what they're thinking. When time is running out in life, it makes sense to cut the small talk.

'He's obviously in port long enough to keep the family line going though.' Rubén slaps himself on the knee, and Julia is grateful for his attempt at humour.

'*Sí*, I'm due in a few months.'

'It will all be fine,' Rubén says gently, his face more thoughtful now.

Julia meets his eyes, letting a few tears come. She thinks of the miscarriages she has had at home on her own, between María's birth and now, and the courage it has taken to fall pregnant again. No sooner had she told Carlos the news of this pregnancy than he accepted his current job on the *Pescador*. It makes her furious, to be abandoned again, but with toothfish selling for upwards of thirty American dollars a kilogram in fancy foreign restaurants it had been difficult to say no. A full hold, Carlos had said, would be worth two-and-a-half million dollars. She knows that if they get away with just some of that, a tenth even, he and Eduardo could pay for a deposit on their own boat. They'd never look back.

She studies Rubén as he watches a boat unload countless tonnes of fish into refrigerated trucks.

'It's a wonder there's anything left in the sea,' he says. 'The boats are hitting the stocks so hard nowadays. No sooner do you hear about a new fishing ground opening up — Crozet, Kerguélen, Prince Edward — than they are having to start on another. That's why your Carlos has gone so far south, you realise.'

'*Sí*, but these foreign boats took our fish. What are we supposed to do?'

'Hmm,' Rubén muses. 'I don't have an answer for that. But I suspect even if all the fish were gone, some of us would still find an excuse to go to sea.' He smiles. 'I was like your Carlos. An explorer. A hunter.' He focuses on something a long way out to sea. 'And what of your parents, Julia? They moved to Tarariras to retire, didn't they?'

'I know it's only two hours away, but I miss them.'

'Of course. I used to see a lot of your father. He sold my fish out of his shop at Puerto del Buceo. You remember?'

María comes back with most of the bread still in her hand. 'They weren't very hungry,' she says.

Rubén laughs. 'For another day then,' he says, taking the bread and packing it back into the plastic bag.

'Can we keep walking, *Mamá*?'

'*Si*, for a little while, then it's bedtime for you,' Julia says smiling at her daughter. 'Take care, Rubén. We'd better keep going.'

The old man gives Julia's hand a squeeze and tips his hat. As Julia walks away, she thinks about what he said. If the stocks are so overfished, perhaps Carlos won't have the choice of going to sea for much longer, anyway. She whispers a small prayer for this trip to provide them with enough financial security for her husband to dry his feet and learn another trade. She could resume teaching, which she had reluctantly given up after María was born. With Carlos spending so long away, it had been impossible to balance work and motherhood.

Julia puts her hands on her stomach and rests for a moment. If this baby is also a girl, perhaps Carlos will have another reason to stay home. Maybe he won't feel the obligation to pass on the family tradition of fishing. Heaven knows there's nothing traditional about it any more. She thinks of Eduardo's wife and how different she is from herself. After two daughters, Virginia is hoping that, should she fall pregnant again, their next child will be a boy. A fisherman. 'It's Eduardo's dream, to have a son,' she had said in a rare moment of candour when they were last together. 'He longs to be able to pass on all that he knows. He just worries that there won't be enough fish left.'

Julia considers telephoning Virginia when she gets back to the apartment, but decides against it just as quickly. With few exceptions, their conversations are forced and short, as if most of the words are being held back. It occurs to Julia that she is no closer to Virginia now than when they first met as teenagers, Virginia already round with Eduardo's baby. It occurs to her, too, that most of the blame for their distance rests with herself: her inability to forgive Virginia for a crime she never even knew she had committed. No, she'll call Eduardo's wife only when she has news of the boat.

'*Mamá*, can Sofía sleep over tomorrow night?' María says, interrupting Julia's thoughts.

'We had her here just two nights ago,' Julia answers, resentful at the thought of having to share the precious *ensopado.* 'I'm sure Sofía's *mamá* will ask us to look after her again soon, anyway.'

Julia thinks of Francisco Molteni, Sofía's father and a senior fisheries manager at Uruguay's Department of Fisheries. He has called in so many times on his way home from work to collect his daughter that she almost regards him as a friend. It's something she could never say about his wife, Cecilia, who, Julia suspects, is wary — perhaps even jealous — of her more natural beauty. Cecilia has remained as cold and unyielding as a dead fish from the day they met outside their daughters' ballet school, which María no longer attends because of the expense. Perhaps, Julia considers, if this trip south goes well, María could re-enrol.

Francisco might know where Carlos is, it occurs to Julia. But for him to confess to her the *Pescador*'s whereabouts, he would have to admit knowledge of its illegal operations. She suspects it's better to let him keep turning a blind eye, if that's what he's doing. For all Julia knows, Cecilia — who must overhear countless conversations between fisheries officials at her frequent dinner parties — might also know the truth about the *Pescador*. Perhaps she is taking advantage of the situation every time she brings Sofía over 'to play' while she wines and dines or plays tennis with friends. If Julia refused to mind Sofía, she is sure that Cecilia would only have to 'accidentally' tell one of her many media acquaintances what Carlos is up to and the government would have no choice but to prosecute.

'Please, *Mamá*. Let me ask Sofía over.'

'No, María. Come on, it's getting dark. See how the boats are turning their lights on?'

'*Sí*. Do you think *Papá*'s boat has its lights on now?'

'I'm sure it does,' Julia says, shivering at the thought of such small lights on a large dark ocean.

MARGIE
Hobart, Australia
20 September 2002

Margie Bates places the sable brush on the wet page and lets the watercolour work its magic. An ultramarine sky bleeds forth, driving clouds and specks of white that could be seabirds, perhaps albatrosses, over the Southern Ocean. She loves the way the paint does the job for her. She may will it to behave a certain way, or even tilt the page slightly, but she resists the urge to fuss. The best results are always when the colour runs free.

An ocean, rough hewn and dark, fans up into the sky with abandon and, in places, runs back down like rain. A small red flash of alizarin crimson disappears behind a watered-down stroke of Payne's gray that resembles a wave. It's her husband's boat, the *Australis*. 'Stop,' she tells herself. 'Don't do any more.' The painting is finished. Anything else and the drama and freshness, best captured by a minimal use of paint, will be lost.

She peers into the wet surface as though it is the real scene. Her information on Dave is limited to what she hears on the radio and via the occasional satellite call from the ship, so she feels justified in conjuring up her own version of reality. Imagining it into being. She could phone Customs in Canberra but has decided to save those calls for a time when she really needs them. At the moment, according to the media reports, the Australian vessel is safe.

Margie curses. Damn Dave for agreeing to a chase in seas that are even less hospitable than the darkest corners of her mind. Corners blackened by the death of her twenty-four-year-old son nearly two years ago in a car crash only a kilometre from their Hobart home. Dave was at sea when Sam borrowed his car. It was to have been a short drive into town with his best friend, William, to take advantage of a sale at an adventure-sports shop, but a P-plate driver ran a red light and ploughed into the driver-side door.

Margie attended the scene after receiving a mobile phone call from William. He had escaped with a broken collar bone, while Sam's life was teetering on the edge of freshly sheared metal that once belonged to his father's Ford Falcon. Margie was there, holding one of Sam's bloodied hands, when he died. She has pushed that memory away as much as she can. Compressed it into oblivion.

Finally, after many long, dark months, she is again allowing tiny beams of light to enter the windows of her mind, creating fleeting moments of illumination and acceptance. On a good day, she may even feel that Sam is still with her in the night sky or in a sunset, as corny as she knows that sounds. Times when she can convince herself that all living, or once living, things are still connected, and that everything is, in a sense, all right.

But she still cries herself to sleep at night, more often than she admits. When Dave is away, she holds the urn containing Sam's ashes, still unscattered, to her, sometimes under her shirt like an unborn baby, and lets herself weep. The grief is somehow easier to bear when her eyes have bled their salty water, and her body has heaved itself free of its deluge of sobs.

It takes a long time to grieve. A long time to forget the horrors of a death and remember all that you can of a life. To realise there is no going back, no flesh in the shape of that person any more. No last kiss or hug or word. A life is simply over, and it's this finality that is so hard to accept, or escape.

That's where painting helps. Margie keeps a small bottle of water, her favourite field brush and a watercolour pad in an old daypack of Sam's, to lose herself when the need arises. She walks along the cliff tracks that begin just metres from her house. There have been times when the cliffs have summoned her, and teased her with the ultimate release they offer. Occasions when her feet have travelled too close to the edge and the sky has promised to lift her like a bird. But she could never do that. Not to Dave. Not after seeing grief in his eyes once already.

Instead, she paints. Something will catch her eye, two eucalypt branches touching with the ease of lovers, or a yellow flower rooted lightly at the edge of a cliff, waving in the breeze despite its vulnerability. Signs of life. She might do a rough painted sketch and perhaps take a photograph, to be followed by more detailed drawings at home, in the warmth of her study-cum-sewing room, with a cup of tea. But the field sketches often capture something that her studio paintings don't. A feeling that she can't describe in words is conveyed in a few spontaneous brush strokes. Some moments can't be improved upon.

It seems her best paintings are those she doesn't care too much about and just lets happen. For Margie, it's a bit like looking at the stars at night. The moment she focuses too closely on a star, it vanishes. She remembers the same thing happening when she played the piano in high school. Whenever she concentrated too hard on the music and the placement of her fingers, she made mistakes. When she removes herself slightly, her creative efforts are rewarded.

It's not that she doesn't get absorbed by her paintings — quite the opposite. She becomes spellbound. And it's a magic to which she surrenders happily. When she is painting, everything else ceases to exist.

She takes a sip of her tea and wonders if she has accidentally used it to wash her brush in. On a particularly intense painting day, she has been known to drink straight from the rinsing water itself. Only when she sees herself in the mirror later and observes the trace of pigment on her lips does she realise her mistake.

She tucks her sable brush behind her ear, unconcerned by the likely smear of colour through her salt-and-pepper hair.

She makes her hands into a tunnel and holds them up to her hazel eyes. By closing one eye and peering down the darkened corridor with the other, she can better see her art. The painting comes alive. It's a little trick she does when she wants to transport herself into the world she has created.

The boat moves, a wave falls, she feels the frosted wind and spray and is deafened by the barrage of ocean noise. Small slices of white paper break through the crimson paint of the *Australis* and the effect is like ice forming on the rails. She is pleased with the happy accident.

A jagged piece of white lunges off to the right of the boat, piercing its hull on the port side. It moves again, jutting out at her. Margie steps backward, dropping her hand-tunnel from her eyes. An iceberg.

DAVE
The *Australis*
21 September 2002

'Jesus!' Dave Bates slams the boat forward even harder and starts swinging the bow to starboard and away from what a moment ago in the fading, sodden light he took for a wave, but now realises is frozen water. A growler.

The ice appears to lunge for a gulp of air before diving beneath the ocean's ragged surface. To complicate matters, a spiralling low has descended, with gale-force southwesterly winds pushing up mountains of water that have travelled thousands of nautical miles with nothing in their way but the occasional iceberg and fishing boat.

Dave knows how perilous his position is. Hitting a growler in these conditions is every sea captain's worst fear. The *Australis*, while ice-strengthened, is no icebreaker. If the growler strikes the boat hard enough, it could puncture the hull and sink them before nightfall.

'Where the hell did that come from?' Dave yells, but on a frigid sea it's a stupid question. He knows that with the approach of summer, the vast expanse of pack ice — the ring of solid sea around Antarctica — will have begun to melt. The edge will have started its retreat towards the cold comfort of the continent, and icebergs that had been frozen into the pack will finally be let loose. Some bergs, he has heard, are so large that they form their own clouds as they exhale the air that was trapped inside them hundreds of thousands of years ago. Others, smaller and slyer, will be lying in wait under the waves, rising up only occasionally like submarines to survey their surrounds. Meeting one now is a sure sign the edge of the pack is only half a day away.

Dave veers the boat harder to starboard but it refuses to move against the storm. The winds gust up to eighty knots and knock the boat sideways into seas rising to more than twelve metres. 'Christ!' This is as close as he has come to survival sailing. He tries to keep the boat headed into the weather to prevent it from broaching, but the waves push it back towards the indifferent mass of the growler. The sunken iceberg, having already made it this far from its glacial home, is in no hurry. It will take many months to leach its ancient freshwater into the surrounding salty soup.

Cactus appears at the wheelhouse door with a sleep crease down his left cheek and a thin smear of blood on his mouth.

'Bit of a gale, Davo?' Cactus shouts over the back of his hand, as he applies pressure to his mouth. 'Fuckin' knocked me out of me bunk.'

'Thought you'd got into your make-up again,' Dave jokes without taking his eyes off the sea. 'Dressing up for the growler.'

'Shit. Where?'

'Portside. Barely.'

Harry is at the door for the second time in half an hour. 'What've we got?' The first mate is focusing hard on the radar but in these conditions there's no way to separate ice from the green field of wave scatter.

'Growler,' Dave says through clenched teeth. 'We're practically on top of it.'

The boat lifts on the starboard side with the force of a wave and is tipped towards the sunken berg.

'Bloody hell, Dave, move 'er forward!' Cactus bellows.

A blow to the hull towards the stern throws Dave against the wheel. A coffee, which he'd placed hurriedly on the instrument table twenty minutes ago, spills across the back of his hand. It scalds, thanks to the wonders of insulated mugs. The boat swivels slightly, before slipping off the submerged iceberg.

'Jesus Christ!' Cactus yells. 'You tryin' to get us killed down 'ere. Go, go, go!'

In a break between waves, Dave pushes the boat into full throttle, before another gust hits. The *Australis* grinds forward and they're clear.

Dave grimaces at Cactus. 'Go and check if we did any damage. As soon as this storm eases up, we'll head north and track the buggers from up there.'

'And what d'you want me to do if we have sprung a leak? Stick me finger in the friggin' hole?' Cactus, not waiting for an answer, leaves the wheelhouse with a grunt, and Dave looks back at the radar. Almost unbelievably, the foreign boat, which they had been gaining on, is moving further towards the pack ice and then disappears out of range, apparently on a death wish.

'Stupid bloody fools,' Dave spits, cursing their brazenness. He knows that, legally, the chase has now been broken and the *Pescador* cannot be prosecuted. Surely he can make a case for not following them blindly into the ice. He didn't sign up for suicide. But he's not giving up without a fight, either. 'Where do they think they're headed?'

'God knows, but you're right not to follow them south,' Harry says calmly, squinting through the wheelhouse windows in the direction of the foreign boat. 'Those bloody bureaucrats in Canberra wouldn't have a clue what we're dealing with here. Check out the size of this mongrel!'

Dave cranes his neck to see the headless wave towering above them, much of it out of view. He grips the wheel as the boat climbs, pivots and then drops through mid-air before pounding into the seas below. Over his shoulder, through the windows along the back wall, he watches the mountain of water recede. Metal heaves and groans, and somehow holds together.

There are another half-dozen such waves before Cactus is back in the wheelhouse. 'Christ all fuckin' mighty! Enough's a bloody 'nough!'

'Any damage?' Dave asks.

'No, but buggered if I know how we avoided it!' Cactus's ruddy face, which Dave has long suspected is a product of his love affair with bourbon, bleaches with panic. 'Just get us the hell out of here!'

Dave grunts as the *Australis* hits another trough. The coffee mug rolls against his feet, having emptied its guts on the floor, greasing the linoleum with its thin brown slick. Dave kicks the mug away.

'Hell of a time to get yourself a hot drink, wasn't it? With that growler under us.'

'Harry brought me the coffee ages ago. I didn't take my eyes off the bloody radar. What do you take me for?' Dave heads the boat straight into the guts of a wave. The *Australis* climbs and the men fall silent until they have made it over.

'Shit!' Cactus shouts, as they bottom out in the trough.

'We'd have been lucky to see that growler on the radar even in good conditions,' Dave continues. 'You know that as well as I do.'

Cactus says nothing, and Dave recognises fear in his eyes. Come nightfall, the icebergs will be as good as invisible, until they're caught — too late — in the ship's lights.

It's some hours before conditions start to ease, and Dave can finally inch the boat northwest, away from the low-pressure system that created the southerly gale. It's a reprieve, but he knows there'll be another low soon enough. The vortexes of foul weather circle the continent like vultures. The trick is to stay either north or south of them. Harry indicates with a slight backward flick of his head that they have company. William, their youngest crew member, is at the wheelhouse door, his eyes wide as he surveys the sea, trying to read its complex language. Dave wonders if he did the right thing putting in a good word for Sam's best mate as trainee crew. He thinks back to how young William went off the rails after Sam's death. How, after gaining a reputation as a fine jackaroo on properties all over Australia, he threw it all away by getting drunk one night and trashing a farm. Dave had seen this trip as a chance to straighten the young bloke out. 'What better classroom is there than the sea?' he'd said to Trish, William's mother. But Cactus has never thought it a good idea having a novice on board.

'What was that God almighty bang a while back?' William asks.

'What d'you bloody think?' Cactus's veins stick out of his neck like fingers under his skin. He is angrier than Dave has ever seen him. 'We just had a cuddle with the coldest bloody mermaid this side of Antarctica. Her left tit's probably still pokin' up through your bunk. Why don't you go back to bed and feast on that till it's all over?'

William, visibly startled by the outburst, turns to leave the wheelhouse. Dave catches his eye and gives him a wink.

'That was a bit rough,' Dave tells Cactus as he passes the searchlight over the ocean. The winds may have eased, but nightfall hasn't waited for the huge seas to subside. With the relentless hammering of the waves, the boat lurches from side to side.

'Well, it doesn't take too many neurons to work out we've hit a berg!'

'Give the boy a break,' Harry says. 'It could've been a whale, or a sunken hull —'

'Or a bloody mermaid,' Cactus jeers in Dave's direction. 'We never should've taken him on. He's a friggin' liability, your surrogate son.'

It's typical of the man, Dave thinks, to launch a personal attack when he's feeling threatened. To fire hostile words ahead of any attempt at good judgment. He ignores him.

'Any sightings of our foreign friends on the radar?' Harry asks.

Dave knows what he's up to. He and the first mate know that when tempers flare at sea, the best strategy is to get everyone focused back on the job at hand. If there's to be a fight, it can wait until they're on dry land. Right now you could cut the air with a knife.

'Nope. They're well and truly gone,' Dave says. He imagines the pack to the south of them — vast chunks of ice rallying for supremacy like feuding tectonic plates. Only last year a German freighter, experienced in Southern Ocean transport, was crushed in the pack, all lives lost.

'It's no bloody wonder a couple of pirate boats go missing every season.' Harry shakes his head.

Dave thinks of the crew aboard the *Pescador*, no doubt hired as little more than slave labour by some foreign owner with his feet up in a comfy pad somewhere nice and warm, maybe Spain; all the owners seem to come from there. He imagines the crew's fatigue, their hunger, their smell. 'It'll be on my head if we push the poor buggers to their deaths.'

'And what about us?' Cactus pipes up. 'The suits up there in Canberra-land wouldn't 'ave a clue what an iceberg was if they had one stuck up their proverbials! And *if* the rotten illegals do reappear, d'you reckon Canberra'll call the naval frigate back from Timor for the boarding?'

Dave remains silent as Cactus's derisive snort hangs in the air like a sick joke. Finally, he responds. 'Like I said before, we'll see what back-up's on offer, but for now we pursue the boat for as long as we can.' Dave hopes he has managed to conceal his own cynicism. 'They'll have to head north at some point, and we'll be here when they decide to reappear.'

'A wild goose chase! Our lucky day,' Cactus sneers. 'It's not as though it's the first bloody boat to take somethin' for nothin' down 'ere. There'll be another ten pirate boats rippin' the guts out of what's left of the fishery while we've got our backs turned playin' politics. It's just not … substainable what they're doing.'

Dave, quietly amused by Cactus's attempt at 'sustainable', maintains his focus. For now he's just relieved the wind has dropped, its monstrous howl having paused to catch its unholy breath.

'Righto, Cactus. Pull your prickles in and grab the helm, mate. I'm going down for a kip while things are relatively calm.' Dave pats Cactus on the back a little too hard and notices the acrid smell of nervous sweat. 'Harry, you right to stay here for a bit?'

The first mate agrees.

'You're worth your weight in hot cocky poo,' Dave jests before climbing down the stairs from the wheelhouse. He passes the officers' deck where his cabin is located, and descends another flight of stairs to the crew's accommodation. There are twenty-one men on board, but only half are in their bunks. The others are out on deck removing polar ice from the rails. It's a constant job, but critical. Boats can capsize under the weight of frozen water.

Dave steps into William's shared cabin, which welcomes him with the stench of stale wet-weather gear and a recently used toilet. William emerges from the adjoining bathroom and makes his way warily to his bunk, not a mermaid's tit in sight. The smell in the room suggests he has probably just had a bout of diarrhoea, the kind that strikes when raw nerves turn bowels to water. William shivers as he lifts the bed clothes up over his face.

'It'll all have blown over by morning, kiddo,' Dave says.

'I hope so,' William's voice groans. 'I don't think my stomach can take much more of this. There's nothing left to vomit up or shit out.' He sticks out his head and Dave sees how pale he has turned.

'Well, I wasn't going to say anything, but I'm not sure how much more we can take of your stomach, either!' Dave laughs, trying to lighten the mood. 'Nobody light a match.'

William's roommates chuckle quietly to themselves. 'I thought we'd sprung a gas leak,' one of them guffaws.

'That's enough now,' Dave says before continuing quietly to William. 'Actually, when I said it'd all blow over, I meant that nonsense before with Cactus. He's a stupid old coot. Can't help himself. Unfortunately I can't promise we won't strike more bad weather, but we're not going any further south, so I reckon we've seen the worst of it. It's just that the seas take a while to get the message the storm's over.'

'Okay,' William says, again covering his head. 'Thanks.'

Dave reaches his cabin and crawls into his bed. As soon as he closes his eyes, Sam is there, laughing and joking. 'Come on, Dad, nothing a hot bath won't fix.' It's one of Margie's lines. Her version of a hot tea to fix all ills. Sam and Dave had used it on many occasions, normally with a tinge of black humour and associated with some grisly injury — a slipped screwdriver, once even a saw, when working on the boat or on one of the investment properties in need of a makeover — or to cheer themselves up when catches were poor the few times Sam accompanied his father to sea. It occurs to Dave that he hasn't heard Margie say it for a while. She's still not herself — hasn't been since Sam died.

But Dave knows he has about as much chance of getting a hot bath as he has of convincing the *Pescador*'s master to head to Fremantle without a fight. Still, he allows himself the luxury of imagining stepping into the claw-footed tub at home. He feels the warm water surround his aching body and surrenders to its safety. He pictures the white bathroom tiles, each with an emerald-green border of gum leaves, and tries to conjure up the scent of the soaps, bath salts and aromatherapy candles that Margie has arranged on the wooden bath shelf. He built the shelf last year from Huon pine he salvaged from one of his off-season renovation projects, and intended using it for storing magazines and newspapers. But there's never enough space for anything other than Margie's bathtub paraphernalia. It's strange, he thinks, how the memory of those feminine objects soothe him.

Dave has always thought of himself as a strong and practical man. Stoic even. Losing Sam was the worst that life could throw at him, yet he had survived. He'd fallen into the raging waves and hit the bottom, and had used the seabed of his grief to push off again. He'd swum back to the surface, emerging like a nearly drowned man, gasping for air but still alive. He *had* resurfaced. And it was with some relief that, bobbing around there in the turmoil of his emotions, he'd realised there was nothing that could hurt him as much ever again. So, it comes as a shock to Dave tonight that, reaching out for sleep from the farthest corner of the globe, he can again taste fear. Fear for the lives of the other men on his boat; fear for what losing them would do to their families; and, if the *Australis* did go down, what that would do to Margie. Fear, too, for the strangers aboard the *Pescador* and for their families on shore. He thinks again of the warm bath in his Hobart home, and of Margie, and lets his memory of both warm him in his cold bunk on a frigid sea.

LOGBOOK OF EDUARDO RODRÍGUEZ TORRES

∾

The ice is thick around us now. It's the beginning of spring, and the pack has reached its greatest extent — stretching across half the Southern Ocean. I've read that the freezing of seawater around Antarctica is the largest and fastest annual event on Earth, and that the pack moves forward at fifty-seven square kilometres a minute. The frozen blanket has become our refuge, our place of escape. From now on, as spring advances, the ice will retreat south. I can hear it groan underneath us, squeezing our hull like a vice, heaving and sighing as we cut our path. It wants to take us with it.

I saw a magnificent iceberg today. Ancient water from another time cut free from a frozen continent, like a giant broken tooth. At this latitude, it could drift for many months, losing water and altering its form — an ever-changing sculpture. A snow-white petrel disappeared as it flew in front of the tabular berg, and then reappeared, as if by magic, on the other side. The Antarctic sun, ringed by a halo of high cloud, barely clung to the horizon. In its haze, here at the edge of the ice, there were seals, creatures that appear to me to be as different from other animals as the Antarctic is from the other continents. Their presence provides unexpected comfort and makes me feel less alone.

*Just before nightfall, there was an explosion of birdlife
— a celebration — as plummeting beaks swooped to spear
fish plump with krill. Adelie penguins reflected metallic
flashes through the water, while fulmars, albatrosses and
whale birds startled the sky.*

*How I would love to soar with these birds. To fly above
all that I know and reach a higher plane. To rise beyond
what my father and his father dreamed of for me. To write.
Perhaps it seems odd for a fisherman to hold such esoteric
ambitions. But do not underestimate us — our dreams, our
experience. There are other artists here, too: poets, painters
and musicians. The sea might flow in our veins, but surely
we are permitted to bleed ourselves of it on occasion. To
express our respect, even our love for it. Instead we are taking
from it all that we can. Devising schemes to make money
fast, so we can one day be free.*

CARLOS
The *Pescador*
21 September 2002

Carlos Sánchez moves his boat through the pack, forcing the ice into a violent series of rifts and ridges. Caught in the ship's lights, immediately ahead of him are two icebergs — one to starboard and the other to port. They jut up through the frozen landscape like static frozen eruptions, blasted off the Antarctic ice shelf.

The boat groans under the weight of nearly two hundred tonnes of toothfish, and countless kilograms of polar ice. The white mass is building on the rails, layer upon layer, threatening the ship in the same way cancerous bones threaten the stability of a human body.

Carlos watches as Eduardo straps his safety line to a rail and begins the hand-numbing job of smashing the metal bars clean. Seventeen crew work alongside the first mate on the flood-lit deck, creating small glassy avalanches that pound the painted metal of the deck. The wind has dropped to a mere thirty knots and the seas have been smothered by the pack. It's a welcome reprieve and the men make the most of the relative calm, even if it is after midnight.

But Carlos can feel the squeeze of the ice beneath him, sucking the boat of speed and threatening to stop them, dead.

At the next opportunity, he'll try to break free. He flicks through his logbook. They've been running south of the Australian patrol for four days. He doubts Julia has even been told of the chase. Why wouldn't Francisco and his department feign ignorance for as long as possible while the palms of officials are being greased with the money of stolen fish?

The master reads the chart and, with his finger, traces the dotted lines that indicate the likely extent of ice throughout the year, before fixing his gaze on the eerily lit pack in front of him. According to the map, it's at its greatest reach and will soon recede. For now though, it's starving them of precious fuel and erasing any advantage they have gained by heading so far south.

Carlos thinks of his crew: four Uruguayans, four Chileans, ten Spaniards, fifteen Peruvians and a Russian engineer, whom Eduardo first met during his time working the Bering Sea fishery three years ago. Normally, a vessel's owner arranges its crew, but Eduardo had put in a good word for the engineer, telling Migiliaro that Dmitri was the best in the business. Carlos had appreciated the recommendation — at these latitudes, a good engineer is the difference between making it home, or not — but, on a personal level, he hasn't yet warmed to the Russian, who strikes him as a law unto himself.

Carlos had warned the crew that the *Pescador* would venture into the high Antarctic if the pickings of toothfish elsewhere had been unfavourable, or if they'd been forced to flee a patrol boat. But the chances of being chased had always been slim. He has never known a boat to be pursued over such a distance. He tells himself that his decision to run south was sound. It has forced the Australians to break the hot pursuit, and now the *Pescador* can't be charged under international law — not as he understands it. As he passes the starboard iceberg, he uses the searchlight and sees an opening in the pack only one hundred metres away, just before the next iceberg. He makes for it.

Carlos watches Eduardo brace himself against the deck rails as the *Pescador* turns, and notices his flapping jacket go still as the wind drops in the lee of the second berg. Even if Eduardo were not wearing the personalised wet-weather jacket, Carlos would be able to tell Eduardo apart from the other orange-hooded forms on deck. There's something unique about the deliberate and relaxed manner in which he works, and the way he seems to move as one with the ocean.

This afternoon, just before nightfall, Eduardo had stopped to watch hundreds of birds launch themselves into the fertile waters at the edge of the ice. The feeding frenzy was of a scale he had never before witnessed, he later said. Eduardo reeled off the various species of birds, embellishing his sightings with facts about where they nest, how often they breed and how their populations are faring. Carlos is well aware that while other crewmen play cards or music or read magazines in their rare moments of recreation, Eduardo makes careful notes, sometimes well into the night, from his small on-board library of science books and magazine articles. In another life, the first mate's love affair with the sea might have seen him graduate with a degree in marine biology, the master thinks as his friend leaves the deck and makes his way towards the wheelhouse.

Carlos again passes the searchlight over the seas, this time illuminating a pod of minke whales. Their shining backs, punctuated by tall, curved dorsal fins, drift out of the beam of artificial brilliance and deep into the night. Eduardo enters the cabin and drops his hammer on the floor. Shards of ice rain out from creases in his jacket, and pool on the fuzz of worn, blue carpet tiles. He throws back his waterproof hood and strips off a woollen balaclava, his face emerging like a sculpture from a mould. He has the perfect skin of a child it occurs to Carlos, as though the wind and salt water have worn away the layers and turned back time. His eyes are deep-set and dark; his only physical imperfection the slightly folded rim of his right ear. Eduardo jokes that it's where his mother used to grasp him when he misbehaved as a child.

'Must be time for me to thaw out,' Eduardo offers, a shine in his eyes. 'Now that we're through the hard part.'

Carlos flashes a good-humoured smile and gives over the helm. He has always marvelled at Eduardo's energy and resilience. The first mate endures conditions that would break a weaker man, and always comes up smiling and asking for more.

'I'm getting that ice off first, though,' Carlos says, pointing at the thick film encrusting the wheelhouse window. 'Can't have us heading to the South Pole! Or do you think that government boat would follow us there, too?'

Eduardo laughs. 'Sorry, I should've cleared it off before I came in.'

Carlos waves away the apology, flips his jacket's hood forward over his head, and does up the zipper. Only his dark eyes and heavy brow are visible as he leaves the wheelhouse, ice scraper in hand.

Outside, the horizontal barrage of stinging water slices at his face. It hurts to breathe. His chest tightens. Salt spray burns his eyes. He chips the ice away as fast as he can, hitting the back of the scraper carefully with the back of a wrench. Already a new thin film begins to form, and through it Carlos can see Eduardo's eyes on the radar, an uncharacteristically troubled expression on his face.

When he has finished, Carlos can no longer feel his fingers. The water and the cold have somehow worked their way in through his gloves. He grips the rails of the narrow wheelhouse deck with ice-blunted hands and guides himself back to the door, lugging it open against the wind. He flicks back his wet hood. 'I can't remember what it's like to be dry,' he jokes, pulling at his clothes, which are heavy with frigid water. His eyebrows and forehead are crusted white with salt, adding decades to his appearance. He moves an already damp towel over his face.

Eduardo is still looking at the radar, which is crowded with the fluorescent blips of wave scatter and perhaps a dozen icebergs. It could be a stellar map of the southern skies.

'You're happy to be this far south?' he asks Carlos.

'Happy? No. But we need to get some distance behind us. Another day or so down here, just tracing the edge of the pack, and we'll lose the patrol, if we haven't already.'

'You'd think so. They can't be as stupid or as stubborn as us!' Eduardo shakes his head, but doesn't quite manage a laugh. 'Mauritius is unlikely then?'

'We might have to find another port. Africa maybe.'

'Migiliaro won't like it.'

'What choice do we have?'

Carlos watches as Eduardo walks to the chart table, takes a sip of *mate*, and uses the gourd-shaped vessel containing the herbal tea to hold open the map. Using his finger, he draws a line from their current position to various alternate destinations: Mauritius, back home to Montevideo, or … Eduardo travels his finger up the west coast of Africa, and stops at Walvis Bay.

'They normally turn a blind eye to unrecorded catches in Namibia,' he says, looking up at Carlos.

Carlos tilts his head to the side, weighing up the risks and benefits of the proposition. 'Maybe,' he concedes. 'Anyway, if you're happy to take over, I'll go and get some sleep.' He shifts his attention out to sea. 'While the weather holds.'

'That's why I'm here,' Eduardo says, waving Carlos to the door. 'Go and dream of that beautiful wife of yours.'

'She'll be worried sick.' Carlos reaches out a gloved hand to touch the photograph of his wife. He circles his finger on her pregnant belly. 'So will Virginia ...'

'*Si*,' Eduardo looks away from the photograph and towards the ice. 'But they'll be happy with what we have in our pockets. Enough money to break free of the Migiliaros of the world.'

Carlos nods. 'I hope that's how it turns out.'

'It'll be okay. Trust me.'

'*Si, Capitán!*' Carlos jokes, making a mock salute with his hand on his forehead as he leaves the wheelhouse, glad to surrender control for a couple of hours.

LOGBOOK OF EDUARDO RODRÍGUEZ TORRES

No attempt at fine prose today. Dmitri Ivanov, our engineer, is proving a major problem. It seems I was wrong to involve him in our plan. I had not long taken over the helm from Carlos when Dmitri entered the wheelhouse and overheard a middle-of-the-night satellite call from Uruguayan Fisheries — Francisco Molteni has ordered us back to Montevideo. Dmitri had paced the floor, insisting we unload in Mauritius as planned. I've never seen someone so emphatic yet so blank, like a sheet of ice. The air in the room was heavier in his presence, and I was suddenly aware of the dank smell of the carpet. Clenching his teeth so hard that the muscles at his temples bulged, he claimed he'd tell Migiliaro about our arrangement to sell behind his back if I broke our deal. He said the South Africans he is on-selling to — thugs he informs me — also have my family's address.

It's my fault. He was my choice. But if Carlos was to be kept out of trouble, he couldn't know who we were selling to. Julia would never have agreed to Carlos's part in the private sale if he had had to do anything other than just turn a blind eye. It was my promise to the pair of them to wear the consequences. Predictably, my oldest friend hadn't liked it when I said I would shoulder all the risk, but I joked that I owed him for a lifetime of misdemeanours that he had wanted no part in. This was my chance to put it all right. I might have laughed, but I have rarely been more sincere. In front of Carlos I had held Julia's hands and looked into her dark, wet eyes and assured her that it would all work out fine.

But now I am not so sure. Dmitri, without the knowledge of anyone else on board, has smuggled guns on to the boat — or so he claims. He won't tell me where they are. Perhaps it's all a bluff. He says he was to sell them to his South African buyers along with the fish, and that they could come in useful if we are boarded. He had the deluded eyes of a madman when he told me that. But I think I have convinced him that Namibia is our safest option. I agreed that Montevideo is out of the question — the catch would be seized — and argued that with the Australian patrol lying in wait, Mauritius is a risk we should try to avoid. Instead, Dmitri's buyers could meet us at Walvis Bay. I'd already discussed this with Carlos just a short while before.

Dmitri still can't understand why I have kept his role in our plan a secret — why Carlos would be content for me to make all the arrangements. Dmitri caught me looking at the photograph of Julia, which is taped to the wheelhouse wall, and said that if he were Carlos, he wouldn't be so trusting.

❧

Julia
Montevideo, Uruguay
22 September 2002

Julia looks at her watch, and back out through the bus window across the seamless stretch of white sand beach that lines the Río de la Plata. The water appears polished in the morning light, and she thinks that, on days like today, the harbour separating Uruguay from Argentina was indeed well named: The Río de la Plata, the River of Silver. If she didn't have to be back home this afternoon, she'd be tempted to stay on the bus for longer, and leave the drab city buildings of Montevideo well and truly behind. She and María could head east along the Atlantic coast to even better beaches. If there was time, they could go all the way to La Paloma.

'We'll have a couple of hours on the beach, and then we'll have to catch the bus home again, *mi chica*,' she tells her daughter. 'Sofía's coming over to play this afternoon, remember?' Julia keeps to herself her annoyance about Cecilia's last-minute child-minding request, taking off her watch and zipping it into the beach bag. She won't let that woman's expectations ruin this precious time. If they get home slightly late, then Cecilia can wait.

'Is she bringing her Barbie dolls?'

'I'm sure she will. She brings them every time she comes, doesn't she?'

'*Si*, and she always has a new one. Why do I only have one?'

'Sofía doesn't need so many.' Julia reaches down, lifting the yellow brim of María's sunhat and kissing her on the forehead. In truth, Julia can't stomach the North American dolls, with their anatomically impossible forms and sparkly clothes and accessories. But she knows she can't force her own values on her child, who seems to derive real pleasure from twisting the long bodies into bone-cracking arrangements of dress and undress.

Julia remembers her best friend Paula's story of giving a Barbie to her son in front of her parents in an effort to break the gender stereotypes that her father was trying to impose. He'd wanted to give the boy a gun, but Paula said no. She couldn't understand why her father, having lived through the years of military dictatorship and having survived an attack by the *Tupamaros*, Uruguay's urban terrorists, hadn't rejected guns for life. Her son had possession of the Barbie for less than a second before he bent the doll backwards, pointed her toes towards his audience, and proceeded to shoot the entire family with his politically correct 'gun'.

Bus number sixty-four grinds to a halt along the coastal highway, and Julia and María step onto the palm-lined esplanade. The sea air whips off María's hat and Julia treads on it, pinning it to the grass.

'That was close,' she says, handing over the hat and fitting it firmly back onto her daughter's head. 'You'll need that today. It's nice and sunny.'

There's no shelter from the wind on the beach, but Julia lays out her towel, anyway, quickly lying on it to keep it from blowing away. Even with the wind, her body relishes the first of the warmer weather, absorbing its touch as if it is a lover's caress. She surveys the families dotted along the sand while María, holding her hat on her head, struggles to make a sand castle one-handed. Julia watches as a man of about her own age massages sunscreen onto a young woman's back. He unlaces her red string bikini and Julia can imagine the sensation of his fingers on her skin. She wonders how much longer Carlos will be away. She thinks too of Eduardo, and how, at first glance, he could be Carlos's brother. It has occurred to her before. Both are dark-featured, large men, although Eduardo is broader in frame than her husband. And Eduardo's face is set more squarely. His hair is short, but his eyelashes, Julia thinks, would be the envy of many a South American beauty. She is still staring at the couple on the beach when the woman looks up at her. Julia turns away, focusing instead on the rhythmic beat of the waves against the shore. She shivers as she imagines how different the seas must be where Carlos and Eduardo are, on a different ocean, on what must surely seem a different planet. She says a prayer for Carlos. And another for Eduardo.

Cecilia arrives late at Julia's apartment, all set for a tennis match. She is a flurry of white shoes, fake-tanned legs and heaving bosom, which bounds under her tight lemon-coloured singlet long after she has stopped running up the front path. Julia can't imagine how Cecilia sees the ball coming beyond that voluminous bust, or how she bends or stretches as she plays without embarrassing herself wearing a skirt that only just covers her backside.

'*Hola*, Julia. The match is about to start. Did I mention we might stay for dinner afterwards? I hope that's all right with you.'

Julia is overcome by a cloud of nauseatingly sweet, but no doubt expensive, perfume. 'Fine.' She forces a smile, adding Cecilia's lack of an apology for her lateness to the growing list of irritations about this woman. 'I'm sure we can scrape together something for Sofía to eat.'

Cecilia scrunches her heavily made-up face, as if momentarily revolted at the thought of Julia resorting to scraping up leftovers out of an almost-bare fridge. Sofía, too, seems nervous.

'Just joking!' Julia laughs. 'There's a lovely fresh apple cake for you girls. But maybe we'll have some *tostados* first. What do you think?' She is annoyed by Cecilia's assumption that she'll always have enough food in the house to feed Sofía, who eats twice as much as María. Cecilia can afford whatever food she likes, placing the shopping order with a live-in nanny who also prepares the Moltenis' meals.

Julia waves a goodbye and is just about to close the door when Cecilia takes a step towards her. The heavy perfume makes Julia cough.

'Terrible business about the boat being chased,' Cecilia says.

'What boat?'

'Oh. I thought Carlos was *capitán* of Señor Migiliaro's *Pescador*.'

'*Sí*, he is.' Julia feels sick. 'What have you heard?'

'Oh.' Cecilia's hands are flat on either side of her face, talons reaching all the way to her bottle-blonde hairline. 'Francisco was talking about it with some workmates a few days ago at one of our dinner parties. I thought you'd have heard by now.' Cecilia seems to be enjoying the torment she's dishing out on Julia's front step. Like it's a game. 'Carlos's boat was caught fishing in Australian waters. They've been ordered to Australia to face charges, but *we've* ordered the *Pescador* home, so we can sort it all out here, under our law.'

Julia's fingers tighten around the door frame, and she feels herself going weak.

Cecilia turns her knife. 'But it seems the Australians are going to chase them all the way here if necessary!' She holds her hands out at her sides to indicate the ridiculousness of the situation. 'You poor girl. What a worry for you. And with a baby on the way.' Her hand is over her mouth now in an unconvincing display of concern. 'But I'm sure the handsome Carlos will be okay. Although Francisco did say the weather can go from calm to gale-force in an instant down there.'

Julia is shaking, but tries to hide it. Of course Cecilia knew that it was Carlos's boat, and that she couldn't have heard about the chase, except through Carlos or Francisco or someone else in the Fisheries Department. Yet Cecilia had been sitting on the news for days, waiting until now to reveal all in this flippant just-dashing-out-to-tennis way. Julia is shocked by the cruelty of the woman. She can hear Cecilia's words, spoken as if she is one of the Fisheries Department officials herself: '*We've* ordered the *Pescador* home.' How dare she? The Barbie of a wife has probably never even seen a whole fish up close, let alone scaled and gutted one.

'How far south are they?' Julia asks.

'Well, Francisco said something about icebergs, so I suppose —'

'Is Francisco at work?'

Cecilia stalls, and for a moment her confident façade wavers. She studies Julia's naturally attractive face closely and an ugly, jealous crease forms in the make-up at the corners of her painted mouth. '*Si*, but he doesn't like to be bothered there. I get into the biggest trouble if I phone him.' Cecilia retreats behind a girlish giggle. 'I'll ask him to call you if there's any news.' She places a perfectly manicured hand on Julia's forearm and Julia resists the urge to bat it away. 'Anyway, I'd better get to this game.' Cecilia combs her fingers through her hair and drags the blonde mane back into a tight ponytail. 'Maybe you should have a lie-down. You're pale. This won't help your pregnancy, will it? And you've had such a bad run in that department, you poor girl.' Cecilia motions to give Julia a vacuous hug and an air kiss, but Julia turns to go inside, closing the door behind her. In truth, Julia is barely aware of Francisco's wife any more. The woman is unimportant, like a small moth stirring up the air around her.

The girls have already disappeared into María's bedroom with the designer shopping bag crammed full of Barbies, their blonde heads poking out, jostling for attention. The resemblance to Cecilia is frightening.

Through the lounge-room window Julia catches sight of Cecilia reapplying her lipstick in the rear-vision mirror of her silver Mercedes. It seems Francisco is well paid for his efforts policing Uruguay's fishing industry. She wonders how much of the money comes over the table, and how much under it. The Mercedes starts up and Cecilia drives too fast down the narrow street. It's surprising, Julia thinks, that she deigns to be seen in this neighbourhood at all.

Julia inhales for five seconds, and counts to seven as she releases the warm air. It's a relaxation technique that Paula showed her. She opens the telephone directory and dials the number for Uruguayan Fisheries, and asks to speak urgently with Francisco Molteni.

He answers the phone without delay.

'*Hola,* Francisco. Cecilia has told me about the chase. What's going on? Are they okay?'

'Cecilia should mind her own business. *Lo siento*, Julia,' Francisco apologises. 'I was going to call you today. They're safe. Carlos is okay. But he's taking a big risk going so far south. We've ordered them back to Montevideo so we can sort out the matter here. Our government is dealing at a diplomatic level with the Australians to try to convince them to get off Carlos's tail. But at this stage they're continuing the chase.'

'Can I speak with him?'

'We've advised Carlos not to make satellite calls, except to us. It's possible the communications will be intercepted, and any conversations he has could be used against the *Pescador* in court. We've officially arrested the boat on the basis of the accusations against it, and the fact that it wasn't identifying itself to the Australians.'

'Do the Australians have a case?'

'We don't know. The vessel-monitoring system was off when the supposed illegal fishing took place. We have no record of the *Pescador* even being in Australian waters.' Francisco's voice softens. 'As I said, I was going to tell you about all this today, now that we've made contact with the *Pescador*.'

Julia thinks of the opportunities Francisco had to tell her about the chase when he collected Sofía just a few days ago. She had invited him in for a drink and he had accepted, relaxing into Carlos's empty chair as if grateful for the chance to chat.

'If you keep me in the dark again, I'll never forgive you, Francisco.'

'I know. Try not to get ahead of yourself. *Señor* Migiliaro's ship is strong —'

'*Señor* Migiliaro can go to hell. You and I both know he's only concerned about getting his hands on the fish. And the *Pescador* is just an old boat dressed up. If she goes down, Migiliaro won't lose a night's sleep. We both know he has plenty more rotten vessels in his fleet. A few months fishing on another boat, and he'll have paid for his loss.'

'You're angry, but remember Carlos agreed to whatever arrangement was made with *Señor* Migiliaro. Your husband is no fool. He knew what he was getting into.'

'Don't think I'm not angry with Carlos too.' Julia's voice is quiet, almost a whisper. 'I'll call the first mate's wife. To let her know. *Adiós*, Francisco.'

'*Hasta luego.*'

Julia ends the phone call, and consciously deepens her shallow inhalations to calm herself. She dials Virginia's number and imagines her answering the call from her small wooden house at La Paloma. Julia pictures the beach where they all met during school holidays, every detail still clear in her mind. She sees the fishing boats and Eduardo's father's fishing shed nestled in its soft bed of white sand. She knows her news will shatter the calm, striking Virginia like a tsunami crashing in from the sea.

'*Hola*, Virginia. It's Julia.' Julia can hear Virginia's daughters laughing in the background. 'I've just had news of the boat. They've been spotted fishing illegally in Australian waters. They're being chased.'

'Oh my God.' There is panic in Eduardo's wife's voice.

'It's not great news, I know. I'm sorry.'

'I have to talk with him.'

'The Fisheries Department has asked them not to make calls. In case they're intercepted. Have you got Francisco Molteni's number?'

'*Sí.*'

'Well, he's probably the best source of information. Call him if you're worried. Carlos and Eduardo are okay though, the stupid fools. It's just not all going to plan. They're on their way back here.'

'So, they're probably a couple of weeks away, do you think?'

'At least. They're a long way south right now.'

'*Jesús.*' Virginia's voice is brittle with fear. 'Eduardo.'

'He'll be all right. They both will. I'll call you if I hear any more.'

Virginia sniffs and Julia realises she is crying. The laughter in the background has stopped.

'*Hasta luego*,' Julia says, but the phone is already dead.

'María, sweetheart; I'm having a lie-down for a moment, all right?'

'All right,' María's voice sings back merrily, unaware of the drama unfolding around her. Julia lowers herself onto the double bed, surrendering her body to the mattress. She thinks of Carlos and aches to be close to him. She imagines that they are lying on their sides, her face nestling into the hairs of his chest and his arms wrapped around her. She tries to recall his scent, but can't capture it. Perhaps she will never again be with him and will be left always trying to remember — forever reaching out for him in the dark. The thought sends her whirling into a panic. She thinks, too, of Eduardo, but pushes those feelings away, instead placing her hand on the skin that separates her from the baby inside. She whispers a lullaby, then puts a pillow over her face so María and Sofía can't hear her sobs.

MARGIE
Hobart, Australia
22 September 2002

Margie Bates hasn't looked at her painting since the iceberg rose off the page at her. And when she read in the newspaper this morning that the *Australis* had struck a growler in a storm, she vowed not to toy with fate again.

Instead she is busying herself cleaning the house and baking. She has invited two friends for morning tea, and the kitchen is alive with flour, eggs, milk and talk-back radio.

She hasn't been sleeping well, but has discovered that there are other ways of deriving strength and energy. Before breakfast today, she did yoga on the veranda and then enjoyed an Earl Grey tea while she watched yellow-throated honeyeaters bathe themselves in the glazed-pottery bath she made for them. The bird bath sits on a flat rock under an old eucalypt at the bottom of her garden, near where Sam's old rope swing had been. As Margie sipped her tea, the honeyeaters drank from nectar-filled grevilleas, whose floral heads, heavy with blossom and birds, kissed the surface of the shallow pool.

Margie remembers having an inner reservoir of calm that she could tap into at a moment's notice. But that was in her other life. Since Sam's death, she has emptied out that reservoir countless times and, unable to find even a drop of life-sustaining liquid calm, has been left dehydrated from grief. Only in recent months has she learned the importance of refilling that pool — with yoga and tea, friends and art — to fortify herself against the bad days. Now is not the time to start depleting it with senseless worries about Dave. That's something else she has learned. Worry about what you can change, not what you can't. Easier said than done.

She struggles constantly to refute the thoughts that catapult her into fearing the worst all the time. *Catastrophising*, she has heard it called. She knows people think of her as a worrier, and she hates it. What's closest to the truth always hurts. Worry is an intruder in her life. A robber of valuable time and energy. A thief of happiness. It drives morbid thoughts and spirals her into anxiety. Like the time, shortly after Sam's death, when Dave was late radioing in from a fishing trip and Margie had been left pacing the house. She saw Dave's hairbrush in the bathroom, his wiry red hair spun around the bristles, and thought how much she regretted never having collected a lock of Sam's adult hair. All she has is a fair wisp from his first hair cut, neatly sticky-taped into his baby journal. In an instant, she'd imagined Dave's boat sinking, her husband lost, these few strands all that she had left of his physical, tangible form.

But thoughts like this serve no one, least of all herself, and she pushes her fears away. If Dave's hairbrush was here now, she would give it a good clean and put the hairs in the rubbish bin. She mustn't let worry get the better of her.

Margie sweeps the floor and rearranges the cookbooks on the shelf, aware that her busyness borders on mania. But so be it. By the time her friends arrive, she will have collected herself. Her house will welcome them with light classical music (she must remember to put a CD on), the smell of freesias picked from her garden, and a tidy kitchen warmed by freshly baked scones doused in her own rich blackberry jam and thick King Island cream.

Bonnie, Sam's golden retriever, is standing at Margie's feet, tail wagging, tongue out, panting hot air against her shins. Bubbles of saliva drop onto the newly mopped Tasmanian-oak floorboards. Margie gives the dog a loving rub on the soft fur at the base of her ears, and gently scolds her for the puddle of drool before encouraging her outside with half a scone. Bonnie takes the offering and moves in the direction of Margie's pointed finger without argument, plonking herself heavily onto the sunny veranda, the scone still bulging under a soggy black lip.

Margie loves having Sam's dog about the house to share her grief. There's an understanding between them. Bonnie lost her whole world too when Sam died. Crusty tears have since formed in the corners of her dark eyes. Margie often spends a good hour on the veranda burying her bare feet into the comfort of the dog's warm stomach, and Bonnie later reciprocates by simply laying her heavy head on Margie's lap. And there's something else. Every now and then, for no obvious reason, Bonnie will suddenly run to the gate, wag her tail furiously, and smile in the way dogs do when they greet someone they love. Margie can never see a cause for the welcome, and allows herself to believe that it's Sam's spirit paying them a visit. Something in her heart opens expectantly, and she imagines seeing her handsome dark-haired son, all six feet of him, crossing the grassy lawn and walking up the front steps, arms outstretched for a hug.

She reads the clock and figures she has half an hour before her friends arrive. They're always a few minutes late. Opening her cookbook, she wonders whether she has time to also make some pikelets. She turns the pan on just as the phone rings. It's Dave. He's okay. The line is rough, and she imagines him at sea.

'Marg, we're still … on track dow … here … Everyth … fine. Just pho … Canberra … if you're … worri …'

'I can't hear you very well,' Margie replies, tears running down her cheeks. 'How much longer do you expect to be away?'

'Not sure … Hon … We didn't ev … get close enou … to … catch … the buggers … fishi … And … we … ha … to break … chase. Canberra want us … to kee … going … though. But … we're … following fr … furth … north. I … hope … all … wor … it.'

'I hope it's all worth it, too!' Margie says, shaking her head. 'How's William doing? His mother called. We heard about the iceberg.'

'News trav … s fast. William's … fine … Tell Tri … in good … 'ands.'

'Just for God's sake pull out if it's too dangerous, Dave. I don't care what the idiots in Canberra say.'

'We're fine. We're not goin … any … furth … south.'

'Well that's something. I love you, you silly old coot.'

'Love you too … sweethear …'

The phone cuts out. Margie sits down heavily and sighs, shedding days of suppressed anxiety. She calls William's mother without delay. Trish answers sunnily.

'Trish, it's Margie Bates.'

'Margie, how are you? Beautiful day, isn't it? I've just been out in the garden. So nice to have the warmer weather. Have you heard from Dave?'

'Yes, that's why I'm calling.' Margie tries to sound calm and reassuring. 'They're fine. They're still pursuing the illegal boat but from further north.'

'Oh good. I've called the Canberra office a couple of times, and they've said everything's fine. This'll certainly put some hairs on William's chest!' Trish laughs.

Margie isn't sure if this is bravado, or if Trish just hasn't realised the danger her son has been in. Perhaps she just believes that everything will turn out well because it always has. Margie wishes she still had the same blind faith that only good things happen to good people. She considers being more honest and telling Trish how fast the situation can change down south. They're in iceberg territory, for heaven's sake. Margie suspects the closest the suits in Canberra will have come to an iceberg are the ice trays in their kitchen freezers. If only someone had warned her about the P-plate driver who was speeding down Goulburn Street on the ninth of October nearly two years ago and ran that red light just when Sam was crossing his path. She would have stopped the car with her bare hands if given the chance.

'Trish, if you're not comfortable with this, you must phone Canberra again and tell them. Let them know that these are people they've sent into the Southern Ocean. People with families. It's not okay to put them at risk for the sake of some political points and a few dead fish.'

Trish hesitates, and when she resumes, her voice has lost some of its gloss. 'I'm sure if there was a problem, the government would bring the boat back.'

It occurs to Margie that some people simply prefer to relinquish control, and to trust that life will treat them well. How much easier that would be. 'Well, Dave won't be kowtowing to Canberra all the way to Uruguay if he doesn't think it's safe, that's for sure,' she says. 'He asked me to let you know that William is in good hands.'

'I'm sure he is.' Trish stops. 'Sorry, Margie, I've got to go. I have to pick up Matt from soccer. Thanks for the call.'

'Okay. I'll be in touch. Bye for now.'

Margie hangs up the phone and wonders whether she could have handled the conversation better, but her thoughts are interrupted by a pungent smell. She runs towards the frying pan and sees the margarine container melting against its metal edge. Fumes of burning plastic compete with the perfume of freesias for custody of her kitchen.

There's a knock at the door. Her friends have arrived.

She throws the smoking margarine container out of the sash window and onto the back lawn where she can deal with it afterwards. She remembers Bonnie's drool on the floor, takes a tissue from her pocket and wipes it away.

LOGBOOK OF EDUARDO RODRÍGUEZ TORRES

∽

The whales are plentiful. Humpbacks particularly. I have read that baleen whales (blue, fin, sei, humpback, minke and southern right) spend four to six months in Antarctic waters, depending on the species. They'll then travel to warmer waters to breed, migrating distances of over ten thousand kilometres. We might also see toothed whales, both sperm and killer, as well as bottlenose whales, whale dolphins and pilot whales.

I envy the whales, being able to dive to great depths to escape life on the surface. How I would love to leave this boat and Dmitri far above and descend into another realm — to travel the vast distances home across more forgiving seas, leaving all this behind. But I cannot do that. Not to Carlos. Not after everything else.

∽

CARLOS
The *Pescador*
22 September 2002

Carlos Sánchez half wakes to the sound of whale song through the steel hull. The humpbacks are close, and numerous. There's no engine sound, not in itself a cause for alarm. The calm conditions have no doubt allowed a rare opportunity for maintenance. If there was a problem, Eduardo would have woken him.

He checks the time and sees that he has been asleep for the six hours since he handed over the helm to Eduardo late last night. He is grateful to his friend for the chance of a proper rest. Their last conversation and Eduardo's idea of offloading at Walvis Bay play on his mind, but the songs of the whales reclaim his attention. He lets them, allowing himself a few more moments to listen to their guttural murmurings, which seem to resonate through his chest. It's a miraculous sound, primal and moving beyond any imagining. The calls are filtered through the sound of the ocean, so constant he almost doesn't hear it any more.

The *Pescador* is still tracing the edge of the pack. Broken ice performs its percussion against the metal skin of the boat. Carlos imagines the broken pieces tapping away less than a metre from his head, and shivers involuntarily.

He can hear the crew speaking in a mixture of Spanish and Portuguese, sometimes both in the same sentence. They sound happy enough. Someone is playing panpipes. He hopes, in time, they will forgive him for bringing them so far south.

Carlos thinks back to a radio call from the Australian patrol last night. The master had said that he was concerned the *Pescador* had ventured into the ice, and asked if they were safe. He had added that it was not too late to turn around and head back to Australia. Carlos hadn't responded, but focused instead on the chart and the distances travelled. Already they were 1700 nautical miles southwest of Heard Island. How could the Australian possibly imagine he would turn back now? He makes his way to the engine room where Dmitri is checking gauges and recording their readings on a chart. The engineer has his back to him and stops to speak in Russian to Eduardo through the ship's intercom. Carlos listens to Eduardo's familiar voice respond in the unfamiliar language and is surprised to hear he's so fluent. Eduardo's time working in the Bering Sea fishery had totalled a year — a year away from Virginia and their daughters. A year in which Eduardo had hoped, in vain, to fill the coffers more than he could by fishing from home. Carlos marvels that he managed to master another language in that time. The varied talents and deep intellect of his friend are a constant source of wonder.

'What's the problem?' Carlos asks Dmitri.

'It not too bad,' Dmitri replies, switching to a jerky Spanish. Carlos rarely has occasion to visit the engine room, and the Russian appears surprised, as if his territory has been invaded. 'I just notice the engine getting hot. The gauges read high. I want to make sure oil purifier working properly. Good time to check while weather okay. I replace some seals, connected again the oil lines and tighten the bolts.'

Dmitri works his spanner on a fitting, giving it one final turn, which Carlos suspects is mostly for effect. 'I think I fix the problem. But maybe it is time we head north. Yes?'

'Not just yet,' Carlos says, sensing the Russian's anxiety. 'But soon,' Carlos gives him a quick pat on the back, but feels the bony scapula recoil under his hand.

Dmitri speaks again, this time in beginner's Spanish, to Eduardo in the wheelhouse, asking him to re-start the engines. He again reads the gauges and listens intently to the pulse of the motors. It occurs to Carlos that it's the first time he has seen the Russian smile. The expression transforms his long, pale face, but appears unnatural. 'That better engine music.'

Leaving Dmitri to his task Carlos winds his way up through the bowels of the ship. The panpipes are louder now and he can hear the Peruvians singing. One of them is playing the *charango*. The music resonates within the tiny guitar's armadillo shell. Through the portholes and the light drizzle, Carlos can see the vast sea of pack ice to the south. He imagines the distant Antarctic continent, with its palette of white and steely blue, glistening in the dawn's light. Somewhere beyond the ice, large stony peaks solidify the horizon.

From the wheelhouse door, Carlos sees Eduardo drinking *mate* at the helm. The first mate seems distracted as he sips the herbal infusion through the purpose-built straw, its sour smell — something between green tea and coffee — hanging in the air. Carlos recognises, too, the smell of Dmitri's cigarettes and realises the Russian must have thought the engine problems significant enough earlier to pay Eduardo a visit while he himself was asleep below.

Carlos sees the pack protruding north ahead of them. To stay at this latitude they'll have to cut across it. He walks towards Eduardo. 'What's on your mind, *mi amigo?*'

Eduardo starts, as if woken from a deep sleep. 'Our Fisheries Department called overnight. They've ordered us back to Montevideo. They say they'll sort out the charges against us there.'

'*¡Condenado!*' Carlos swears. 'What about our twenty tonnes?'

'We could say we'd made a mistake in our logs.'

'Not a twenty-tonne mistake! We'll be caught out, for sure. Guilty on two counts, illegal fishing and an unrecorded catch.'

'Or we could offload in Namibia, like we talked about before. Get rid of the evidence.'

'And ignore the order to return home?'

'If we head northwest, it looks like we're following orders. Then, at the last minute, we could claim engine trouble. Make a dive for Walvis Bay.'

'What, and get Dmitri to lie for us?' Carlos asks.

'He would. He's desperate to head north.'

Carlos nods, recalling the conversation he just had with the Russian. 'We're up to our necks, aren't we?'

'*Si.*' The first mate lifts the binoculars from his chest, where they hang from a frayed strap, and studies the sea and the approaching protrusion of ice. 'You want to cut through it?' he asks, pointing to the fat extension of ice that is jutting out ahead of them. It's as though the pack is feeling the temperature of the surrounding water, like a finger testing the heat of water in a bathtub, determining whether it is safe to continue its northern march.

'*Si*, then straight to Namibia. With any luck, we'll be far enough west by then to miss the Australians, if they're still following us.' Carlos reads the date on his watch: 22 September. It's five days since they were spotted by the patrol.

'Francisco Molteni says the Australians are planning to follow us all the way home, if necessary.'

Carlos raises his eyebrows. He thinks of the distances involved, and how much fuel they have wasted by waging war on the ice. Never did he anticipate they would be forced so far south for so long. He walks back to the chart table. By the time they round the Cape of Good Hope, they'll have travelled over four thousand nautical miles since leaving Heard Island. Four thousand nautical miles more than he had counted on. And then there's still another thousand nautical miles, travelling up Africa's west coast, before they reach Walvis Bay. He hopes the fuel will stretch that far.

'Do you ever wonder what this place will be like when our kids are old enough to come down here? What we'll be leaving them?'

Carlos is surprised by his friend's questions, which seem to come out of nowhere. 'Well I *had* hoped we'd be so wealthy by then we could pay for them to come down on a cruise ship.' Carlos laughs. 'Can't you just see our girls sunning themselves in deck chairs at minus ten degrees?'

Eduardo smiles briefly. 'I could live with that.' He views the pack through the portside windows. 'But I think the future won't be so rosy. We'll have taken all the damn fish, for starters. But it's worse than that.'

'Go on, cheer me up. You're doing well so far!'

'The ice shelf is breaking away faster than anyone predicted. Carving off like old loose teeth. The rot of global warming.'

Drizzle gives way to rain as Carlos notices the slurry of ice in front of him. Vast chunks of the continent's edge bob around in the ice soup like giant, soggy croutons. He reads Eduardo's uncharacteristically sombre mood as a sign of stress. 'Sounds like Julia and I might have to move up from the ground floor!' he says, but his attempt at humour doesn't register on Eduardo's face.

Humpback whales cross the ship's path, the same whales, presumably, that stirred Carlos from sleep less than an hour ago. Their dorsal fins seem too small for the size of the beasts, which emerge now like surfacing submarines. Glossy backs arch monstrously as the mammals feed on fish that have gathered at the edge of the ice. Then, as if performing their grand finale, two of the whales raise their vast sculpted flukes high out of the water and execute deep dives. Carlos imagines them descending beneath the ship, and feels the hairs rise on the back of his neck. 'Quite the performance,' he says. 'They don't seem too afraid of us.'

'It's what has made them such easy prey. No wonder they were almost fished out. We saved them just in time.' Eduardo tries to locate the humpbacks again but they've gone. 'We'll wipe out the toothfish next. We're just as bad. Soon there'll be nothing left.'

'Dmitri was a good find,' Carlos says, trying to change the subject. 'He listens to that engine like a mother listens to her baby's breathing.' He studies Eduardo, waiting for a response but the first mate is silent. 'It looks like you were right to recommend him to Migiliaro.'

'I hope so,' Eduardo finally replies, fixing his binoculars on the ocean.

Carlos senses that his friend has done enough talking and watches him walk towards the door that leads to the deck. The worn knees of his plastic wet-weather gear have been reinforced with rubber, and his gloves look like they could steer the boat themselves if he strapped them to the wheel. A short beard keeps the ice from his skin.

If Carlos had to describe his first mate, he would say that he was a decent man, working hard to provide for his wife and two young daughters in a profession that has forced him to move with the times: to fish on bigger boats, with bigger gear, and fill deeper holds. He knows that if Eduardo had a choice, if he owned the *Pescador*, he'd have made different choices. It has been Eduardo's motivation for selling some of the catch behind Migiliaro's back. 'We could use the profits to pay for a deposit on our own boat,' he had said to Carlos. 'And a permit to fish. One good season down here and we'd pay it off. After that, it'd be money in our pockets.'

Carlos remembers Eduardo's face when he had had the next idea. The mixture of cunning and satisfaction. 'If we're *really* smart, we'd use what we learn on this trip to report illegal boats like the *Pescador*. Sink the Migiliaro's of the world who don't give a shit for the stocks. You never know, if enough legal operators get on board, if we formed a coalition, the toothfish might have a hope in hell of surviving. And, God willing, if we have sons, they'd have a fishery to inherit.'

It had seemed a good idea. A way of insuring themselves, as well as the stocks. After all, fishing is all they know. They would curl up and die without their regular coating of salt, seawater and fish grime.

Julia had shaken her head at the proposition. She said they were taking enough of a risk in the first place fishing illegally. 'Why go behind *Señor* Migiliaro's back as well?' she'd argued. But Eduardo had persisted, trying to convince them that this was the easiest money they would ever make. Carlos remembers how Eduardo had stared at Julia's pregnant belly and the anxious tears in her eyes, before taking her hands and promising that he alone would make the arrangements. Carlos wouldn't need to know anything of the deal — nothing of who was buying the unrecorded catch, or whom that buyer was on-selling to. All he would have to do, Eduardo insisted, was steer the boat. If the sale went awry, his first mate made it clear that he would wear the consequences himself. Carlos remembers feeling torn between loyalty to his best friend and concern that Julia's pregnancy not be further burdened with worries about this voyage, not after the miscarriages she has already been through. Eduardo reminded them of all the times when Carlos had saved his skin. 'I owe you,' Eduardo had said.

The memory of returning the bike Eduardo stole as a boy in La Paloma floods back to Carlos. There were other times, too, when he had had to rescue his friend from his seemingly insatiable appetite for risk. Once, as a teenager, he hauled Eduardo from an ocean rip during a storm, despite having warned him that it was too dangerous to swim there that day. The seaward current had almost pulled them both under. Carlos wonders now if his friend had been as sure of success in this most recent venture as he had sounded when they were back on dry land.

The Uruguayan master contemplates, too, Eduardo's deep love for the sea and how the first mate feels the contradiction between this adoration and his occupation more than most. Carlos curses, to himself, the wealthy Americans, claiming to be conservationists, who will feast on the toothfish in the *Pescador*'s hold: the catch that he and Eduardo have risked everything to claim. A whale resurfaces in front of the boat, and Eduardo delays his departure from the wheelhouse to study the majestic creature through the binoculars.

'The whales are coming back; so will the toothfish.' Carlos tries to sound optimistic. 'Pretty soon it won't be worth it for illegal boats like this one to come down here. Did you see how many of the larger fish already had hooks in their mouths? The fishery will be commercially extinct before the last fish is caught. The stocks will rebuild.'

Eduardo shakes his head. 'Not if prices keep going up. If toothfish don't interbreed between the islands, it's only a matter of time before we wipe out local stocks. From what I've read, they produce large numbers of eggs only once they reach a good size.' He allows himself a smile. 'Unlike us, they reach their sexual peak in old àge.'

'Something for them to look forward to.' Carlos, grateful to see his friend's humour back, extends the joke. 'What's their secret?'

'What I'm saying is that if we take all the large fish now, then we've taken the best breeders. There goes the fishery. *¡Basta!* It's not as though it'd be the first time. Think of the cod. And the Bering Sea fishery wasn't faring too well when I was there. According to the scientists, ninety per cent of the populations of the large fishes have been wiped out.'

Carlos says nothing, allowing Eduardo to vent his spleen and rid himself of a poacher's guilt.

'Toothfish were fished out off Patagonia after only a decade,' Eduardo maintains. 'Now we're ripping the guts out of this magnificent place.'

Carlos switches the ship's lights on and watches through the now heavy rain as the whale descends deep below them, its gut full of krill.

'And then there are boats coming down here for krill. *'¡Pendejos!'* Eduardo swears. 'The krill drive the entire system. It'd be like us removing all the grass from a paddock and then wondering why the cattle died. It's madness.'

Dazzled by the lights, a south polar skua flies above the deck, narrowly missing the communication tower.

'The ocean needs *real* fishermen, people who've spent

their lives pressed up against the sea, living its weather and feeling its pulse. If we owned the boats, we'd look after the fish. Instead, we're stuck working for rogues like Migiliaro, and, in the eyes of the world, *we're* the vandals.'

After a long silence, Carlos again addresses his friend. 'What would you do if you weren't fishing?' he asks gently.

Eduardo seems to be peering deep into the soul of the sea. 'Write a book.'

The answer comes as a surprise. Having known this man all his life, Carlos had assumed he knew his best friend's dreams. He remembers the book Eduardo wrote for María, but that was just a children's story and he always assumed it was a one-off present — the kind an uncle might give. He thinks too of a comment Julia once made that, given other opportunities, Eduardo could have been a fine writer. Perhaps he had confided his ambitions to her; perhaps because she is a teacher and he thought she would understand. 'A book? What about?'

'Fishing. What else?' Eduardo lets loose a small laugh. 'The way my father fished, and his father before him. How different it was from the way we fish now.'

'Ah. The notes in your logbook. I've been wondering what you've been up to with that. I was starting to think they were love poems to Virginia.' Carlos grins.

Eduardo studies Carlos, as if trying to determine whether he is joking, or fishing for personal musings that he'd rather keep private.

'So, would it be a true story?'

'No. A novel. I'd want it to come alive.'

'Why haven't you told me before? Were you afraid of what I'd say?'

'No. It's just too early. I haven't even discussed it much with Virginia. It's just a few notes so far, but I'll weave them together one day.' Eduardo laughs. 'Probably when I'm too old to stand on a fishing deck.' He stoops over as if holding a walking cane and wrinkles up his face into a mock toothless grin.

There is a cough at the doorway and Carlos turns to see Dmitri, who is clearing his throat as if trying to get their attention. Carlos notices how quickly Eduardo reverts to his sober mood, visibly stiffening in the Russian's presence.

'Sorry to disturb your joke,' Dmitri says coldly. 'The engine, it runs good again, but we need to go north now in case we have more trouble. If engine temperature starts rising, I have to take oil purifier apart and rebuild on board. We do not want to stop engines down here.'

'The Uruguayan Department of Fisheries has ordered us back to Montevideo,' Carlos says. He sees Dmitri shoot a hostile glare at Eduardo. 'But if you think there's a problem with the engine, of course we'll stop earlier. One or two more days down here and then we'll head north. Sooner if we have to. Namibia is probably the best option to avoid the Australians. Are you happy to do any repairs in Walvis Bay?'

'I would prefer Mauritius, but if that is not possible, then Namibia is okay.' Dmitri gives Eduardo a firm nod as he departs. As always, it seems that the engineer prefers to communicate with Eduardo, and Carlos assumes it is because his friend speaks Russian.

'Seems like Plan B is falling into place, *mi amigo*,' Carlos says to Eduardo. 'And we don't even need to ask him to lie for us. Are you sure you don't want to be *capitán*?'

'No. That honour is all yours.'

Carlos laughs quietly and whispers behind his sea-roughened hand, 'He's a serious fellow isn't he? Those Russians must have only been allocated a set number of smiles at birth. A good character for your novel, maybe?'

'Probably,' Eduardo says, but a sudden slowdown in the boat's speed interrupts the conversation. The *Pescador* has entered the pack again, and the ice is thicker than both men had anticipated.

The steady irregular rapping against the hull has become a steady groan. 'Seems we might have to head north now anyway,' Carlos observes. 'If we stay here much longer, we'll be staying here for good. A well-preserved feature of the Antarctic landscape.'

'There has to be an easier way to look young forever!' Eduardo teases, as if relieved to finally be changing course.

In under half an hour, they're free of the pack once again but are exposed to the waves a new gale has whipped up.

'Watch out,' Carlos shouts too late as a sudden shift in wind direction pushes the starboard side of the *Pescador* into an iceberg. The boat shudders with the impact, but Eduardo manages to move it away from the berg and into open seas.

Minutes later, with the iceberg behind them, Dmitri is back in the wheelhouse, waving a damaged hand, which he has wrapped in a greasy rag and bound with duct tape.

'I demand you head this boat north. Immediately! No more delays,' the Russian shouts. He faces Eduardo directly, continuing in Spanish. 'I play no more games. You tell Carlos, or I will!'

Carlos looks to Eduardo for an explanation but the first mate directs his attention only to the Russian.

'Enough,' Eduardo commands.

Carlos is struck by the hardness in Eduardo's voice. He watches as the first mate holds up his hand in front of Dmitri's face, silencing him.

'We've *already* changed course. Look!' Eduardo points to the compass.

Dmitri reads the direction, but says nothing.

'What happened to your hand?' Carlos asks the Russian.

The veins have risen in Dmitri's neck. 'The spanner slipped. Cut me,' he replies in Spanish before turning to face Eduardo and switching to Russian. Carlos doesn't understand the sudden barrage of words, but cannot miss seeing Dmitri slice a finger across his throat in Eduardo's direction.

Dismayed, he looks to the first mate who seems to know how to manage the truculent engineer. They need Dmitri back on side.

'Go and clean it before it gets infected,' Eduardo says, his monotonal words delivered as if a threat. Carlos feels the heat of the anger in his friend's eyes.

When Dmitri has left the wheelhouse, Carlos faces Eduardo, incredulous, his unspoken earlier misgivings about the Russian vindicated. But there is something else — an unwelcome concern that he has been insulated, by language, from discussions with Dmitri, perhaps even shielded by Eduardo from the worst of their engineer. Carlos wonders whether, because Eduardo had been the one to recommend the Russian, the first mate feels he must wear the consequences of that decision too. 'What was he going to tell me? Why is he so angry?'

'I have no idea.'

JULIA
Montevideo, Uruguay
24 September 2002

Julia Pereira de Sánchez is watering the potted hibiscus on her small back porch, when the *gorrión* chick falls from its nest in the apartment's roof. It is dead on impact and cuts a forlorn picture on the lawn. Blue skin stretches over eyes still closed to the world. The orbits bulge from the meagre skull against a broken, featherless backdrop of a body. The chick's bent wings and rudimentary tail are reminiscent of the prehistoric fossil skeletons of the archaeopteryx, that Jurassic cross between a dinosaur and a modern bird, which Julia has seen at the museum. It's uncanny, she thinks, how closely an embryonic form can resemble that creature's extinct ancestor. Even in humans, the stages of embryonic development (from egg to tadpole-like being, to forms resembling frogs, then lizards, and, finally — a complete, hominid foetus) repeat the sequences seen in evolution (from unicellular organism to fish, to amphibian, to reptile, to mammal). 'Ontogeny replicates phylogeny' was the shorthand way she described it to her biology students. It never ceases to amaze her.

Using a hand trowel, Julia collects the bird's tiny floppy form and buries it under the single *Tipas* tree in the shared back garden. The mother bird is nowhere to be seen. How can she be so uncaring? Doesn't she know her own flesh and blood is being buried? Raucous cries erupt from the rooftop nest, interrupting Julia's thoughts. The mother bird skims overhead, her beak ajar with a fat insect. She's feeding her surviving chicks, Julia realises. God knows there's little time for grief when there are other young to nourish. Nature horrifies her sometimes, biology teacher or not. Using a branch of the tree, she hoists herself up from the ground and looks down at the tiny grave before going inside to console herself with a warm drink.

She takes her favourite ceramic *mate* gourd from the shelf and prepares the herbal tea, methodically tipping the gourd back and forth until the dried herbs are properly dispersed in the hot water. Before inserting the metal straw, she adds a spoonful of honey, her mind already elsewhere. She ruminates over the phone call she received yesterday from Francisco. He said he had had another conversation with Eduardo and been assured that the *Pescador* was on its way home. There had been some minor engine trouble, but fortunately all was well again.

The conversation has left Julia restless. Only another couple of weeks and Carlos would be home. Eduardo too. But the thought of engine trouble turns her stomach to water. She doubts Migiliaro would have spent one more peso on the boat than he had to. If the mechanics fail again, and conditions are bad, the *Pescador* could go down. Carlos, Eduardo and the entire crew would have only moments to reflect before their lives froze over. Maybe that would be the government's preference. And Migiliaro's too, for that matter. No scandal. No court case. Just an unfortunate incident at sea. The catch would be buried with the men, making it impossible to prove whether the vessel had been fishing illegally. *Señor* Migiliaro would escape fines and, through his middleman, claim insurance on his boat. The Uruguayan government, she suspects, would hide their knowledge of the *Pescador*'s illegal operations behind a smokescreen of fabricated concern for the tragic loss of life. It would be in bad taste to sully the dead men's names with slanderous allegations.

Julia shakes her head. Here she is worrying herself sick, while Carlos and Eduardo are no doubt still scheming about how to sell part of the catch without Migiliaro finding out. Ever optimistic. Overly optimistic. Eduardo may have promised to keep Carlos out of those arrangements, sparing him — and her — the consequences, but she is angry at the pair of them, and at herself, for agreeing to any of this. She finishes her *mate* and empties out the gourd, tipping the spent herbs down the sink and swirling her finger in the plughole to help the slurry disappear. For now, she has day-to-day life to contend with. She peruses the calendar. There is an antenatal appointment at the hospital at two o'clock, and she needs to be back in time to collect María from school. With a thick black pen, she crosses off another week of her pregnancy. Today marks the beginning of week twenty-six. For the baby's sake, she tries not to think any more about Carlos and Eduardo at sea.

The phone rings. It's the school. María has a high temperature and is vomiting. 'I'm on my way,' Julia says, hanging up the phone without even saying goodbye. She checks her watch. The next bus to the school leaves in fifteen minutes, enough time to reschedule her antenatal appointment. But the receptionist at the Hospital Maciel says they are fully booked for another two weeks. Julia writes the new date on the calendar, and hopes Carlos will be back by then. She clutches the small cross that he had fastened around her neck on a fine silver chain just months ago. 'For our baby,' Carlos had whispered. She holds it to her lips and utters a small prayer for their unborn child, for María, and for the safe return of her husband.

It takes three days for María to regain normal colour in her face. Over the phone, Julia's mother had scoffed at the doctor's diagnosis of a virus. To her, a virus is a convenient label for any illness the doctor doesn't know the cause of. There was no such thing when she was young, she insisted. How can something invisible to the naked eye wreak so much havoc? It doesn't fit with her robust, practical, hands-in-the-dirt view of life. 'No, it must be something María ate,' she'd said emphatically, the fact that food poisoning is also caused by microbes apparently lost on her. Julia let her mother's opinion lie. Sometimes it's better not to bring biology classes home, she has learnt. It was her mother's chicken soup she had phoned for, not an argument.

Julia opens María's bedroom window and lets the afternoon light spill inside. María wastes no time in leaning out over the sill to take in the view of the back garden. The mother *gorrión* snatches an insect from the *Tipas* tree and María twists her head around in the direction of the chicks' hungry calls. 'The nest's too far away. I can't see,' María complains, squinting into the sunlight.

'Watch out or they'll make a nest in your hair,' Julia teases. 'It's such a mess. Come and I'll fix it.' She taps the bed beside her and waves the hairbrush. María eventually obliges and Julia forms two straight plaits with practised hands. 'It always makes you feel better to have your hair done, *mi chica.*'

'Can Sofía come over and play?'

'Let's give it a couple more days,' Julia answers. The last person she feels like seeing now is Cecilia. 'Just to make sure you're all better. Here, I'll read you a story. Which one would you like?'

María reaches for *El Pez* (*The Fish*), which Eduardo wrote and illustrated for her when she turned two. It's still her favourite.

It makes Julia laugh as well. Laugh and cry. It reminds her of all the things about Eduardo that she can't share with another living soul. In the book, Eduardo has drawn perfect line-illustrations of his father's boatshed at La Paloma. The boatshed's back window shutter is open to the breeze, and there are footsteps, two sets, in the sand. The pictures, Julia knows, were drawn for her. A secret code.

María turns the page and Julia thinks back to her holidays as a teenager at the small fishing and surfing town just a few hours' drive from Montevideo. She is transported back to the long summer days of sand and swimsuits, of sipping soft drinks on La Paloma's shores. She remembers, too, the hours spent with Eduardo in the boatshed.

As she touches the pages of the book that his hands made, Julia feels again the deep ache in her womb that would build as her parents drove the family car along the Atlantic coast towards her favourite headland, kissed by the ocean on both sides. As the beaches grew whiter and the ocean clearer, she recalls how the flame in her heart rose up into her neck, warming her face until she could see it in the rear-vision mirror — her cheeks red at the thought of seeing her young lover again. Eduardo would let her know if his father was out fishing by leaving the boatshed's shutters open. (Eduardo's father always kept his shed closed tight like a clam, even if he was busy repairing nets inside. Julia supposed it was a relief for him just to be out of the wind, having spent so much of his life braced hard up against it at sea.) Seeing Eduardo's secret sign to her as they passed in the car, Julia would quickly help her parents unload the luggage, stacking it neatly against the wooden walls of the small rented bungalow. Then, announcing that she was going for a walk to stretch her legs, she would make her way down to the boatshed, shrouded by windswept pines, and to Eduardo.

They would climb in behind an old dinghy and lie together on a pile of salty, dry netting. She would feel his rope-calloused hands under her blouse, first on the small of her back, then on the sensitive skin of her stomach until, finally, with her silent encouragement, they brushed against her breasts. She liked the roughness of his palms and fingers worn from fishing nets, and projected onto her young lover a physical maturity beyond his years. They kissed and talked, dreamed and touched, but they never made love. Julia was terrified of becoming pregnant, a fact that sits uncomfortably with her now. Instead they discovered other ways to satisfy their young ardour. Ways that wouldn't result in a baby, but that, she realises now, would be the envy of many a staid and married couple who had run out of time, ideas and passion. Afterwards, the shutters would be closed, and Julia would leave the boatshed, her face glossy with its thin veil of sweat as if she had, indeed, just been for a walk.

Julia's family, devout Catholics, would never have approved of such a love before marriage, and so, at Julia's insistence, the young couple kept their holiday romances a secret. Not even Carlos — who Eduardo introduced to her as his best friend — knew.

Every school holiday for two years, Julia returned to La Paloma, her heart beating hard to see Eduardo, her face flushed in anticipation. It was on the first day of one such vacation that she learned their love affair was abruptly over, their future undone, torn apart and cast aside like an unravelling, old fishing net. Eduardo had become involved with another young woman and she was expecting his baby.

Virginia had moved to La Paloma with her parents only four months before. She was tall and tanned, and difficult to ignore. Julia later found out from friends in La Paloma, who knew nothing of her own love for Eduardo, that Virginia had sat beside him in class from her first day. On weekends she had sunned herself near his father's boatshed. It was love at first sight, they had said.

Julia hid her devastation well. She had no choice. Virginia was pregnant. Eduardo was to marry her.

Soon after, Carlos innocently asked Julia out, his invitation made casually in front of Eduardo. It was clear that Carlos still hadn't the faintest suspicion that she and Eduardo had been anything more than friends. Even if her first love had not remained faithful to her, he had at least kept his promise to keep their relationship a secret. And, from the sadness in his eyes, Julia knew that he still had feelings for her. Perhaps he even regretted his situation — bound to a new girlfriend forever by a child. Nevertheless, she punished him for his infidelity and accepted, on the spot, Carlos's invitation to see a film: a love story.

But she couldn't sustain her anger. She still cared for Eduardo and, it had to be said, respected his commitment to the mother of his unborn child. And there was something else that softened the hurt. In the months that followed, Carlos persisted in his attempts to woo her, and she began to enjoy his attention. He found fishing work in Montevideo and invited Julia for long walks along the riverfront and cheap meals in the Ciudad Vieja. He was solid and dependable, and seemed incapable of causing her the hurt that Eduardo had inflicted. The physical side of their relationship was slow to develop, but perhaps that was a good thing.

When she turned twenty, a marriageable age, both sets of parents approved of the union. Carlos asked Julia to be his wife and, on the same day, asked Eduardo to be best man. In the weeks leading up to the wedding, Julia tortured herself with a Catholic's guilt about her secret first love. In truth, part of her still yearned for him, a sentiment that was only heightened by Eduardo's speech on the day she and Carlos married. Julia was sure that Eduardo had been talking to her when he told the gathered guests that 'real love only happens once'.

As the years passed, there were other times when she felt tempted to tell her husband the truth about Eduardo. Times when their marriage felt so strong that nothing could rock the boat, and times when the motivation was completely different: when Julia felt that Carlos was taking her for granted and spending too long at sea. But to admit the truth would change everything: Carlos's friendship with Eduardo, Eduardo's relationship with his wife, and Julia's relationship with all three. It would also draw a line through her intimacies with Eduardo forever, and they were not all ancient history.

Just six months ago, when Eduardo casually mentioned that he had almost finished restoring his father's old wooden dinghy, the one they used to lie behind, Julia found herself asking if she could come and see it. She told him she could catch an early-morning bus to La Paloma and be home in time to put María to bed. She'd ask a neighbour if they could take María to school and mind her afterwards, she'd said out loud as she thought it through.

When they met at their teenage hideaway — their bodies older, their smiles complicated by thoughts of spouses and children — what followed was no accident.

Eduardo had replaced the old nets behind the restored dinghy with a mattress and a sea blanket. Perhaps it was spare bedding for the boat, but Julia suspected they were new additions. She wore a soft sandalwood perfume and a white, knee-length dress dotted with red flowers. Thin straps dropped easily from her shoulders, and the zip at the back was loose from wear. It was all too easy. Neither one of them held back their desires, instead letting years of suppressed passion and curiosity carry them forward to the natural conclusion for the first, and probably final, time.

Part of Julia had hoped the encounter would settle her physical longing for Eduardo once and for all, perhaps even be an anticlimax. That would have been easier. But he was the relaxed and natural lover she had always suspected he would be. They moved together without haste or anxiety, savouring the chance to uncover the treasure they had been searching for all their lives.

Afterwards, Eduardo had convinced Julia to let him take her photograph. 'You look so beautiful today,' he had said.

They left the boatshed separately, just as they had when they were teenagers, before returning home to their families, this time as the parents. Julia had told Carlos she was going to La Paloma for a day trip and that he would need to collect María from the neighbour. He hadn't questioned her for a second.

A week later, Eduardo's photograph had arrived in the mail. For six months she kept it hidden in a book under the bed she shared with Carlos until finally deciding she should send it to her parents. It was too dangerous having such evidence in the house. When Carlos found the photograph the day before he left for the Southern Ocean she had panicked, yet he regarded the picture with the same trust in his eyes that was always there for her. She thinks of that photograph now on the ocean with Carlos and wonders if Eduardo has seen it in her husband's hand.

It isn't that life with Carlos is without passion. They remain intimate after all their years together, their losses and their joys, but in a stop-and-start kind of way. Marriage has allowed her to fall in love with her husband many times over. Their best moments are the homecomings, when Carlos returns after weeks at sea.

She longs for such a reunion now, and remembers when his boat last docked, just two months before he left port aboard the *Pescador*. María had been at school and Julia had watched her husband walk up their street with his fishing jacket and overpants slung over his shoulder — his hair hard with the sea. He had smelt raw and real and she allowed him only the briefest of showers before welcoming him onto newly washed sheets. They lay together, fanned by the afternoon breeze through the apartment's billowing bedroom curtains, making love with a fresh sense of urgency. The physical reconnection came as a relief — a transfusion of intimacy that gave their marriage vital blood and reassured her that she had married the right man. She had let Carlos push Eduardo from her mind, and surrendered into their rolling, lilting unison. It felt, she thought at the time, as if the sea was still flowing in Carlos's blood and entering hers.

DAVE
The *Australis*
24 September 2002

The weather has turned southerly again and, with the chase
nearing the end of its first week, Dave Bates wonders what
the hell he's still doing out here. The *Australis* rolls in the
heavy seas, pitching from one side to the other, on the edge of
iceberg territory. He makes a satellite call to the Australian
Customs Service, and is surprised when Roger Wentworth
answers. According to Wentworth's secretary, he had been on
stress leave for the last two days. Dave had laughed bitterly
when he heard this the previous day.

'It's still pretty ordinary out here,' Dave says, struggling to
steer the boat with one hand on the wheel. 'Any news on the
illegals? Because if they're still poking along in the pack ice,
maybe we should let them go. I don't want to be responsible
for driving them to their deaths.'

'Affirmative, Dave. We intercepted another call between
the *Pescador* and Uruguayan Fisheries. I was just about to let
you know. Sounds like they've had a bit of engine trouble, but
they're on their way to Montevideo. They were too far south
for anyone's liking.' Wentworth pauses. 'That why you pulled
the pin on the hot pursuit?'

'Too bloody right. That and the fact we hit a growler that

could've sunk us before we had a chance to ask the government's permission.' Dave tries to contain his anger. 'Look, I realise you'd prefer us to have stayed within spitting distance of the illegals, but it's a death sentence down there. We're not out of the woods where we are.'

'I know that, mate. But once they do reappear, it'll be in our interests to keep them in your sights if you can. The word is that the *Pescador* is just one of a fleet of boats run by a bloke in Spain, a Mr Migiliaro. The Minister's pretty keen to put the pressure on him.'

'I'll do what I can, but I'm not going to endanger my crew.'

'No. Of course not. We'd never ask that,' Wentworth splutters. 'Be assured we're doing all we can to convince the illegals to call it quits and bring this all to an end. For everyone's sakes. Needless to say, they're not answering our satellite calls. We've advised the South African navy about the chase, and they're prepared to help apprehend the vessel once it gets closer.'

'Okay. Just let me know if the plan changes. We've got some crusty old seadogs on board and none of them have seen seas like the ones we've been copping. It's beyond me how the illegal boat's still afloat, to be honest.'

Dave ends the phone call just as William appears at the wheelhouse door, pale again. Dave isn't sure if he has heard any of his conversation with Customs.

'Feeling a bit rough, lad?'

'Just a bit,' William says with a burp. Dave figures he's moments away from vomiting and looks for a bucket. 'The weather's pretty bad again. D'you reckon we've seen the worst of it?' William asks, picking at a hole in the sleeve of his polar fleece.

'It has picked up a bit again. Nothing the boat can't handle, though. She'll blow over.' Dave relaxes the muscles of his face in a deliberate attempt to appear reassuring. 'The autopilot normally takes care of the steering for us, but in storm conditions I like to keep control of things myself. It's hard work though, after a while.' A large wave pushes the boat sideways and Dave struggles to keep his balance. Once the boat is back on course he checks on William, who is bracing himself against the door frame, staring open-mouthed at the sea. 'See what I mean?' Dave says. 'Here, come and feel her.'

William appears unsure, but Dave knows that taking the helm will distract the lad from his nausea.

'Come on. You've got to have a few stories to tell your mates back on dry land.'

Dave lets go of the helm, and the boat falters slightly. William takes hold, just as a large wave strikes the bow. 'Geez, there's some power in those waves,' the young man says, gripping the helm harder than he needs to. Dave watches his fingers turn white.

'Just get the feel of it, lad. And don't hold the helm so tight. It's all controlled by hydraulics. You can't prevent the boat being knocked; just gently correct her course each time. And see if you can keep the knocks from coming side-on. We don't want to broach.'

Cactus is at the wheelhouse door now, shaking his head. 'Not really conditions for an L-plater.'

William turns to Cactus behind him and heads the boat the wrong way into a wave. The *Australis* is knocked sideways.

'Bloody hell,' Cactus swears.

William takes his hands off the helm like a scolded child, and the boat lurches again. The men grab hold of anything they can to stay upright. Dave takes over and tries to correct the course. Eventually the boat comes around.

'Now I've seen it all,' Cactus scoffs.

'You were learning once, Cactus. Pull your bloody head in.'

Dave hears a guttural surge rise from William and the young man vomits onto the wheelhouse floor. It's clear he hasn't eaten much in the past few hours. Meals have been pretty basic since the weather turned foul: bread, cheese, canned ham, some soup to keep them warm, baked beans and powdered mashed potato. But it doesn't appear that William has tried much more than bread and soup today.

'We'll have to get some kilojoules into you on the journey home, lad, or Trish'll kill me, if Margie doesn't first! There's enough sausages, steak, eggs and bacon in the freezer to feed a small army. Good sailing grease.' Dave says the last few words just before William vomits again. 'Sorry, that was a stupid thing to say. Just thinking out loud. Go down to your bunk and lie on your side for a while. And if you can eat some dry biscuits or bread and cheese, it might settle you down, son.' As soon as Dave says the word 'son', he wishes he could reel it back in.

William wipes his mouth and chin with the back of his hand and leaves the wheelhouse without a word.

'*Son* now is it?' Cactus raises his eyebrows.

If it wasn't for the twelve-metre seas, Dave knows he'd give the stupid bastard a piece of his mind. It's not as if he doesn't have it coming. Less than a decade ago, Cactus and Dave had each owned orange-roughy trawlers, and spent weeks at a time fishing for the brilliant-coloured fish off seamounts south of Tasmania, often within coo-ee of each other. Cactus made a packet of money before he retired, just before roughy catches fell, quotas were set and boats sold. He timed his exit perfectly. Rumour was that he'd had inside knowledge. Dave, on the other hand, had been slow to get out — Margie had called it stubborn — and sold his boat for a song. Cactus rubbed Dave's nose in his success, but within a year had gambled away all of his fishing money. A week after he was declared bankrupt, he had a heart attack.

'The stupid bugger brought it all on himself,' Dave had told Margie more recently. 'He needs to look around sometime and see that other people have their stresses too. Losing a son is hardly a bed of roses. Dave knows now that much of his anger at Cactus stems from his silence after Sam died. He could've bloody stretched himself to sign the card they sent, he thinks. But no, good old Connie did it for him as if he were a big bloody kid.

Margie had excused him. 'Deep down he's probably just frightened of having another heart attack.' And Dave suspects she was probably right. Cactus has certainly told him, on more than one occasion, that there are, in the surgeon's words 'only six seconds between his next heart attack and death'.

Perhaps that's why Cactus is so hard on the big, strapping William it occurs to Dave for the first time. William has his whole life ahead of him, and a body that resembles a Greek god, while Cactus, with his white hair and withering muscles, probably feels he's on borrowed time. But whatever his hang-ups, Dave wants to shake Cactus until his self-centred head falls off. He wants to shout at him that no life is guaranteed, young or old, and that he should just get on and live his and quit the victim act. Instead, Dave settles for getting him to clean up William's vomit.

'Go and get the mop and bucket, Cactus,' Dave says without looking at him.

Cactus swears out of the corner of his mouth, creamy with wasted spit.

Dave scans the radar as Cactus leaves the wheelhouse. A new neon-green blip appears on the screen. He dismisses it as another iceberg, as it bobs in and out of range. But the next time he looks down, the light has inched forward.

'I'll be buggered,' he says under his breath, studying the distances. The *Pescador* is only ten nautical miles from them. Dave feels a rush of adrenaline at seeing the boat again, and is relieved to see for himself that they're still afloat. If he was honest, he'd even admit to being pleased to have the company on this remote stretch of lonely sea. Perhaps this is how rival astronauts would feel if they met each other on Mars. The *Pescador* appears to be cutting north across his path, and he wonders at their sudden change of heart. According to Roger Wentworth, they're supposed to be heading back to Montevideo. Maybe they sustained damage and are making a run for a closer port. Perhaps somewhere in South Africa.

Cactus reappears with the mop and bucket.

'Get a load of this!' Dave points at the radar.

'Bloody oath. It's not a phantom friggin' chase after all!' Cactus shakes his head.

The *Pescador* makes its way across the radar screen, aided by the southerly behind it.

'They're not afraid of much.' Dave imagines the *Pescador* with the seas — like nature's own patrol boats — behind it, pushing it out of Antarctic waters for trespassing.

'They're tough buggers. I'll give 'em that,' Cactus concedes. 'But I'm not sure if they're being brave or bloody stupid runnin' with the weather blowin' up their backside like that.

If the seas get any bigger, she'll be pitched arse over tit.' He sniggers. 'Where d'you reckon they're headed?' He scrapes up the worst of William's vomit with a bread knife and a dustpan before getting the mop onto it.

Dave scratches his head at Cactus's choice of implement, but keeps his thoughts to himself. Cactus always makes harder work of things than he needs to.

'I don't know, but it won't be long before we can ask them ourselves,' Dave jokes. 'We'll be on her tail soon enough.'

'Canberra'll be happy,' Cactus says.

'We'll see. Wentworth's pretty pissed off at us for breaking the chase. Reckons we might've screwed up our chances of getting a prosecution.' Dave attempts a satellite call to Canberra, but there's no dial tone.

'No go?' Cactus asks.

'Satellite's out. I'll wait a while.'

'Fan-bloody-tastic! Just us and a bunch of pissed-off South American cowboys,' Cactus says. 'Reckon they're armed?'

'There's a better than even chance. Most hard-core illegals carry guns, according to Wentworth anyway.' Dave's expression suggests that Wentworth might not be the most reliable source of information.

Harry enters the wheelhouse. 'Must be your turn for a break, Davo.'

'Cheers.' Dave hands over the helm. 'Just don't slip on the floor there.' He points to the spot in front of Cactus. 'Young

William has been marking his territory. And, by the way, we've got company.' He points to the radar.

'Well, I'll be blowed.'

The deck of the *Australis* is awash with foam and water. Dave watches as the whole bow goes under and, for a long moment, he wonders if the boat will just keep going down. An arrow destined for the deep. The boat re-emerges like a drunken cork. He can almost hear her gasp for air.

'I'll leave you with it, mate,' he tells Harry before taking his leave from the wheelhouse. He checks in on William, who he finds already asleep in his bunk, and wonders if he's being too soft on the boy. But he can't help fathering him. He's the closest thing he has to a son now.

Dave makes his way back up to his own cabin and surrenders himself to his bunk. He imagines spooning with Margie in bed, the sound and smell of the eucalypts swirling outside the bedroom window, Bonnie scratching at the door to be let in. In his mind, he opens the door for the dog and allows her wet tongue to greet his face. There have been times since Sam's death, when Dave has let Bonnie right up onto the bed. 'Who's been sleeping in *my* bed?' Margie would say playfully, when she discovered the dog's blonde hairs on the doona cover. Dave can see her now, holding up a sample of offending hair.

'At least it's *dog* hair!' he'd answer back. 'Don't know what you're complaining about.'

Dave knows that their friends think it odd that Margie and he can joke about infidelity. No doubt they are jealous that, after twenty-seven years of marriage, he and his wife still hold hands and kiss in public. Their bed is as sacred as the day they first laid upon it together. It still even has its moments of true passion, although the grief they've shared with the loss of Sam has dulled that in recent times. Making love has become more of a comfort than an excitement.

He covers his face with the blanket, blocking out the smell of the ship, and brings to mind the early days of his courtship with Margie. It was their last year of high school and neither of them had known love before, but they found their way with each other. Nervously, they had their first kiss behind a dance hall. They took things slowly, cautiously. Back then, Dave thinks, life was a horizonless sea. There was no hurry, and no end in sight.

He relives the night they graduated. They had taken a drive in his new Volkswagen Beetle and parked at Hobart's Domain to watch the moonlight play on the river. He remembers seeing the silver light dance, too, in Margie's smiling eyes when he told her, for the first time, that he loved her. He had been surprised by the weight of her breasts in his hands as she allowed him under her woollen twin-set. It was a night he'll never forget.

Now, as Dave closes his eyes, he can smell Margie's familiar scent and feel the softness of her skin against his. Sleep advances like a gentle wave and washes over him.

LOGBOOK OF EDUARDO RODRÍGUEZ TORRES

～

The waves here are immense, larger than any I have ever seen. Dizzying walls of water, thirty metres high, build behind us, lifting the Pescador *as if it is a toy, and throwing us to the gaping sea below. I think the ocean is angry, fuming at us for stealing what it holds dear.*

～

CARLOS
The *Pescador*
28 September 2002

The *Pescador* surfs in the following seas, which chase it with the ferocious force of rearing, wild-eyed horses. The waves pedal their rising hooves against the stern of the boat, beating it in a storm of rage for straying into their territory. Carlos checks the GPS, watching the boat's speed climb feverishly on the descent of a wave: ten, twelve, fourteen knots. Water engulfs the stern in a barrage of heavy attacks and, with the weight of ice on the port side, it's an effort to keep the vessel from broaching. The wave lets go, its fingers torn and ragged from holding on too tight. Carlos relaxes his grip on the wheel.

Eduardo enters the wheelhouse, wrenching on his sea jacket. He speaks hurriedly to Carlos. 'We have to get that ice off — now!' He runs the heavy zip up almost the full length of his face, so that only his eyes are showing beneath the jacket's hood. Perhaps it's because they've been friends since childhood, or perhaps it's because Eduardo's eyes are indeed the windows to his soul, that Carlos believes he can read his friend's state of mind from just this narrow strip of exposed face — Eduardo appears without fear, focused and determined. Carlos doubts his own eyes are as reassuring.

'Make sure you use safety lines. No heroics,' Carlos says.

'You think I'm a fool?' Eduardo asks, feigning offence.

'*Loco*,' Carlos teases, twirling a finger at the side of his temple.

Eduardo laughs. 'I've already spoken to them down below. The crew will meet me out there.' He studies the vast amount of water washing over the deck. If he is at all nervous, Carlos cannot tell. Eduardo makes a brief study of the instruments, processing what he needs to know of the boat and wind speeds.

'You don't have to go too, you know,' Carlos says. 'I could do with the help here, to be honest. And I promised Virginia I'd bring you back in one piece.'

'I can't ask them to go out there if I'm not prepared to go myself.'

'All right,' Carlos concedes. He knows the crew will waste no time in assisting their first mate on deck, and wonders if Eduardo would have made the better master. They revere him like a god.

Dmitri enters the wheelhouse, and says something in Russian to Eduardo. Carlos thinks he hears the word 'Mauritius' before the engineer leaves again.

'Why does he do that? Speak in Russian when I'm here?' Carlos asks.

'He's a good engineer. I didn't say he had good manners,' Eduardo says, his eyes smiling.

'What was he saying about Mauritius?'

'He's still harping on about offloading there, the stubborn idiot. He says we're stupid fools.'

'Well, he's probably right about the second part.'

Eduardo laughs again and, continuing his earlier joke, bends forward, pretending to hold a walking stick. He hobbles towards the door, takes the hammer from a side hatch, tips an imaginary hat and goes outside. The gusting wind crashes the door shut behind him and Carlos watches his friend make his way down the metal stairs and onto the deck.

In his wet-weathers, Eduardo is a small orange blur as he braces himself against the full power of a wave. Water crashes over the stern, thrusting the bow skyward. Eduardo rides the wet rising deck, which rears now like a harpooned whale. He clips his safety line to the portside rail, holds his footing and, between waves, takes short firm steps through falling water towards the bow of the boat.

Carlos searches the radar screen, which is green with wave scatter. On the outer reaches he makes out another vessel. It has been drifting on and off the radar for a few days and appears to be tracking his course. '¡*Maldito!*' he mutters. He's surprised the Australians have stood it out. It's difficult to imagine there's enough in it for them.

He watches the men on deck and sees Manuel, one of the Spaniards on board, hauling himself along the rails. Like Eduardo, Manuel has made sure that he is identifiable from the wheelhouse when working on deck. The word '*Padre*' is painted in black on the back of his jacket, helping those in the wheelhouse to know where their most experienced crew member is at any one time. It's Manuel's idea of a joke. He likes to think of himself as father to them all.

Behind Manuel are another fifteen crew members, lining up behind their first mate like ants, swinging their clubs at the ice on the rails and returning it to the sea. Carlos feels the boat lift abruptly and turns his head to see a wall of water gaining behind them. Eduardo sees it too, a giant wave, gathering the *Pescador* up and carrying her forward with such momentum that the bow of the boat is out of the water, soaring. The men on deck check safety lines and hold the rails, which suddenly seem to belong to a skyscraper, such is the gape of air beneath them.

When they hit the trough, gulping water swallows the crew, surging across the deck. Carlos maintains the boat's course and, when the bow of the *Pescador* finally resurfaces, he counts his men. To his horror, two are missing.

Eduardo gets to his feet and is hauling at a line stretched tight over the side. Carlos can't see Manuel. Eduardo slips on the wet deck, but manages to catch himself against the rails. The bow lifts higher out of the water and more of the crew get to their feet to haul at the straps that dangle two of their own over the ocean's open mouth. Flashes of white foam fly onto the deck, the spittle of a rabid sea gnashing its jaws below them. Finally, the jacket with the painted word '*Padre*' reappears as

Eduardo and another crewman haul Manuel back on deck. Carlos sees the old Spaniard raise an arm to let him know he is okay. Within seconds, the other seaman is also landed, slapped on board like an exhausted fish. He isn't moving.

One of the crew puts an arm around Manuel and hauls him to his feet, guiding him back along the rails to the door that leads down to the cabins. Another crewman, who Carlos recognises from his size to be the Peruvian they call El Animal, carries the limp crewman in his arms. It could be a war zone, El Animal pausing only when the battleground receives another assault from behind. Eduardo and the remaining crew continue on the front lines, hammering off ice, finishing only when the job is complete.

It's half an hour before Eduardo reports back to the wheelhouse. He has changed into dry clothes: a fleece and pants. Carlos notices that he has even combed his hair, perhaps in an effort to reassert a sense of normality on the extreme situation.

'They're both okay,' Eduardo says, rubbing his gloved hands together to improve their circulation.

'Thank God.' Carlos looks back at the sea and corrects the boat's course. 'I recognised Manuel, but I didn't make out the other one. He seemed in a bad way.'

'It was the young Peruvian — José. I'm surprised he wasn't washed off long ago, to be honest.' Eduardo chuckles. 'Flyweight that he is.'

'For a minute there, I thought you were going over, too.' Carlos slaps Eduardo on the back. '*Jesús*, don't scare me like that again. What would I say to Virginia? Or to Julia for that matter? They'd both kill me. Life wouldn't be worth living!'

'Looks like you're stuck with me.'

Carlos grins and finds himself thinking back to the long summers he spent with Eduardo, Julia and Virginia all those years ago. Happier, simpler times. 'Remember when we all used to hang out together at La Paloma. Those holidays seemed to go on forever.'

'They were never long enough.'

'It took me years to pluck up the courage to ask Julia out. I still can't believe you didn't beat me to it. You two always got along so well.' Carlos reaches over and messes up Eduardo's hair. 'It wasn't like you to be slow off the mark.'

'I guess not.' Eduardo's smile is wistful. Carlos imagines that his friend is also reminiscing about better days, wishing he was back there.

'God I hate being away from her. I just want to hold her again, to curl up beside her and know that she is safe. To know that María and our baby are safe.'

'We'll be home soon,' Eduardo says, putting a hand on Carlos's shoulder. 'Anyway, I'm going below. I'm exhausted.'

Carlos winks, 'Dream of that lovely wife of yours.'

MARGIE
Hobart, Australia
1 October 2002

Margie's fingers play in the warm velvet of Bonnie's ears. The newly washed golden retriever gleams in the morning sun. Margie's engagement ring, polished from the combination of dog shampoo and Bonnie's fur, glints, too, in the honey-coloured light streaming onto the back veranda. She studies the ring, its small, sparkling diamond set simply in a wave-like curve of white gold. It sits neatly against her matching wedding ring, reminding her, as it has always done, of spooning lovers. Of David.

White gold, Dave has said, is also what fishermen call the lucrative flesh of toothfish. Who would have thought such an ugly creature, caught in the deep, dark waters off Antarctica, would cause so much fuss? Margie shakes her head at the nonsense of it all at the same time as she watches, through the large Tasmanian-oak kitchen windows, her two pet goldfish in a bowl on the kitchen bench. They are swimming around and around, as if trying to find a way out, their shadows flitting across the white wall behind the bowl — there one moment, gone the next.

She has just heard from Customs that they have lost contact with Dave's boat 'for the moment'. She had called

Roger Wentworth in a moment of anxiety, and now wishes to God she hadn't.

She wishes, too, that she had more self-control when panic strikes. She shouldn't blindly follow her feet to the phone, and speak after her fingers have dialled the number. She wonders if her anxiety is obvious to the person at the other end, or if she manages to hide it behind a sufficient number of light-hearted jokes. Not that she cares a hoot what Roger Wentworth thinks. He had managed to piss her off royally, as Dave would say.

Wentworth has told her that Dave's decision to break the chase hadn't pleased the Fisheries Minister 'one iota'. 'Losing sight of the illegals has seriously compromised our chances of a prosecution,' he had said.

'Well, it's better than being seriously dead,' Margie had snapped back. 'I, for one, am pleased that Dave stuck to his guns. Surely you can appreciate he's responsible for more than twenty lives down there. He isn't going to follow some minister's orders if it means endangering his crew. Believe me, if it was safe to continue, he would have done so. With bells on!'

'Yes, Mrs Bates. Of course.' Roger Wentworth had backed off like a chastised schoolboy.

The phone call has left Margie sick with concern. She knows conditions must have been pretty rank down there for Dave to have pulled the pin. She flicks through a newspaper to distract herself, and to fool her anxiety into focusing its attentions elsewhere. In her current frame of mind, she knows that keeping busy is the best way to keep her own head above water.

She comes across a full-page advertisement for a private health fund. It seems to have been written for her. There's a picture of a road sign that reads STOP, and in small letters under it, WORRYING. The implication, of course, is that if you sign up to the health fund now you can say goodbye to your anxieties forever. It's an attractive promise. If Dave was here, he'd cut out the page and pin it up somewhere for her to see. Perhaps it's not a bad idea, she thinks, going to work with the kitchen scissors and securing the advertisement to the fridge door with a set of kitsch fish-shaped magnets that Sam bought for her as a joke. She makes a mental note to take the ad down when visitors call in.

Margie looks across the lawn to the eucalypt-fringed Derwent River. She watches a sailboat dance on frilly waves whipped up by the spring winds. Turbulent Tasmanian spring, she thinks. Yesterday was stiflingly hot, the air so dry that vapours from eucalypts had sparked bushfires across the State, yet a heavy frost this morning had damaged fruit trees and destroyed half the expected summer harvest of apples, pears and cherries. Today, there's snow on Mount Wellington and more snow is forecast for tonight, right down to sea level. Spring in Tasmania is a bit like grief, she decides. Just when you think the worst of winter is over and that summer has arrived, a sudden storm will strike from an unexpected angle with such ferocity that the only option is to drop the sails and ride it out.

She phones Joan, a woman she has known since Sam was born, twenty-six years ago. Joan was in the bed beside her at the maternity hospital. Their children had been born five hours, and a whole world, apart.

Joan's daughter, Beth, has Down's syndrome. Margie remembers feeling for the new mother beside her, watching her determination to celebrate the birth of her first child, while mourning the loss of the one she'd imagined.

Most visitors to Joan's bedside didn't acknowledge the baby cradled in her arms. Margie could hear the older, hard-of-hearing, ones talking conspiratorially outside, their voices echoing carelessly in the corridor louder than intended. They told each other how it would have been easier if the mother and child had never met. How the baby would have been better off in a home. Like they knew.

Margie would sometimes catch Joan staring at Sam in his hospital cradle, peering over the glossy white crib when she thought Margie was asleep. She remembers feeling guilty about her perfect bundle. At his potential. Life had dealt them such contrasting hands.

Heads or tails. Light or dark.

It occurred to Margie at the time that nothing else in life placed you so much in the lap of the gods as having a child — carrying it, bearing it and raising it through the early months.

She remembers panicking that the two babies might have been mistakenly given to the wrong mothers. Sleep deprived and hormonal, Margie had been terrified that the nurse could one day breeze in, fluff up her pillow and say: 'I'm terribly sorry, Mrs Bates, but that little girl is actually yours. Silly me. Let me bring her over to you.' It bothers her, to this day, that she doesn't know what she would have done. Does that make her a bad person?

Margie recalls the expression on Joan's face when someone finally did ask her if she was keeping 'the baby'. Joan later told her she could have been kicked in the chest, the impact was so great. On the day they both left the hospital, Joan told Margie there was never a doubt in her mind that she would keep her child. The trauma was in completely redesigning her life. Forgetting the future she had wished for. Margie promised herself silently then and there that she would spend a morning a week at her new friend's house looking after Beth. It would give Joan the chance for a break, to do something for herself.

Margie's still not sure if the promise stemmed from her own guilt at having had a perfect baby, or her fear that life can so easily turn on you, and that perhaps good deeds, in some way, provide a degree of immunity against misfortune.

Today, Margie parks outside Joan's white fibro house in Moonah, on Hobart's outskirts, ashamed that she has not honoured her commitment of late. It has been a month since she last visited, and she makes another pact with herself to reinstate the weekly relief care. She hasn't been at all reliable since Sam's death. But it goes deeper than that. It's ironic, but she feels jealous now when she visits Joan and Beth. Jealous because Joan still has a child. It's as though the hands dealt to them have indeed been switched.

Heads or tails. Light or dark.

Joan and Beth are closer than most adult mothers and daughters and still enjoy an enviable level of physical affection. Margie has been left with just the memory of Sam — nothing warm that she can touch. Resentment sneaks up on her, and in her darkest moments Margie is distressed by black thoughts about why it had to be Sam that died in the car crash and not someone else's child. She elbows the thoughts aside as she pushes open the car door and crosses the small square of mown front lawn stabbed with a white, rusted wrought-iron letterbox. Number 42. It's the same old fibro house that Joan had brought Beth home to all those years before. The same house in which her husband, Charlie, had died from a stroke ten years ago while they had all slept.

Margie sees Beth at the aluminium-framed window, her pale skin fringed by the fleshy pink camellias that grow near the front steps hiding the tired paintwork. Margie hears her shout excitedly to her mother, and pictures her running down the well-worn carpet of the hallway before she appears at the front door, which yawns precariously on its loose hinges.

Flushed and gasping, Beth fills the doorway, and Joan moves her sideways to greet Margie with a kiss and a quick, oven-mitted hug.

'Come in. I just have to get a cake out of the oven.' Joan jogs quickly towards the kitchen. 'It's a new recipe. Orange cake. Hope it's okay,' she calls behind her.

Margie inhales the warm, citrus aroma that greets her. 'If it tastes half as good as it smells, it'll be fabulous!'

There's a new flush of art on the walls, and an Indian yellow beaded throw strewn across the couch in the lounge room. A purple ikat tablecloth covers the dining table, clashing awfully, and wonderfully, with the couch cover.

There's a sense of life here, Margie thinks. A pushing of the boundaries, and a celebration of difference. Survival against the odds. Despite caring for her handicapped daughter within these same walls for more than two decades, Joan has rejected the temptation to become resigned and bitter. She has played the hand dealt to her and, if anything, has become positively defiant. Always exploring new horizons, trying new things. Challenging others out of their conservative cocoons. It occurs to Margie that the ever-changing, life-affirming décor in this house is an outward expression of Joan's resilient soul.

'How's Dave, Marg?' Joan asks, placing the sliced cake on the table between them and sinking into her 1970s lounge chair. 'I've read in the paper that he's caught up in a bit of drama down south.'

'That's putting it mildly,' Margie says, rolling her eyes. 'It's a stupid situation they've got themselves into.' Margie sees Beth through the window, running her plump hands over the red tulips that border the lawn. The flowers are planted thickly alongside daffodils in a bed of black, well-watered soil. Margie begins to weep from nowhere. Raw emotion that finds acceptance in Joan's home.

'Margie, love ...' Joan holds out a tissue as Margie succumbs to her fears for the first time since the beginning of the sea chase.

'What right does the illegal boat have to risk another crew?' Margie holds the tissue under her dripping nose. 'Selfish bastards. And what about *their* families? Don't they care about them, either?' Margie blows her nose on the sodden tissue and Joan passes her the whole box. 'I phoned Customs and they had the hide to tell me that Dave was in trouble with the Minister for not having followed the illegal boat further south. He's been chasing them for two weeks, for Christ's sake! Those bureaucrats need a bucket of iced water tipped over their heads.'

'And down their pants,' Joan chortles, obviously trying to lighten the mood. 'Too much testosterone, that's the problem. Bloody men!' Joan focuses on the gaily painted teacup in her hand, studying the scene of Dutch windmills, flowers and children in traditional dress. 'All this over some dead fish!' She attempts a laugh, and then grows more earnest. 'Why don't you contact the foreign master's family? Can't be that hard to track them down. Where did I hear the boat was from … Uruguay, wasn't it?'

'Yes, but …' Margie raises her eyebrows at her friend, disarmed and confused by the naïve comment. Joan's advice is normally so sensible and well considered. She looks at the clock on the wall.

'I know what you're thinking,' Joan says. 'How could I ask such a damned stupid question? But why not contact the other family? Give me one good reason.'

'I wish it were that simple. But, chances are the boat's flag state has nothing to do with where the master and crew are from. It's just a convenience thing. A Get Out of Jail Free card. Illegal boats like to register with countries that either haven't signed up to, or choose not to honour, the international fishing agreements. The master can be from anywhere, and the poor old crews are a melting pot of desperadoes from all around the world.'

'You could google the Uruguayan Fisheries office. They'll have an email address on the web. It'd be a start.'

Margie is surprised at her friend's persistence. 'Joan …'

'Look, life is simpler than we sometimes choose to believe. The other master's wife will want her husband home, too. Your agendas are the same. If you lived across the road from each other and your husbands were at each other's throats, wouldn't you invite her over for a cuppa to see if you could help sort out the mess?'

'Even if I did get a contact address for the illegal guy's wife, what would I write? "Dear Mrs Illegal Guy's Wife, I'm the wife of the man who's chasing your husband halfway around the world. Please tell him to surrender so we can fine him to within an inch of his life and confiscate his catch, and the boat. Oh, and he'll probably be held in detention in Australia until the trial is over, and if found guilty, could be put in jail. Sincerely, Margie Sticking-Her-Nose-In-Where-It's-Not-Welcome Bates."'

Joan appears somewhat put off, but carries on. 'Don't be like that. Just tell her that nothing is worth dying over and that you'd like to work with her to come up with a solution to resolve the situation. Maybe you could suggest that the Uruguayan boat docks in neutral waters. Somewhere where the case could be heard independently.'

Margie opens her mind fractionally to the idea just as Beth throws open the flyscreen door and charges inside, crying in big snorts. The door crashes tinnily behind her and Margie feels a spray of moisture across her arm. Beth, clawing at her face, lands heavily on her mother's lap.

'For heaven's sake, Bethie! What's wrong?' Joan shouts, the air pressed out of her.

Beth points to her left nostril and Joan, holding the right side shut, asks her to blow out. Margie hands over a fresh tissue just in time to catch the fresh onslaught of spray and a small, shiny Christmas beetle, which lands dazed and glistening upside-down on the Kleenex. Its wet wings are glued together and its back legs inscribe circles in the air above it. Beth's mood changes dramatically. She is mesmerised by what she has produced. The beetle, presumably no less startled, rights itself, and spreads its wings to dry.

'You're amazing, Joan Summers,' Margie chuckles, wiping away happy tears and reaching over to embrace her friend.

'What, for liberating a beetle from a fate worse than death?'

'That and a lot more.' Margie holds Joan by the top of her well-muscled arms. 'Can I mind Bethie again for you soon? To give you a break.'

'That'd be great. But let's wait until Dave is back. You don't need more on your plate right now.'

Margie, grateful for such a friend as Joan, gives her another hug. Over her shoulder she sees Beth, still completely absorbed by what her nose has produced. The insect, now sufficiently dry to become airborne, leaves Beth's pink hand and makes for the open louvred window. It negotiates the glass panes perfectly and escapes outside.

LOGBOOK OF EDUARDO RODRÍGUEZ TORRES

∾

She is in my heart, so deeply that I sometimes cannot breathe. When I close my eyes it is her face that I see, her voice that I hear. I am starting to wonder if I will ever be able to touch her again.

∾

CARLOS
The *Pescador*
4 October 2002

Manuel is at the helm when Carlos creeps playfully into Eduardo's cabin. The first mate is lying on his bunk writing in his logbook, his back to the door. Curious to sneak a glimpse at the early notes for his novel, Carlos waits until he is only a metre away before declaring himself, the hint of a joke in his voice. 'Let me guess, love poems?' he teases.

The *Pescador* hits a trough and Carlos watches Eduardo's pen slide across the page, drawing a line through several neat entries. Carlos, emphasising his jest, cranes his neck forward, pretending to read what Eduardo has been writing, but Eduardo claps the book shut.

'It's nothing,' Eduardo answers hastily.

Confused by his friend's coyness, Carlos presses on. 'How long have we known each other now? Twenty years.'

An almost shameful expression breaks over the first mate's face and Carlos instantly regrets his intrusion. He had hoped that, by making light of it, Eduardo might feel more inclined to confide in him some of his prose, but it is clear that these notes are personal. He has overstepped the mark and struck a raw nerve. Perhaps Eduardo's logbook doubles as a diary, a place to purge himself of thoughts and feelings that he is unable to share, or perhaps he believes that sharing them would help no one and get him nowhere. Eduardo never complains, but Carlos knows his friend must also be aching for home.

'It's okay. You can admit to me that you're missing Virginia,' Carlos says, gently. 'I'm sorry I interrupted.'

Eduardo rubs his eyes, and Carlos thinks he sees relief.

'Do you remember what you said in your speech at our wedding?' Carlos asks.

'Which part?'

'You said that finding love was the most precious gift we are granted, and that it happens only once.'

'*Sí*.' The emotion returns to Eduardo's face.

'Well, you were right. I don't think I ever told you that.' Carlos smiles. 'We will get back to them and to our children. It's all going to work out.'

The boat pitches suddenly and is buffeted by a succession of waves, as if Manuel has let go of the helm. Carlos grips the door frame of Eduardo's cabin, and feels the boat settle on to a new course. Through the porthole he reads the direction of the seas. The *Pescador* is heading northeast. He thinks he sees something like fear cross Eduardo's face. It's the first time he has seen the expression.

'Oh no!' Eduardo covers his face with the logbook, hitting it hard against his forehead. 'The idiot!'

'What does he think he's doing?' Carlos says. 'He knows to talk to us before changing course. We're back-tracking.'

'It's not Manuel,' Eduardo says, standing up and throwing the logbook on his bunk. He looks directly at Carlos. 'I think Dmitri might've taken matters into his own hands.'

'But we were heading to Namibia. He agreed.'

'He never gave up on Mauritius.'

'The stupid fool! It's out of the question. We'll cross the path of the Australian boat. We have to assume they're armed and capable of boarding. *¡Maldito!*' Carlos pounds his fist against the frame of the door. 'He listens to you. Come on.'

Carlos turns to leave, but Eduardo grabs hold of his jacket, stopping him. 'He might have a gun,' Eduardo tells him.

'What?' Disbelief is written across Carlos's face.

'I've been hoping he's bluffing, but Dmitri told me a few days ago that he has hidden weapons on board.'

Carlos regards Eduardo with a deep, confused frown. 'You should have told me.' The master's voice is measured and quiet. Disappointed. He stares back through the porthole and out to sea, at the waves rushing at them from behind, pushing them towards Dmitri's preferred destination. An albatross keeps pace with the boat and turns its head momentarily towards him. He finds himself wishing that he was the bird, free to plot his course home to his mate. 'We have no choice. We have to change his mind, guns or no guns.'

Carlos turns once more in the direction of the wheelhouse, aware of Eduardo's silent presence behind him. He thinks again of Julia and María. He has never felt more vulnerable, or out of control, and can imagine nothing worse than leaving his wife and daughter without a husband or a father. He forces his feelings for his family from his mind as he hauls open the wheelhouse door.

Dmitri is at the helm, a semi-automatic weapon slung across his body with a strap. José, the young Peruvian, is similarly armed. Manuel is lying on his side on the floor, blood seeping from a wound just above his eye. José takes a few steps back, the gun held awkwardly at the ready. He could be a child who has just wet the bed.

'You stupid fool,' Carlos says to Dmitri, who meets his eyes and replies with a defiant smirk. 'What game are you playing?'

The young Peruvian, his gun still cocked, takes a step towards the vessel's master.

'It is all right,' Dmitri says to the youth, '*Capitán* Sánchez and his friend are going nowhere.'

'I thought more of you than this,' Carlos tells the engineer, flicking a glance at Eduardo, frozen in the doorway.

The normally humourless Russian is wearing a cold smile. 'From now on you might take my suggestions on our course a little more seriously.'

Carlos is struck by the sudden improvement in Dmitri's Spanish. His deception. He wants to fly at him for what he has done to Manuel, but as he steps forward he is held in place by the barrel of José's gun. He looks through the rear windows of the wheelhouse and sees the Australian patrol gaining on them.

'We already have our enemy. They're behind us, on another boat.' Carlos reaches for the Peruvian's gun, as though attempting to confiscate a child's toy. José jerks the gun away and fires a shot into the wheelhouse wall in panic. Carlos almost feels sorry for the misled fool. But his sympathy is short-lived as José digs the weapon into his chest. '*¡No me jodas!*' Carlos curses at the youth with half his wind.

'You've let me down,' Eduardo says, his voice remarkably steady as he glares at the Russian.

'And you me,' the Russian metes out the words like punishment.

'And what exactly is your plan now, big man?' Carlos asks. 'Are you going to just hide behind this boy with a gun?'

'We are going to Mauritius as first planned. I'm going to sell the entire catch there. And, of course, the guns. There are more where these came from. Anyone who helps me to get the boat safely to port can have a share of the profits. Manuel tried to stop me but I think he has learned his lesson.' Dmitri kicks Manuel in the stomach to bring home his point. Manuel coughs and draws his knees to his chest.

'Enough!' Carlos shouts. 'What will you do if he dies? You can't use the autopilot the entire way. Don't think Eduardo and I are going to help you.' He looks again at Manuel, who is motionless on the floor, and then back to the Russian. 'How dare you bring guns on to my boat!'

'It's *my* boat now.' Dmitri smirks. 'And you can ask Eduardo about the guns. They were *his* idea, *his* business on the side.'

Carlos doesn't bite. Doesn't even acknowledge Eduardo's protestations.

'Didn't he tell you? There are hundreds of them under the floor, right where you are standing. They are worth a lot more in Mauritius than fish.' Laughter erupts from the Russian, who uses the back of his index finger to wipe away a smear of foamy saliva from under his bottom lip.

'Don't listen to him,' Eduardo says, his voice carefully controlled.

'I'm not a fool,' Carlos tells the Russian. 'Do you think I'd believe anything you tell me?' Carlos hears Eduardo step forward. The first mate stops beside him. 'Eduardo is my oldest friend,' Carlos maintains. 'He's like my brother. You think you can drive a wedge between us with a blatant lie?'

'I am no fool either,' Dmitri says. 'I know about your unrecorded catch. Twenty tonnes, wasn't it? You were going to sell it in Mauritius. To a Russian buyer. Am I right?' He is speaking quickly in fluent, slightly formal Spanish, as if he has learnt the language from a book.

Carlos is caught off-guard but tries to hide it. Perhaps

Dmitri overheard them talking. He clearly understands Spanish better than he let on. 'Eduardo organised the sale. He didn't discuss with me who the buyer was. I left it to him.'

'The buyer is me.' Dmitri beats his chest triumphantly, as if declaring a winning hand. He plucks a small flask from his jacket pocket and takes an ample swig. When he talks again, Carlos smells vodka. 'It was Eduardo's idea. I was to fall ill and leave the boat in Mauritius. But instead of finding a hospital, I was to onsell the twenty tonnes, *your* twenty tonnes.' He takes another swig from the flask. 'Along with the guns, of course. My buyers are South African. Everything was planned.'

Carlos remembers Dmitri's earlier threat that if Eduardo didn't tell Carlos then he would. So, this was the secret: Dmitri was the buyer from the start. But surely Eduardo would have raised the alarm if he'd known about the guns. Carlos feels a surge of anger towards his oldest friend, but tries to conceal it.

'Your wife didn't want you involved, did she?' Dmitri eyes Eduardo suggestively and leers back at Carlos. 'I know about the promise Eduardo made to her.'

Carlos takes a moment to try to understand what Dmitri is insinuating. He looks at the picture of Julia. At the warmth in her eyes.

Eduardo puts his hand on his back. 'I'll explain it all later.'

Carlos shakes his head in dismay and turns to leave.

'Sit down!' Dmitri shouts. 'You are staying here.' Again the gun is pointed at Carlos. José, no doubt promised a share of the sale, is fast if nothing else. Eduardo steps forward, but Carlos pushes him back.

'*¡Jódete!*' Carlos swears again at the Peruvian. As master, he has always prided himself on the loyalty of his crew and the camaraderie on board. Until now, their boat has stood apart from other pirate vessels. But with Dmitri at the helm, the *Pescador* is like all the others with its drunken captain and downtrodden crew. He turns reluctantly towards Eduardo, the friend he thought he knew, and reads the regret on his face. 'So let's hear this plan of yours,' he says to the Russian. 'Do you think we'll still be allowed to unload in Mauritius with the attention this chase will have attracted?'

'Of course. They rely on these illegal catches. If they make a public outcry about us, what message does that send to other pirate ships wanting to offload in Port Louis? Much better for them to keep us happy and keep the ships, and the fish, rolling into port.' Dmitri makes a small adjustment using the manual helm, ensuring that the *Pescador* is making a direct route to Mauritius, before flicking the steering back to automatic. 'It is free advertising.'

Carlos knows it's true, and was counting on the same welcome, if not in Mauritius, then in Namibia. 'What if the Australians catch up with us and want to board?'

'They won't have weapons. They're just a patrol vessel.' Dmitri is grave again.

'So you're prepared to use your guns? They're not just for show? A little prop to make a small man feel larger?'

'You think I haven't killed a man before now?' Dmitri's face contorts into a derisive mask.

'Fine. Good luck. The crew won't help you. And neither, of course, will I. You're asking us to become murderers now, as well as thieves. I — we — will never do that.'

'That is your business. Just do not get in my way. Or a bullet may get in yours.'

Manuel moves on the floor, rising to his knees. Carlos, relieved to see that he is again conscious, takes a better look at his injury, which has caused his eye to disappear into the swollen flesh around it, like a wounded barnacle retreating into its broken shell.

'Go and cover the name of the boat, before the Australians see it,' Dmitri orders Manuel. 'And then come straight back here.'

'They've already seen our name, you idiot,' Eduardo says.

'Do as I say!'

'He isn't up to it. Have you gone blind?' Carlos shouts, helping Manuel to his feet.

'I am in charge now.' Dmitri aims an outstretched finger at Manuel and then at the door, indicating that he should leave.

When Manuel reappears half an hour later he is saturated and shivering uncontrollably.

'The Australian boat is close behind us. Our name is covered,' Manuel reports through blue lips.

Carlos shakes his head. 'You really have no idea, do you, Dmitri? All you're doing is giving away what rights we have left. And confirming our guilt. Without a name, anyone can board at any time, and it's not considered an act of piracy. Why do you think we didn't do it in the first place?'

'All right. Manuel, you heard what the good *capitán* said. International law dictates that we display our name. You had better get out there again. We do not want to be bad international citizens, do we?'

Carlos sees the Russian's delight at the frigid torture he is meting out to the Spaniard and realises that Dmitri doesn't care if the ship's name is displayed or not. The mutineer is interested only in showing them the lengths he will go to to assert his authority.

Manuel turns unsteadily to go back outside, to single-handedly uncover the name of the boat in conditions that would make it difficult for two able-bodied men to accomplish.

'Manuel, wait. I'll help you.' Carlos makes to stand up.

'No. You stay right there, *Capitán!*'

'*¡Condenado!*' Carlos swears. He struggles out of his jacket. 'Here, take my coat,' he tells Manuel. 'You're saturated.' But the Spaniard ignores him. Carlos wonders what game he is playing. Perhaps he is bluffing compliance, biding his time until they can talk in private. Unless, Carlos considers, after hearing Dmitri's accusations against them, his loyalties are now elsewhere.

'He is fine. Keep your coat,' Dmitri orders Carlos, before pointing to the ship's intercom. 'Tell El Animal you want him up here now. I have a proposition for him and his Peruvian friends.'

Carlos does as instructed. Perhaps he underestimated the Russian, he thinks. El Animal, as the leader of the largest — and poorest — group on board, would be key to a successful mutiny.

At least the Australians appear content to remain astern. If they were armed, and serious about attempting a boarding, surely they would have made some attempt to cut them off at the pass.

Five minutes later, El Animal is at the door, stopping abruptly as he makes sense of the chaos in the wheelhouse. The long-haired Peruvian shouts in his native tongue to José, who is pointing his gun directly at him. Carlos makes out the angry words: 'I saved your life!'

'Stick to language we can all understand,' Dmitri scolds, shaking a finger. His voice is punctuated by the punch of the boat's hull against the troughs as the autopilot works hard to steer the vessel northeast towards Mauritius. 'We have been ordered back to Montevideo by Uruguayan Fisheries but we are running low on fuel after our time in the ice. The Australians are still pursuing us. If we are caught, we will lose our catch. We will each be individually fined and imprisoned.'

'That's not true,' Carlos finds himself shouting, and quickly moderates his tone in an attempt to re-assert his calm authority. 'Only the first officers will be charged. You have nothing to fear.'

'Your future poverty *would* be sealed. I've seen it happen,' Dmitri insists. 'However, we do have an advantage over the Australian boat.' He breaks his speech for dramatic effect. 'As you will have noticed,' Dmitri holds up his weapon, 'we have guns. Many guns. Your first mate was trafficking them.'

'He's lying! They're his,' Eduardo spits, glowering at Dmitri.

The boat clashes with the unforgiving ocean and Carlos notices Dmitri rubbing his stomach through his clothes. It's something he has seen him do before. It's as if the Russian has an ulcer that is eating him from the inside — as if he is, in fact, consuming himself in a lunacy of self-destruction.

Dmitri perseveres, looking squarely at El Animal. 'But, if we can help it, I'd rather not use the weapons. The solution is to head to Mauritius, as first planned. Once we are there, the Australians cannot touch us. And, at Port Louis, the authorities will turn a blind eye. We can sell the fish and the guns, and split the profits between ourselves. You would never have seen so much money.'

Carlos can see the appeal of the plan. The way out. 'He's asking you to become a murderer if we are boarded,' he says. 'We knew nothing of these guns.'

'They don't deserve your loyalty,' Dmitri presses on. 'What your master is not telling you is that he and Eduardo used you. You owe them nothing. While you are being barely paid for your work, they were going to privately sell some of the catch that *you* caught.'

'I will talk to the others,' El Animal says, turning to leave the wheelhouse.

Carlos, unable to find words to help his case, shakes his head and turns his attention to an albatross, visible through the wheelhouse windows. Its markings are different from others that he has seen. He sees Eduardo watching it, too. Normally the first mate would comment on the species, its habits even, but he is mute beside him. The bird veers off to the northwest, away from the *Pescador*, in the direction of home.

Carlos thinks how disastrously Eduardo's plan has come unstuck and dwells uncomfortably on Dmitri's knowledge of Julia's reluctance to go along with it: her plea that her husband not be involved. Eduardo must have felt the need to explain to the Russian the promise that he had made. But there was something else that the Russian was insinuating, something less virtuous — an attempt, perhaps, to divide and conquer: to create a schism between the friends.

Carlos's eyes return to the picture of his wife and he smiles, determined not to give the Russian the satisfaction of appearing unnerved. He tries to predict how Julia will react when he tells her the lengths Eduardo went to to honour their agreement. For himself, however, Carlos isn't sure whether their friend's behaviour reflects extreme loyalty, bad judgment, or, worse still, a form of betrayal. How could Eduardo not have told him their buyer was on the same boat: the gloomy Russian, their engineer? When Eduardo had so keenly recommended Dmitri to Migiliaro for this voyage, was he already setting him up for this role? Surely it was taking their pact too far to keep this fact hidden. And the guns, even if Eduardo didn't know from the outset that they were on board, why didn't he say something a few days ago when, he claims, Dmitri told him? 'I'll explain it all later,' Eduardo had said. Later, Carlos thinks, can't come soon enough.

JULIA
Montevideo, Uruguay
4 October 2002

Julia rolls over, heaving her pregnant belly from one side to the other. In recent nights she has been waking with backache and has resorted to sleeping on a folded blanket on the lounge-room floor, the hard surface easing the discomfort only marginally. She peers through the ground-floor window to the world outside. The apartment's small, shared garden with its clothesline and *Tipas* tree gazes back at her blankly. She extracts her diary from under her makeshift mattress, and attempts to organise life into neat little squares. She counts back the days, and calculates that it has been two-and-a-half weeks since the Australians started chasing Carlos's boat. Surely they have given up by now. But then why hasn't Carlos contacted her to let her know that he is safe?

Julia's stomach, scoured from anxiety and hunger, growls. For the first time in days, she feels hungry. A good sign. But the gastric virus that María brought home from school and passed on to her has left her two kilograms lighter, and she worries for her baby.

It's days like these that Carlos's absences make her want to scream from the injustice of being left alone at home. It's like she is already a fishing widow, one of the scores of wives who've been left looking out to sea forever, waiting, wondering, grieving, resenting.

Yesterday Julia even resorted to phoning Cecilia to ask if María could stay there for the night. It wouldn't nearly begin to equal the tens of nights she has minded Sofía. Cecilia eventually agreed, but not without letting Julia know it was an inconvenience.

If only Paula was in town. Her best friend, another teacher, is in Spain for four months' long-service leave, and her absence has made Julia realise just how small her circle of friends has become since becoming a mother. She has many acquaintances, but no close friends who she can ask to help out when life turns on her, baring its teeth.

She misses her parents, and can't help feeling that they have also abandoned her. It was her father's decision to move to the country to manage a farm. He said it was the perfect way to pay for retirement: a way to secure an income at a time when Uruguay's economy was on a downward spiral. Julia knows it tore at her mother to leave her only child, but still she went, loyal to her husband to the end. When they visit, with their fragrant boxes of fresh-picked oranges and peaches, they only ever last one night on the mattress on the lounge-room floor — the same place she is lying now. Julia kisses them goodbye again through the window of their small farm truck, so out of place in the city street, and, with a lump in her throat, tells herself that it's the way of the world now. People move away from family for work all the time, but she wonders if that makes it all right.

It's eight in the morning and, with María at Cecilia's, Julia enjoys the rare opportunity for a slow start to the day. She turns a page in her diary. Her obstetric appointment isn't for another few days. With any luck, the doctor will have some drug-free suggestions for relieving the back pain.

From her ground-level vantage point, Julia studies the long shadows in the grass and opens the window to the wet smell of soil after rain. The mother *gorrión* is rifling through leaves for insects just a metre from her face. Its deep, brown eyes are the same colour as María's. She wonders if this mother thinks of her lost chick, or if the daily chores help her to forget. A resilience born of necessity. The bird skewers a moth that rested a moment too long on the lawn.

Julia's stomach growls again, reminding her of her own young's need for nourishment. Thankfully she only need venture into the kitchen, no hunter-gathering required. As she throws back the blanket to rise, the bird starts and then drops the moth, its morning's work. The insect leaves a puff of dust in the still air and flies free.

'*Lo siento*,' Julia apologises, before making a beeline for the kitchen. She promises the bird that she'll return with a crust from her toast to make amends.

As the kettle boils, Julia turns on her computer, deciding to send an email to Paula over breakfast. The computer, a relic from the school office, fires up noisily and three new messages gleam at her in bold lettering. One is from Paula, speak of the devil. The second is from Julia's mother, who has only recently discovered that she can search the internet and send emails from her local post office. Her mother seldom offers any significant news, and her written language is more formal than her speech, but Julia looks forward to the messages nevertheless. The final email has been forwarded by Francisco. She opens that one first.

Dear Julia,

I haven't been able to make contact with Carlos's boat today and am suspecting a problem with the satellite. I am sure there is no need for concern.

On another matter, I'm forwarding a message from the wife of the Australian vessel's master. It seems she found my email address on the internet. My manager doesn't know I'm passing this message on to you. See what you make of it. And would you please contact me before you reply?

Cordialmente,

Francisco

Dear Sir/Madam,

(Can you please pass this message on to the wife/family of the Pescador's *master? Perhaps she/they would be able to convince him to end the chase peacefully and quickly.)*

My name is Margaret Bates. I am the wife of the Australian master of the Australis, *the vessel pursuing the Uruguayan-flagged* Pescador. *I'm writing to ask your assistance in ending the high-seas chase. I hold grave concerns for the safety of our loved ones and their crews, and simply wish for them to reach port safely.*

It appears that my husband, David Bates, is under instruction to pursue the Pescador *all the way to Uruguay if necessary. It would also seem that your partner/family member has no intention of returning to Australian waters, as is the request of the Australian Government. I wonder if there is a chance that the two boats could instead go to a neutral port to resolve the issue. If you could please assist me in getting this message to the appropriate people, I would be most grateful.*

Sincerely,

Margaret Bates

Julia is unsure what to make of the message from the Australian woman. She is grateful for the human contact from the other side of the world, but is suspicious of this woman's apparent concern for Carlos. Perhaps the Australian boat has lost sight of the *Pescador* and this is a ploy of the Australian authorities to extract information on the vessel's whereabouts. She certainly can't see how either she or Margaret Bates could influence the outcome of the chase. Still, she responds directly, in English, without first contacting Francisco. There's nothing to lose.

Dear Margaret,

(I am sending this message directly to you, not through the authorities here.)

I, too, want this chase to end. I have not, however, been able to speak with my husband now for almost a month and fear for his safety. The Uruguayan Fisheries office wants the boat to return to port here in Montevideo where our courts can decide whether or not they were fishing illegally.

When I speak with my husband again, I will be asking him to go to the nearest port. But I can make no promises. I hope that by the time I hear from Carlos again, the closest port for the Pescador *will be here in Montevideo.*

Perhaps you will have better luck convincing your husband to end the chase and deal with the matter in a court of law. I wish your husband and his crew a safe return.

Regards,

Julia Pereira de Sánchez

Julia presses send and watches the message disappear from her computer screen. She imagines it making its way to Australia, a place she has never been and has only clichéd imaginings of. It strikes her that she doesn't understand how email technology works. Are there cables carrying the small concerns of mankind under the floor of the sea? Or is the electronic chatter of Earthlings relayed through space? If she and Carlos were both watching the sky at the same moment, would they both see the satellite that carries her message?

Julia opens a new email message and types in Virginia's address, then sends her a quick note relaying the latest news from Francisco.

Next, she opens the message from Paula. Her best friend is asking for some bibliographic details of classroom biology texts. There is a school in Madrid where she is interested in doing some work while her husband takes a university course.

Julia reaches up higher than is comfortable and drags the dusty school texts down from the bookshelf. She lowers herself heavily into the wooden chair beside the computer and forwards the publishers' details with a note telling Paula that she is only allowed to take the Madrid job for the duration of her husband's course and not a day longer. 'I'll miss you too much,' Julia types, transmitting the message quickly before she can change her mind.

The third email contains a new recipe that Julia's mother writes 'will be good for María's school lunches'. Julia prints it out and decides to make a batch of the fried biscuits for María when she arrives back home.

When she again stands, Julia is overcome by vertigo and she berates herself for delaying breakfast. She makes herself a *mate* and a piece of toast, sipping the tea slowly while she re-reads the Australian woman's email. She will contact Francisco tomorrow, she decides, after she has slept on all of this. He was in no hurry to let her know about the chase. Perhaps the two women can achieve something the authorities, weighed down by bureaucracy, can't. Stranger things have happened.

Julia feels a tightening in her abdomen as the baby moves. They are strange and wonderful, these little reminders of a life in the making. Stirrings of being, providing reassurance that her baby is fine. Hope dispels fear. It's a line she recently read in a novel and has found herself repeating like a mantra. She hasn't had an ultrasound scan because of the cost, but the pregnancy seems uncomplicated enough so far.

She decides to go for a short walk down to the docks. Perhaps it will help ease her backache. At least it will make her feel closer to Carlos to be around all the things that he loves: the creaking boats, the nets, the salt-hardened ropes and the fish. Then again, sometimes the Puerto de Montevideo has the opposite effect on her, evoking instead a maddening feeling of being left behind. Marooned. She is jealous of the pull that the sea has on her husband, and hates the control it has over her life.

Before leaving the house, Julia makes a trip to the bathroom and feels her body vacate itself of fluid. Too much fluid. The copious gush doesn't stop.

'No.' Julia's voice is quiet and pleading. Like she's in a dream. But this is all too real. She tells herself to stay calm as she walks gingerly to the phone. There is a trail of amniotic fluid on the tiled floor. 'Please, no.' Her baby is not due for another thirteen weeks.

She dials for an ambulance and hears herself tell the operator in a high, trembling voice that her waters have broken prematurely. 'I'm only twenty-seven weeks' pregnant,' she cries, her legs shaking.

She lowers herself onto the ground and removes her pants, which are drenched with hot fluid. She reaches for a hand towel and places it beneath her while she waits for assistance. The operator offers to stay on the line, just in case. She accepts the company, and lies down, holding the receiver to her ear. Her other hand seeks out her abdomen and she's alarmed at how much smaller it has become, and how much more vigorous the baby's kicks seem without the cushion of amniotic fluid. Almost panicky. She talks soothingly to her frightened child as the fluid leaves her body. The operator tells Julia to stay calm. 'Help will arrive soon. Every moment that you delay labour will help your baby to survive.'

And there it is. Life and death, served up to her by a stranger on the other end of a phone line. Her baby could die. It's all being decided here on the tiles of her kitchen floor, right where she stands each morning to make breakfast. With her head on the ground, she can see crumbs of white toast gathered in sympathy, like grieving relatives, under the cupboard doors where her broom has failed to reach. She exhales hard and the crumbs flee.

DAVE
The *Australis*
4 October 2002

Dave is dreaming about Sam when he hears Cactus crowing nearby. 'We're right on 'er tail, Davo.' Dave opens his eyes and sees the prickly, red-skinned face above him. 'You can see the buggers on the back deck, clear as day. Closest we've been in the whole seventeen days — but who's counting? Seems they're heading northeast now though. D'you reckon they're on their way back to Oz?'

Dave brings his wrist close to his face to better see his watch. He has been asleep for less than three hours and feels nauseous from tiredness and the sudden shot of adrenaline. Straight away he notices that the seas have again picked up. The *Australis* is bobbing like a Halloween apple in a deep barrel of water. He can hear waves tearing at the boat, like the chasing teeth of hungry children keen for a bite of the prize.

'Well at least they're heading in the right direction,' he declares to Cactus, who appears high on life. It makes a welcome change.

Cactus indicates his agreement with a click of his tongue. 'I'll leave you to get your gear on,' he says as he departs.

Dave struggles to pull on his track pants and sweatshirt as the boat pitches and dives. His eyes fall on a novel on his small bedside table. The book is by Joseph Conrad, his favourite author, and Dave surprises himself by remembering the writer's description of the sea being the 'irreconcilable enemy of ships and men ever since ships and men had the unheard-of audacity to go afloat together in the face of its frown'. He wonders what Conrad would have made of this chase — making an enemy of a boatload of men for a hold full of fish. Back in the novelist's day it was thought that the ocean was a bottomless source of seafood. How wrong they had been.

He makes his way to the wheelhouse, where Harry is watching the illegal vessel through binoculars.

'They're not entirely of one mind, Dave,' Harry says.

'How do you mean?' Dave takes the binoculars that have been handed to him. He locates the rocking red-and-white vessel, steaming ahead against swollen seas. It's perhaps three hundred metres from them. The huge waves are exaggerated through the lenses, and the sight of vast white seas consuming the pirate boat somehow makes his own boat feel smaller. It's as if he is watching a film that has been slowed for dramatic effect.

'When we first caught sight of them, the name was being covered. Now some idiot has uncovered it again. He's still on deck. Can you see him?'

'Yep,' Dave answers. A small tremor has started in the muscles at the corner of his eye. He has felt the faint twitch before when he has been particularly tired, or nervous. 'Crazy fools, buggerising around with the name in these conditions. Whoever's giving the orders doesn't know if he's Arthur or Martha. Wouldn't mind being a fly on the wall, though. Something fishy's going on.' He laughs at his accidental pun. He imagines the mayhem on board. The foreign voices swearing. The fury at being chased. The panic at being caught. He wonders if they're still carrying their stolen cargo, or if it has been dumped in frozen waters. Wasted, like everyone's time.

'Get a load of the damage on the starboard stern,' Harry says. 'Reckon something gave them a pretty good whack down south. Bit of Southern Ocean corporal punishment. Probably what made their minds up to head north.'

'Yeah, I saw that. Looks like she copped a bit of a ding.' But Dave is distracted. He is watching a lone hunched figure dressed in the familiar safety orange making his way along the *Pescador*'s deck towards the cabins. There's something painted on his back: '*Pa—*' Dave can't make it out.

The pirate looks like any other seaman battling the southern seas as he slips and skates on the icy deck: tired but determined. Dave sees him lose his footing as the ship swerves unpredictably to port. The figure hits the deck hard, the waves washing him towards the painted white rails. He clearly isn't strapped on.

'Stupid fool,' Dave mutters.

The man remains lying on the deck against the rails, not moving.

'Jesus! Stupid bugger's on a death wish.' Dave feels a panic swell inside him, and is caught off-guard by the memory of Sam's dead face in the hospital morgue. He feels himself go faint. A large wave hits the *Australis* and he falls heavily against the instrument table.

'You right, mate?' Harry reaches for the binoculars but they are still glued to Dave's face.

Cactus enters the wheelhouse.

'He's giving up,' Dave says, seeing the figure as someone's son or father. He wants to reach out an arm to hold him. The orange body wraps around the metal of the rails with the force of water running off the deck.

'Who is?' Cactus asks.

'Some codger on the aft deck,' Dave replies. 'Get up, you stupid fool!' he yells in vain in the direction of the *Pescador*. 'What the hell does he think he's playing at?'

Dave makes a radio call to the foreign vessel. '*Pescador, Pescador, Pescador*, this is the *Australis, Australis*. You have a crew member in danger on the back deck, portside.'

He waits for a response for several long seconds before repeating the call. Still there is silence.

Dave hangs up the radio and looks again through the binoculars. To his relief, he sees the endangered crewman raise a hand to hold onto the rail, just as he has willed him to do. The weight of the boat shifts and the man is given a moment to decide his fate. He chooses life and drags his sodden body back up, gripping the metal bars separating him from the sea. No one has appeared on deck to offer assistance. Instead, the cold steel guides him along until he nears the aft door, where he lets go of the rail and takes a few slanted steps towards safety. It seems to take all his effort to prise open the door, and then he is gone.

Dave drops the binoculars against his chest. 'He's inside,' he says, exhaling volubly. 'Thank Christ for that.' His heart is pounding. It is clear they are chasing a broken and defeated crew, and part of him just wants to let them go back to their distant, desperate lives. Let them keep the bloody fish.

'We should probably let Customs know we've caught up with them,' Harry says.

'You make the call. I don't feel like suffering Wentworth's bullshit right now,' Dave replies, taking over the helm.

Harry punches the number for Customs into the satellite phone and almost immediately Roger Wentworth's voice comes down the line, which is flooded with static. Harry adjusts the settings to speaker-phone before arcing up the volume.

'Roger, this is Harry Perdman, first mate of the *Australis*. We've caught up with our friends. Thought you'd want to know.'

'Good-o. I'll inform the South African authorities. They've confirmed that their naval boat the *Bremner* can assist. It's probably only half a day away, if that.'

Dave feels the mood in the wheelhouse lighten. They've almost made it. With the news of the imminent arrival of the South African navy, Cactus is standing tall, his chest stuck out with achievement.

'Music to our ears,' Harry says. 'It'll be good to lay eyes on them.'

'You just keep trailing those illegals.'

'We'll do our best. But if they pick up their boat speed too much more, we'll be backing off again. It's not safe with the seas behind us like this. What's the plan once the South Africans are on the scene?'

'We obviously need the boat and the catch brought back to Australia as evidence. The *Bremner*'s offering to put armed personnel on the *Pescador* to confiscate any weapons the illegals might be carrying. By the time your men step aboard, it'll all be safe as houses. And a few of the South Africans will stay on the boat to keep things in line on the journey back here. The master and crew you send over won't have any trouble.'

As Harry finishes the satellite call, Dave switches to autopilot and re-examines the *Pescador* through his binoculars. He wonders about the fate of the crew on board. Who are they, these men whose lives are just fodder for some wealthy boat owner? Who is waiting for them back home? But it's an affinity that's tempered with anger as he thinks of young William downstairs, still scared to his core that he mightn't live out the dreams he'd imagined for himself on dry land. Dave knows the Southern Ocean has left its mark on the young Tasmanian. But then William is different from the rest of the crew. He was in the car when Sam died and has seen the face of death first-hand. It has left him vulnerable.

'You happy to take the helm again for a few more minutes, Harry?' Dave asks. 'I'd like to go downstairs and let the boys know we're almost home and hosed. That the cavalry is on its way.'

'Sure thing, boss.'

When Dave enters William's shared cabin, he is overwhelmed by the responsibility for the lives of these men, and the relief that he'll have them home soon. They are lying about on damp bunks, playing games of solitaire and reading magazines. One bloke is drawing pictures of seabirds. They're a good bunch mostly, Dave thinks. Rough diamonds who aren't afraid of hard work and who believe in taking responsibility for their own actions. In their thermal undergarments and fleeces, they look nothing like the seamen that Dave saw around the docks as a boy. Back then, sailors worked wet, weighed down by wool. Here, on the *Australis*, there are luxuries like clean clothes and showers, but still the smell of diesel, salt and sweat lingers. It's at once unpleasant and reassuringly human.

Dave eyes the tired, unshaven faces. Some of the younger crew are wearing beanies, the hats cocooning their salty hair.

In these seas there's nothing the men can do on deck, and they're enjoying these moments of enforced recreation. William still appears anxious and out of place — like a calf in the holding pen of a slaughterhouse, it occurs to Dave. He's noticeably paler and thinner than when he boarded.

'You'll be pleased to hear we've caught up with our Uruguayan friends and that the South African navy is on its way to help apprehend the vessel.'

The men look up and cheer, whistling loudly through cracked lips.

'We're almost there, lads.' Dave holds onto one of the bunks as the boat falls through the air and smashes into a trough. 'Umph,' he grunts. 'We're almost there.'

Dave watches William's demeanour change. The young Tasmanian swings his muscular legs over the bunk, and sits upright. He rubs his stubbled jaw back and forth with his thumb and index finger, processing the news. The fear that moments ago racked his face ebbs away.

'Saved by the bloody Springboks!' William jokes. Dave sees his bluster for what it is: an attempt to regain some blokey respect after his failed attempt to find his sea legs. William's relief is palpable. Dave has heard some of the crew calling the young lad a 'pussy', given his frequent retreats to his bunk. Good on him for trying to make light of things now, he thinks. On land, Sam had always been in awe of his best mate, his preparedness to take risks and throw himself head-first at life. But the sea is another story, and the Southern Ocean a baptism by fire. Dave realises he should have started the lad off on something gentler. But then, how was he to know they'd end up having to chase the South American buggers? Time will tell if this is going to be young William's first and last trip.

Dave considers his own future and can't see himself quitting just yet. The sea is in his blood. Like Sam, he has always needed a challenge, and isn't happy if he's not pushing boundaries — testing his capabilities. He'll tell Margie it's his job, and that he doesn't have a choice, but deep down he knows that he's hopelessly addicted. Being at sea is one of the few things that makes him feel alive. And since Sam's death, it's one of the only ways he knows to truly escape. Out here, it's as if time stops. Nothing else matters, except what's happening on the boat.

'Harry and a few of you blokes'll be going on board to help steam the *Pescador* home, but only after the South Africans have got the situation on board under control,' Dave tells his crew.

One of the few ratbags aboard performs a convincing act with an imaginary machine gun, while his mates fall about in a mock show of agony to underline the point.

'Before you all get too carried away ...' Dave holds off until his crew settles down. 'I've been assured that every effort will be made to avoid injury. And, in any case, we'll have done our job by then and will be staying right out of that side of things.'

'Typical. Just when it gets exciting.' The bloke with the pretend gun feigns disappointment. Dave knows his bravado is purely show and that the young sailor would be the first to falter in the face of a real gun.

'Just keep your wits about you over the next little while, lads. Help is at hand, and we'll soon be heading home. But don't take your eyes off the ball just yet. And I'll need some volunteers to put their hands up to accompany Harry when the time comes. For now, though, rest up, and thank your lucky stars you're not on that Uruguayan boat.'

Dave watches as William again loses colour and lies back down on his bunk. He waits until the other crew are distracted with their yahooing before leaning towards him. 'It won't be you going over,' Dave says, ruffling the young man's hair. 'You'll be back home and having a beer at Knopwoods before you know what hit you.' Dave thinks that he could do with a drink himself at the old sandstone pub. 'You won't be the first sailor to drown your sorrows there.'

He ponders how much the world has changed since the days when Knopwoods fronted directly onto the water, before the river was pushed back and reclaimed as parkland. Back then, it was the whalers who came to drink their pints while overlooking the steel-blue finger of water that had carried them safely from the Southern Ocean to Hobart, where they unloaded their oily spoils. He tries to imagine what the waterfront was like when the whaleboats docked directly in front of the pub, attached like tethered giants to the sandstone by large metal loops that are still in place today. Now fishermen stand out like sore thumbs amidst the fashionable clientele. In neighbouring restaurants, well-heeled city slickers dine on the fish these men have caught, never asking, or even considering, where it has come from.

MARGIE
Hobart, Australia
4 October 2002

Margie, unable to sleep, climbs out of bed and wraps Dave's dressing gown around herself, tying the cord in a tight bow. She grabs a banana off the kitchen bench and eats it in the time it takes to heat a cup of milk in the microwave. She notices the answering machine light flashing frenetically, and presses play. How could she have forgotten to check the messages? It seems the more anxious she is, the less functional she becomes — even if that means failing to check whether Dave has called, the very thing that could calm her overtired, harried mind.

The sound of static fills the kitchen and Margie wonders if the machine has malfunctioned. But then she hears Dave's voice. With the interference, it's difficult to decipher what he's saying. She holds her ear close to his voice, imagining him beside her.

'Margie, we're … doi … fine. It looks li … South Africans are com … to our aid to br … this bullsh … to a close. Any moment … heading back ho … Can you pleas … Trish … William is okay? Love you … Please … Bonnie … cuddle for me.'

'Thank God,' she says to the empty room as the answering machine clicks off and whirs in rewind mode. Her body aches with the weight of days of tension. She needs a hot shower, something to smooth out the muscles across her neck and back that have forgotten how to relax. Something that will help her surrender to sleep. She makes her way to the bathroom and turns on the shower taps above the bath, undressing as she waits for the hot water to come through. Her skin tingles in anticipation before she dives under the rush of warmth as though she is letting herself be soothed in Dave's embrace.

Standing under a warm shower gives her as big a lift as any yoga class or meditation practice, she thinks. If they weren't on tank water, there are times when she'd be tempted to stay under the shower all day. Joan told her once that the rush of water creates a source of negatively charged ions in the air, and that it's those ions that make people feel so wonderful — creative even. Who knows if it's true. Joan says the same thing happens at the bottom of a waterfall. It seems strange that negatively charged ions can make someone feel good, but she lets herself be swept along by the mysteries of the universe.

From the shower, she looks through a tall double-glazed window to the flashing light of the Iron Pot Lighthouse on an outcrop at the mouth of the Derwent River, warning boats away. Her mind returns to Dave at sea. She lifts her face into the spray of water and lets it wash away her worries. She is wasting water, but isn't ready to leave the sanctuary of its warm caress.

To hell with it, Margie thinks as she takes the bath plug between her toes and slots it into the plughole. She leaves the shower running and also turns on the bath taps. The spent water can be re-used on the garden, Margie tells herself.

She opens a dusty jar of dried flowers and berries, which she had kept, largely for decoration, beside the bath, and sprinkles them onto the water's surface. The earthy sweet scent, mellowed with age, is subtle and pleasing. If the flowers block the drains, so be it. Dave can deal with that when he gets home — his penance for putting her through all of this. When the bath is full, she turns off the taps, and leans across to take a box of matches from the bathroom drawer. She lights the row of candles that sit along the Huon pine shelf, and traces the wood's pale vanilla growth rings with her finger. How old was this tree before its wood became this piece of bathroom furniture, she wonders. Some Huon pines can live for a thousand years, each growth ring a memory of a distant time. She marvels that one of these rings might have formed in the same year that the Battle of Hastings took place. Another will correspond to the year that Captain James Cook sailed into Botany Bay. A number of growth rings away would be wood that formed at the same time that Tasmania's notorious Port Arthur jail impounded its first convicts; and, later, the month when armed soldiers and settlers marched together, in what was to become known as the Black Line, down the same colony in an effort to herd its first occupants

— its Aborigines — onto the Tasman Peninsula at the southern tip of the island. How strange that times past are captured in a block of wood in her bathroom, Margie muses. She thinks of Dave building the bench, a project to occupy his hands and his mind after Sam died. He'd said Huon pine was perfect for using near water. It's what boats were once built from.

Lavender petals and juniper berries kiss Margie's legs as she lowers herself into the bath. She can soak in here as long as she wants tonight, she thinks. These moments of inner quiet are to be celebrated and savoured. She knows that now.

She focuses her mind on relaxing every inch of her physical self. She remembers Dave's request to phone Trish, and makes a mental note to do it first thing in the morning. 'Relax,' she reminds herself. Trish won't be sitting by the phone, waiting for her call. She's the sort of person who seems to go through life blissfully unaware of potential tragedy. Margie envies her.

She squashes a juniper berry between her finger and thumb and rubs the juice onto her stomach and across the caesarean scar through which Sam was removed from her womb twenty-six years ago. She remembers the first time she saw the curved scar in the mirror. It seemed to be smiling at her. Without too much imagination, her torso morphed into a whole face. Her breasts became the scar's eyes and her naval its nose. But seeing it now from above, the scar resembles a downturned mouth — forlorn. Without too much imagination, her wrinkled knees become frowning eyes, warning her to seize life, this moment, for it will pass like a ship in the night. She touches the scar of Sam's birth and imagines, for a moment, that her baby is still safe inside her. He will always be with her, she thinks as she leaves her hand there. He was made of her, after all. Her blood, her flesh, her bone. Nothing can take that away.

She thinks of Dave and how losing Sam has changed him, too. How he is more likely now, than before, to tell her that he loves her. Perhaps some good can come from bad. But still there is the pain of what can never be. She has seen the sadness in his eyes when he sees young children and is reminded that he will never have grandchildren of his own. Perhaps they'd been jumping the gun, but they had thought they'd come close to it with Sam's girlfriend. Sascha had been almost part of the family until just before the accident.

Margie thinks of Sam's face the day he told her that Sascha had broken up with him. It was so different from his face the day before, when he confided that he was about to ask her to be his wife.

Margie pushes the flowers around on the surface of the water, making patterns out of the chaos.

Sascha still hasn't been back to the house since the funeral, and Margie couldn't face her that day. If she is honest, Margie would say that she blames Sascha for the accident. If Sam had been thinking straight, he would have seen the P-plate driver coming. And, within months of Sam dying, to add insult to injury, Margie learned from a friend that Sascha was pregnant to her new boyfriend. The news came as a betrayal. How could Sascha, whom she had welcomed into the house like a daughter, have moved on so quickly? Did Sam, her first love, mean so little to her? At least Sam never knew of the pregnancy, Margie thinks. It's a small blessing.

A heavy drop of water falls from the old brass tap into the bath and Margie lets the sad thoughts of Sam slip away. She sinks her head under the warm water, and looks up through the scatter of flowers on the surface, thankful that the aged pot pourri has lost any capacity to sting her searching eyes. As she releases her breath, bubbles rise and push the petals around like small painted boats.

When she comes up for air, Margie bids a fond farewell to the soft light of the candles, luminous on the bath's edge. She begins to blow them out, but the last one resists. It flickers but then stands tall. It's as if it doesn't want to go out. Margie opens the window slightly and lets the cool, dark wind from the Southern Ocean extinguish it.

She stands and runs her fingers over her scalp, studying herself in the mirror. With the petals and berries in her hair and her skin turned red from the heat, she is a human echo of an overcooked crayfish. She laughs out loud, picking the flotsam and jetsam from her body. If it were a fancy restaurant, the sort where they serve toothfish but call it something more exotic, like Chilean sea bass, they'd say she'd been slow-cooked and served with lavender essence and juniper *jus*. She turns the shower on hard and lets the water pummel her head, teasing out the spent petals and berries. Her mind again flies thousands of nautical miles west to Dave at sea. She imagines his fingers massaging her. Is it possible (she asks herself, or God, or whoever is listening) that Dave — stubborn but honest, hard-working and hers — was placed on this earth at the same time as her to share life's experiences, some good and some so terrible that no human being could endure them on their own? But that would suggest that life is fated, and that Sam was always going to die. She's not sure she can believe that. Still, no one else understands her as well as Dave, and that, she decides, is enough. He accepts her as she is, her ups and downs, her need to paint and to sometimes disappear for a whole day on a local bushwalk to combat her grief. A doctor had warned them to keep talking to each other after Sam died, and they did — every day.

As she turns off the shower, Margie wonders how Julia Pereira de Sánchez is faring. Her email response had been brief and Margie wonders if she should warn her about the involvement of the South African navy. Perhaps it would help ensure that the Uruguayan master surrenders peacefully, no guns fired. It doesn't feel right to have extended the hand of cooperation, friendship even, to another woman, and then to have withdrawn it just as quickly when circumstances turned in her favour. She thinks of Dave telling her she'd have made a good Catholic, with her guilty conscience. He's probably right.

Margie wraps a crisp white towel around her torso and winds another one, turban style, around her faintly silvered hair. She'd escaped grey hairs completely until Sam died and then managed to produce a small shroud of them almost overnight.

No, she decides as she rubs moisturiser onto her face, she won't warn Julia that the navy are on their way. Who knows, the information could start another chase, making the situation worse for everyone. The important thing is that the hot pursuit, as the government insists on calling it, is drawing to a close. It's what she and Julia both wanted. Margie unwraps the towel from her hair, takes the blowdryer from the drawer and bathes her head in its warmth. Finally her body feels ready for sleep.

LOGBOOK OF EDUARDO RODRÍGUEZ TORRES

∽

It's strange to think there are fish at the base of the ocean older than me. Some of the larger ones we've caught must be nearer to my father's age. I imagine myself there sometimes, in their realm, where no man has been before.

I had a dream last night that I joined the fish … I was washed overboard. Three times I managed to glimpse sky and flashes of the red-and-white hull, and breathe foaming air, but the waves struck again. Carlos was there, trying to save me. I could see his distraight face through the foam as I was battered against the hull by the weight of rushing water. I felt myself losing power and sensation in my arms and legs as the cold took hold. My mind blurred. Icy water paralysed my body and my lungs ached from a lack of oxygen. Seawater swelled my stomach until it was solid. I couldn't cough. There was no air left. I thought of my girls at home. Of Virginia. My beautiful daughters. And Julia. I was a fish on a line, hanging by a thread. Suspended between life and death. The pain was intense. I managed to unfasten my safety clip and the sea welcomed me home. The pain stopped.

∽

CARLOS
The *Pescador*
4 October 2002

Carlos looks past Dmitri to the ice that has again built up on the rails. He knows, from the concerned expression on his first mate's face, that Eduardo has seen it, too. The southwesterly weather is showing no sign of abating and the boat is wearing its fury like a white badge of honour. With the sea behind them, he knows it would take just one bad decision at the helm to twist the boat up into a wave and roll her under, finishing this off for the lot of them. He checks the seas through the rear windows of the wheelhouse and is relieved to see that the *Australis* has resumed its place as a distant presence behind the waves.

'I'm going out to get that ice off,' Eduardo says. 'Or we won't be going anywhere.'

Dmitri clenches his jaw and rubs at his stomach, as if weighing up the risk of letting the first mate back into contact with his men.

A wave lifts the *Pescador* and pushes it towards Mauritius. 'The crew can do it,' Dmitri says. 'Carlos, you order them out.' The Russian points at the intercom that connects the wheelhouse to the men tucked away in their cabins. 'They're used to following orders from you.'

'You don't know them,' Eduardo says. 'They won't cooperate unless I'm out there, too. I always go on deck with my men in bad seas. It's why I have their respect — something you'll never have.'

Dmitri goes to speak but stops. Something changes in his face, a flicker. 'Very well. Go.'

Eduardo gives Carlos a straight smile so full of remorse that the master is left wondering if there is something else his first mate is not telling him. When he is gone, Dmitri continues. 'And you,' he says to Carlos, 'take the helm. I have to use the bathroom. When I am back, you can call the crew. But not before.' Dmitri uses his finger to beckon the young Peruvian to stand closer to Carlos. 'Keep an eye on him,' he tells José. 'And if he tries anything …' Dmitri makes his hand into the shape of a gun, and leaves.

Carlos watches Eduardo make his way down the external stairs to the deck. He watches his determination as he clips his harness to the rails and lurches towards the bow of the boat. A wave breaks unevenly on the stern, catching Carlos off-guard. The boat swings fast to starboard and Eduardo lands hard on the deck, skidding into a metal strut that he clings to like a long-lost lover. It takes another minute for Carlos to correct the boat's position, and for Eduardo to get to his feet.

'I need to call the rest of the crew out there,' Carlos tells José, reaching for the intercom.

'No.' José raises the gun higher, onto his shoulder. 'Not until Dmitri gets back.'

'Don't be an idiot!' Carlos lifts the handset, but José forces the end of the gun barrel into the back of his hand.

'I said no!'

Carlos draws his bleeding hand to his mouth for an instant before placing it back on the wheel. His attention is firmly back on Eduardo, alone on deck. The first mate begins work as soon as he reaches the bow, swinging his hammer at the bone-white rails. His whole body works the blows, and chunks of ice fly into the sea. The wind and waves serve some of it back up on deck. The bow resembles a sideshow ride arcing high into the sky before plummeting in a death-defying dive. Eduardo braces himself against the rails as he works. Seawater falls away in torrents from around his legs and then swamps him up to his thighs.

Dmitri is back at the door, and Carlos reaches again for the intercom.

'Leave it!' the Russian orders.

'Eduardo can't do this on his own. You said —'

'I know what I said.' Dmitri grabs hold of the helm. 'Your job is done.' He flicks his head in the direction of the wall. 'Get back there.'

Carlos feels the boat pitch to port when his back is turned. With José's gun digging into his side, he looks up in time to see the wash of a large wave over the bow. Eduardo is off his feet and sliding. The boat leans heavily under the weight of water and ice and sucks Eduardo under the rails.

'*¡Jesús!*' Carlos shouts. He casts José aside and sprints the few paces back to the instruments, pressing the man-overboard button on the GPS to mark Eduardo's position. 'I'm going out there! Turn the boat.'

Dmitri lets him go.

Carlos pushes open the wheelhouse door, grabs the dan buoy and throws the float over the side. There's no time for his safety harness. Eduardo has only minutes to live in these frigid seas. Every second counts. Carlos drags himself along the rail against the barrage of waves to where Eduardo's line is twitching, tightly stretched, against the hull with the combined weight of the large man and the monstrous seas. Eduardo is a flash of orange jacket and a grabbing hand. Carlos claws at the safety line. Without gloves, it's difficult to gain any purchase. The rope tears at numb flesh. Another wave is breaking over them. Eduardo's body is beating against the side of the boat like a slain fish. Carlos signals at the wheelhouse with one hand to slow the boat, pushing the air back repeatedly in Dmitri's view. But the *Pescador* pounds forward regardless.

'*¡Mierda!*' Carlos swears.

Carlos reaches for Eduardo's hand again, but it is gone. He can no longer even see the orange jacket.

Carlos is deaf to his own cries over the roar of water and wind. He unties a life ring and throws it, too late, into the hungry sea, but inflated plastic is a poor meal compared with a human soul. Huge waves gulp behind him, consuming their prey. Carlos looks towards the dan buoy to see if Eduardo finds it as the ship moves forward, but there's no sign of the first mate. He squints in the direction of the *Australis* but it is too far away. Eduardo will be dead and gone by the time the Australian vessel catches up.

The *Pescador* is still surging forward. 'Turn the boat,' Carlos bellows hopelessly, drawing a circle with his arm to Dmitri in the wheelhouse. But he's signalling to an icy window five metres above the deck. He knows Dmitri would see him only as a mute, orange blur. Carlos pulls the empty safety line, easily now, onto the deck. The carabiner is bare of Eduardo's harness. He holds the naked line up in full view of the wheelhouse.

'*¡Condenado!* Turn around!' he screams against the wind, tossing the safety line into the ocean to illustrate Eduardo's fate. Carlos knows Eduardo would have released himself as a last resort in the expectation that they would attempt to retrieve him. If he had stayed attached to the safety line any longer, he would have drowned anyway, or died from the blows he suffered against the hull.

Carlos again tries to make out the shadow of Dmitri in the wheelhouse but is knocked down by the relentless seas, pressed flat under the icy assault of yet another wave. Water washes over him as if he is a mollusc, loosely secured, on a beach rock. Each wave prises him off the deck and then slaps him back against it.

'*¡Capitán!*' someone shouts. But Carlos is aware only of the growing distance between the boat and his life-long friend. A wall of water, a trough, a wall of water, a trough. Eduardo is gone, consumed in the *Pescador*'s wake.

Carlos sees Manuel standing over him and feels himself dragged to his feet. It hurts to move his eyes because of the ice encrusting them. His long hair, too, having escaped its leather band, is frozen to his plastic jacket. He is lifted and carried back inside. Manuel peels off the sodden clothes before wrapping a blanket around the master. Another senior crew member, a Spaniard called Roberto, the oldest man on board after Manuel, removes his own beanie and puts it on Carlos's shivering head. Carlos examines the faces of the other ten crew who are watching on. They appear confused.

'It's good that you're shaking. It's when you stop that we worry.' Manuel grins broadly, causing the wound above his eye to weep fresh blood.

'Eduardo?' The name is misshapen by Carlos's numb mouth and jaw.

'He must still be in the wheelhouse,' Manuel answers.

Carlos shakes his head.

'Well, he's not on deck,' Manuel contends. 'It's *you* we're worried about. You're lucky we found you. What were you thinking going out there alone?' He spins his finger at his temple. '*Loco.*'

Carlos shakes his head. He had made the same joke with Eduardo only days before. Hypothermia and shock compress his chest and cloud his thoughts. Is he dreaming? Carlos sees Eduardo disappearing through the wheelhouse door, smiling and acting the fool. He thinks of him now, leaden with seawater and death, and sobs.

'Hey. You're okay now,' Manuel says with a bemused chuckle, attempting to reassure the deposed fishing master. 'We'll deal with Dmitri in good time. None of us want what he's offering.'

Carlos holds his hands in front of him, motioning Manuel to stop. He opens his mouth, but no sound escapes.

'Don't try to talk. Just get warm,' Manuel instructs.

'Eduardo.' Carlos lowers his head and tilts his shaking bare hands open on his lap. 'Gone.' The word is so quiet it's barely audible. '¡Me jodí!' He blames himself.

The air in the room seems to change as the crew process what Carlos has told them. Carlos sees them finally comprehend what has happened. He wasn't alone on deck. Eduardo would never have allowed that. Not when he could go.

Manuel's face drops. 'Oh God,' he whispers, resting both hands on the side of Carlos's chair and hanging his head heavily between his arms. The room is silent, but for the incessant howl of the wind punctuated by the boom of thundering waves.

JULIA
Montevideo, Uruguay
4 October 2002

When the ambulance arrives, Julia is still lying on the tiles of her kitchen floor, the hand towel decorated with red roses now sodden between her legs. She has heard the siren's oscillating crescendo building from the direction of the port: first in the distance, rushing along the riverfront Rambla as if in a dream, then turning right and becoming more insistent until she has had to cover her ears with her hands. The scattered toast crumbs on the floor are drenched in her fluid. So is the lower part of her dress. The baby's kicks and rolls hit hard without the liquid cushion. She tries to soothe her child and herself by rubbing her stomach in large, sweeping circles and whispering to the tiny life that is warm and nurtured within her. She imagines her child extracting oxygen directly from her blood, not yet ready to breathe, not yet ready to be born.

Julia opens the front door to the paramedics, leaving a line of amniotic fluid along the hallway. There are no hellos but the older man offers a polite smile as he carries the stretcher inside and sets it down on the floor.

'So, you're only twenty-seven weeks' pregnant,' he confirms as he guides her onto the stretcher and places a welcome hand on her wrist to take her pulse. His brown eyes are deep and kind. He reminds her of a middle-aged Carlos.

'*Sí*,' she says. There are hot tears on her cheeks. 'It's not enough.' The sound of her own voice, small and frightened, comes as a shock.

'No.' The response is honest. 'We'll do what we can.'

The other paramedic asks Julia to roll onto her side. 'It's better for the baby,' he says as he places a drip-line in her arm. 'This is in case they need to give you IV drugs in hospital.' He takes her blood pressure, and makes notes on a plastic clipboard attached to the end of the stretcher.

Outside, Julia is aware of someone stopping beside her. She sees short black shoes and beige stockings and hears the voice of her elderly neighbour. 'Oh, Julia. The baby?'

Julia's hand is across her face.

'You will be all right. Both of you.' The woman holds Julia's hand in her own arthritic one and gives it a slight squeeze. 'I will pray for you,' she says as the stretcher is lifted into the ambulance.

It's just what Julia needs to hear. Blind faith and optimism. The ambulance doors close. She feels a warm hand reassessing her pulse. 'It's a bit quick,' the older paramedic says. 'Just relax.'

'I'm trying to.' Julia then repeats to herself a calming mantra. She learned meditation when she was trying to fall pregnant again after María was born. Relaxation, she was told, would help. But, as she focuses her mind, she feels her abdomen harden, drum-tight. '¡Ay, no!' she cries.

'A contraction?' the more senior attendant asks.

'Sí.'

'Painful?'

'Not very.'

'Well, they mightn't become regular. Just relax. Chase them away in your head.'

Julia lies quietly, trying desperately to soothe herself with her silent mantra. 'Ommm, ommm, ommm.' It becomes an internal clock, ticking off the minutes between each tightening. She wills the contractions away.

To distract herself, she thinks of her parents' home in the hills. She sees chooks squabbling and hears the rustle of leaves in the orchard. She imagines sinking her teeth into the soft downy flesh of a peach, tasting its sweetness. In the orange groves, she can smell the summery fruit. She scrapes the heavy globe of an orange with her fingernail, filling the air with the perfume of better times. Her father is talking, but she can't make out what he's saying. Her mother is there too, telling her she will be all right. María is playing on a swing in the dense shade of the grapevine that shrouds the courtyard.

But the daydream is interrupted by light so bright it penetrates her eyelids as the doors of the ambulance are flung open. She is lifted out of the vehicle and can hear the men's footsteps on the bitumen change to the sharp, efficient clicks of shoes on a polished vinyl floor. She is in the hospital, she realises without even opening her eyes. She hears nursing staff direct them through the echoing corridors and into a quieter place, perhaps an examination room. Information is relayed on blood pressure and heart rate. Someone takes her hand. Julia opens her eyes and sees the older paramedic's face.

'You just relax. My wife had the same thing happen. You'll be okay,' he says. 'And remember, God won't deal you anything you can't handle.' He clasps her hand firmly.

'*Muchísimas gracias*.' She shuts her eyes again, and hears the door open and close. She wonders what horror she is capable of enduring. What hand will God deal her? How cruel can He be? She isn't even sure that she believes in God, but decides to give prayer a chance one last time. Now or never. 'Please let this baby survive,' she utters quietly to any god who may be listening. '*Please* let my baby live.'

'Do you want me to call your husband?'

Julia opens her eyes, surprised that the nurse is still in the room and has heard her small prayer. 'He's at sea. I can't reach him,' she answers, turning her head away.

'How long is he away?'

'A couple more weeks, at least,' she says through tears. It's impossible to stop the flood of salt water from her eyes now, just as she can't stop the constant trickle of amniotic fluid from the broken bag of waters within her womb.

'He's a nice fellow, that ambulance man,' the nurse says, changing the subject as she places a monitor around Julia's stomach to trace the baby's heart rate and any further contractions.

Julia realises she didn't ask the paramedic if his own baby had survived.

'The doctor will be here soon to take a look at you.' The nurse tips the contents of a medicine bottle into her hand. 'Luckily he's on the ward this morning. He asked me to give you these.' She places two small white tablets on a tray. 'They should help settle the contractions.' The nurse makes a note on the medical chart. 'I'll be back with the steroid injection. It'll strengthen your baby's lungs.'

About five minutes pass before the nurse re-enters with a large syringe and a vial, which she pierces with the needle. She fills the syringe to the brim before unloading it slowly and painfully into Julia's thigh. Julia feels the nurse's hand rub at her leg, spreading the drug throughout the muscle and easing the discomfort. She wonders how long it will be before her blood carries the steroid to her baby's lungs, pumping them up in readiness for life outside the womb. The nurse covers her again with the sheet. 'So, your husband is away. These men sure know how to pick their times, don't they?' The nurse pulls a face that is both bemused and disapproving. 'I had both my children when my husband was out of the country. Is there someone else I can call for you?'

'*Si*. Can you please call Cecilia Castillo de Molteni? I don't have her telephone number with me, sorry. The address is Buschental Avenue, number six, I think. It'll be in the phone directory. She's looking after my daughter and was expecting me to pick her up this morning. She'll have to keep her there for a few more days, I suppose.'

'*Si*, at least. Leave it to me. And what about your parents? Are they close by?'

'They're in Tarariras. But there's no point worrying everyone just yet. The contractions might stop. Mightn't they?'

The nurse doesn't meet Julia's eyes. 'You just relax and think of somewhere nice,' she says warmly. There's a brief knock at the door, and the doctor comes in. 'Here he is. *¡Bueno!*' Her face softens with relief.

The obstetrician introduces himself briskly to Julia before studying the printout spewing from the monitors. His face doesn't give much away. He readies the ultrasound machine for an examination. 'Let's see what's going on in there,' he says.

The doctor's presence, alone, provides comfort, but Julia knows he's no miracle worker. 'What are the chances if my baby is born now?' she asks.

'Well, all babies are different. But statistically, about seventy per cent born at this gestation survive.' He squeezes a tube of lubricant onto the ultrasound device and passes it over Julia's belly. He clicks away on the machine, measuring the baby's length.

'Your baby is a good size for its age. We might be all right.'
He slides the ultrasound over Julia's glazed skin. He glides it
down low on her abdomen and presses firmly just above her
pubic bone. Julia watches his face.

'The baby is certainly on its way, but we'll see if we can
hold it off for a day or so. The nurse has already given you the
steroid injection, so it will just be a case of wait-and-see now.
The longer the drug has to work the better, but there's also a
risk of infection for the baby now that your waters have
broken. It's a balancing act.'

'Why has this happened?'

'It's difficult to say. Premature labour isn't something we
have a good understanding of. Be assured it's nothing you've
done. You didn't have a scan before presenting here, though,
did you?'

'No. I was due for an appointment a couple of weeks ago
but my daughter was ill and I had to put it off. I got sick, too.
A gastric thing. Could that have brought this on?'

'It's possible, but chances are we'll never know the cause, to
be honest. Babies are just born too early sometimes.
Unfortunately, things are rarely as black and white as we
would like. See if you can get some rest. There's nothing you
can do now.'

The doctor gives Julia a pat on the knee and leaves.

The nurse re-enters. 'Just thought I'd turn these bright
lights off for you,' she says before flicking three switches,

extinguishing all but one of the lights. 'Sleep now.' She closes the door.

The room hums with the sound of the air conditioner, the electronic beeping of the monitors, and the whir from the printer. The printout's squiggly line, the baby's heart rate, is broken by sudden jagged peaks of uterine contractions. It reminds Julia of the graphs that record the seismic details of an impending earthquake. Sleep seems like a sick joke.

Julia watches the clock on the wall. Never before has each minute been so important. It's difficult to believe it's not yet nine o'clock. Not even an hour has passed since she woke and watched the *gorrión* bird catch its breakfast on the lawn. Yet already the lights have been switched off and she has been put to bed on this, the shortest — and longest — day of her life. Julia strikes her hand against the mattress, resentful that Carlos isn't here. But how could he have known this would happen? How could anyone have known?

She tries to think of the things that make her happiest: searching the beach for shells and polished glass with María, and playing tea parties with her on the picnic rug under the *Tipas* tree. Julia thinks, too, of Carlos arriving home in earlier years, and the languid afternoons they spent together making love. And she thinks of Eduardo, and the deep ache that invades her body every time she stands too close to him. When she's with Eduardo, it's as though they're teenagers again, naïve and optimistic. With him, everything feels as if it will turn out well. Perhaps this premature labour is her penance for her love for him, she thinks. Punishment for their affair. But she pushes the idea away. No god would be so cruel as to punish an unborn child for its mother's sins. No god that she wants to know.

There's a knock at the door and an old woman in a crisp white apron delivers a cup of tea, but no breakfast. 'I was told fluids only,' the woman whispers. 'In case you have to go down to theatre. You'll have your baby soon.' She rubs her hands together gleefully, unaware of what is at stake, and shuts the door smartly behind her.

Julia sits up and sips the tea but it's cold and too strong. She goes to put it back on the side table, but is overcome by a low ache in her womb. The tea spills down the drawers, bleeding all the way to the floor. The squeeze in her abdomen intensifies. It's unmistakable, a true labour contraction. She lies on her side. Five minutes pass and she feels another. Then a third, more painful now. Her internal birthing clock has found its rhythm, and is locking it in.

The nurse arrives and reads the expression on Julia's face before investigating the monitor's latest output. The graph confirms what Julia already knows.

'We'd better call Doctor. I suspect he'll want to get things underway as soon as possible now. It'll need to be a caesarean at this gestation.'

'So I've just been told.'

'You've already seen the doctor?'

'No, the tea lady!' Julia says, through gritted teeth, her face screwed up in pain.

'Oh, I'm so sorry. A normal birth would be too stressful for the baby. It's for the best.' The nurse writes something on Julia's chart and hurries away.

Julia, left alone again with the machines, is aware of the familiar sting of tears on her cheeks. The baby is going to be taken from her body within the next couple of hours. She finds herself saying another prayer. She doesn't have much else to call on. If only Carlos were here.

The examination room is suddenly abuzz with preparations and staff. Julia is dressed in a gown and is shaved and washed with iodine. The doctor enters the room, swinging the door wide, and inspects the graph. He twists his mouth sideways, and holds the head of the ultrasound against Julia's uterus, just as another contraction takes hold.

'He's still all right, but we'll need to be quick.'

Julia catches a glimpse of the baby's face in profile on the monitor for the first time, and sees a tiny hand give a floating wave.

'*Hola*,' Julia whispers to her child as she waves back.

'Your baby is distressed with these heavier contractions,' the doctor says. 'I have to make some calls. I'll be back in a couple of minutes.' He is already on his way out the door, and seems to have changed modes, viewing her now as a patient to be cut and sewn. He can't afford to be distracted by sympathy or personal concern.

His words are ringing in Julia's ears: '*He's* still all right.' Is the baby a boy, she speculates, or had the doctor just used the generic *he* that everyone seems to apply to unborn children? Julia's parents have been calling the baby 'he', too. Perhaps they are hoping that if they say it enough times, their wish might come true.

Until now, Julia hadn't wanted to know the sex of this child. After the miscarriages, she'd needed to be sure the pregnancy would end happily before making plans. It was simply too painful to build castles in the sky for her baby's future only to have them demolished and burned. Turned into ash like her tiny, lost babies. She supposes she was trying to keep a small distance between herself and the little life within. But seeing her baby's face on the monitor has evaporated any chance of self-preservation. She must love him now, not later. Whatever happens.

In minutes, Julia is hurried to theatre and the anaesthetist is asking her to sit up and bend forward so he can insert a needle deep into the space between the bones of her spine. The contractions make it difficult to keep still. She feels the coolness of an alcohol wipe and the prick of a local anaesthetic. There's a deep, nauseating feeling of fullness in her back. She is laid down and observes the flurry of action, blurred through tears, in her peripheral vision. She weeps quietly.

The doctor, now fully gowned, is scrubbing at a sink, his back to her. Her baby's life is in his hands. He turns to face the surgical bed but avoids meeting her eyes.

The paediatrician introduces himself before attending to a small Perspex trolley fitted with tiny tubes, drip bags and a heat lamp. The baby's soon-to-be new home is no substitute for her loving belly, she thinks.

The surgeon begins. Julia feels a tugging sensation, but can't see beyond the screen that has been erected on her chest. A bloodied glove reaches for an instrument and Julia focuses instead on the ceiling. Nausea overcomes her and she vomits. A nurse deftly catches the tea-stained bile in a bowl. Some of it sticks in Julia's hair. She feels a cloth wipe her face.

There is a small mewl and Julia realises it's her baby crying. The doctor lifts the tiny, red-skinned form from her and passes it to the paediatrician who places it quickly into the Perspex humidicrib.

'He's very small,' the doctor says.

'*He*,' Julia whispers. So it *is* a boy. A son.

She sees the intensive-care nurses and the paediatrician huddling around the humidicrib. There's a sucking sound as they work to clear her baby's lungs.

It's odd, Julia thinks, that her baby can survive so many months surrounded by water, and then be in danger of drowning only when he is brought up and into the air. It strikes her as the opposite of what happens when an adult drowns. Eduardo once admitted to her that it was his greatest fear — to fall deep into the earth's watery womb.

Julia lifts her head but a nurse warns her to stay still. 'The doctor hasn't finished stitching you up,' she is told.

But, with the anaesthetic, Julia couldn't reach her son even if she tried. It's as though she has been assaulted and robbed — left paralysed, body and soul. The paediatric team swiftly moves the baby out of the theatre and into a lift that will take him to the neonatal nursery. It's so strange, Julia thinks, to be so instantly separate. To feel the distance forcibly stretched between her and her baby. To realise that she is now a mother of two, for however long this baby survives.

Julia looks back at the obstetrician's face and sees that he is starting to appear more at ease. He tells the nurses a joke and Julia is struck by how quickly his part in this ordeal is over. Her nightmare, she suspects, is just beginning.

LOGBOOK OF EDUARDO RODRÍGUEZ TORRES

❧

To drown at sea. We all fear it. All of us fishermen. From the time our grandfathers struggled through surf in small boats that they launched off the beach, to now, on factory ships, a million miles from our homes on shore. We call the sea our second home, but none of us want to go to Davy Jones's locker. I have read that 'Davy Jones' probably derives from 'Duffy Jonah', a west Indian term. Duffy means a ghost. Jonah was the prophet who was thrown into the sea.

❧

CARLOS
The *Pescador*
5 October 2002

Carlos dreams of Eduardo sinking. He becomes Eduardo. His orange sea jacket fades to a muted blue before turning ink-black, in the way the deepening ocean bleeds all life of its colour. A final cry departs his gaping mouth as a rising, expanding bubble. Empty lungs collapse under the water's weight. Strange life forms inspect him at close range. Hagfish nibble on fronds of waving hair. A parasitic lamprey attaches to a sunken cheek. Above him lies the swollen belly of an iceberg. Finally, his large body gives way to the seafloor.

He opens one eye. Then both.

His legs merge into a tail fin.

He communes with fish, removing hooks from black, rubbery lips. He plunges a hand down torn throats and into soft stomachs to remove the remains of poorly digested chicken bones, food tins and plastic bags, all discarded by fishermen. Antifouling paint, containing toxic tributyltin from the hulls of icebreakers, coats the seabed with its sickening film, causing some life forms to die and others to mysteriously change sex. The reach of humans is everywhere.

A procession of toothfish approaches him. There are perhaps five hundred. Each gaunt specimen hooked via a short nylon rope to a longer, sturdier line. It's the longline he had cut only two and a half weeks before — the line he had let fall, fully laden, back to depth.

The fish queue patiently for him to release them, one by one. They are thin from being enslaved, unable to feed.

He hears the familiar engine noise of a boat above. Naked hooks, the size of fists, appear. He takes the end of one in his mouth and lets it pierce his cheek. He warns the other fish away. Hours pass as he waits, suspended. He is patient.

Finally he is brought to the surface. Once handsome, he is now reduced to a ghoulish mess of matted hair and gouging fish hooks tearing his broken face. His sea jacket hangs like shreds of sunburnt kelp. He gloats as he spins on the line, dancing a series of macabre pirouettes from an avant garde ballet. Slowly he stops spiralling and faces the fishermen on deck. His audience.

'Soon there will be no fish left. Go home or you shall die.' His curse is clear. Emphatic.

The fishermen hurriedly cut the line and he falls heavily back into the ocean. His turgid tail splashes water at the shaken men, who are left in doubt of their minds. He is gone, this soothsayer who can divine the number of fish left in the sea.

He has learnt to breathe the air dissolved in seawater, but it will not always be so easy. The deep sea, so rich in oxygen, is finally releasing the life-giving gas. As the earth warms, and ocean circulation patterns change, less oxygen is being transported down to deep-ocean currents. He wonders how long it will be before the strange world around him suffocates.

He rides the Antarctic circumpolar current full circle, allowing himself to be caught at every opportunity — at the islands of South Georgia, Prince Edward, Crozet Kerguélen and Heard. He moves further south to Ob and Lena Banks, where illegal fishers are already exhausting new grounds.

Sometimes deep-sea nets are used instead of longlines. But they are no barrier to this keeper of the deep. He climbs into their open mouths and cuts holes in their fouled rope to let the fish escape. Occasionally he is spilled onto deck and takes a blow from a gaff or a bullet to the head, body or tail. He bleeds thick blood, stocked high with anti-freeze borrowed from his Antarctic toothfish cousins. But he can't be killed, for he lives in every fisherman. He is their collective fear of the ocean, of drowning, of becoming monstrous. He propels himself back into the sea.

Tales of this denizen of the deep spread. They converge in the bars of Port Louis, Durban, Walvis Bay and his home port of Montevideo. In these places, the illegal fishers gather to drink their fill of spirit, and to warm aching bones and souls weary from chasing fish across lonely seas. Each time his ghost visits a boat, the vessel inevitably suffers misfortune: sometimes the loss of life, sometimes an injury, always poor catches. It's hardly worth going to sea.

His curse is realised. The boats scared away, he begins the long task of nursing the stocks back to health.

Carlos wakes in a lather of salt water, his mind and body thick with the effects of hypothermia. He struggles to shake off his nightmare of the ghoulish Eduardo and for a moment wonders if his friend's death may also have been a dream. He glimpses relief. But it is a mirage. It vanishes like the flashes of Southern Lights that grace the Antarctic sky, teasing fishermen with the luminous greens — the colours of grass and trees — of home. He can't lie, not even to himself. The details of the dream recur with sickening, spiralling clarity. Not as a fluid film of events, but rather a succession of short takes of the drama that unfolded. The order is jumbled, as he tries to make sense of what has happened.

An unstoppable barrage of memories place him once again on the frozen deck, reaching out for a disappearing hand. It's as though by retelling the story, he hopes to discover a detail that will reverse events and bring Eduardo back.

His thoughts drift now to Eduardo's wife and daughters. He'll have to make a satellite call to break the news, a call that will reveal the *Pescador*'s position to the world — not that it's a secret any more. And if the call is intercepted and used somehow to incriminate him, then that is the price he must pay. The fate of the boat and the catch now seems less important. He covers his face with his hands, blocking out the world. Perhaps he should give Virginia and the girls one more day in which to believe that Eduardo is still alive, a brief peace before their hollow grief undoes them forever. Carlos knows that from the moment they learn of Eduardo's death, their lives will be divided neatly into before and after. Everything will change.

The boat is travelling perilously in the following seas, and Carlos thinks of Dmitri at the helm, steering the boat northeast, at right angles to the waves behind them. How could he have failed to see the Russian's vile potential? He pounds his fists hard against the inside wall of the hull. He recalls the accusations Dmitri made against Eduardo and wonders if any were true. Perhaps none of it matters now. He feels sick with grief and panic and the knowledge that he has failed his crew. Carlos lowers himself out of his bunk and feels his body ache under its own weight. There's a sharp pain each time he draws air into his lungs, and he realises he must have bruised or cracked a rib when he was reaching over the deck yesterday, reaching down towards oblivion for Eduardo. He closes his eyes against the pain and the truth.

Someone knocks on his cabin door and he hears the hinges creak as the door opens and closes. 'We're going to pretend that it's a divided camp.' It's Manuel's voice coming towards him. 'That the Spaniards aren't yet convinced of his plan, and that the Peruvians are for it. If we all pretend to be behind Dmitri, it'll look too suspicious.'

'What he said about us planning to sell some of the catch behind your backs was true.'

'Most of us would have done the same.'

Carlos opens his eyes to study Manuel, trying to comprehend the loyalty of his crew. 'I didn't know about the guns.'

'I know. Neither did Eduardo. I overheard him talking to Dmitri. Not the whole conversation — most of it was in Russian — but he let slip in Spanish a few times, to swear mostly.' Manuel makes a poor attempt at a laugh before his grave expression returns. 'Eduardo was furious that Dmitri had brought guns on board.'

'So he *was* telling the truth.' Carlos rubs his forehead and studies Manuel.

'*Si*. But we have to focus on Dmitri now. He has been at the helm for nearly twenty-four hours. He'll be getting tired and dropping his guard. You go up there, and tell him the Spaniards won't talk to you. He'll take it as encouragement and call us up to the wheelhouse — I'd bet on it. But we'll play hard to get so that when the Peruvians offer their support, he'll lap it up. When he hands out the guns, that'll be our chance to overthrow him.'

'You've given this some thought then?' Carlos manages a weary smile, but inside a part of him has died. Being at sea doesn't feel the same without his best friend. But even Eduardo had struggled to make light of the grim situation they'd become embroiled in. Carlos suspects this would be one of the few occasions that he would have admitted he'd bitten off more than he could chew.

He thinks back to being a boy at La Paloma, larking about with Eduardo — the trips too far from the coast in Eduardo's father's dinghy, and the nocturnal dives (Eduardo always went first) off the pier to commune with the ocean's night-dwellers. It's true that Eduardo took bigger risks than he himself was ever prepared to take, but it's also the case that Eduardo was prepared to wear the consequences. Whatever secret arrangements his friend made for this trip, Carlos consoles himself, were to protect him.

Carlos pays a short visit to the crew's cabins below deck, acknowledging each man with a short dip of his head. He sees their silent grief at losing Eduardo. He opens his mouth to speak, but shuts it again. Words are inadequate. In silence, he makes his way along the corridors and back up the three flights of stairs to the wheelhouse.

'What the hell happened yesterday?' Carlos fires the question at Dmitri as if it were him, and not the Russian, holding the gun. He knows that the treacherous conditions on deck would have hampered visibility from the wheelhouse, but the Russian must have seen two men become only one. 'Why didn't you turn the boat around? We could have saved him.'

'Not in those seas.'

'You didn't even try. You killed him.'

The Russian sneers. 'Do you think I need either of you?'

Carlos glances briefly through the rear windows and sees that their lead on the Australian boat has narrowed while he has been asleep. To hell with them. He reaches for the satellite phone. 'I'm calling Eduardo's family.'

'I don't think so.' Dmitri holds up a small piece of wire, no doubt taken from the guts of the Inmarsat communication system, from his jacket pocket. He takes a final mouthful of vodka and feeds the wire into the empty bottle. 'We cannot transmit using VHF radio, either. We can, however, listen to incoming calls on both, just to keep ourselves entertained.' He laughs.

Carlos takes a step towards Dmitri, but José threatens him with the gun. Carlos holds up his hand in surrender and steps back. To be shot now would serve no one, bar Dmitri. And with the shortage of helmsmen on the boat, not even him.

Carlos leans his back heavily against the wall nearest him and slides down to the ground. He rests there on the wet carpet, his knees drawn up, hands hanging over them. His body is still exhausted from the day before, and he squeezes shut his eyes as he tries to block out the piercing pain in his ribs.

'So, what's the feeling among the crew?' Dmitri asks. 'I thought El Animal might have been back here with an answer by now. What's taking him so long?'

'I don't know. The crew aren't talking to me.'

Dmitri guffaws. And Carlos watches him reach for the intercom. 'Manuel, bring the Spaniards up to the wheelhouse. I want them to hear from me what is on offer.'

Within minutes, the ten Spanish crew arrive edgily at the door. Their eyes go straight to the guns slung across Dmitri and José, and then dart around the room as they try to conceal their fear. Most of them, Carlos realises, are seeing the wheelhouse for the first time. They take in the bird's-eye view that the windows afford of the fore and aft decks, and Carlos imagines that each of them is reliving the last three weeks from his perspective. He questions whether they would have made different choices.

José is watching their eyes too, and twitching with adrenaline. He points his gun anxiously at the men.

'Take the helm, Manuel,' Dmitri orders, before turning to speak to the assembled men, his own gun hanging by his side.

The Spaniards jeer collectively at Dmitri and swear at José, who is waiting on the Russian for direction. One of the younger crew spits at Dmitri's feet. It's not the reception the mutineer had expected.

'Do not mock us, my friends,' Dmitri warns. 'And do not think for a moment that my colleague here does not know how to use that gun.' His expression hardens. 'Show them, José. There must be someone here who has angered you over the last few weeks. Perhaps they have taken more than their fair share of food, or made you look a fool.'

José appears confused about what Dmitri is asking him to do.

'Go on. Show them you can do it. Or are these men right? Are you afraid to use the gun?'

Carlos notices Manuel tensing visibly at the helm. This was not part of the plan. 'There's no need for that,' Manuel speaks quickly. 'Listen, men, to what Dmitri is offering you.'

'Shut up. I want them to see I am serious.' Dmitri repeats his instruction to José. 'Go on!'

José raises the weapon and looks down its length to the men in front of him. He surveys the group, one by one. Carlos has paid little attention to José until now. He strikes him as a loner, and wonders if the young Peruvian can claim to know any of the men in front of him — if anyone inspires hatred or admiration. Or are they just a blur of fishermen, desperate souls crewing the same boat on the same stretch of ocean?

'I said go on!' Dmitri bellows.

The gun is trained on the oldest fisherman, Roberto Cruz.
Carlos has never seen José even speak to him.

'Do it!' Dmitri roars.

'No!' Manuel shouts from the helm.

José panics and Carlos hears the gun explode.

'*¡Jódete!*' Carlos swears. He hadn't expected the fool to do it.
Not in the chest. Perhaps over his head, or into the floor. He
goes to the old man. Roberto's son — a young man of perhaps
twenty — is on the opposite side, holding his hand to his father's
bleeding chest. His other hand smooths the wounded man's
time-worn forehead, and strokes his thick, silvery waves of hair.

'*Padre,*' the young Spaniard cries.

Roberto is still alive, but is managing only shallow airy
gasps. His lips and skin are fading to a bluish white. There is
blood at his mouth. He says something quietly to his son and
touches his cheek. Carlos is holding Roberto's other hand and
feels it release. The wheelhouse falls silent.

José staggers backward, seemingly bewildered by what he
has done. He almost drops the gun, but Dmitri takes it before
it hits the ground.

'I did not think you would actually do it, I have to admit,'
Dmitri says, slapping José on the back. The young man leans
into the furthest corner of the wheelhouse and vomits.

Carlos glowers at Dmitri with wet eyes, his arm flung
around Roberto's son. 'You've taken our friend and this man's
father. How will you ever sleep again?'

'You think this is the first man I have had killed!' Dmitri's laughter hisses like shards of ice in a fire.

José, vomit still clinging to the sparse hairs on his chin, has slunk to the floor, cowering from Dmitri and the angry Spanish crew.

'And you,' Carlos says, glaring at José, 'you might try to hide, but you'll be haunted by what you've just done for the rest of your life. You've killed a man, and nothing you ever do will put that right.'

'Enough!' Dmitri spits. 'I hope I now have your full attention. There is something important I have to offer you.'

Carlos watches the Russian who has so misjudged his audience. He may have won their fear, but he is as far from gaining their respect as a man can be. How could he have ever thought this would convince them? It occurs to Carlos that Dmitri would be the sort of person to beat his dogs, coercing them into submission. But beaten dogs feign loyalty only while their master is awake. The moment he falls asleep, they'll tear him apart.

'But before I start,' Dmitri says, 'you might want to question your loyalty to your *capitán* here.' He points at Carlos. 'What he is not telling you is that he himself is a murderer.'

'What?' Carlos clamours, incredulous.

Dmitri tells the Spaniards what he has already told the Peruvians about Carlos and Eduardo's plans to secretly sell part of the catch. 'But,' he goes on, 'it seems that wasn't enough for him.' He eyes Carlos. 'What better way to secure the full amount than by pushing Eduardo overboard when it was just the two of them on deck.' Carlos feels the crew watching him, narrowing their eyes and the terms of their loyalty. 'I saw it all from up here. It's a good view, you must admit.'

Carlos is on his feet now. 'You're suggesting I killed my best friend? These men know that's absurd.' But he senses his crew's allegiances swaying, back and forth. He is losing ground, metre by metre, just as he lost sight of Eduardo in the waves only yesterday. A wall of water, a trough, a wall of water, a trough.

'We all know Eduardo would never unclip himself from the safety line. It was unclipped from the rail. *You*,' Dmitri glares at Carlos accusingly, 'reached down and did that for him. *You* killed Eduardo.'

Carlos shakes his head. There's nothing he can say that will help his case. He was a fool to toss Eduardo's empty safety line into the sea. He knows that now. But how could he ever have anticipated that he would need to account for himself? He watches the men slip away from him. They, too, are unclipping themselves from their safety harnesses and sinking. And he can do nothing about it. He wants no more of this trip, or of the fish. He just wants to go home to María and Julia and the baby in her womb.

'So, men, you decide where your loyalties lie. If not with

me or Carlos, then at least with yourselves. What I am offering is this.' Carlos listens to Dmitri outline the promises he made to the Peruvians: a share of the proceeds from the sale of the fish and the guns, which he still claims Eduardo smuggled on board. 'But only if you help me get this boat to Mauritius. You decide. But before you go …' Dmitri measures his shoe size against the dead man's foot and orders Roberto's son to remove his father's sea boots. 'I will take his overpants, too,' Dmitri says. 'Unfortunately the jacket has a hole in it.'

Roberto's son lunges for the gun, but Dmitri cocks it fast.

Carlos restrains the young Spaniard. 'Don't!' he shouts at him. 'He's not worth it.'

The young man squats on the floor, his arm bent across his face, and weeps unashamedly.

'I said undress him!' Dmitri hollers.

Carlos places a hand on top of the grieving youth's head, before beginning to undress the dead man. Slowly, the young Spaniard lifts his face and whispers to his father. '*Lo siento*,' he apologises, before surrendering to the task.

'And when you have finished, throw him overboard,' Dmitri orders.

'Let us at least wrap him in a sheet,' Carlos implores as Dmitri squeezes Roberto's boots onto his own feet. The boots are in good condition, probably new. It occurs to Carlos that the old man must have figured he had some years of fishing left in him yet.

'The fish will not mind how he comes; just get him out of here,' Dmitri snaps. 'Now!'

Carlos again puts a steadying hand on the bereaved son's bowed head and then says a small prayer, despite Dmitri's protestations. Like pallbearers at a funeral, six of the men help to lift the body.

'Do not think *you* are leaving this wheelhouse,' Dmitri tells Carlos.

Carlos observes Manuel as the men open the door to the outside. The Spaniard's face is contorted with deep pain. Not just physical pain now but soul pain with its own distinctive ache. Carlos knows that Roberto and Manuel were old friends, and that Manuel will be feeling responsibility for his death. It had been his idea to suggest that they play 'hard to get'. If it hadn't been for that, Roberto might well be alive. Carlos knows the guilt of not being able to save a friend is almost worse than dying yourself.

Through the ice-lacquered glass of the wheelhouse, Carlos watches the blurred figures carry the body along the deck. He sees them stop and then move in unison, swinging the old man like a wave advancing and retreating, advancing and retreating, until they have built up enough momentum to cast the dark shadow over the rails. The body plummets below the side of the boat out of sight from the wheelhouse, but the men remain reverently on deck for some minutes before drifting, like ghosts, back inside.

DAVE
The *Australis*
5 October 2002

Dave Bates is watching through binoculars at dusk when the Spaniards aboard the *Pescador* heave the old man into the sea. At first he thinks it's a bag of evidence such as logbooks and computers, or maybe just kitchen refuse — the sea is littered with it — but something about the way the men carry the weight and the reverential way in which they unload it tells him otherwise. Men don't stand motionless on frigid decks watching the ocean for longer than they need. They have conducted a burial and he is an uninvited mourner, looking on from the outer edges of the graveyard.

Dave keeps the binoculars pinned to the orange shape flashing in and out of the waves like a torch running out of batteries. He loses sight of the body, but then there is a flicker against the dark sea and the torch is again alight. Normally a corpse would be wrapped but, in the middle of a sea chase, Dave supposes there is little time for ceremony. The body rises on a wave and for a sickening moment he considers that the man cast into the sea might still be alive.

The wheelhouse door opens behind him. 'What you found, boss?' Harry asks, seeing that Dave is focused on something in the water behind the foreign boat.

'The bastards have dropped a man over.'

'Bloody hell.'

'I reckon he's dead, but I won't sleep tonight unless I know for sure.' Dave passes the binoculars to Harry and points in the direction of the body, which Harry promptly locates.

'You gonna launch the rhib?' Harry asks.

'You're reading my mind, mate,' Dave says reaching for the ship's intercom. 'All crew on deck. We need the rhib in the water. The *Pescador*'s got a man overboard. Cactus to supervise proceedings, please.' He switches off the intercom. 'It wouldn't be the first time a pirate ship has topped one of its own,' he says to Harry.

The satellite phone rings. It's Roger Wentworth. 'I've got some good news for you, Dave, mate,' he chirps. Dave hears him smacking his lips as if tasting success. 'The South African naval vessel the *Bremner* has confirmed that they're set to board —'

'Good, but I can't talk now. We've got a man in the water.'

'Christ! You should've said.' The pitch of Wentworth's voice climbs. 'Who is it?'

'One of the illegals.'

'Shit, I thought it was one of ours!'

'A life's a life. We're just getting the rhib — our inflatable — in the water now to attempt a retrieval.'

'Be bloody careful. We don't want you losing one of our men for the sake of one of theirs.'

'I'm not planning on endangering anyone.'

'Okay, do the good-citizen thing, but I need to remind you *again* that we're supposed to keep this chase continuous —'

'A man is in the water!' Dave cuts him off, irritated. 'If I jeopardise the damned legal case, so be it. Are you suggesting we do nothing?'

'I'll let the South Africans know what you're up to. They might even have the boarding all stitched up by the time you're back on the scene. Over and out.'

Harry tells Dave to slow the boat. Cactus is waving at the wheelhouse and pointing to the man in the water.

'I don't want to run over the poor bugger,' Dave says without taking his eyes off their target.

The man is face-down, being pushed and pulled by the waves, already part of the sea. Dave heads the boat away from the body and feels the bucking ocean taking on a new, smoother rhythm as the boat speed drops. He brings the *Australis* broadside to the waves, creating relatively calm conditions in its lee where the rib will be lowered. Out of the corner of his eye, he is aware of Cactus preparing the deck crane and attaching the launch. Most of the crew are on deck. He diverts his attention from the body for a moment, to locate William, whom he spots beside the rails. The young lad is wearing Sam's wet-weather jacket with its extra reflectors sewn onto the hood and collar courtesy of Margie, but it is the long coil of rescue rope hanging from William's hand that is alarming Dave. Cactus hands William a lifejacket.

'Shit, no. Not William,' Dave protests. 'What the hell does he think he's doing? You go out and give them a hand, Harry. I'll be okay here. And tell William to pull his head in and let one of the more experienced guys go over. I'd tell him over the radio, but I don't want to embarrass the lad. He doesn't know what he's getting himself into.'

But William proceeds quickly towards the deck crane, and boards the rhib with two other crew before Harry gets close enough to tell him to stop.

Too bad if it embarrasses him, Dave thinks as he switches on the deck radio and projects his voice to the outside. 'I want an experienced seaman over the side. Not William!' But the rhib is already being lowered, and is disappearing from view.

Dave's legs turn to jelly. He sees Sam in front of him, asking permission to use his car: 'Just while you're at sea, Dad. I'll get my own after that. I promise.' Sam's hand had been on his heart for effect. 'Yeah, right,' Dave had said, handing over the keys. It was the last conversation he'd had with his son. After the accident, nothing mattered for a long time.

Cactus shakes his head and looks up at the wheelhouse, hands in the air in an effort to ask Dave whether he should bring the rhib back on board.

Harry is at the deck intercom, lifting up the plastic cover that seals the electronics from the weather. 'We'll lose the body if we try to bring the rhib back in now, Davo,' he says, steady as ever.

'I know.' Dave's voice over the radio is frail and hollow against the weight of the wind. 'It's too late.'

He feels the rhib fall as if it's passing through the pit of his stomach. It's as if *he* has gone over. Or Sam. He watches through binoculars for the inflatable to reappear a safe distance from the *Australis*. He sees William holding out the coil of rope. The rhib is almost on top of the body. There is no time.

The body is still floating face-down. William hangs over the side in preparation, and is pummelled by breaking waves. The body hits the side of the rhib hard and seems as if it might go underneath. But William propels himself forward and grabs hold of an arm. The rope is expertly applied, and the body is brought on board with little help from the other men. Perhaps it was his recent practice wrestling bullocks into branding crushes as a jackaroo, but William makes it look easy.

Dave hasn't seen this side of Sam's best friend before. Something resembling pride rises inside him. He remembers Sam telling him how capable William was when put to the test. That he'd scaled some of Tasmania's most challenging mountain peaks with just a set of climbing ropes and a bag of chalk. He had been teaching Sam to rock-climb in the months leading up to the car accident. The pair were planning to tackle Mount Wellington's organ pipes, the dolerite columns that form an imposing primeval mass, like toppling candlesticks, behind the seaside city. Dave had been quietly proud of his son's adventurous spirit, too, and tried to suppress any feelings of concern. 'Can't wrap kids up in cotton wool,' he'd told Margie when Sam was growing up. And, as it turns out, he was right. It was more dangerous just letting him get in a car.

Dave watches William turn the body over to face him. Even from this distance, he can tell the man is dead. The contrast couldn't be more stark: William's supremely fit form and bronzed face beside an old man bleached alabaster. Life and death entwined in a boat together. The rhib is driven back towards the *Australis* and disappears from view.

Within minutes, the deck crane delivers the rhib and its cargo home. Cactus turns to face the wheelhouse, carving his finger dramatically across his throat to let Dave know the retrieved man is indeed dead, as if there was any doubt. The rest of the crew are slapping William on the back, registering their approval.

Dave, relieved to see William back on board in one piece, forgets to turn off the deck radio and barks, 'Thank fucking Christ!' It's the first time that most of the crew have heard Dave swear and he imagines them smiling at the novelty of it. 'Superb effort, William,' he says, correcting himself.

Dave knows that William will be cold and numb, but recognises from his body language that he's on a high. The young man has risen to the challenge, adapting his skills to the job at hand. His legs will be shaking beneath his plastic overpants from shock and relief. Dave remembers Sam admitting that after a climb they could barely walk from delayed nerves.

The corpse is lifted from the rhib and brought on deck. Dave turns his binoculars to it. It occurs to him that, if this chase is a war against illegal fishing, then this body belongs to the enemy. Suddenly their foe appears fragile and human. The dead man is no youth. His hoary mane is longer than men his age typically wear their hair in Australia. It resembles well-used steel wool, matted from seawater and the struggle to get him into the raft. His mouth and one eye are open as if surprised, awoken from the most permanent of slumbers. In this light, against the backdrop of the ocean and sky, his white skin is so pale that it's almost blue — the colour of the icebergs that dot these frozen realms. Dave doubts whether the body would bleed if the flesh was cut, and notices that the fisherman, while still wearing a wet-weather jacket and thermal long johns, has no overpants or boots. His naked feet are even whiter than his face. William and three other crew lift the body and carry it along the deck and up the stairs to the wheelhouse. Cactus, Dave notices, is keeping his distance, focusing instead on resecuring the rhib.

Dave hasn't seen a dead body since he saw Sam at the hospital morgue, and is overcome with a crippling dread. The men lower the sodden mess of a man onto the floor respectfully, like hunting dogs delivering their punctured prey to their master. 'Jesus,' Dave says. 'Poor bugger.'

'I know.' Harry's voice is almost a whisper. The men have all fallen quiet, the shock of death having silenced their collective tongues.

Dave begins to move the boat forward again in the direction of the *Pescador* and the South African vessel that has come to their aid. 'Wonder what happened to the poor old bloke,' he continues. 'Maybe he just died of natural causes. A heart attack or something. He's no spring chicken.'

'Why'd they throw him in, though?' William asks.

'I don't imagine we'll ever know,' Harry replies. 'You'd better keep your theory of a heart attack to yourself, Davo. Cactus is already scared shitless about having a coronary at sea.'

'Well, at least he knows we wouldn't toss him into Davy Jones's locker in his undies.' Dave flicks a look at the dead body, and then back at William, who is shivering more acutely now. 'You go below and get warm, lad. There's not a lot we can do for this poor bugger. Glad you're okay, though.' He turns to face his first mate. 'Harry, see if there's anything in the bloke's pockets to identify him, would you, mate?'

William is at the door of the wheelhouse when Harry unzips the dead man's sea jacket and stops stock-still.

'What you got there, Harry?' Dave asks.

'This tear here's a bit suspicious,' Harry says, jerking back the jacket and hoisting up a heavy woollen vest.

William steps back into the room.

'And look here.' Harry uses his finger to trace the outline of another hole, this time in a woollen undergarment. 'Just thought I'd see where it leads …' He manages to raise an old-fashioned thermal singlet, which the sea had twisted tight, to expose the dead man's chest.

'Holy shit,' William rasps. A large hole washed clean by the ocean gapes back at them. 'He's been bloody shot.'

LOGBOOK OF EDUARDO RODRÍGUEZ TORRES

∾

There is a strange cloud in the sky tonight, a shiny blue magical form. I've read about clouds like this — noctilucent clouds, they're called — visible at the Poles, high in the atmosphere after dark. The blue clouds are thought to be one of the first manifestations of climate change. But I fear there are other, more imminent, changes in the air.

∾

CARLOS
The *Pescador*
5 October 2002

As Carlos stands to stretch his legs, he catches a glimpse of the radar. The *Australis* has backed off again but another boat has appeared on the screen about twelve nautical miles away. The new arrival is ahead of them on the port side. Carlos notices that Dmitri has spotted it, too. 'You'd better hope it's just another longliner heading south,' he tells the Russian.

Dmitri looks out to sea before fixing his stare on the bloodstained carpet. He throws Manuel a towel that was stuffed under the instrument table. 'Clean it up,' he orders. 'I do not mind if it leaves a stain. It will serve as a useful reminder. But I do not want it to start to smell.'

Manuel catches the towel and lowers himself onto all fours to clean up his friend's blood. Carlos imagines Roberto's body — stiff in death — being buffeted by the seas. The blood would be cooling rapidly, and congealing like the blood on the rag in Manuel's hand. As if reading Carlos's mind, the Spaniard gags but manages not to vomit.

'And when you have finished there, wipe up José's mess in the corner,' Dmitri barks.

A voice crackling over the radio fills the wheelhouse.

'*Pescador, Pescador, Pescador.* This is the South African naval vessel *Bremner, Bremner.* Do you read us? Over.'

Dmitri moves his eyes to the horizon. The boat is faintly visible. '*Ahueyet!*' he curses, striking the instrument table with his fists. 'It seems we have more than the Australians for company. *Poshel k chertu!*' He swears again as the South African naval vessel repeats its radio call. There is a delay as the *Bremner* waits for a response. Dmitri makes no attempt to enable the radio.

The voice continues. 'The Australian government has asked us to apprehend your vessel on their behalf. We have agreed to do so. We ask you to assist us when we board. Please follow our instructions. Our men are armed. Over and out.'

'Manuel, lift up the flooring over there,' Dmitri instructs, pointing to a place where a carpet tile is lifting at the edges, 'and take out the weapons. You too, Carlos. But do not get any bright ideas. They are not loaded.'

Carlos shakes his head in disbelief. So the weapons had been there all along. He wonders which crew Dmitri will decide to arm. It's an insane plan, to take on the South African navy.

'Are you still of the opinion that it is better not to help me?' Dmitri asks Carlos, the panic in his voice barely concealed.

'I will never help you,' Carlos answers, watching as Manuel reveals the stash of automatic weapons. They are stacked, one on top of the other, in piles of ten. God knows how many more are secreted elsewhere around the ship.

'Fine. Your choice.' Dmitri says coldly. 'Manuel, bind Carlos's hands and feet. Use those.' He points to the ropes securing the guns. 'If you are not going to help me, you are not going to get in my way either.'

Manuel does as he is ordered. Even at such close range, the Spaniard fails to make eye contact with the man who, only a day ago, was the ship's trusted master.

There's a knock at the door, and El Animal, the Peruvians' leader, enters. He is large but moves smoothly, as though hunting. Carlos can see where he got his name. The Peruvian scans the wheelhouse stopping when he sees the bloodstain on the floor.

'An unfortunate incident,' Dmitri answers El Animal's querulous glare. 'We have lost one of the older Spaniards. But that is behind us now. We have a new problem on our hands. But I will tell you about that in a moment. How did you get on? Are you with us?'

'*Si*.' El Animal looks up from the bloodstained floor. 'You have our support.'

'Good.' Dmitri eyes Carlos. 'I knew these men were not stupid.' Then, to the Peruvian: 'We have company.' He points at the radar, and then to the horizon. 'The South African navy, no less.'

El Animal raises his eyebrows.

Dmitri throws the new recruit one of the guns that Manuel has laid out. 'Be careful. It is loaded,' he lies, before turning to speak to José. 'Go and clean yourself up. And get me some coffee. Make it strong. Manuel, you go too and bring back only those men willing to defend our boat.'

Manuel nods and leaves the wheelhouse. José stands to follow him. As he does, Carlos notices a wet patch on the floor and the smell of urine.

El Animal takes up his weapon and inspects it. Dmitri again turns his back to him and Carlos realises he is testing the Peruvian; there is no way he would give him such a perfect opportunity to use the gun. In the reflective glass of the wheelhouse, Carlos meets the uncertain eyes of El Animal and shakes his head with the minimum of movement. The gun stays at El Animal's side. Dmitri waits a few moments longer, to be sure, before showing the Peruvian the stash of bullets in the floor. 'You will need those too when the time comes,' he winks. 'Sorry, but I had to be sure you would still be loyal when I was looking the other way.'

Dmitri studies the radar and Carlos does a quick mental calculation. In this good weather and the more manageable seas, the South African vessel will be upon them within half an hour.

'It's game over, Dmitri,' Carlos taunts.

'Shut up, unless you want to join your Spanish friend and your first mate in the sea,' Dmitri spits back.

Carlos thinks of Julia and imagines her glaring at him, warning him to be quiet. He stifles the verbal attack on his lips, swallowing it down. There's a bitter taste in his mouth — the bile of his anger and his anxiety about how this all might end. Julia, he knows, would pray, but for what? To be saved from Dmitri only to be delivered to the Australians and jail? Or, simply, to survive, so that one day he will be returned to his family? With Eduardo gone and Dmitri having shown the ruthlessness he is capable of, nothing else matters.

José arrives at the door in clean trousers and bearing a steaming coffee, which he hands to Dmitri. 'Now,' Dmitri tells him, 'start loading the guns. You too, El Animal. '

The Peruvians do as instructed, first propping their own guns against the green vinyl chair that has been José's fearful post since Dmitri took command a day ago. Dmitri pushes the boat at full speed towards Mauritius, studying the chart and the approaching naval vessel with nervous darting eyes. In different circumstances Carlos would be amused by the Russian, reminiscent as he is of a chihuahua bracing itself to outrun, or, if need be, confront, a rottweiler.

Carlos observes the Peruvians, the tiredness in José's face, his mental slowness as he loads the bullets clumsily. José doesn't notice Manuel coming around behind him like the walking dead. Carlos watches Manuel stalk his prey and is aware of his own body alive with adrenaline. Surely Manuel won't kill the idiot. It's all happening too fast.

Manuel picks up José's gun and strikes him hard over the back of the head with the butt. In the same arc of movement, he points the gun at Dmitri who had turned his head at the sound of the blow to José's skull. Manuel fires, square at the Russian's back to the left of his spine. Dmitri gasps and falls against the instrument table, his eyes meeting Manuel's as he registers that it is the Spaniard who discharged the gun. He lands heavily on the floor and Carlos is struck by how closely he resembles a dying fish, quivering and eyes glazed. Within a few long moments, his hissing ceases. Manuel steps over him to take the helm. He drops the boat speed as a sign to the South Africans of surrender, before untying Carlos.

'I wondered how long you were going to take, you old dog.' Carlos shakes his head at Manuel. 'You could get an Academy Award for that performance. You too, El Animal.'

More of the crew, having heard the shot, are now flowing up the stairs towards the wheelhouse and crowding inside, congratulating Manuel and El Animal with slaps on their backs. 'And now, *Capitán*?' Manuel asks. 'What fate awaits us?'

Carlos observes the naval boat gaining on them from the horizon. After nearly three weeks of seeing only water, ice, sky and, periodically, the Australian patrol vessel, the massive warship resembles something from another planet. He looks through the rear windows of the wheelhouse but can't make out the Australian patrol. It can't be far away. The sky, too, is closing in. It's getting darker with the approach of night, and rain clouds are gathering around them like heavy wet blankets. It's as though the hands of God are descending, setting boundaries, reining them in.

'We've reached the end of our journey,' Carlos says, rubbing hard at his forehead with blunt fingertips. 'Not quite the one I'd imagined, I have to confess. But it's the risk we take fishing down here. At least we've survived to tell the story. One of Migiliaro's other boats hasn't been so lucky.' Carlos looks at Roberto's son and thinks of Eduardo at the same time. 'Not that we have been without loss.' There is an extended lull in the wheelhouse. A silence born out of respect and exhaustion.

'The South Africans have radioed their intention to board.' Carlos links his fingers together on top of his head, resigning himself to this unimagined destiny. 'I'm sure you agree, there's no point resisting arrest.' The men shift on their feet uncomfortably. 'I want you to know that I take full responsibility for the decision to fish in Australian waters. Of course, I was under instructions from the owner but he'll have covered his tracks.'

'*Bastardo*,' Manuel curses.

'You might remember seeing an Australian boat fishing near us off Heard Island,' Carlos says. 'I suspect they're the ones who reported us. Maybe they even filmed us fishing.'

'Just a moment,' Manuel interrupts, stepping forward. 'We brought the line in off the starboard deck and they were off to port. I remember it well. If they did film us, they wouldn't have been at the right angle to see us fishing. It's not illegal to be passing through their goddamn waters. It's ridiculous, anyway, that they can lay claim to all the ocean around Heard and McDonald Islands. A little country like Australia. What right do they have?' He scratches his chest. 'Maybe we should just say that we caught the fish further south and were just sheltering at Heard to fix engine trouble. Dmitri said something about the lube-oil purifier malfunctioning. We could blame that.'

'Our engine was running when we were spotted,' Carlos says, dismissing Manuel's fabrication. 'They would have tracked our course on radar, and it would have been obvious we were moving along a longline. And if there had been a problem with the oil purifier, the engine would have been off.' Carlos surveys his crew, trying to discern their mood. 'Anyway, it's not your problem. It'll be me who'll face the charges and we —'

'With Eduardo gone, I'm next in line,' Manuel interjects again. 'Do you really believe one scalp will be enough?'

'We don't have a choice. We surrender, simple as that. But as soon as it's dark, give these a swim.' Carlos kicks the guns, at the same time wondering how much worse his sentence would be if he was also found guilty of trafficking weapons. It's often assumed that fishing vessels will carry one rifle to kill any seals found taking fish from the lines, but Eduardo and he had never even agreed to that, let alone the scores of guns their engineer was responsible for bringing on board. He frowns down at Dmitri's bloodstained body and then at the piles of fire-arms. 'And, for the record, I didn't know about those. Neither did your first mate. I won't have Eduardo blamed for that. As far as I'm concerned, the guns — bar one — didn't exist. But that's the only lie I'm prepared to tell. We will claim that Dmitri brought a single weapon on to the boat to achieve his mutiny — the same gun that was turned against him in self-defence. We'll tell them we threw it overboard. As for him,' Carlos's gaze again skims over the dead Russian, 'put him in a freezer.'

'What do we tell them about Roberto?' Manuel asks.

'The truth: Dmitri ordered José to shoot him and dispose of his body. Are there any more questions, *mis amigos*?'

José groans as he regains consciousness. He opens one eye fractionally, and takes in the room, chameleon-like. His eye widens when he sees Carlos out of his ropes, and Dmitri lifeless on the floor. Relief passes over his face, before he collapses again into a kind of sleep. A few of the men shake their heads in apparent disgust.

'Forget José, too, is my advice,' Carlos says. 'For now, anyway. When we are on shore, the authorities can deal with him. He'll pay for what he has done, but let's not have anyone else's blood on our hands.'

Carlos focuses his attention momentarily on Roberto's son. 'I know it will be hard for you to have the man who killed your father still with us on this boat, but your family will need you when you get home. Don't give anyone a reason to lock you away as well.'

Roberto's son stares at the floor in reluctant agreement.

'When the South Africans board, you'll assemble along the decks,' Carlos instructs, watching the sea-hardened faces of the crewmen who are crammed into the wheelhouse like sardines. 'They'll be armed, but shouldn't bother us if we offer ourselves peacefully. I expect they'll escort us back to port, probably to Australia. But the worst is over. With any luck you'll be flown back to your homes fairly swiftly.'

The men seem to relax in unison. Carlos feels the weight of their trust and marvels that they followed him to the ends of the earth, without argument, when there was little in it for them. If they had refused to flee south, he would have had no choice but to surrender to the Australian patrol, then and there. The crew would have been flown home, their only sacrifice the loss of their meagre wages from Migiliaro.

The staccato voice on the radio breaks in: '*Pescador*, *Pescador*, *Pescador*, this is the South African naval vessel *Bremner*, *Bremner*. Do you copy? Over.'

'Shouldn't we tell the South Africans we're surrendering?' El Animal asks, his large frame propped against the wheelhouse wall.

'We're receiving both Inmarsat and VHF radio communications but can't transmit anything, courtesy of

Dmitri,' Carlos explains. 'If any of you know anything about electronics, be my guest. It might help things go more smoothly.'

The *Bremner* keeps on, '*Pescador, Pescador,* I will repeat my earlier call. Given your proximity to South African waters, we have offered to lead the boarding of your vessel on behalf of the Australian Government. It is in your interests to cooperate. We are assuming your communications are down. Perhaps you cannot answer our radio call. We will be sending a boarding party at 0900 hours. It is not safe to attempt a boarding in the fading light now. We would ask you to begin to turn your vessel around and head due east. We will take that action as agreement with our request. Over.'

Carlos steers the boat as instructed in a neat and obedient arc afforded by the calm seas. He is surprised to feel the relief of surrender, the ease of simply following orders and handing himself over to fate.

The South African voice resumes. '*Pescador, Pescador, Pescador,* this is the *Bremner*. It appears you have received our request and have responded favourably. Please continue on this course. We will resume communications in the morning. Over and out.'

Carlos's face folds into an exhausted smile. He holds out a hand to Manuel who shakes it reluctantly. 'It's over.'

'I'll have a go at fixing the radio if you like,' El Animal offers. 'If someone wants to receive messages but not transmit, there are only a few ways to do it. It should be fairly easy to figure out.'

Carlos, visibly impressed, steps back to allow El Animal access to the communications systems. 'Please, do what you need.'

Two of the crew lift Dmitri and carry him from the wheelhouse. Carlos imagines the Russian turning ice-cold in the freezers, and feels no regret. As the other crew members return to their cabins, El Animal disconnects the handset and takes it away. In less than an hour he is back in the wheelhouse.

'It should work now,' he tells Carlos with a glimmer of pride. 'Dmitri had cut the handset microphone wires.'

'Well, it's good to have you on our side.'

El Animal reconnects the handsets and signals to Carlos with a nod when the job is complete. Carlos attempts a satellite call to Uruguay's Fisheries Department. He suspects, however, that with two nations now involved in the apprehension of the *Pescador*, the department has been kept abreast of developments.

Carlos's call is answered and he gives the Peruvian the thumbs-up. El Animal salutes light-heartedly and takes his leave.

'What the hell happened to you?' Francisco sounds annoyed. 'We've been trying to reach you.'

'It's a long story, but it's over. We're being boarded in the morning. No doubt you know that.'

'*Si*. But why were communications down? It looks like you were avoiding our calls for you to return here. How are we supposed to help you?'

'There was a mutiny. Our Russian engineer cut contact. Francisco … we've lost the first mate and one of our Spanish crew, as well as the engineer, Dmitri Ivanov.'

'*¡Mierda!* How? What happened?' Francisco stops himself. 'Wait, Carlos, there's something else … It's Julia. She has gone into labour early.'

Carlos is silent. He can hear a coursing pulse of blood in his ears as panic takes hold. It's almost as though his heart stopped with the news and is now racing to make up the missed beats.

Manuel enters the wheelhouse, the wound above his eye freshly bandaged, and Carlos indicates for him to take the helm.

'Is she all right?' Carlos finally asks.

'*Si*. She was taken to hospital yesterday morning but they couldn't hold things off.'

'And the baby?'

Francisco hesitates. 'Obviously he's very small. He's in intensive care.'

'A boy … But will he be okay?'

'We're all praying for him, Carlos.'

'*Jesús*,' Carlos cries, his free hand holding his forehead, covering his eyes. 'I have to get home. We're being sent back to Australia. No doubt you know more than we do. Please. I have to get home.'

'We're doing all we can. We have to take this one step at a time.'

Carlos wipes tears from his face with the sleeve of his polar fleece and kicks at the loose carpet tile with his boot. 'Please, just explain the situation to the Australian officials. I'll face whatever charges they like, but I need to see Julia first. Can I answer the charges from Uruguay?' Carlos is overcome with a sudden urge to head the boat back around, but contains himself. He has no choice.

'I'll see what we can arrange. Just keep your mind on the job there as much as you can. You still have a boat of men under your command. I've contacted the owner for you and have let him know what has happened. I'll also need to inform the relatives of the deceased. I have a crew list here. Can you repeat the dead men's names?'

Carlos's nose is dripping from emotion, and he wipes it again with the back of his sleeve. 'Eduardo Rodríguez Torres, first mate. But now that communications are restored, I'd like to tell his wife myself. He was my best friend. We go back a long way.'

'Eduardo, *si*, I spoke with him over the satellite phone. How did he die?'

'He was trying to chip ice off the deck. He was the only one out there. Our Russian engineer made sure of that. Eduardo was washed overboard. I did everything I could.'

'I have no doubt. But there will be some formalities, of course. All the deaths will need to be properly reported once you reach port. What are the other names?'

'Dmitri Ivanov, the engineer who took the helm at gunpoint. He brought the weapon on board without my knowledge. And Roberto Cruz, a Spaniard. Dmitri ordered him shot.'

'*¡Ay, mierda!* I'll arrange for a representative from the Uruguayan consulate to be present during questioning back in Australia. But that's enough for now. Have you got any questions, Carlos?'

'Have you heard anything of Migiliaro's missing boat?'

'He hasn't reported any vessels missing.'

'You should be holding an inquiry into those deaths, too.' Carlos says, his anger building. 'Or are you just going to let Migiliaro get away with it? He sent those men to their deaths. He's the one telling us where to fish — or don't you want to hear that?'

Francisco says nothing.

Carlos picks at a piece of dry skin on his lip, drawing blood. 'How's María? Who's with her?'

'She's fine. Cecilia is looking after her until Julia's parents arrive. We're taking good care of her.'

Carlos feels sick at the thought of not being able to comfort his daughter. At the thought of shallow, cold Cecilia, of all people, taking his place. Cecilia and Francisco, who Carlos knows will do nothing to try to bring him home, are no substitute for family. 'Can I phone you tonight so I can speak with her?'

'*Sí*, of course.'

'And Julia. Can you find the hospital number for me and have it when I call?'

'I have it here,' Francisco says, and gives it to Carlos. He also gives Carlos his home number. 'By all means phone us tonight. I'm sure it'll help María to hear from you.'

'*Sí*. And Francisco, please don't tell Cecilia yet about Eduardo. Julia and I were both close to him and I want to tell my wife that news myself.' Carlos ends the satellite call and covers his face with his hands.

'Your boy will be all right,' Manuel offers, placing his hand on Carlos's shoulder. In the confines of the wheelhouse, the Spaniard has heard the whole conversation. 'If he's anything like his father, your baby boy will be all right.'

Carlos nods appreciatively. He dials the number for the maternity ward and asks to speak to Julia. She answers quietly.

'Julia, my love,' Carlos says, fighting back tears.

'Carlos.'

Carlos hears that she is crying too and fears the worst for his son, but is relieved to hear her continue.

'He's so small. He's being kept alive with machines. Why didn't you answer my calls?'

'Our communications were down. I'll explain later. Don't worry about that now. Everything will be all right. Francisco says our baby is getting really good care.'

'He's in a humidicrib, behind Perspex! I can't even hold him. They keep taking blood from his tiny arms and legs, wherever they can find a vein large enough to take a needle. And chest X-rays. His lungs are so immature. There's no bleeding in his brain though. The doctors said that's one of the biggest risks. Still, he could be blind from all the oxygen he's getting. He hasn't even opened his eyes yet, Carlos. The lids are still fused. He should still be inside me!' Julia sobs. 'When are you getting home?'

'I've spoken to Francisco to see what he can do.'

'What do you mean? I thought you were on your way back here.'

Carlos feels his chest tighten. 'We're being escorted back to Australia.'

'No. Carlos … We need you here. Your baby!'

Carlos doesn't even bother to wipe the tears away now. 'I'm doing everything I can to get home, believe me.'

Julia is distraught on the other end of the line. 'I can't talk now,' she says. 'It hurts to cry … because of the caesarean. It's all so horrible.'

Carlos hears her crying fade and then a series of rustles and thumps, as if she is struggling to hang up the handset.

'*Te quiero*. It will be all right,' he says loudly into the phone, but she has gone. He strikes the instrument table with the receiver, before Manuel gently takes the phone from him. 'I didn't tell her about Eduardo,' Carlos says. 'She knew him too.'

'Probably a good thing.' Manuel says. 'She doesn't need any more sadness. It won't help her now.'

Carlos's chest feels as though it might collapse under the weight of the news from home. He makes his way out on to the deck to force his lungs open with a shock of cold air. The Southern Ocean wind tears at his skin. He lifts his face to the heavens and sees a strange cloud high in the darkening sky. It's silvery blue, and he remembers Eduardo saying something about seeing a cloud just like this a few long days ago.

MARGIE
Hobart, Australia
6 October 2002

Margie opens the front page of the *Mercury* newspaper and sees a photograph taken of the *Pescador* on the high seas. Dave's boat is nowhere to be seen. Margie burns her lips on her coffee as she reads the accompanying article.

Historic Sea Chase Over

The longest sea chase in history is expected to finish today at 0900 hours (local time) with the boarding of a Uruguayan vessel accused of illegal fishing in Australian subantarctic waters.

The boarding by armed South African naval personnel will bring to a close a three-week, 4000-nautical-mile Southern Ocean pursuit of the Uruguayan-flagged *Pescador* by the Australian patrol vessel *Australis*.

The *Pescador* is to be charged with poaching Patagonian toothfish worth an estimated $2.8 million off Australia's Heard Island, 2000 nautical miles southwest of mainland Australia.

According to the master of the *Australis*, Captain David Bates, the chase saw both vessels strike icebergs in subantarctic waters, where seas reached in excess of 15 metres, with winds gusting up to 90 knots.

'The conditions were extreme, with temperatures on deck often reaching as low as minus 20 degrees Celsius with the wind chill,' Bates said.

'We are pleased to have made it through with little damage to our vessel, and no injuries to those on board our boat.'

On behalf of the Australian Government, Fisheries Minister Mr Mark Somes has publicly thanked the South African navy for its assistance in apprehending the *Pescador*.

'I hope the chase will send a clear message to others involved in illegal fishing that they will be pursued and they will be caught,' he said.

'The Australian Government is committed to curbing the loss of our valuable marine resources and will not tolerate illegal fishing, which is a threat to our fishermen's livelihood and the sustainability of these vulnerable deep-water stocks.'

Somes said it is likely that the senior members of the crew will be heavily fined, and the vessel will be forfeited to the Crown and destroyed.

'Investigations will also be made following information that the ship's owner, a Mr Migiliaro, is in Spain,' Somes said. 'It's possible that he is operating a fleet of illegal boats and that the *Pescador* is only the tip of the iceberg.'

On seeing Dave's name in print, and reading that he and his crew are safe, Margie reaches down and hugs Bonnie, who responds by resting her head on Margie's lap.

'Your grand-daddy's coming home soon, sweetie,' Margie says, holding the dog's dreamy face in her hands.

She studies the newspaper photograph of the *Pescador*, imagining Dave on board the *Australis* just out of frame. The ocean and sky are gun-metal grey, imposing. According to the caption, the photograph was taken from the South African naval boat. Margie takes another sip of her coffee and imagines the dark-featured faces of the Uruguayan vessel's crew, sombre in their capture. She pictures Julia's husband in his wheelhouse. What has driven these men to risk their lives for fish? Are they that desperate? That poor? Perhaps they are. She feels a welling of sympathy for the bedraggled bunch and wonders what fate awaits them. She suspects, however, that if Dave's boat had run into major trouble during the pursuit, sympathy would be the last thing she'd be feeling for this lot.

The phone rings. It's Dave, and the line is clear.

'Oh, love …' Margie hears her voice wavering with emotion. 'You know I'm convinced we've got ESP. I'm holding a picture of the *Pescador* as we speak. Front page of the paper. It seems you're famous.'

'I'm not sure about that. Tomorrow everyone'll be wrapping their fish scraps in that story. Anyway, the good news is we're just about done here,' Dave stalls. 'Does the article say anything about us plucking an illegal crewman out of the water?'

'Dave! My God. He's lucky you were there. Did he fall overboard?'

'No. And he's not that lucky. He's in our freezer, dead as a doornail. Would you believe he was shot?'

'For heaven's sake!' The waver is back in her voice. 'What, by his own crew?'

'Looks like it. Poor old codger. We'll know a bit more about it all after the boarding.'

'*Please* tell me you're not going to be involved in that.' Margie scans the article again. 'Says here it's at nine o'clock, your time, so that's …'

'About four in the afternoon for you. We're about seven hours behind. And no, love. We'll leave the boarding to the armed professionals. Harry and our young fisheries officer will go over only after things have settled down.'

'Well, if you hadn't taken it this far, they'd have got away,' Margie says. 'And you've kept your crew safe. That's the main thing.'

'You almost sound like you think chasing the buggers halfway around the world was a good thing now!' Dave chuckles. 'Actually, between you, me and the gatepost, I feel a bit sorry for the Uruguayan master. Carlos Sánchez his name is. The South African boat intercepted a call he made to Uruguay and overheard that his wife has had a baby — very early. It's all a bit touch and go for the little one. Australia will be the last place he'll want to end up.'

'Oh no.' Margie sighs. 'Poor Julia. That explains why I haven't heard back from her.'

'What do you mean?'

'I emailed her — Julia Sánchez. It was a crazy idea of Joan's to see if the women couldn't get you blokes to put an end to the whole stupid chase. Secret women's business.' Margie hears Dave laugh again in the background. 'I didn't know she was pregnant, though. God I hope I didn't add to her stress. I was going to tell you I'd contacted her, but nothing came of it.'

'You girls. Maybe we'd all be better off if you were in charge.'

Margie can hear the relief in his voice that the chase is over. He's lighter and chattier, like he has a head full of champagne. She feels the knot in her own stomach begin to loosen.

'How did William get on?'

'Surprisingly well when the chips were down. I'll tell you about it later, love. It's after midnight here, and tomorrow's going to be a big one. I'd better try to catch some shut-eye. Love you. And give Bonnie a hug for me.'

'Love you, too.' Margie ends the call and reaches down to hug Bonnie again. A tear runs off her cheek and splashes onto the dog's ear, glittering there like a tiny jewel. It pains her when Dave talks about giving Bonnie a hug for him. She suspects it's his way of sending his love to Sam. A way of making a connection with his son without saying his name. It's the second anniversary of Sam's death on Wednesday, and she knows it will be on Dave's mind too. It's not right that they should endure that day, of all days, apart.

Margie kisses Bonnie on a twitching eyebrow and stands up to face the rest of the day. Bonnie gets to her feet, too, and walks over to a sunny spot near the back veranda. She lies down heavily, resting her head on an old pair of Sam's walking boots that still sit by the cedar French doors. Margie has been planning to get rid of the shoes for some time, but Bonnie seems to have formed such an attachment to them that she can't bring herself to do the deed. Well, it's a convenient excuse.

The well-worn hiking boots, Margie notices, are bleached from the sun and emptied now of all their leather's natural oils. Sam wouldn't be happy with the state of them. He was meticulous with his camping gear, carefully washing the tent and cleaning the stove equipment at the end of every trip. He'd only ever had one pair of hiking boots, and joked that he liked the rugged, well-travelled image they gave him. She can see him now, warming the old boots in front of the fire while he watched TV. He used to bury his bare toes into the warm fur on Bonnie's belly, and the dog loved every minute of his attention. Every so often he would check to see if the leather was warm enough for the next layer of beeswax sealer. She remembers his toes tracing the scar on Bonnie's stomach where she was de-sexed as a puppy. 'You poor thing,' he'd said. 'Never getting the chance to have puppies.'

Margie's eyes burn from staring into the space where Sam's boots lie. She blinks dryly and rubs her eyelids. She decides, on the spot, to pull out some of Sam's camping gear and give it all a proper airing. She'll use it herself for an overnight walk this week, on Wednesday. What better way to acknowledge her son's life, and the second anniversary of his death.

Sam had always teased her that she was a homebody, leaving it to he and Dave to do the adventuring. 'You're missing out, Mum,' he'd said, kissing her on the cheek as he set out on yet another bushwalk. He'd invited her on the last hike — Dave had been at sea — but she'd declined, for reasons she is still unclear about. This week though, she decides, there will be no excuse. She'll make her son proud.

JULIA
Montevideo, Uruguay
6 October 2002

Julia peers into the humidicrib at her tiny baby, and sees nothing of herself or Carlos in his miniature features. She puts her face closer to the Perspex to study the baby which, she realises, would fit along Carlos's outstretched hand. His small red form appears barely human. Tubes in his nose provide oxygen from a ventilator and his chest, frail as a bird's, rises and falls with each mechanical expansion and contraction. Thin aluminium bars secure narrow plastic tubes to the veins of his arms. Every so often the young doctor comes and takes blood from the lines for testing, and then gives a transfusion to replace the blood that has been taken. A small clasp is attached to her son's foot to measure the levels of oxygen in his blood.

The incessant beeping of the monitors drills holes into Julia's skull. She extends her hand shakily through the porthole in the side of the humidicrib to touch her child, to stroke his downy body and hold his fragile hand. A nurse tells her it will help. And indeed when she holds his hand, the neon numbers on the machines — his oxygen levels, and heart and respiration rates — all respond positively. Does he really know it's her?

Love and hope rise up in her like giant waves, spilling over into tears. But coming at her from the opposite direction are equally large waves of fear and despair. Fear that if her baby survives, his quality of life could be so impaired that death may have been preferable. Despair that if her baby dies she'll never know true happiness again, that she won't even know how to put one foot in front of the other. How would she even draw breath? She strokes her child's forehead — already wrinkled like a worried old man's — and tries to straighten out his crumpled paper-thin ear, but it bends forward again. The doctor says his body is still developing and that she should be patient.

But he has also made it clear that they need to get the baby off the ventilator as soon as possible. It is keeping him alive, but at a cost. Each forced inhalation puts enormous strain on his tiny lungs, which, from time to time, are displayed as an X-ray on the light box in the nursery for all to see. And there is another problem, the doctor said. Just as too little oxygen is a bad thing, so is too much. 'We hope it's not the case, but oxygen toxicity could send your baby blind.' Julia knows that the paediatrician was just trying to prepare her, but part of her hates him for it. She doesn't have space in her head for anything other than the here and now. Will her baby survive the next hour? She urges her son on. Tells him she needs him to live.

'Have you named him yet?' a nurse asks as she rushes past to the neighbouring humidicrib where an alarm is sounding.

Julia feels herself panic. To give her baby a name would make losing him even more painful. And what will she call him? Carlos had favoured naming a son after his best friend, and had suggested, before he left, also making Eduardo the baby's godfather. But she's not sure if she can go through with that. Maybe it's tempting fate to honour a man she has always secretly loved. In her irrational state, she still wonders if the premature birth is her punishment for the affair.

'Not yet,' Julia answers.

LOGBOOK OF EDUARDO RODRÍGUEZ TORRES

〜

No wonder we have had to travel so far to find fish. I read today, in one of the science magazines I have on board, that ninety per cent of the populations of large fish have vanished from the world's oceans since high-seas commercial fishing began, and that it takes just fifteen years to catch eighty per cent or more of any one species. Yet here we are …

Is it any wonder I lie awake?

〜

CARLOS
The *Pescador*
6 October 2002

Carlos hardly slept overnight and struggles to keep his mind on the job at hand. The sea chase and the fate of the fish are unimportant now compared with his son's battle to survive. Still, he keeps his head, for the sake of his crew.

Through binoculars he sees the rope ladder strike the midship rails at the same place where the longlines are normally brought in over the side. Within minutes he sees the first of the South Africans, dressed in full riot gear, haul himself on board. One after the other the men climb on deck, clutching machine guns. It's as though the fish that were landed one after the other in exactly this spot are finally fighting back — escaping their hooks and seeking revenge.

Memories of the military dictatorship that stained his youth until the age of ten come flooding back. Carlos relives his fear when friends' parents were imprisoned, some even tortured or killed, for their political views. He later learned that Uruguay, in the mid-1970s, had more political prisoners per capita than any other nation in the world. He remembers what it felt like to be a young boy afraid that his own parents could be taken away. To be powerless.

He watches as four of the South Africans make their way to the stern of the boat where his crew are waiting, lined up and silent, like obedient children. The remaining three naval men make their way towards him.

He thinks again of Julia and the baby, and powerlessness takes on a new dimension. He pushes the thought away, but, like a searchlight, it seeks him out, until he is caught in its glare, stunned and shaking. He pulls the photographs of Julia and María off the wheelhouse wall and puts them into his pocket. If he thinks any more about his family now, he'll be no good to anyone. He owes it to his crew to have his wits about him. As the South Africans reach the top of the wheelhouse stairs they raise their weapons and Carlos knows they will be quick to use them, given half a chance. If lives are lost, no one will ask if his crew deserved it. There is no such thing as a good pirate.

Manuel is standing on the bridge deck, and as the first South African approaches, Carlos sees the Spaniard hold out a conciliatory hand. The naval officer returns the handshake and sights the Uruguayan master through the wheelhouse windows. Carlos holds both his hands in the air to show that he is unarmed. The South African, instantly at ease, drops the weapon to his side. The men behind him follow suit with the precision of a school of fish changing direction. Carlos hears a booming Afrikaans accent and then a good-natured burst of laughter as the first man enters the wheelhouse, Manuel close behind. Manuel must have told a joke outside and delivered the punch line just before he opened the door, Carlos thinks, marvelling at the Spaniard's cool-headedness.

Three fair-haired and ruddy-skinned naval men, who could be front-rowers in a rugby team, fill the room. Carlos eyes their bulletproof vests and helmets and wonders if he is a disappointment to them — not quite the villain they were expecting. He sees the men registering Manuel's bandaged head and the bruise that's forming around his eye.

'I suppose this is checkmate,' Carlos ventures in reasonable English.

One of the men in the boarding party steps forward. He removes a large black glove and extends his hand to meet Carlos's. 'Lieutenant Commander Jan de Ridder, Executive Officer.' His eyes are the blue of warmer seas, Carlos notices, as he introduces himself. 'So you speak English.'

'Yes, but not as good as Manuel. I am *Capitán* Carlos Sánchez,' Carlos announces as their hands meet. 'Sorry to take you away from your regular …' Carlos hesitates as he searches for the word, 'duties. Or were you in the area?' he says, continuing Manuel's efforts to lighten the mood. To thaw the ice in the air.

'It has been a relatively minor diversion,' de Ridder answers with half a smile. 'You certainly gave the Australians a run for their money.'

'We had much to lose.'

'*Ja*,' de Ridder agrees. 'You still do.'

Manuel steps forward, confident in his English after a lifetime of driving taxis for tourists in Spain when not out fishing. 'That is what you get for being stupid, stubborn, Spanish-blooded fools!' His comment gets another laugh from the South Africans. He seems to know what to say. 'We crossed through the Australian Fishing Zone, and stopped to fix some engine trouble. All the fish on board were caught in international waters. Not there. Not in the Australian sea. It was a stupid — we can see now — but perfectly legal shortcut for us.'

Carlos is caught off-guard by Manuel's fabrication and glares briefly in his direction. But the Spaniard continues talking, steering them deeper into trouble, magnifying their crime. Carlos wants to tell him to stop. One lie breeds another; everyone knows that.

But Manuel has taken the situation into his own hands, and Carlos hasn't got the energy to argue. 'When the Australians saw us in their sea, we knew it did not look good. In fact, it looked very bad,' the Spaniard adds, a flicker in his eye.

The South Africans exchange good-humoured glances.

'Who would believe our story?' Manuel continues. 'We have families back home, children. We could not afford to be wrongfully accused of illegal fishing. We do not have the money to pay the large fines. Have you any idea how poorly we are paid? We did what any self-respecting fisherman would do. We took a gamble and ran.'

Carlos tries to conceal his annoyance. Why is Manuel doing this? Is he trying to protect himself, fearing the consequences of being the *Pescador*'s new first mate? At any other time, Carlos would have corrected him, but he lets it go. Lets that single moment decide his future. Perhaps Manuel knows what he is doing. Perhaps this is the only way to get back to Julia. Right now, nothing else seems important.

'The decision was not without its price though, let me tell you. We have lost three men,' Manuel says gravely.

'*Ja*, we heard. Our condolences,' de Ridder replies, his face dropping with genuine feeling.

Carlos is momentarily confused by the South African knowing this, but then remembers the satellite call that he made to Uruguayan Fisheries just yesterday. It must have been intercepted, or the news relayed. 'Well then, you will also know about our Russian crew member, Dmitri Ivanov. Our engineer,' he says. 'He took control of our vessel and cut our communications. We did not know the Australians were still pursuing us until two days ago.'

'And where is this Russian now?' the South African asks.

'I shot him with his own weapon,' Manuel says, regarding Carlos out of the corner of his eye. 'We have him, I think you would say, "on ice".'

One of the younger South Africans sniggers, but de Ridder glowers at him.

'And you didn't recover the other bodies?' de Ridder looks searchingly at Carlos.

'No. What do you want us to do now?' Carlos can hear his own voice, but feels strangely removed from it. It's as though he is watching the whole scene on television. Detached. Paralysed.

'Just continue on your current course,' de Ridder answers. 'The Australian fisheries officer will be boarding later today to officially apprehend your vessel. An Australian master and crew, plus three of our men, will accompany you to Fremantle, Australia. The *Australis* will be the escort ship. Our vessel will resume former duties. Presumably you need more fuel to get you back to Australia?'

'Yes,' Carlos answers.

'There is something else,' Manuel says, holding out a hand in Carlos's direction. 'Our fishing master here has just had very bad news from home. His wife has delivered their baby early and the child is very ill.'

Carlos feels weak at the mention of his son. A dizzying surge of panic rises inside him.

'Is there any way he could be escorted back to land on your ship?' Manuel beseeches. 'He could then get a flight home and answer any charges from there. It might be the only chance he has to see his little boy.'

'Our sincerest condolences, Captain Sánchez,' de Ridder says with what seems like true compassion. 'But our boat won't be in port for another month now. In any case, decisions like that rest with the Australians.'

Carlos feels his future slipping away from him. As if he is Eduardo overboard, unable to reach the life ring.

'None of us will be the same after this trip,' Manuel offers, patting the master's back.

The South African addresses Carlos. 'Would you be able to show us over the rest of the vessel now, Captain Sánchez?'

Carlos starts to walk to the wheelhouse door but Manuel stops him with a hand on his chest.

'You stay here, *Capitán*,' Manuel says. 'I will go. But first I would like to tell the crew, in Spanish, what is happening. Unless any of your men speak Spanish?'

'No, I don't expect so. Go ahead,' de Ridder answers, tipping his naval cap briefly at Carlos before signalling to the door and following Manuel on to the deck. One of the South Africans remains in the wheelhouse, his gun by his side.

Carlos watches the men leave and wonders how his crew will react to the revised plan and Manuel's fabricated version of the truth. A light rain begins to fall from an almost cloudless sky, and several of the crew instinctively flick their wet-weather hoods over their dark hair as if expecting worse weather.

Through binoculars, Carlos sees Manuel addressing the crew. He also says something to the South Africans, one of whom — a brutish youngster — throws his head back in a guffaw. It's the same man who sniggered so inappropriately in the wheelhouse moments earlier. One of the Peruvians appears to spit at his feet. Manuel steps forward and says something that seems to bring the discussion to a close. The crew are taken back inside and Manuel appears to be given permission to return to the wheelhouse.

'What did you tell them there at the end?' Carlos asks as the Spaniard enters the room.

'That it's not only guilty people who flee. Sometimes they run because they are being chased and have no other choice.'

DAVE
The *Australis*
6 October 2002

Dave Bates brings his boat alongside the *Pescador* in the startled light of a new day at sea. It's three weeks since he spotted the *Pescador* off Heard Island. He radios de Ridder who is in the apprehended vessel's wheelhouse. Another of the South Africans has taken the helm.

'The *Pescador*'s officers are denying they were fishing illegally,' de Ridder informs the Australian master. 'They say they caught the fish in international waters and were simply sheltering at Heard to attend to their engines. Over.'

'And pigs have wings,' Dave quips. 'Of course they'll deny it. If they're prepared to risk their lives in pack ice, they're not going to give in now. Anyway, that's not our problem.' He wonders how the case will play out in the courts; if all of this will be worth it. He watches a fine curtain of rain fall on an ocean that appears to be made of countless silver coins angled to catch the first rays of light. 'Have you told them about the fellow we have on ice? Over.'

'No. Thought we'd leave that to you.'

If he had said no to the chase, Dave thinks, the three dead men might still be alive. He steers his concentration back to the job at hand. 'Anyway, we're just about ready to send over

Harry Perdman for a reconnoitre before he skippers the boat home tomorrow. Our fisheries officer's pretty keen to check out the catch, too. Label and catalogue the evidence — all that jazz.'

'No problem. We'll send over our launch, seeing it's already in the water. No point getting yours wet,' the South African says with a jocular air.

'Much appreciated. Over and out.'

Dave ends the radio call as Cactus enters the wheelhouse.

'Need another man to go aboard, Davo? I'm happy to put me hand up if necessary.'

Dave tries not to laugh at Cactus's efforts to sound only moderately interested. 'She'll be right, mate. We'll need you here to help Harry and the others into the launch. I've got to have at least one experienced seaman on deck.' He hopes the last comment will stroke Cactus's ego enough to stop him from becoming a nuisance. He uses the intercom to let Harry know the plan and follows the approaching launch with binoculars until it's beneath them. The door shuts noisily and Dave realises that Cactus has left to join the others on deck. The rain has stopped and he watches Harry ordering the deck crane operator into position.

In under ten minutes, the launch is back in the water with Harry and the fisheries officer on board. It travels the short distance to the *Pescador* and lines up with a rope ladder that has been dropped from the midship rails and descends all the way to the sea. Harry begins to climb and Dave wonders how it must feel to finally be in physical contact with the boat they have chased almost to Africa. The ladder swings out from the side of the ship and Harry collides with the hull, swinging like a fish on a line. Dave hears the wheelhouse door open and shut again and assumes that it's Cactus.

'He'll be shitting himself, I reckon.' It's William's voice beside him in the wheelhouse, watching through his own set of binoculars.

Dave laughs but doesn't take his eyes off Harry until two South Africans hook the Australian first mate under the arms and drag him on board, landing him like a great big trophy of a fish. Dave scans the deck and finds himself looking, for the first time, into the dark, glaring faces of several of the *Pescador*'s crew.

Harry and Dougal McAllister, the fisheries officer, arrive back on board the *Australis* just before nightfall. 'It's a bloody dog's breakfast over there,' Harry tells Dave in the wheelhouse. 'Can't believe they've made it as far as they have.'

''Specially given the weight of toothfish they've got on board,' Dougal adds.

'So they haven't ditched the evidence then?' Dave looks at the two boats — the *Pescador* and the *Bremner* — lit up like floating oil rigs. If he didn't know better, he'd say the *Pescador* even appeared welcoming. The lights flicker on the darkening blanket of sea, which is calmer than Dave has seen it for the duration of the chase. It's as if even the ocean is appreciative of the chance to bed down and ready itself for a rest.

'Nope, got enough evidence to sink a ship,' the fisheries officer answers, pleased with his accidental play on words. 'I've started labelling it, and grabbed a few samples and measurements as an insurance policy. There was one fish, two metres long, that they'd had on ice to be made into a wall trophy. What a beauty. Should have seen the size of those child-bearing lips! I kept thinking of her cruising around down there in the pitch black just a few weeks ago —'

'Anyway, mate,' Harry says, 'you go and make a start on cataloguing those samples. I'll be down in a minute to lend a hand.'

'I reckon he'd talk at fifty fathoms with a mouth full of marbles,' Dave jokes as soon as the young man is out of the room.

Harry snorts derisively.

'Tell me about this Carlos Sánchez character. Is he what you expected?'

'Not at all. Spent most of the time in his bed, such as it is. The Springboks have booted him out of his cabin, so he's sleeping in the crew's quarters. You've got to feel sorry for the lot of them, really. They're just a downtrodden bunch of blokes trying to scratch out a living.'

'You going soft on us, Harry? They're scratching a living out of *our* fish. Our livelihood. This fishery will be buggered in under a decade if the illegals don't back off.' Dave bites at the ragged corner of his thumbnail, and tears a piece off. 'I know what you're saying, but *they* chose to be here, and *they* started the chase. If they'd just accepted their fate earlier, three people might still be alive. We're just lucky our lot made it through okay.'

'I told them about the body we recovered,' Harry tells Dave as if seeking his permission retrospectively. 'I said it looked like he'd been shot and they gave me the whole sorry story. It turns out the Russian bloke — the mutineer — smuggled the gun onboard. The deceased fellow we have down below — Roberto Cruz was his name — was killed in front of his son. Poor kid.'

Dave goes quiet again. He knows it could have been worse. In those seas, with a madman in charge, it's a wonder the *Pescador* hasn't made a grave on the bottom of the ocean for the lot of them.

'A Spanish guy called Manuel was at pains to let us know how much it meant to have the old man's body recovered. He told us a story — I'll never forget it actually — about a fishing boat that went down off Spain. His brother and father were among the missing. Anyway, when none of the bodies washed up on shore, a team of divers went searching for them. Found them lying together on the seafloor like they were just asleep, as if the ocean had "sung them a lullaby", in Manuel's words.'

'An eddy must have kept them together.'

Harry nods. 'The divers strung all the bodies along a rope, like a bunch of fish on a line, and towed them back to shore. As the divers swam and dragged the load, the bodies all rose to their feet and bloody walked along the seafloor behind them. Or, so it seemed. I can't get that image out of my head. Can you imagine?'

'I'd rather not.'

'No, sorry. But the point this Manuel fellow was making was that if the divers hadn't gone to such lengths, those men would never have been returned home to their families. It was his way of saying thanks, I s'pose, for recovering his friend.'

Dave shakes his head and thinks of the other body still out at sea. The South Africans told him it was the *Pescador*'s first mate. He thinks of the first mate's family, and how they will always be left wondering what became of him. His bones and skin and hair. At least he knows where his son's remains are. At least he gave Sam a proper burial. Dave can hardly believe it's almost two years since he died. It still feels like yesterday.

'Not a bad yarn, is it? Not one for the grandkids, though.' Harry goes quiet as if hearing his words too late. He scratches his head, and Dave can tell he's preparing to change tack. 'It's interesting, the science stuff,' Harry announces quickly, latching onto his new subject. 'I hadn't really known what young Dougal gets up to until now.'

'The genetics and so on?' Dave asks.

'Yeah, and the way they can tell the age of a fish by counting the growth rings in its earbones, of all things.' Harry chuckles. 'Bit like counting the rings in a tree trunk, apparently. And get this: really old fish still contain radioactive markers in the growth rings corresponding to the years of atomic testing. So the scientists can check their methods because they know the dates of the blasts.'

'Well I'll be blowed.'

'To be honest, I hadn't realised just how little we know about species like the toothfish. The boffins still haven't got the foggiest idea how often they reproduce or how many eggs they make. We'll be playing Russian-bloody-roulette if we give out too many licences or set the quotas too high around Heard and McDonald. Especially with the illegals getting their paws in. Boats like the *Pescador* are only getting stuck into Australian waters because they've buggered up the subantarctic stocks further west. It's no wonder the French and British and South Africans have naval boats regularly patrolling their territories. Dougal reckons toothfish numbers around Prince Edward are just ten per cent of what they used to be, and around Crozet it's only about twenty-five or thirty per cent.'

'You saying this chase hasn't all been a waste of time then?'

'Not if they get convicted.' Harry shrugs, as if to say that they have no control over that part of the equation. 'Not sure I go along with all the genetics stuff, though. Seems like a lot of fuss just to prove the fish they've got on board came from our waters. I mean, to state the bleeding obvious, an Aussie trawler saw them there, for Christ's sake.'

'Yeah, but they didn't actually film them fishing. Wentworth said the angle of the boat was wrong. To anyone watching the footage, the boat could just have been doing some routine maintenance in our waters like they're claiming.'

'Whatever happened to common sense? Honestly, the world's gone mad.' Harry scrubs at his short blond beard. 'Anyway, like I said, I'd better go and help the young lad out. A promise is a promise.'

As Harry leaves the wheelhouse, Dave notices, for the first time since they left port, how tired the first mate is looking. Dave knows that Harry is the sort of man who would give his right arm to save a friend. He is dependable and loyal and as honest as the day is long. If Harry was asked to take the helm for twenty-four hours straight, Dave has no doubt he would do it, no questions asked. It's a steadfastness that Dave hopes he hasn't abused by asking too much of him — this man he would be proud to have as a brother.

The *Pescador* has drifted so that it is side-on to the *Australis* and Dave ponders on the future that awaits the men bunkering down inside its metal walls. The ship's owner, he suspects, will get away scot-free. Dave supposes it's the same in the drug trade. The small-time pushers get caught, while the drug lords run amok. As he watches, a light in one of the cabins goes out and he imagines it's Carlos Sánchez finally surrendering to his fate.

MARGIE
Hartz Mountain, Tasmania
9 October 2002

The moment Margie Bates steps out of the car at the Hartz Mountain carpark she knows the hike is a good idea. The air is crisp on her face and a soft white mist is descending, caressing her with its downy dew. Individual particles of water are visibly suspended in the still air, muting the silvery sheen of tea trees — blushed pink with new growth — and surrounding them like feather cloaks.

'Thanks so much for agreeing to come, Joan,' Margie says, framing the scene in front of her with her hands to see how it would reproduce as a painting. 'I hope you're feeling all right about leaving Beth with that carer.'

'She'll be fine. It'll be good for the pair of us,' Joan says, tying a double knot into the laces of her hiking boots.

Margie takes a photograph from her jacket pocket and studies it closely. It shows a millpond-smooth lake within which is reflected a jagged mountain ridge dusted with snow. Beside the lake is Sam's tent and balanced on a rock at the water's edge are his boots. A wallaby is staring at the camera. Staring at Sam.

Margie rediscovered the photograph in one of Sam's albums just days before, and remembers what he told her when he first showed her the picture: 'You could do that walk, Mum. You'd love it. I'll take you myself one day. I promise.' She returns the print to her pocket and pats it through the Gore-tex with her hand. Well, Sam, she thinks, here I am.

Margie can only see five metres in front of her, and imagines painting the veiled scene in watercolour. For the background, a wash — a mix of ultramarine blue and madder brown. While the paper is still wet, she would make soft shadows with tiny dabs of the brush. She'd continue the wet-on-wet technique to build up the tea trees in the foreground, allowing the pinks and green-greys to blend naturally. It would be a challenge to achieve an ethereal quality while still providing enough definition to give the painting some substance. Above all, she mustn't let it get muddy, always a danger when working wet. She would add highlights of raw sienna in the foreground, as though the sun was just making it through the mist to light the rocks closest to her.

She takes her camera from the top of her backpack and fires off three shots, already excited by the prospect of painting the scene when she gets home.

'We're not even out of the carpark, Margie hon!' Joan laughs. 'I hope you've got a lot of film in that pack!'

'Plenty.' Margie chuckles, thinking of the six packets of film stuffed into her sleeping bag for safe-keeping. 'It's reference material for painting. But if I stop too much, you just go on ahead.'

Margie remembers Sam complaining about Sascha wanting to stop too often on hikes, to watch a bird, or to eat, or drink, or have a wee. She remembers urging him to be patient and enjoy the journey. It had been good advice.

'Okay, we'd better make tracks,' Margie says. 'So we're not setting up camp in the dark.'

'Ready when you are.' Joan swings the pack onto her back, as if she's done it a million times.

Margie struggles into her own pack, and suddenly understands the merit in Sam's dehydrated food. Joan has a few packets of the stuff stowed deep in her pack, but Margie has secretly taken the cans of soup and beans. She takes a few steps towards the start of the track and hopes she'll survive the walk.

'Okeydokey,' Joan says, springing weightlessly into her first steps as though she is moon-walking. Margie watches her stretching out her short legs in Sam's oversized wet-weather pants and jacket. Both sets of cuffs, at the ankles and at the wrists, have been rolled up two or three times. The pack itself reaches almost to the top of Joan's head, so that all Margie can see of her friend are a few piebald curls bobbing about.

It had been a last-minute decision to offer Sam's hiking gear to Joan. At the time it seemed a sensible and obvious gesture, but now she can't help thinking about the last time Sam wore it, where he had been and what he'd been thinking. A large lump forms in her throat. She focuses on each step and the calming surrounds, allowing herself to be lulled by the simple act of walking up the winding track. Peace descends and she releases a long sigh. Underfoot, rocks, slippery with moss, dot the red clay like dollops of fresh green paint.

A scarlet robin flits onto the track and drinks hurriedly from a pool of water. Margie gasps, and, telling Joan to stop, crouches down to better see the bird. The lump returns to her throat.

'It's Sam,' Margie whispers. 'I saw a robin at the house the day he died. Every time I see one now I think it's his spirit paying me a visit.'

'I'm sure you're right,' Joan says, resting her hand on Margie's forearm. The robin vanishes into the undergrowth and Margie rises to her feet. Joan takes her cue and walks on without words. They have been friends for long enough to know when to talk, and when to be silent.

At the top of the incline, Margie drinks in the vista rising up above her. Hartz Mountain looms majestically over what is now a level, duckboard track. Off in the distance, Margie glimpses Sam's beloved southwest wilderness.

'You don't get away from it all, you get back to it all,' Joan says.

'I've heard that somewhere before.'

'Peter Dombrovskis, the landscape photographer.'

'That's right. Sam had a poster with that quote on it.' Margie shakes her head in wonder, taking this as another sign that her son is with her, here and now. She peers down into the crowns of regal forest giants in the valley below. The treetops merge into one another in an ancient mosaic of every imaginable green. She wonders which of the trees rallying for supremacy are myrtles and which are sassafras, Huon and King Billy pine. Once they are in timber form, made into tables and chairs, Margie can pick them a mile off, but seeing them here, in their natural state, she is at a loss. Sam would have been able to show her, she thinks.

'Isn't it incredible that these forests have been growing since before white man even set foot on this island?' Joan says. 'Do you know there are animals down there that are no longer found on the mainland?'

'No, I didn't,' Margie says. It is as if she is sailing above the sea of green. 'Can you smell smoke?'

'Yep,' Joan says, as they wind their way around the mountain track. She points beneath them and both women stare at the ugly blackened scar of clearfelling still smoking from a recent forestry burn.

Margie feels personally assaulted, her inner peace shattered. It's a bit like a death when a forest is logged, she decides. All the structures, the complexity, that were a person or a landscape are erased in one fell swoop.

In silence, the women wind their way further around the mountain, leaving the deforested valley in their wake. They walk for another hour across an undulating plateau, before being greeted by a perched lake nestled at the base of a rocky peak. Margie recognises the campsite straight away. She pulls Sam's photo out of her jacket pocket and uses it to locate his exact tent spot, and the rock where he left his boots. It sends a sharp pain through her like an invisible winged arrow. Sad, yet strangely happy at the same time.

'Here we are.' She stops in front of the lake, close to where Sam must have stood to take the photo that now rests in her hand. 'Our campsite. Sam's campsite.'

Joan releases the hip strap of her rucksack and lets the weight of it fall heavily to the ground. 'And a beautiful one it is.'

Margie unloads the tent and starts to erect it, fibreglass poles and pegs going in all directions.

'I take it you didn't do a practice run in the lounge room?' Joan teases.

'I did actually, but you're one of the few people I'd admit that to.'

A fine rain starts to fall as the tent is raised and the two women make for its cover, dragging their packs in behind them.

Through the smoky haze of the tent fly, Margie watches the rain fall on the lake. She imagines that each delicate drop of water will be casting minute ripples over the dark surface. Perhaps, in some immeasurable way, the tiny ripples will make it to the other side. A feeling of peace again washes over her, a feeling that she might just survive after all.

'I'll get some water for a cup of tea,' Joan says, grabbing the pot and squeezing herself out of the tent. Margie watches her pull the hood of Sam's jacket over her head and crouch beside the rock where her son sat his boots a lifetime ago. Tears well in her eyes as she imagines that it's Sam collecting water for her. She can't even remember what she said to him when he promised to bring her here one day. She'd probably made a joke that he'd have to carry her half the way. How she wishes she had simply said yes.

As the women boil the billy, Margie wonders how Dave is coping today, Sam's day. Whether he can take a few moments to lose himself in the stars and shed a few tears, or whether he'll be having to be Mr Cool in front of his crew. She doubts he'll mention Sam's anniversary to any of them.

She serves the tea in metal mugs, handing one to Joan. 'Do you mind if I light a candle? It's something I do every year at this time.'

'Of course not. You don't have to ask my permission. Would you like some time on your own? I could go for a walk around the lake.'

'No, you stay put. I'd like the company.' Margie reaches into the side of her pack and locates a large candle the colour of a summer sky strewn with clouds. She climbs out of the tent and walks over to Sam's rock, placing the candle carefully in a hollow that seems to have been ground out of the stone for just this purpose. Once lit, the candle forms a beautiful beacon in the fading light, attracting moths and small insects that fly to the borders of its warmth before disappearing into the night.

It is in this space, that ancient lichen-encrusted rocks and gnarled, wind-worn alpine vegetation speak their stories to her, and, along with the ripples on the lake, cast their hypnotic spells. All things seem connected, and, for just a moment, she almost forgives the world for what it has taken from her.

JULIA
Montevideo, Uruguay
10 October 2002

Six days after her baby was taken from her body and placed in the humidicrib, his artificial uterus, Julia is back at home. They hadn't wanted her sleeping in the chair beside the humidicrib at the hospital, and she hadn't been able to face another night in the maternity ward, surrounded by the sound of healthy new babies crying for their mother's milk. It is surreal to be back in the outside world, as though someone has turned the lights up before the end of a movie. She thinks of her baby still in neonatal intensive care, where the drama is not yet over.

She stares at a Polaroid image of her son to stimulate the oxytocin-driven let-down reflex, which will start the flow of milk, and she holds the plastic pump in position, ready to draw the life-giving fluid from her breasts. The release of hormones feels like someone is pouring warm treacle down the back of her head and neck. She imagines the milk flowing into her full breasts and then into the mouth of her baby. The visualisation works. To start with, the milk appears thick and yellowish in the sterilised bottle attached to the pump. After a while, it thins out to a bluish white.

She sips on a weak coffee and assures herself it won't harm her baby. Caffeine is given intravenously to the infants in the nursery to stimulate their breathing, she was told just yesterday by a nurse, so a small amount in her breastmilk will be of little consequence. Perhaps it could even help. When Julia asked what other drugs her child might be given, the list was long: steroids, antibiotics, surfactants to clear his lungs and, if necessary, morphine for pain.

'It's a wonder they don't come out of here as addicts,' Julia had said.

'It's a wonder some of them come out of here at all,' the nurse had replied, and then, as if sensing the harshness of her words, continued. 'They're such little miracles, every one of them. I've often thought that these babies have fought more battles just to make it into the world than many of us face in a lifetime.'

Last night, Julia's first night at home, she woke with a sense of dread. She phoned the hospital, to check that everything was all right. It wasn't. Only moments before, the paediatrician had been called to investigate a sudden drop in her son's oxygen levels. When she arrived, her baby boy was blue and being ventilated with a hand pump. The sight of so many medical staff around the humidicrib had sent her into a terrified spin. The intense concentration on the paediatrician's face said it all. A nurse took Julia by the arms and backed her away to the waiting room. There was nothing she could do, and no room for her anyway at the bedside. In those few minutes, while she sat staring at a wall poster of a smiling breastfeeding mother, her son would either live or die. Life on a knife edge. Just when she had thought he was out of the woods, he was back in them again, and it was darker in there than ever. She had been warned that this was the nature of such extreme prematurity: no guarantees, just sudden turns.

The nurse told her afterwards that one of the tubes into her son's lungs had been too deep, blocking the supply of oxygen, a relatively common occurrence. The tube had been repositioned quickly, and a brain scan showed there was no damage. By then it was four in the morning and Julia steadied herself with a warm, sugary tea and a cream biscuit before going to see her baby.

He appeared peaceful again, although a deep furrow persisted on his tiny brow. How she longed to hold him to her, to feed him, and rock him and sing him a lullaby. How she longed to be held and rocked and sung to herself.

'Would you like some *tostados*, Julia?' her mother calls out from the kitchen. She'd arrived two days ago to mind María and to help with the cooking and washing. But her presence in the house, while an enormous help and support, has left Julia feeling more dependent and less strong, as if she is a child again. For reasons Julia doesn't understand, the maternal sympathy and concern seem to magnify her own anxieties rather than reduce them.

'When I get back,' Julia answers.

'When can I visit my baby brother?' María hollers, bursting into Julia's bedroom.

'Soon, sweetheart. When he's a bit stronger,' Julia replies, deciding to hold María off for a few more days. To protect her, in case the worst should happen. Who knows if it's the right decision.

Julia places the expressed milk in a small esky containing a freezer brick and prepares to take it to the hospital. Only tiny amounts of breastmilk have been given to her son so far, and her supply in the nursery freezer is becoming embarrassingly large. The nurses have assured her she should keep bringing it in: 'It's too precious to waste. He'll use it. You'll see.'

Julia opens the door to the nursery and washes her hands automatically at the basin. The routine has become second nature. A curtain is drawn around one of the other humidicribs and Julia can hear a woman crying. The voice of the paediatrician is soft and low, comforting. A sick feeling pervades Julia's stomach and she notices that her hands are shaking as she dries them on a paper towel. The curtain is drawn back and a mother and father are handed a small bundle of baby wrapped in a tiny hospital blanket. Julia sees the dead infant's face buried into its mother's neck. The tubes have been removed but the baby is ghost white. The tearful parents are shown to a private room at the side of the intensive care area. Their baby, born only a few days ago, and smaller than her own, has died. It's all over. All their hopes, dreams and fears.

Julia thinks she can see, amidst the profound grief, something resembling relief on the mother's face. No more wondering if her baby will survive, or be permanently disabled from the early birth. No more rushing to the hospital at three o'clock in the morning to be told that the baby had given them a scare but that everything is again all right — for now. It's all over. Everything but the loss, which will be there forever.

Julia feels herself holding onto the bench by the milk freezer. She is swaying. How much can people be asked to bear? How cruel can life be?

She places her newly expressed milk in a sterile freezer bag, seals it carefully and writes on the label: 'Baby Sánchez Pereira, 10/10/02'. Beside her supply is a collection of bags carefully labelled 'Esmeralda Brovetto Alves'. Julia recognises the name from the humidicrib that now lies bare. She wonders what will happen to the breastmilk.

Making her way to her own baby, Julia passes the room where the bereaved parents are washing and dressing their child for the first and last time.

'He's breathing by himself today,' one of the nurses says to Julia, bringing her attention back to her son. 'Some good news for us.' The nurse discreetly wipes away a tear. It occurs to Julia that their job must be one of the hardest. Nursing tiny babies to their early graves. Perhaps the nurse questions whether there was more she could have done for little Esmeralda and her parents. 'A good day for your first cuddle. What do you think?'

Julia is excited and nervous all at once. 'Are you sure he'll be all right? I don't want to hurt him.'

'He'll love it.'

The baby is cautiously taken from the humidicrib with his trail of intravenous lines, and the nurse motions to place him in Julia's arms.

'Just let me sit down,' Julia says, scrambling for the hospital chair. 'All right. Ready.'

She takes the baby and holds him against her body. He wriggles his tiny legs against her stomach, this time from the outside. His little eyes are open now and he makes a small cry. It's the sweetest sound she has ever heard. '*Te quiero*,' she whispers, placing a kiss on his forehead. The respiratory monitors sound their alarm.

The nurse reaches for the baby. 'Each day the cuddles will get a little longer, and he'll get a little stronger,' she says, promptly returning him to the humidicrib. His respiration rate returns to normal. 'He loves his *mamá*. You got him all excited and he forgot to breathe.' The nurse checks the monitors. 'Have you decided on a name yet?'

'No,' Julia says, remembering to breathe herself. 'Well, almost.' She inhales deeply. 'Eduardo,' she says, her voice cracking with emotion.

'Eduardo Sánchez Pereira. That sounds perfect,' the nurse says, as she takes the blank name card from its slot at the end of the crib and cements the baby's identity in black permanent ink. 'Is Eduardo a family name?'

'It's the name of my husband's best friend, and this little one's godfather-to-be. It's what we'd spoken about.'

'*Bueno,*' the nurse says, returning the card to its slot and then attending to the next baby.

'*Sí.*' Julia feels a sense of relief. 'Eduardo,' she whispers, happy that her child has a name. He deserves that. Just as Esmeralda did.

Julia strokes her baby's hand before leaving the hospital for a waiting bus. She finds a seat to herself beside a window and presses her forehead against the glass. Tears wet her cheeks — tears born of relief that her baby will probably now survive, and tears of exhaustion from nearly a fortnight of little sleep. She cries too for Esmeralda, and her parents, and the knowledge that it could so easily have been her facing that bottomless pit of grief. Julia can still see the parched and drained expression on Esmeralda's mother's face. Her robotic steps to the small private room. Her dead baby in her arms. Life can be so cruel. How will those parents recover from this? How will they ever trust in life again? Julia closes her eyes and tries to relax her aching muscles. Life has lost its innocence for her too, she realises. It can all change so fast.

She should count her blessings, she tells herself. Her baby is doing well. She pictures his name, newly printed, above his humidicrib. The worst is over.

The bus turns a corner and is flooded by light — the glare off the Río de la Plata. She has a son, she tells herself. She must allow herself to start believing it.

At her apartment door, she sits on the step, taking a few moments before going inside. A blur of cars and buses rush by as they have always done. People are living their lives. Can't they see how radically hers has changed? That she has been to hell and back with these trips into the hospital, hoping with every inch of herself that her baby will survive? That little Eduardo's life has been balanced on the thinnest of blades? An old woman bustles past, blotting her wet eyes with a handkerchief. At her side, being dragged along by the hand, is a small boy. Julia wonders for a moment what their family's story is. Perhaps they have just visited the boy's mother in hospital, or perhaps the boy has been orphaned and is now his grandmother's charge. She turns her attention to a man of about her own age. His hair is prematurely white and the skin under his eyes unusually dark. Perhaps he too has been dealt a raw hand and survived. It occurs to Julia that she is not alone, but closer to humanity than she has ever been. She has been awakened to the precariousness of life, and that knowledge, she realises, is a gift.

She thinks how much she and Carlos wanted this baby, and how difficult it had been to conceive. She remembers the pain of endometriosis as a teenager and the doctor's warning, in her early twenties, not to delay having children. In ten years of marriage, even without contraception, she still only fell pregnant four times, and two of those pregnancies had ended in miscarriage. The multiple pregnancies have somehow eased the pain of endometriosis, but left the ache of lost babies in its place. It's a miracle that little Eduardo had been born at all.

Julia opens the apartment door and is greeted by her mother's voice.

'I've made you a *chivito*.'

She enters the lounge room in time to see her mother smack the steak sandwich piled high with cheese, bacon, tomato and lettuce on the table.

'I thought you'd be hungry. And there are *empanadas* too.'

María is playing on the lounge-room floor with some Barbies on loan from Sofía. She runs to Julia and gives her a tight hug around the legs, before returning to the dolls.

'How's the baby?' Julia's mother asks guardedly.

'He's doing well. I held him today.'

'Praise God!' She clasps her hands together in thanks, and in the same moment tells Julia that she has run out of ingredients for a batch of fried biscuits. 'The mixture is half ready in the fridge if you feel like going out and buying some more eggs.'

'*Madre*, just leave me for a moment. I need to have a warm shower. I'm exhausted.'

'But your lunch?'

Julia closes the bathroom door and eyes the bathtub. In another week she'll be able to have a soak in there without causing problems to the caesarean scar. It seems like an eternity away. She undresses, inspecting the wound, which is just starting to heal, and thanks God that her baby has, so far, been blessed with life. She turns on the shower taps and steps under the stream of water, letting it wash away days of tension from her body.

When she finally emerges, Julia puts on Carlos's dressing gown and goes straight to her computer, hoping for a message from her husband. As she scans down the emails, she is surprised to see a second message from the Australian woman, Margaret Bates, which she opens.

Dear Julia,

Perhaps I am the last person you want to hear from, but I felt I had to contact you.

You have no doubt been told that your husband's boat has been apprehended and is on its way now to Australia. Thankfully the chase is over, but I do hope that he is returned safely to you soon.

I have also heard that you have had your baby prematurely and I just wanted to let you know that there are people on the other side of the world who are feeling for you, and sending you all our positive thoughts.

I didn't know you were pregnant when I emailed you previously. If there is anything at all that I can do to assist you at this troubling time, please let me know. Please excuse me for seeming so bold, but I know how precious children are, having lost my only son, and feel enormously for what you must be going through.

Kind regards,

Margie Bates

Julia is again confronted but warmed by the concern from the other side of the world. It's more than her best friend, also on the other side of the world, has offered. Perhaps there *is* something Margie Bates can do. She sends an email back, pleased that she made an effort with English classes at university:

Dear Margie,

Thank you for your kind letter. My son, although born thirteen weeks early, is now doing well. It has been a daily struggle for us, but we are surviving.

The greatest gift at the moment would be to have my husband home. According to the authorities here, there is no record of his boat fishing in Australian waters. I do not know what influence you have, but if there is any chance of convincing the Australian authorities to try my husband here in Uruguay, that would be the best help you could give.

Regards,

Julia Pereira de Sánchez

Julia presses the send button and watches the message disappear from the screen. When she looks up, she sees her mother in front of her, the uneaten *chivito* on a plate in her hand.

'It's cold. After all the trouble I went to to make it.'

'Sorry, *Mamá*. I'll have it now.' Julia gives her mother an apologetic hug and sits down at the table to eat.

María migrates up from the floor to sit beside her, walking the Barbies around on the table top as if it was a catwalk. 'Has our baby got a name yet?'

'*Si.*' Julia kisses María on the forehead, leaving behind a smudge of cold bacon grease. 'I meant to tell you. It's Eduardo.'

'Like Uncle Eduardo?'

'Just like that, *si,*' Julia says, reaching over to wipe her daughter's face clean.

LOGBOOK OF EDUARDO RODRÍGUEZ TORRES

⌇

I dream sometimes that I am an albatross, surveying the world's largest ocean from the air. Albatross sighted this trip: southern royal albatross, wandering albatross, white-capped albatross, white-capped mollymawk, black-browed mollymawk, grey-headed mollymawk, light-mantled albatross and sooty albatross. These most admirable, most noble of birds can live for up to fifty years, spending the majority of this time at sea. They sail with grace through the most treacherous turbulence life can deal them, and when they return home it is to their lifelong partners.

⌇

CARLOS
The *Pescador*
11 October 2002

Carlos's sleep is fitful — a pitching, diving struggle between competing worlds: conscious and unconscious. He is like a seabird caught on a fishing line and trying to surface. Each time he breaks through, unseen nocturnal waves pull him back under. He dreams of his newborn child, too sick to be kept alive with the ventilator. The machine is switched off. Long tubes that had pumped air into his tiny lungs are extracted slowly. The baby is handed to his father and attempts to breathe on his own, but he can't. He's too small, too immature. Carlos feels the baby's tiny legs struggle against him briefly. Has his baby died? Surely he would have felt some change. Some small weight — his son's soul — would have shifted and left. He is offered a swaddling blanket and asks permission to take the infant outside the hospital and into the light for the first time. A nurse agrees.

Outside, the tiny form is shown a world he will never see. The wind ruffles his fine, short hair. Carlos wishes he could breathe for his child who is so blue now that he must surely be dead. But he refuses to believe it. He promises God he will exhale warm life-giving air into the baby's empty lungs forever if necessary. But he knows there's no use. He thinks he sees his son's spirit fly from his body, soaring higher and higher into the sky, like an albatross.

The hospital doctor had asked Carlos to return with the dead infant when he was ready. A funeral will need to be arranged. But he's not ready to let go — not yet. He takes the tightly wrapped form down the street, hiding his blue face and lips from passers-by. He walks the whole way like this to the Puerto de Montevideo, to his father's old fishing boat. He unties the weathered ropes and starts the engine. Julia is beside him now. She had heard this is where he had gone with their child. María, safe with Julia's parents, waves from the shore.

The seas build and Julia asks where they are heading.

'I just want him to see the ocean,' Carlos answers.

Carlos doesn't have a destination in mind and simply motors out to sea. Cut adrift. A day passes, then two. Carlos knows the hospital staff will be wondering where they have gone. Julia says they should return, but Carlos keeps going. He puts the baby in the cold hold to preserve the body, deciding never to go back. The three of them will remain at sea. Until the pain stops. Julia weeps and grows thin. He has forgotten to provide for his wife. He has failed her. He holds out his arms but she pushes him away.

Carlos sets a fishing line, but there are no fish. Something large takes hold of his hook, and he reels it in. It's Eduardo. The first mate climbs up the line. He seems fine. The Eduardo of old — handsome and happy. He says he has been looking after the fish.

'I tried to save you,' Carlos tells him, relieved to have the chance to explain. 'What happened? Did the harness break?'

'I unclipped myself. I thought the boat would turn. But when it didn't, it was okay. It's not your fault, Carlos,' Eduardo answers. 'I shouldn't have been out there alone. I should have warned you about Dmitri. But I'd made that promise to you and Julia.'

Carlos dreams then that Julia is on deck too, holding their dead child. She runs to Eduardo and lets him comfort her.

Carlos wakes in stages, but each time the dream pulls him back down under its liquid skin.

Finally he wakes completely, shaken and confused. Has his baby really died? Was this some kind of premonition? He needs to call Julia and groggily makes his way up to the wheelhouse where the most senior of the South African naval officers on board is talking to Harry Perdman at the helm.

'I need to use the phone,' Carlos pleads, his face awash with tears. A thick rope of mucus extrudes from his nose, before falling to the floor. 'My wife. I need to call her. Please.'

'We need to get permission from Customs for you to use the phone,' Harry tells him. 'Now that I've taken over as master, I'm under strict instructions —'

'Please,' Carlos begs. 'I need to know if my son is all right.'

He watches the South African mime, for Harry's benefit, the action of putting a stitch in his lips.

'Okay. But I know nothing about it,' Harry says as he points to the phone.

'*Gracias*,' Carlos whispers. '*Muchísimas gracias.*'

Julia answers from their apartment.

'Julia, sweetheart. *Que tal*? Is our baby all right?'

'*Si*. Well …' She falters and Carlos holds his breath. 'He has given us a few scares, but he's stable now. He's through the worst. He's a week old today.'

Carlos is without words for a few moments. 'When did you last speak with the hospital?'

'This morning. I was in there. Taking up some breastmilk. Why?'

Carlos knows better than to tell his wife about the nightmare. She is superstitious enough already.

'I just needed to hear he's all right. *Lo siento, lo siento*,' he apologises. 'It's all my fault, all of this. I miss you so much and wish I could be there with you. *For* you.'

Julia pauses. 'So do I.'

'How's María doing?'

'Fine. She's my strength.' Julia's voice trails away and, in that small space of silence, Carlos imagines his beautiful daughter smiling. It almost breaks his heart. 'Carlos, I've named our baby Eduardo. I hope that's all right. It was what you wanted last time we spoke about it.'

A maelstrom of emotion whips up inside Carlos. '*Si*. But …' He remembers that Julia still doesn't know of their friend's death. 'Julia, about Eduardo …' Carlos's voice breaks and he is aware of the deathly quiet on the other end of the phone.

'Julia?'

'*Si*.'

'Eduardo was lost at sea a week ago. I couldn't tell you the other day. Not on top of everything else.'

Again, silence. Louder, if that is possible, this time.

'Julia?'

'*Si*.' Her voice is constricted, choked. Barely audible.

'I'm so sorry to have to tell you over the phone. But I didn't want you to hear from Francisco or Cecilia.'

Carlos presses the phone hard to his ear, but hears only the static of the line. Quietly, he begins to cry. 'We'll be together again soon, my love. Our little Eduardo will be fine. He has a very special godfather protecting him now. I've phoned Virginia already with the news, but can you tell her again how sorry I am? And, if you get a chance, can you email a photo of our little boy to the ship …'

'I'll try. *Hasta luego*, Carlos.'

Carlos is still holding the satellite phone after Julia hangs up. He thanks Harry, who goes to speak but stops short. What is there to say?

Carlos walks numbly back towards the bunk that used to belong to Roberto but has now become his own. He passes Eduardo's cabin, which is filled with the personal effects of the *Pescador's* new Australian master. No one will ever fill the void left by his friend, Carlos realises. Every time he calls his son's name he will be reminded of the vacated cabin of the boy's godfather. He descends another flight of stairs and keeps his eyes low as he passes his crew in their bunks. At least the less senior Australians and South Africans have opted to camp out in the mess, he thinks.

He mentally replays the sound of Julia's voice over the telephone. He has never heard her like this before. So detached. He lowers himself onto his bunk and hauls the sea blanket over his legs. He thinks of his son, still alive. He should be happy, but it's as though someone has dimmed the lights and everything is now overcast and muted. Perhaps he'll never feel happy again? He takes the photograph of Julia off the wall beside him and holds it to his chest.

Leaning into the light, Carlos examines the peeling paint on the wall beside his bed. With the Australians now in control of the ship, he has barely left this spot. He studies the now familiar dark shapes that the absent paint has left behind. The longer he stares at the patterns, the more disturbing are the creatures his imagination conjures: there are grimacing faces and twisted bodies, crashing waves and frightened animals running. He takes the silver stud from his earlobe and uses the sharp post at the back to scratch letters into the white paint: E.D.U.A.R.D.O. He writes the name almost subconsciously.

He studies the photograph in his hand, the picture of Julia in what appears to be a boatshed. Using the crisp light through the porthole, he delves deeply, for the first time, into the background. He makes out the blurred shape of a dinghy and recognises it as belonging to Eduardo's father. Eduardo had been restoring it. The boatshed too, Carlos realises, is theirs. He remembers Julia taking a day trip to La Paloma and arriving home in that red-flowered dress. She must have paid them a visit. Perhaps this picture was taken then. He turns the photograph over. In a flowing hand is written: 'For Julia'. He had seen the writing before this but had thought little of it. He takes his earring again and, for reasons he doesn't understand, scratches out Eduardo's name from the paintwork, leaving behind an empty square of black metal.

MARGIE
Hobart, Australia
11 October 2002

Margie Bates closes the email, and checks her address book for Roger Wentworth's phone number at the Australian Customs Service.

He answers promptly. 'Oh, Mrs Bates. I thought it was going to be another media call. We're being flooded with them.'

'Sorry, only little old me,' Margie says, annoyed by his patronising tone.

'No, you're fine, Mrs Bates. I'm glad you've phoned. Your husband should be congratulated for his handling of events over the last few weeks.'

Margie takes a deep breath, in no mood for platitudes. 'On the matter of the trial …' she begins. 'You'd be aware that the Uruguayan master's wife has delivered a baby very prematurely and that there's still every chance the child might not survive.'

'Yes. Dave told you that, did he?' Wentworth's voice is brittle and escalates unnaturally in pitch.

'No, *I've* been in contact with her.' Margie proceeds quickly. 'Is there any way that Carlos Sánchez could be tried in Uruguay? Are you even the right person to be asking?'

'I can't see it happening myself. And yes, you should be talking to me — for starters at least. My understanding is that there has to be a preliminary hearing to determine if we've got the grounds for a full-blown trial.'

'Are you saying all this could have been for nothing?'

'Well, if Dave hadn't lost sight of the boat …'

'Yes, I know what you're about to say.' Margie inhales the breeze through the open window, focusing on the cooling scent of eucalypts. 'But what do I tell Julia Sánchez?'

'You shouldn't be discussing this with her at all. She needs to be talking to the lawyers who'll be handling the illegal boat's case, but, to be honest, I can't see there's any chance that her husband will be allowed to return home at this stage. This is an important test case for us.'

Margie sniffs sharply. 'Perhaps I should contact the media myself and let them know that no one actually saw the *Pescador* bringing in fish.'

Roger Wentworth says nothing.

'David told me,' Margie adds, declaring her hand.

'That probably wasn't appropriate.'

'Appropriate? I wonder how appropriate it was to spend taxpayers' money chasing a ship halfway around the world when it wasn't even seen illegally fishing! And Dave's unarmed crew were never in a position to board. You're just lucky they chanced upon that naval boat. And what about the hundreds of thousands of dollars that'll be spent on the legal case? And they could still get off the hook. If you'll excuse the pun. The papers will have a field day.'

'Mrs Bates, if I may say, your level of concern for this woman seems unusual. Her husband certainly wasn't thinking about you or David when he fled south and provoked this chase.'

'I'm not saying Carlos Sánchez shouldn't be held to account. He certainly should. As should all the others who are illegally fishing out there right now while we argue about this one boat. I'm simply saying that there are some things — like a father meeting his critically ill child — that are bigger than all this.'

Margie hangs up the phone, proud of her assertiveness, even if it is largely bluff. It won't hurt Roger Wentworth to sweat a bit. She puts the kettle on for a cup of tea and watches the goldfish swimming in their bowl. Around and around they go. Blub, bloody blub. All this for some stupid fish, Margie thinks. Bonnie wanders over to a patch of sun on the kitchen floor and rolls over to expose her soft underbelly. Margie uses her foot to stroke Bonnie's smooth stomach and waits for the water to boil. How happy Sam's dog had been to see her after the hike, she thinks. As she pulled into the driveway, Bonnie had swung her tail in such rapid, excited circles that Margie was sure the dog would take off, propelled upwards, back legs first. She hopes it didn't give Bonnie a false sense of hope that Sam would one day appear up the driveway again.

Dave once told her that when he was a boy, the family dog, a labrador, had been lost off the back of his father's yacht during a storm. The conditions had been too rough to attempt a rescue, his father had said. Margie knows it's why Dave never let Sam take Bonnie with them on the roughy trawler. Sam had insisted that she would be fine on the boat, but Dave was never prepared to put himself in the position of having to make a decision like the one his father had made all those years ago. Margie is pleased now that Dave spared their son that potential loss. After Sascha left him, Bonnie was Sam's whole world.

The kettle reaches its familiar crescendo and Margie pours the boiling water into a mug containing a Darjeeling teabag. She made the ceramic mug during an adult education course some months after Sam died. Margie inspects her design of black swans swimming around the perimeter. Like most of her art at the time, it used only black — the absence of colour — and white. Recently her paintings have again embraced blues, greens, reds and even a splash of yellow, and she welcomes this as a kind of progress. A rediscovery of colour in her art and in her life.

Margie takes her steaming cup of tea into Sam's bedroom, which she has kept largely as he left it, although she does come in here to paint and sew. It keeps the room alive.

Today she peruses his bookshelf, almost without realising she's doing it. Books on hiking in Tasmania, travel and rockclimbing are stacked neatly beside university biology texts and a small collection of novels. She puts down her tea and opens a backpacker's guide to Uruguay, Paraguay and Argentina, and finds several pages bookmarked with scrap paper. They are pages on Uruguay, with sections underlined in pencil. Her son was clearly some way along the path towards organising a trip there. Margie feels the hairs rise on the back of her neck.

A black-and-white photograph of Bonnie devouring a bone stares at her from Sam's noticeboard. Beside the picture, Sam has written: 'Life's short, suck the marrow.' He was right, her philosopher son. When all this is over, and Dave is back on *terra firma*, she'll take a leaf out of Sam's book and organise her own trip to South America. She thinks back to her hike with Joan and how rejuvenating it was. By embracing Sam's life and the things he loved, she has found a way of dealing with his death.

She takes a long sip of tea and carries the travel guide into the lounge room. Through the windows, silvery green eucalypts wave their long, thin flags above the velvet water. The afternoon light strikes two kayakers as they paddle at the base of the cliffs in front of her house. Each dip of the paddle flicks a tiny beam of light her way, a flashing morse code. She can see why people get addicted to adventure. It brings them back to life — makes them focus on the here and now.

There's a knock at the door and Margie heads down the hallway, guidebook still in hand. Through the glass panelling she recognises the outline of Sascha, Sam's ex-girlfriend. Beside her is another figure — a small child. Margie takes a step back. Perhaps she could pretend she's not at home. She feels her heart quicken. How can Sascha just turn up without warning, her child in tow, after not saying a word since Sam's death? Just when I was starting to get my life back together, Margie thinks. She curses under her breath and shakes her hands at her sides, attempting to flick away her annoyance and the underlying fear of facing Sascha again. She sees Bonnie race up the front steps to greet Sam's one and only true love. Bonnie is all over the child too, turning circles on the front veranda like she used to when Sam arrived home. Margie had forgotten those excited, welcoming turns until now.

'Hello, Bonnie,' Margie can hear Sascha saying, her voice frail with emotion. 'How are you, old girl?' Sascha crouches down and gives the dog a hug. 'This is little Scotty.'

Margie wipes her sweaty palms on her trousers and opens the door. Sascha looks up and Margie sees that her face is streaked with tears. The little boy seems confused by Bonnie's affection, and is using his hands to bat away her licks.

'Hello, Margie,' Sascha says, filling the void. 'I'm sorry I've taken so long to come and see you. It's taken me two years to build up the courage.' She is crying now and buries her face in Bonnie's fur. 'You must hate me.'

Margie feels the tears on her own face. She thinks of Sam and how much he loved this girl. But it's as if her feet are planted in concrete. She can't move towards Sascha or even away, and simply stares at the young woman distraught on the doorstep. Sascha's clothes — a white linen shirt and jeans — are fitted and fashionable, just as she had always worn, and her hair is still long, but, as she stands up, Margie notices small lines around her eyes and a loss of fullness in her cheeks. Sam would want me to give her a hug, Margie thinks, finally extending her arms.

Margie draws Sascha towards her. She smells her familiar summery perfume and realises that she never saw Sascha alone, without Sam. They were a pair: soulmates. Margie feels a gaping pain in her chest, as if she has taken a wound to the heart. She ends the embrace and tries to collect herself, but the hole in the universe beside Sascha where Sam should still be is almost unbearable. 'How could I hate you when Sam loved you so much. You were a part of our family, like a daughter.'

Sascha wipes the tears from her face with the back of her hand and reaches down to pick up her child.

'I did wonder though why you never visited after —'

'Margie, I'd like you to meet my son, Scotty,' Sascha says, brushing a red-blond wisp of hair from his forehead.

Margie leans forward and strokes the boy's hair. 'Hello, little man. You're a sweet little fellow, aren't you?'

Bonnie reaches up and licks Scotty's leg.

'Bonnie likes you too,' Margie says.

Face to face with Sascha's young son, Margie can't begin to imagine the pain Sam would have felt upon such an encounter. It was enough that he found out Sascha had left him for someone else. Unsure what to say next, she keeps her attention on the little boy. She places the travel book down on the Huon pine dresser by the front door and uses both hands to tickle the toddler's tummy. He giggles, and Margie is struck anew by the intoxicating laughter of childhood.

She lifts her damp eyes back to Sascha who is biting her top lip, as if trying to stop herself from crying again. Sascha is focused on the travel book. 'We were planning on going to South America together, before I screwed things up.'

'Oh, I'd forgotten that. What a time we've all had.' Margie gives her another hug, with Scotty squirming in between. 'Anyway, what are we all doing on the front doorstep. Come inside. Here, I'll take the little lad for you.' Margie lifts him onto her hip. 'You go ahead, Sascha, into the lounge room and we can have a cup of tea. The kettle's still warm.'

Sascha walks obediently down the hall, her blue eyes darting into the open doorway of Sam's old room. Margie watches her in profile as she turn quickly away, focusing instead on the rest of the house. It occurs to Margie that little has changed since Sascha was last here. The black leather lounge suite is still in the corner, and there are the same photos of Sam as a boy in silver frames. Sascha picks up one of the pictures and studies it closely.

Margie puts Scotty on the lounge-room floor and opens a cupboard, reaching up high for a box. 'I thought I still had them,' she says, putting some of Sam's old toys in front of Scotty, whose eyes light up.

Sascha smiles. 'Thanks.' She pauses. 'I'm sorry to land on you like this. After all this time.' She chews at her fingernails, then closes her eyes and blows her nose hard into an already wet tissue.

'Well, you're here now.' Margie walks into the kitchen and re-boils the kettle. As she makes the tea, she can see Sascha handing Scotty Sam's toys in the lounge room. 'Are your mum and dad well?'

'They're all right.'

'They're very lucky to have such a lovely grandson. *Very* lucky.' Margie puts Sascha's tea onto the table beside her.

'You don't see it, do you? I thought you'd pick it straight away.'

'What do you mean?' Margie takes a sip of her tea before placing it alongside Sascha's so she can get down and sort through the toys with two hands. Her heart feels like it will burst with sadness at seeing all the things that Sam used to play with.

'He's *your* grandson too.'

Margie hears the words just as she hands Scotty a wooden

train. She freezes for several seconds, before letting go of the toy. Her legs weaken beneath her and she sits on the floor beside him. He gazes up at her face.

'Ohhh,' Margie gasps, lifting the boy onto her lap. It's as if the universe has been created anew right in front of her, as if all the elements have been thrown up into the air and have landed in a different order. The shock is as great as somebody telling her that Sam is, in fact, still alive. She holds the small child close and cries over his shoulder. The smell of his hair brings back a flood of memories. Overwhelmed by the attention, Scotty struggles out of her arms and Margie tries to hide her tears from his worried eyes.

'Are you sure?' Margie asks, but she knows it is true.

Sascha nods twice. A small nervous smile has formed on her face. Apprehensive, but hopeful. Her tears, Margie can tell, are again just below the surface.

'Sam's boy.' Margie says the words out loud to cement them in her brain. Looking at him now, his blue eyes and reddish-blond hair, Margie can't believe she didn't see it immediately. But she had always assumed that Sascha had fallen pregnant to the young man she had left Sam for. 'I hadn't even considered it. Not for a minute.'

'I found out I was pregnant after Sam and I broke up. And then he died …' Sascha is crying openly now. Margie puts out an arm and Sascha joins her on the floor, welcoming Margie's arms around her. Bonnie trots through the back door and, seeing the commotion, joins in.

'Oh, Sascha. Is that why you haven't been to visit? Were you scared of what we'd say?'

'Yes. And the longer I left it, the harder it got.'

Margie waits a moment before asking her next question. 'And your boyfriend, does he know the truth?'

Sascha wipes her nose with the back of her hand. 'We broke up long before I had Scotty when I told him I still loved Sam, but by then it was all too late.' Sascha plucks a fresh tissue out of the box on the coffee table and sobs into it.

'Then why did you break up with Sam in the first place?'

'I don't know. I think I was afraid of how serious we were getting. He was my first real boyfriend. Mum and Dad were telling me I should meet other boys too. Sam said he wanted us to get married, and I was so confused.'

Scotty searches his mother's face and she holds him tight.

'Do your parents know who Scotty's *real* father is?' Margie asks.

'Yes, of course ...'

'Why on earth didn't you tell us?'

'I thought it'd just make things harder for you. I thought it'd be the last thing you needed to hear and I wasn't sure you'd accept me or Scotty into your lives after everything you'd been through. And after everything I put Sam through in his last few weeks. Mum said to just leave it be.'

'Well she was wrong! How could we not want to know that Sam had a little boy? That we have a grandson?' Margie's sadness fuses with anger.

'I'm so sorry …'

Margie shakes her head. 'The main thing is that you've told us now …' For a second time, she buries her nose into Scotty's curls and their comforting scent. 'My grandson,' she says quietly, 'I can't believe it. Neither will Dave. We've also been grieving for the grandchildren we thought we'd never have …'

'Do you think he'll be okay about it?'

'It'll take a while to sink in, but he'll be thrilled.' Margie thinks of Dave and wonders if what she has just said is true. If he'll be ready yet to open his heart again. Whether she herself is ready. With love comes the risk of loss. She knows it only too well. But closing her heart is no way to live. Given the choice to love again or not, she will always choose to love.

LOGBOOK OF EDUARDO RODRÍGUEZ TORRES

∽

*Most seabirds have salt glands, allowing them to drink
seawater if necessary. How marvellous is nature, how clever
to devise such a system. As for me, I think I will be eternally
thirsty, never sated.*

*I have it all with Virginia and my beautiful daughters,
but it is still not enough. Not enough when I know how
perfect love can be. I have had to choose, and in choosing
I have closed down a part of my heart. Even here, at sea,
I have had to decide between right and wrong, and I fear I
have made the wrong choice.*

∽

CARLOS
The *Pescador*
12 October 2002

Carlos Sánchez is roused from sleep by the brutish young South African, one of the three armed South Africans assigned to the *Pescador* for the two-week journey back to Fremantle.

'There's an email from your wife, with a picture of your baby. Doesn't look too flash,' the South African says provocatively, looking for a reaction from the inert fishing master who has barely spoken since the *Pescador* was apprehended.

Carlos feels his heart race. He spoke to Julia just yesterday and their baby was okay. A week old, she said. 'You opened my email?'

'Of course. What did you expect?'

'*¡Pendejo!*' Carlos curses, throwing back his sleeping bag and filling the small cabin with the smell of stale sweat and unwashed skin.

'There's not much to see anyway. It'd fit in my boot.' The South African holds up his foot.

'*¡Vete al infierno!*' Carlos rises stiffly from his bunk, and makes his way to the computer at the corner of the mess. Before the boarding, all the crew had been able to send and receive emails from a communal address, but an unspoken rule dictated that no one would stoop so low as to read the personal messages of their crewmates.

Carlos opens the email, the South African still at his side like a vulture clawing at its injured prey. He reads the short message from Julia and opens the attachment, his index finger shaking as it hovers over the mouse. The picture emerges line by line from the top of the screen. There is a faint spray of very short dark hair, not the mop that María was born with, but then she was born full term. He makes out a rounded forehead, eyes squeezed shut against the world, and a nose largely covered with sticky plaster, which appears to be holding in place a small plastic tube. Scrolling down he sees his son's delicate mouth, the tiny red lips parted as if yawning or gasping for air. He hopes it's the former.

When the whole picture has downloaded, Carlos sits back in the plastic seat and stares at the screen. The baby's head is partly turned to the left, revealing a crumpled right ear that is folded over, as if glued down, at its outer rim. Carlos feels an immense rush of love and a need to protect this tiny creature. A pen has been placed beside the baby for scale. It is half his son's length, he realises with a start. The baby *would* fit in a man's boot. What chance does his son have?

He re-reads the first part of Julia's message: 'Little Eduardo still weighs less than one kilogram, and is just thirty centimetres long.' It hadn't meant much until he had seen the comparison of his baby with the pen.

'Looks like a skinned rabbit, doesn't it?' the young South African taunts, just as his superior arrives at the door.

'Give the man some peace!' the older man orders.

'I was just making sure —'

'Making sure of what? That this man isn't allowed an ounce of human dignity? That he knows, without a doubt, that you're a pathetic excuse for a man? What's he going to do, dispose of his illegal catch via email? In any case, he's innocent until proven guilty.'

'Shall I go then?'

'Your powers of perception astonish me. Yes, go. As far away from me as this boat will allow.'

The young South African leaves the room like a scolded child.

'I apologise,' the senior naval officer says, seeing the picture on the screen. 'Some of these lads still have a fair bit of growing up to do.' He shakes his head. 'Your son will pull through. They work miracles these days, the doctors.'

'I hope so,' Carlos says in stilted English.

'There's nothing you can do from here. There'd be nothing you could do even if you were there.'

'I could touch him. I could hold my wife.'

'Yes. Of course. Well, let's hope this illegal-fishing matter can be resolved swiftly in the Australian courts.'

'*Gracias.*' Carlos prints out a copy of the picture and tries to imagine the tiny form, his son, growing into a sturdy man who will accompany him on fishing trips. It seems impossible.

No longer permitted to remain in the wheelhouse, and with no desire to be there anyway, Carlos returns in silence to the crew's quarters.

He closes his eyes, but doesn't sleep. Obsessive, anxious thoughts engulf him. How can Julia deal with all of this on her own? How can she have anything left emotionally for María? '*¡Me jodí!*' Carlos swears out loud at himself, taking the blame for the entire mess — the disastrous expedition, Eduardo's death and his baby's premature birth, brought on, he fears, by the stress this chase has caused his wife. If he was at home now, he would hold his wife and daughter and only let go to take María outside to play in the back garden, where he could pretend, for just a moment, that life was still good. He wonders if it will ever feel good again. He imagines Julia smoothing his brow, kissing his eyelids closed. He imagines stroking her long hair and consoling her in return. At least his mother-in-law is there now, he thinks. Julia will be able to drop her guard from time to time. Keeping a lid on this level of emotion would poison his wife.

Carlos imagines their baby in the humidicrib, struggling for oxygen. He pictures his miniature face, with its squinted eyes, and slightly misshapen ear, no doubt bent from lying too long on one side. The ear's crêpe-like skin appeared so thin in the picture that it was transparent. He could almost see the tiny veins transporting their cargo of bright red blood — his own blood.

Carlos finds himself talking with God, uttering a prayer for the first time since he was a boy. At the end, he asks what he has done wrong to deserve this ultimate of punishments — the potential death of his child. Is he a bad person? Why is Julia also being forced to suffer? But there is no answer.

He feels betrayed. Betrayed by God and angry at life for what it is asking of him. If his son dies, he doesn't know if he has what it takes to survive. What does it take? Would he even want to go on living? For the sake of María and Julia, the answer must be yes, but he suspects such sadness would turn him into a different man.

He looks out through a porthole and prays to the sea instead. He asks it to lull him to sleep, to numb his mind and ease his pain. He contemplates the photograph — taped now to the hull wall beside the porthole — of Julia at Eduardo's father's boatshed. He takes it from the wall, again studying the handwriting on the back. It's odd, he thinks, that she didn't mention going to the boatshed, but then what was there to tell? He wishes he had alcohol with him to deaden the answerless ache in his soul.

He dreams he is again visited by Eduardo. This time the first mate's face is gnarled and worn away by the ocean. His once-handsome friend teases him with his newfound ghoulishness. Eduardo opens his mouth and a small fish swims out in a trail of black filth that stains the water like squid ink. Eduardo reaches out his hand, but it's not for him. It is for his tiny child.

'No!' Carlos wakes with a start, shocked by the loudness of his own voice. He doesn't understand the dream. He doesn't understand reality. The space between the two seems infinitesimally small.

Manuel brings him food, but he rejects it, taking only a sip of warm, over-sweetened tea. The effect is nauseating. He has dealt with much in his life at sea: enormous waves, extreme weather, ice and injury. He pleads to be dealt another challenge like that. Something he can recognise and fight. Instead fate is toying with the most vulnerable member of his family, and tying his own hands at the same time.

Hope, Julia wrote in her email to him, is a powerful force. At the moment, Carlos realises, it is all he has. He dares to dream again that one day he will take his son fishing. He would give his right arm to have the chance to teach the boy how to read the clouds, the sea, and the birds that speak of fish. How to tie ropes and fix salt-encrusted engines; to work with men on the most levelling platform on Earth. He rolls onto his side, re-attaches the photograph of Julia to the hull wall that separates him narrowly from the ocean, and, with his fingers gently touching the image of his wife's face, lets the tears come.

LOGBOOK OF EDUARDO RODRÍGUEZ TORRES

∽

In another world we are together. I can touch your hair and enfold myself in its scent. There are no boundaries keeping us apart. It is as it was supposed to be.

∽

JULIA
La Paloma, Uruguay
20 October 2002

Julia is waiting outside the Hospital Maciel in the old part of the city for a bus to the open-air markets at Plaza Cagancha. It's a warm day in the Ciudad Vieja and the sunlight touches her bare arms with the familiarity and grace of an old forgotten friend.

Two weeks and two days have passed since her baby was born and the doctors have told her they would stake their reputations on him coming home within a couple of months. The good news has seen her begin to emerge, little by little, from her cocoon — her self-spun protection. After so many days crouched beside the humidicrib — wet with anxious perspiration and tears under the cold, artificial lights of the hospital — she is finally testing her wings again in the outside world, wondering if they will hold her. She stands tall and surveys her surrounds from her new, higher vantage point, as if she is, indeed, a newly emerged winged insect — a moth or perhaps even a butterfly. The resilient antique beauty of the old Spanish buildings, which have endured so much, resonates with her. She notices, too, old men and women, who would have lived through Uruguay's political uprisings, walking hand in hand with small children, perhaps their grandchildren, leading them forward towards brighter futures.

With her baby doing better, Julia's thoughts are now on his namesake. Until today, she hadn't had the energy for both. She could only deal with one trauma at a time. When Carlos told her, over a week ago, that Eduardo had died at sea, she had felt unusually calm, but completely empty. Part of her had died too, she realises now. Carlos had cried when he passed on the soul-shattering news, something she had known him to do only twice before in their marriage: once, five years ago, when his father died, and then when he phoned from sea earlier this month, after hearing that their son had been born prematurely. Her tears — the proper ones — she knew would come later.

She reads her watch. It's still early. Maybe today is the day.

She walks a few paces to a phone box and dials her home number. Her mother answers. 'Julia, is there a problem? Is our little boy all right?'

'*Mamá*, stop asking me that. Everything is fine. Our little boy is going to make it.'

Julia hears her mother whisper a small prayer.

'I'm taking a bus to La Paloma. I need to get away for the day.'

'Why there?' her mother asks.

'Because I have to.' Part of Julia longs to tell her mother more. To admit to her that she needs to confront her grief over Eduardo's death head on. To admit having loved him. To let her know that she can't go forward without meeting his ghost and saying goodbye. 'I'll be home later tonight. Don't wait up. And if there's no bus tonight, I'll see you tomorrow.' Julia ends the phone call before her mother can say anything else, and peruses the bus timetable posted on the wall of the phone box. There's a bus heading north along the Atlantic coast in ten minutes. Her shopping trip can wait.

The beaches bleach white as the bus propels her back through time. The water becomes clearer and cleaner, and there is the dusty smell of coastal vegetation through the open bus window. Julia doesn't even feel herself fall asleep.

His hand slides up the inside of her arm, and she can taste salt on his lips. Her fingers are in his hair, drawing him closer as he bites at her neck. He takes her hands in his, pinning them above her head as he lifts and consumes her. Her ring finger is in his mouth, her wedding band touching Eduardo's lips.

When she opens her eyes, it is the woman on the bus seat beside her who is touching her hand, rousing her from sleep.

'La Paloma,' the woman says. 'Didn't I hear you tell the driver you were getting off here?'

Julia checks her watch. '*Gracias,*' she whispers as the familiar headland comes into view. There's a rush of blood through her veins, but it is from dread this time, not excitement. Those teenage flutters have finally been extinguished. Even the more recent memory of an afternoon spent here with Eduardo is now infused with sorrow, and the dream, just moments ago, is already a relic from another time — a parallel universe. She steps out heavily onto the uneven pavement and makes the short walk across town to the northern beach. The surf is breaking unforgivingly against the sand, paring back layers, stripping back the years.

Eduardo is calling her.

She can see his father's boatshed, nestled in the bushes. The dinghy is now on a trailer outside, the varnish beginning to peel from the gunnels. The last time she was here, Eduardo had just finished restoring it. How quickly it has begun to deteriorate. The window at the back of the shed is shut, probably forever. She inhales the salty air released by exploding waves, and closes her eyes as the wind pushes her along the sand, its soft warmth filtering through her leather sandals like someone's loving caress.

Finally she begins to let go of her emotions. Her head spins and she steadies herself against the boatshed's front door. The salt-white wood is chalky against her hand and reminds her of blackboards from her teaching days, a lifetime ago. For all of Eduardo's father's best efforts, the building is crumbling into the sand. Salt has wedged itself firmly into the grains of wood, creating time capsules of winds and storms past. Even now, as she braces herself to enter, sharp crystals tear at the wood, cutting and splitting it as the timber expands and contracts with the warmth of sunlight and the chill of shade.

Julia pushes against the unlocked door, and the boatshed welcomes her home with the smell of nets and bait boxes, a smell she wouldn't have been able to describe had she been asked before now. In an instant she remembers it all. She sees herself walking this same path in March, her hair hanging loose, her legs and arms bare except for a hint of sandalwood perfume and the caress of her red-flowered dress. She longs for Eduardo, her first love; she longs to be safe again in his arms. She leans back against the heavy door, closing it behind her, and begins to weep deeply, loudly. 'Eduardo!' she cries out, airing her grief.

'Who's there?' a female voice ventures from the back of the shed. 'Who is it?' The woman is standing now, and, with a start, Julia recognises Eduardo's widow, Virginia.

'*Hola.*' Julia fails to hide the surprise in her voice. She feels naked, caught out. 'It's Julia, Virginia. I'm so sorry. I thought I was alone. Carlos told me about Eduardo. I'm sorry I haven't been up to see you yet. I was on my way. *Lo siento,*' she apologises again.

Eduardo's widow flicks on a light and Julia observes that she too has been crying. Virginia is pale and tired, and obviously confused. Julia rushes to embrace her, but it's an awkward, one-sided gesture. The two women have managed a measure of friendship over the years, but, for reasons neither of them has ever articulated, it has always felt strained. No more so than now.

'But why are you here?' Virginia's voice shakes. She looks Julia up and down, as though seeing her for the first time.

'I needed to gather myself first,' Julia lies. 'I didn't want your girls seeing me like this and I didn't know where else to go.'

Virginia frowns, unconvinced. 'When is the *Pescador* due back?'

Julia wipes her dripping nose on the back of her hand. 'They're on their way to Australia.'

'*Si*, Carlos told me. And you still don't know how long they'll be kept there?'

Julia shakes her head. 'We'll all miss Eduardo terribly.' Caught in the frame of Virginia's suspicious stare, it is all she can do to stand still and not flee. 'Carlos didn't tell me how it happened. How he died. Do you know?'

'Conditions were bad. He was clearing ice off the rails,' Virginia says, her face wincing as if she is feeling the bite of a Southern Ocean gale herself. 'The boat pitched and he slipped and went over. His harness failed somehow, or … Carlos said he might have released himself, believing that the boat would come back to rescue him.' Virginia uses a white linen handkerchief to absorb the tears from her eyes. 'The seas were big and he was being beaten against the hull.' She covers her face with her hand. 'I came here to have a few moments to myself. Away from the girls. We've all been crying together, of course, but I've been trying to stay strong for them. It's terrible. I haven't slept.' She looks at Julia and her expression softens marginally. 'I heard about your son being born early. I'm also sorry *I* haven't been in touch. Carlos had just told me about Eduardo and I was still in such a state of shock. Is he doing okay, your little boy?'

'*Si*. He'll be in hospital for a while yet, but he's doing much better. *Gracias.*'

'Strange that he was born the same day that Eduardo died.'

It feels to Julia that time has stopped. 'My God,' she whispers shakily. She falls silent, taking it all in. 'I didn't know.' She searches for something else to say. 'We were going to ask Eduardo to be his godfather. We've named our son after him.'

'You've called your baby Eduardo?'

'*Si*,' Julia answers, fishing for acceptance. It occurs to her that perhaps this fact alone might be enough justification for why she was here, calling out the name of Virginia's husband. She takes a step closer and rests her hand on Virginia's forearm. 'And I know what you're saying about staying strong. About keeping your emotions bottled up. I've been the same way in front of María.' Julia's eyes drop to the place on the floor where she made love with Eduardo earlier this year. She steps away again, sickened by her own dishonesty. 'I'm sorry to have intruded. *Lo siento.*' It occurs to her for the first time that this place was probably also sacred to Virginia. How could she have assumed she was the only person to have been here with Eduardo? His wife probably made love with him among the nets countless times. 'I'll leave you now. This is your place. And Eduardo's father's.'

'*Si*, he was here earlier today. I saw his car.'

'Of course. Let me know if there's anything I can do to help,' Julia says as she walks, backwards, to the door.

'You don't want to come up to the house? It's a long way to come just for the afternoon?'

'No, I've seen you now, so I should get back. *Mamá* is minding María. *Hasta luego*.' Julia sees Virginia sitting back down, her normally trusting face torn apart by doubt as well as grief. She wants to sprint but forces herself to walk back along the beach — this time the wind is in her face — until she is out of sight of the boatshed. As she leaves the beach, the sand drains from her sandals and she knows that she will not return here. She looks at her watch and breaks into a run. If she goes straight to the bus station now, she should be home again by nightfall.

LOGBOOK OF EDUARDO RODRÍGUEZ TORRES

❧

From the decks of the Pescador *I've now seen both species of Antarctic skua: the southern skua and the Antarctic skua. These birds mate for life, and migrate between hemispheres.*

❧

CARLOS
The *Pescador*
24 October 2002

The sound of a helicopter flying low overhead wakes Carlos, who is on his back on his bunk in the crew's quarters. The other three men in the shared cabin — Roberto's son and two other young Spaniards — are still asleep. It's a different feeling, being down in the bowels of the ship, separated from the wheelhouse by three flights of stairs. One of the crew joked with him that he'd fallen from grace and descended into hell itself, and it seemed the truest thing that anyone had said for days. Carlos stands and walks out into the passageway, but is met by the young South African naval officer and his gun.

'I just want to get some air,' Carlos says.

The South African follows him out on to the deck and stands over him as he walks to the rails and grips the cold metal that separates him from the sea. Carlos puts a foot on the first rung, and the South African grabs hold of the Uruguayan master's jacket.

'Don't do anything stupid.' The naval officer uses his gun to push Carlos's foot off the rails.

'I am not going to jump.' Carlos attempts a laugh, but it sounds more like a cry. He looks out across the pale green sea to the Australian coast. His last dream comes to him. It's

Eduardo again, pointing the finger of blame at him for suggesting this trip in the first place. Life would have turned out very differently for all of them if they'd stayed on shore.

He thinks of home — of Julia, María and the new baby. They need him, but he wonders if he is worthy of their love. What sort of father robs another man's fish so he can feed his family, only to fail? In the end he has taken the food from his own family's mouths. How will Julia support the children on her own? And God knows how much he will have to pay in fines and legal expenses before he returns. Migiliaro won't cough up. Carlos kicks his seaboot against the rails, the same rails that stole Eduardo from him only three weeks ago.

A dolphin appears beside the boat, shooting out of the water and into the air. It spins in mid-flight before piercing the ocean and swimming towards the bow. He can see it, between the waves, just under the surface. A second dolphin appears, then a third and fourth. A family, Carlos supposes, playing together. He tells himself to be patient.

DAVE
The *Australis*
24 October 2002

With the sandy, flat coast of Western Australia now in their sights, Dave allows himself a moment to realise that the sea chase is almost over. He sees the *Pescador* ahead of him in the early-morning light and wonders what her crew will be feeling at this moment.

Television helicopters circle in large sweeps overhead, buzzing the sky like overgrown dragonflies. Cameramen hang out the sides taking footage of the two vessels advancing into port — the bad guys and the good guys.

A seagull is just ahead of the boat now, heading for shore. How easily it flies, Dave thinks, watching through binoculars as it pierces the dark water and surfaces with a small fish flapping for dear life. Only a few nautical miles ahead the water changes colour from its inky oceanic lacquer to a lighter, more inviting blue (Margie would know the exact name of the colour), and, finally, to a luminous green close to shore. Dave tries to focus on the job at hand, but Margie's news, delivered via satellite phone nearly two weeks ago, is still consuming him, buoying him with a fresh sense of optimism. The impossible seems possible. A grandson. Scotty.

It almost feels like Sam has come back to life, and, in a sense, Dave supposes, that is true.

The *Pescador* docks at Fremantle Harbour ahead of the *Australis*, which berths only metres astern of her. Dave can hardly believe the two boats are finally stationary, and in such close proximity. If they'd been this close on the high seas, they would have had only seconds before a collision.

Television crews mill about the concrete pier. Freshly coiffured journalists eagerly deliver their pieces to camera with the blood-red hulls as a backdrop. Dave wonders what they have found to report — what version of the truth their news services will broadcast. He observes a collection of swarthy suits mustering in readiness for interviews, and recognises the Fisheries Minister and various other bureaucrats keen for their moment in the sun. Roger Wentworth is no doubt among them.

The Australian crew aboard the *Pescador* expertly work the deck, securing the mooring lines. Dave watches as the three armed South Africans appear, herding the illegal vessel's crew in a straight line towards the rails. He wonders which of the Latin faces belongs to Carlos Sánchez.

On his own boat, the crew is also at work securing the vessel to the pier. Cactus, hands cupped around his mouth to direct his voice, appears to be calling out to the South Americans at the rails of the *Pescador*. Knowing Cactus, the comments will be childish and inappropriate, but the *Pescador*'s crew ignore him. Dave hopes the television cameras do the same, although attracting their attention will be precisely what Cactus is hoping for. Anything to get himself on the evening news.

Two refrigerated trucks pull up alongside the *Pescador*, disturbing a flock of seagulls. Reporters, too, squawk, disband and regroup. They smooth down their hairdos as though unruffling feathers. The truck drivers lumber onto the pier and unlock the back doors in readiness for receiving the now confiscated catch. Dougal McAllister leaves the *Pescador* via the gangway and the TV cameras meet him as he steps onto the dock to supervise. Dave is quietly amused by the way the young fisheries officer seems to savour the media attention, growing several centimetres in stature, and assuming an air of heroism. The South Africans also seem to have found an excuse to move closer to the cameras. They are on the dock, helping to fasten lines to the bollards, weapons still at their sides. Only the men charged with illegal fishing seem unaffected by the media circus.

An Australian Federal Police car is parked alongside a coroner's van, presumably to take the dead Spaniard and Russian away for examination. Dave suspects it will be weeks, months even, before the families of the deceased finally receive the bodies. He thinks, too, of the dead first mate, lost at sea, and wonders which, if any, of the *Pescador*'s crew will be charged with the deaths. He again scans the people gathered on shore. Somewhere amidst the hubbub will be a representative from the Uruguayan consulate because, in the eyes of the law, deaths on a vessel at sea are seen to have occurred in the country where that vessel is registered.

Two Australian Federal Police officers approach the *Pescador* and make their way up the gangway, no doubt to lay the official charges for illegal fishing. Their black suits look absurd on the decks of the working boat. Dave knows the police will have no understanding of what the men aboard the *Pescador* have just endured — the massive seas, the ice, the fear, the deaths — but his thoughts are interrupted by a radio call from Harry in the illegal vessel's wheelhouse.

'The Minister's office has been trying to call you, Davo. You'd better check the satellite phone.'

Dave does as Harry suggests and sees that it is still off the hook after a dawn phone call from Margie. 'Sorry, mate. My mistake.'

'He wants us all to assemble here for a media conference.'

'I'll leave that to you blokes, I think, thanks,' Dave answers. 'No need for us all to put in our two bobs' worth. I'm sure the Minister will be pleased for the opportunity to give the Australian point of view.'

'No doubt,' Harry says with a laugh. 'But the media have asked specifically for *you*. And if they don't get you here, they'll be chasing you on shore, *and* in the hotel, *and* back home. You won't have a moment's peace. Might as well get it out of the way. Can you get here in ten minutes with Cactus and maybe one other?'

Dave runs his fingers through his rough beard, thinking he'll just have enough time to shave. 'Righto, see you in ten.'

He puts a call out on the intercom for Cactus and William to make their way to the wheelhouse.

'Looks like you'll have your chance to get on the telly, Cactus,' Dave tells him when he barrels through the door.

'I would've killed you if you didn't ask me.'

'I know,' Dave jokes. 'Wasn't worth the angst. Anyway, I'm just going to have a shave and change my shirt. Can you man the radio for a few minutes? You're looking pretty spruced up already.'

'Fancy meself a bit of Fremantle skirt tonight, that's why.' Cactus winks suggestively and takes up his position by the radio.

'Spare me the image.' Dave grimaces good-naturedly. 'We'll meet at the top of the gangway in ten. I'll get one of the other lads up here to take any calls while we're gone. Unless, of course, you'd like to stay on the radio yourself.'

'No thanks.' Cactus winks again and clicks his tongue. 'She'll be right.'

Dave hurries to his cabin and flattens out a clean shirt with his hands. Not ideal for a TV interview, he thinks. Margie will have a pink fit, but he's been at sea for six weeks, three of which have been taken up with this chase. What can she expect? If it were cooler, he'd probably try to hide the shirt under a jumper, but the west coast of Australia has turned on a spring day to rival the high summer temperatures of just about anywhere else. He'll simply have to be crumpled. Weathered.

He takes his electric razor and peers into his hand-held mirror. It's days since he's seen his own face and he's surprised by what greets him. His beard is fuller, and greyer, than he had realised. It's certainly too thick to do away with quickly now.

He thinks of Margie and imagines her frowning at the growth on his face. He wonders how she's dealing with the news of Sam's baby and whether she is also feeling torn — pleased about the offer of rescue, of a new future, but unable to decide whether to risk accepting, for a second time, the hand of fate. Dave feels as if he has been drifting in a life raft, having had his own boat sink from under him. As if, suddenly, from nowhere, a ship's searchlights are on him and the full weight of the vessel is bearing down towards the raft. He was almost getting used to the confined space, the closeness of his crew and the distance from everyone else. Now he has to choose whether to catch a lift back to shore.

Part of him wonders if it's Sam up there behind the searchlight, directing the beam.

He inspects his beard in the mirror. At least the grey gives him a distinguished quality befitting a sea captain, he thinks. He opts to simply neaten the edges, laughing out loud at his own vanity.

When he reaches the gangway, Cactus and William are already waiting. Cactus sets off down the ramp, ensuring that he is received fairly and squarely by the hungry line of television cameras. He takes his hand off the rail to wave at the media scrum, but is distracted by someone shouting his name.

Dave sees Connie, rosy-cheeked and cheerful, waving amidst the sea of television cameras. Cactus sees her too and catches his foot on a raised join in the ramp, falling face-first onto the concrete pier. Connie is there in an instant and the television cameras film the whole thing. Some of the cameramen are laughing.

'Come on, up you hop,' Dave says with a smirk as he gives Cactus a hand up and delivers him into his wife's loving embrace. Dave leans over to give Connie a kiss on her hot, fleshy cheek. 'It's good to see you, Connie. Do you mind if we steal him for a few more minutes? We're needed for interviews on the other boat.'

Connie gives Cactus's hand a visible squeeze. 'Sounds like you're going to be famous, Jackie boy.'

A television journalist asks Cactus what it feels like to be on dry land.

'Hard,' Cactus, says, rubbing a bruised forehead. The media contingent laughs again. Under the watchful eye of a government minder, they agree not to ask further questions until they are aboard the *Pescador* for the official, pre-arranged media conference.

Roger Wentworth thrusts a flaccid hand at Dave. 'Well done, David, mate. Good effort. We've done it.'

'Yes *we* have,' Dave confirms, bristling. He turns to walk up the gangway and on to the Uruguayan-flagged boat. It catches him off-guard to feel that he is now the intruder on foreign territory. Armed South Africans stand between him and the illegal vessel's crew. Dave's eyes scan the row of assembled men and fall on a defeated-looking South American who is being closely guarded by a young naval officer with a brutish air. The *Bremner*'s officer appears to be taunting the fisherman, who isn't responding. The South American has dark hair drawn back into a ponytail, which is how Harry had described the *Pescador*'s master. Dave recognises depression in his eyes and in his stooped posture, and notices the respectful way he is regarded by the crew. He steps forward, extending his hand.

'*Capitán* Sánchez?' Dave asks, but he already knows the answer.

The Uruguayan master meets Dave's hand reservedly.

'My apologies, Captain Bates,' the South African naval officer intervenes. 'This is the *Pescador*'s fishing master, Car—'

'Yes, I gathered.' Dave looks into Carlos's eyes and ventures a small respectful smile as he places his other hand on top of the handshake. 'That was quite a chase,' he says.

Carlos nods, his full lips pursed in agreement.

'Sounds like you've been having a pretty rough time of it, all round,' Dave acknowledges, speaking more slowly and clearly than normal. But, from what Harry has said, the Uruguayan master speaks reasonable English. 'I'm sorry to hear about the loss of life on your boat. And I hope things turn out all right for you and your family. For your baby son ...'

Carlos's face registers surprise at the Australian master's genuine concern.

'*Gracias*. Please, if you can help me to get home —' he manages to say before the government's public-relations officer, having noticed the interaction, claps his hands together.

'Might be time to get started.' He motions for Dave to move away from the Uruguayan master and to return to his side of the deck.

The media rallies like rounded-up sheep. Most of the cameramen missed this most newsworthy of encounters in their efforts to get cameras secured to tripods, batteries checked and light levels set. And the journalists — all hair, lipstick and power jackets — seem content to wait for the official government story to be told. When it comes to getting access to federal ministers, they know how best to play the game.

'We decided it's better to have the media conference out here in the light where there's more room,' the PR officer says to the waiting media contingent. 'That way you can get some shots of the full crew of illegals. Is everyone ready?' He raises his eyebrows expectantly at the Minister.

The Minister clears his throat and begins spruiking in the language of politics and propaganda. He portrays the *Pescador*'s crew as the greedy bad guys. Terms like 'terrorists of the sea', 'illegal aliens' and 'pirates' are bandied about while the cameramen scan up and down the line of assembled South Americans and Spaniards.

The Minister then mentions the determination of the selfless Australian crew, pointing to Dave, Cactus, William and Harry, who has just appeared on deck. Harry waves a hello to Dave, and the television cameras film them obligingly.

'These men have risked their lives to defend Australian waters and our valuable fisheries,' the Minister continues. 'They have ensured that we send a strong message to other illegal boats who might consider poaching in our waters.'

Dave is uncomfortable with the attention and wishes he could be swallowed into the cracks of the deck. He suspects Harry feels the same. Cactus, on the other hand, has regained his composure after his fall, and is having one last shot at glory. He is standing impressively tall and Dave notices that the small graze on his forehead is attracting the cameramen's attention. No doubt the reporters will use it to illustrate the case that the crew risked life and limb to bring the illegal boat home. No one need know that the graze was the result of a graceless disembarkation onto the Fremantle pier. That wouldn't fit the story.

The Minister's minder addresses the media again, pointing out David: 'Captain David Bates here, master of the *Australis*, will gladly answer your questions. However, I would like to remind you that because the illegal boat's master has not yet been formally questioned, neither he nor the *Pescador*'s crew are available for interviews at this early stage.'

'No, we can't have them being seen as human beings,' Dave whispers in William's ear. The media scrum breaks up and heads first for the Fisheries Minister, who, Dave suspects, will be out of here within a few minutes and on the next plane back to Canberra.

Cactus, Harry and William are then asked to stand out of the way, as the PR officer directs the cameras' glassy eyes towards the Australian master. Carlos, having been paraded for long enough in front of the cameras, is being shepherded back inside. Dave wonders when, or if, he will have the opportunity to speak with him again.

The journalists fire a barrage of mostly predictable questions. Only one reporter, a middle-aged dark-haired woman with a Spanish accent asks him a question he hadn't expected. 'Captain Bates, I noticed that you shook the hand of *Señor* Sánchez. Was that out of respect or sympathy?'

'I think that will be all.' The government minder claps his hands again. 'The police need access to the boat now. There will be an opportunity for further questions soon. We'll advise you of a time.'

Dave watches as Carlos disappears inside the *Pescador*, the young South African naval officer's gun at his back for effect. It's difficult to believe this defeated Uruguayan is the same man who mastered this vessel through some of the worst seas on the planet.

Dave turns back to the Spanish journalist and answers quietly: 'A bit of both.'

MARGIE
Hobart, Australia
30 October 2002

Margie Bates studies her husband in profile as he sits, bathed in golden afternoon light, on the back veranda. She can hardly believe he is finally back on home soil. His hair is longer than he normally wears it and he has grown a short beard, but she has decided not to say anything. In fact, she thinks, she could almost grow to like it. He is facing out to sea and leaning forward, elbows on knees, tying knots in the ends of a piece of rope. It's what he does when he's nervous. She checks her watch. Sascha and Scotty were due to arrive a few minutes ago. She tries to distract him.

'When do they want you back in Fremantle for the hearings, love?'

'Not for at least a month — maybe two.'

'Right.' Margie struggles to think of what to say next, her mind also preoccupied with seeing her grandson again.

Bonnie wanders over to Dave and licks his hands. He gives her a pat and looks out to the water, to a swarm of boats gliding downstream on the wide, gentle expanse of the Derwent River.

'A grandson, can you believe it?' Margie says, deciding to articulate what they're both afraid of. 'A little Sam.' Tears well in her eyes and, she suspects, from the way her husband tips back his head, also in Dave's.

'Nope. It's pretty damned amazing.' Dave's tears overflow.

Bonnie slinks off the veranda, towards an old bone on the lawn, and Margie turns away while Dave blows his nose and wipes his face dry. She goes to sit on his lap, brushing back his faded red hair with her hand.

'Any more news of the Uruguayan master's son?' she asks.

'Still hanging on by all accounts.'

'Listen, there's something I have to tell you about all that …'

'Let me guess. You've been emailing his wife and have been putting a cat amongst the pigeons in Canberra, trying to get Carlos Sánchez sent home to be tried in Uruguay.'

Margie fails to hide her grin. 'You've heard!'

'Yep.'

'Are you cross?'

'Nope.' He smacks a kiss onto her lips.

'I didn't want to get you into trouble. But I'd promised Julia Sánchez that I'd see what I could do. To ask the stupid idiots in Canberra if there was any way Carlos could see his little boy.'

'Not much chance of pulling it off though, I gather?'

'No. Callous pigs.'

'I made a few enquiries myself in Fremantle. There's Buckley's of him being allowed home, even if it's only for a few days. It doesn't fit at all with the government's hard line on the illegals.'

'I'm surprised.'

'I'm not.'

'No, I mean I'm surprised at you looking into it. That bloke nearly led you to your death!'

'Don't get me wrong. I think he should get what's coming to him if he was fishing illegally. I just don't think we need to be completely heartless about it. The poor bugger's in a really bad way. Anyway, it's the owner of the boat we should be dragging over the coals. Not Carlos and his crew.'

'I love you, Dave Bates.'

'You too.' He shifts uncomfortably in his seat.

'You okay?'

'I think my leg's gone to sleep. I might have to get you to hop off for a while, love. I'm not as tough as I used to be. And you're a *grandma* now, don't forget.'

'And that makes me heavier, does it?'

'Apparently.' Dave winces, complaining of pins and needles in his leg. Margie laughs at the grimace on his face.

'By the way, how do you feel about having a holiday in South America?' she asks.

'To pursue this legal stuff?'

'No, just a holiday.'

Dave stretches his leg back and forth.

'Do you remember Sam had plans to go there?'

'Vaguely', Dave says, trying to stand.

'I came across an earmarked page in one of his travel books. I'd really like to go. And I'd quite like to track down Julia Sánchez, but only as a social visit. I don't want to make it a hugely long trip, not now that we have little Scotty.'

'When are you thinking of going?'

'Sometime within the next year or so.' Margie hesitates. 'But I'd like Scotty to get to know us first. What do you think?'

'Maybe. But we'll have to see where I sit with the trial. Let's play it by ear.' Dave is finally standing on both feet evenly, the pins and needles evidently gone.

'I could be waiting forever.' Margie laughs. 'Maybe I should go on my own. It'll do you good to be worried about *my* safety for once.' She watches him closely for a reaction. None is forthcoming. 'But you probably wouldn't even give it a second thought, you ratbag. You'd enjoy the peace and quiet!'

The telephone rings and Margie runs to answer it, after realising that Dave, who was closer to the phone, wasn't going to. He had met her eyes and stepped out of the way, and she saw just how nervous he was about even talking to Sascha again.

After perhaps thirty seconds, Margie reappears on the veranda and takes Dave's hand. 'They'll be here in about five minutes. She apologised for being late. Scotty has only just woken up.'

Dave opens his mouth to speak, but his voice catches in

his throat. He coughs and tries again. 'I'm just going to do a bit more work on that swing.'

Margie watches Dave make his way to the bottom of the garden and adjust the ropes on Sam's old tyre swing, which he has tied to the branch of a large eucalypt. It's the same strong, horizontal branch that Sam used to swing from — the first rung in a ladder of branches that spiral to the top of the gnarled old tree. It's ancient, Margie suspects, this stoic giant. What changes it must have endured. For twenty-seven years now, she and Dave have watched the tree shed kilograms of bark — like tired, worn suits — with the seasons. Each shedding exposes smooth white bark underneath, as perfect as the skin of a baby. A previous resident had cut firewood beside the tree and must have lodged his axe in its trunk for safekeeping. In places, these deep, old wounds have penetrated through to the new skin, like memories, but mostly the old bark has taken the scars with it. The giant has healed itself. She respects its resilience. Its capacity to recover and continue to grow. Its preparedness, year after year, to expose its soft inner layers. To be vulnerable.

She hears a car pull up outside. 'I think they're here, love,' she calls out from the veranda.

'I'll be right up.' Dave doesn't move. He remains ankle-deep in old bark. 'I'll just finish tying this off. It's not quite straight. And I have to fix the belt. Can't have our boy falling out.'

Margie watches as his practised, sea-worn hands work the knots and secure the ropes, and she imagines that they shake, just a little. It's nerve-racking, she concedes, meeting one's past and future all at once.

LOGBOOK OF EDUARDO RODRÍGUEZ TORRES

⌒

She was so beautiful that day, more beautiful even than when we first met. Her skin, softer than I remember it when we were teenagers, her hair still like silk. I'll never forget the way her dress, dotted with red flowers, fell from her shoulders.

⌒

JULIA
Montevideo, Uruguay
10 December 2002

Finally, Julia is bringing her baby home. She is nervous and excited in the same heartbeat. As she enters the hospital nursery, this time with both her mother and María, the nursing staff are waiting for her. They have dressed little Eduardo in the clothes Julia had brought in for him and are enjoying a final cuddle. These are the high points for them too, Julia realises. The rewards of working in a high-pressure environment where life and death are such close neighbours. To some extent, little Eduardo must also feel like *their* baby.

Julia is handed her son and gives him a kiss on the forehead. Her mother leans across and strokes his hair.

'Beautiful baby,' she says through tears.

'It's the first time you've seen him, isn't it?' one of the nurses asks Julia's mother.

'I thought it was better luck to wait until today, the day our little boy is coming home,' Julia's mother says. 'I didn't want to believe it until now.'

'Can I have a hold, *Mamá*? Please?' María is jumping up and down in anticipation. Julia tells her to sit in a chair before handing her the baby. The nurses remark on the resemblance of the siblings.

'Can we keep him now, *Mamá*?' María asks, losing herself in her brother's eyes.

'*Sí*,' Julia says, but she knows it will be some time before any of them really believe that little Eduardo is now theirs to keep.

The baby turns his head to the side and María notices his folded ear. 'Look, *Mamá*. His ear is all bent. Just like Uncle Eduardo's!'

'So it is,' Julia says, wondering why it hasn't yet flattened out. The doctor had suggested it would, given time. She is aware of her mother scrutinising her.

'Is that why you called him Eduardo?' María persists. 'Because of his bent ear?'

'No.' Julia laughs, but there is a sinking feeling in her belly. '*Papá* chose that name because Uncle Eduardo was such a good friend of ours. Do you think it suits your baby brother?'

'*Sí*,' María says, bending down and kissing him on the ear.

Julia gently straightens out the folded cartilage with her fingers, but when she lets go it bends over again, just as it did when little Eduardo was first born. Maybe the doctor was wrong, she thinks.

She feels the hairs rise on her forearms.

'Here's his medical book,' one of the nurses says. 'See how much he has grown since he first arrived. He's three times the size!'

Julia kisses her son on top of his downy head as she scans the information recorded in the book:

Name: Baby Sánchez Pereira
Date of Birth: 4.10.02
Gestation: 27 weeks
Birth Weight: 890g
Gender: Male
Blood group: AB positive

His birthdate seems a lifetime ago but it is his blood group that has caught her attention. Her own blood group is A, and Carlos's, she remembers, is O. She had committed these facts to memory in case of an emergency. The sick, panicky feeling grows, crowding Julia's chest and throat. She has taught biology for long enough to know that in no circumstance can parents with blood groups O and A produce a baby with the blood group AB. She examines her baby's face and scrutinises his bent ear, which, she realises now, has nothing to do with prematurity and everything to do with his father.

She feels the hairs rise again on her arms but this time the panic creeps all the way to her shoulders and across the back of her neck.

'*Jesús*,' she says out loud.

The nurse turns quickly to the baby. 'What's wrong?'

'It's nothing,' Julia lies.

'It's sad that Uncle Eduardo has died,' María says. 'He won't be able to make my baby brother a book the same as mine.'

Julia's throat constricts, suffocating her with concealed emotion. 'Maybe you can share yours with him,' she manages to say before standing up and walking quickly to the bathroom to let out the sobs caught in her throat.

Back at home, Julia lies on her bed and nurses her son, following the contours of his malformed ear with her finger. Had she been in complete denial, even to herself, not to have made the connection before now? But it hadn't even occurred to her. With her medical history, she'd always assumed that she was wholly to blame for the fertility problems that had plagued her marriage to Carlos. She'd thought it was next to impossible to fall pregnant after a single encounter with another man. She'd never really even considered the possibility.

'Eduardo,' she whispers into his hair. Perhaps she's the only one who needs to know. It's her doing; why should anyone else suffer the consequences? Carlos doesn't deserve this, and neither does María, or Virginia and her daughters. Least of all this new little life in her arms. How could she have been so stupid?

María and her baby brother will only ever be half-sister and -brother, Julia thinks with a shock of guilt. She fears the secret will stand between them like an invisible wall, keeping them always apart. It's her punishment. Something she'll have to live with. She remembers that Eduardo's son was born the day he died. It's as if their baby was taking his earthly place.

Julia wipes at her eyes, and thinks of Eduardo's parents, and the fact that they will never know that they had a grandson. They will never hold little Eduardo and, in smelling his soft, baby head, know that their own son lives on. She contemplates the comfort — the future — she is denying them.

The phone rings and Julia's mother answers it. 'It's Carlos,' she calls out.

Julia swaddles her son in his blanket and takes him with her to the phone, blotting her eyes again with the tissue. Her mother looks at her aslant but says nothing. Perhaps she knows the truth, somehow. Perhaps she has always known.

'So, his first day at home,' Carlos says from a detention house in Fremantle. He and Manuel have forfeited their passports but are, for now, free to move about town. The rest of the crew has been flown home. 'Is he doing okay?'

'*Si*. It's wonderful to have him here. María adores him. She won't leave him alone.' Julia wonders whether he can discern — by some change in her voice — her secret.

'I've been meaning to check if you've managed to see Virginia yet?' Carlos asks. 'She's much too young to have been made a widow.'

'*Sí*, I saw her,' Julia replies, not wanting to elaborate on their encounter at La Paloma.

'Is she doing all right?'

'I think so. As well as can be expected. I only saw her briefly. She needed time to herself, and I felt I was intruding.'

'Well, at least you've let her know you're there for her if she needs you.'

Julia is relieved to hear the familiar strength in her husband's voice and hopes to never again hear him cry. She won't let that happen. She signals to María to come and talk to her father, to deflect the attention from herself. 'There's someone here who really wants to talk with you.'

Julia holds the phone out to María but crouches down so she can hold it to her own ear as well. Her mother takes the baby without saying a word.

'*¡Papá!*' María squeals. 'Little Eduardo has come home. Did *Mamá* tell you?'

'*Sí*, I can't wait to meet him,' Carlos replies, his voice soft and gentle for his daughter. 'And to give *you* a huge cuddle.'

'When will you get here? *Mamá* says she doesn't know.'

Julia runs her hands through her hair, her fingernails travelling in parallel paths over her scalp, from her forehead to the nape of her neck. She thinks of how many times she has leant on Carlos — her anchor — and how few demands he has placed on her. She has taken him for granted.

'Just as soon as I can, my beautiful daughter. *Mamá* will explain more soon. It's complicated, but just remember I love you and I'll be there with you as soon as I can.'

'All right. *Papá,* Cecilia says you're in trouble for stealing fish.'

Julia is surprised. How dare Cecilia talk with María about any of this.

'Well, that's what the Australians are saying,' Carlos responds. 'But it's a big ocean, and it's not always clear whose fish are whose.'

'Do people own the fish? I thought they were everybody's.'

'I wish it were that simple. They're so yummy that everyone wants them.'

'Aren't there enough?'

'No, *mi chica*. There aren't enough. Not for everybody. Not any more.'

'Does that mean you'll stop going away, *Papá*?'

'When I get home, María sweetheart, I'll make sure I don't go to sea again for a long time.'

'Never?'

'That's something I'll have to talk to *Mamá* about. Can you please put her back on, my love?'

'I'm still here,' Julia says as María lets go of the phone. She stands up straight, and María skips back to the book she was reading: *El Pez* by Eduardo. 'Children certainly ask the hard questions,' Julia says, attempting a laugh, but it sounds forced, even to herself. 'So what do you think? Will you be fishing again?'

'It's not that simple. You know that. But I won't fish if you don't want me to.'

'Maybe María is right. Maybe it *is* that simple. But let's just take one step at a time. We need to get you home first.'

Julia tries to visualise her husband by the phone in the Western Australian detention house and wonders how long it will be before she sees him again. He has emailed some photographs of himself on expansive beaches and in the shopping malls of a neat, clean-looking city. The locals are all well-dressed. Affluent. Perhaps it's because they have never travelled abroad together, but when Julia looked at those pictures, she was surprised to find herself feeling jealous. Jealous that Carlos could be in such a place without her, and jealous of the seemingly carefree lifestyle of the locals.

'What are you doing for the rest of the day?' she asks.

'Probably going for a walk on the beach. God knows how much longer I'll have even this much freedom.'

Julia pictures Carlos dressed in his cap and sunglasses walking alone on the Australian sand. She sees him anew and wonders, for the first time, if her handsome husband will attract the interest of any of the local women.

'*Te quiero,*' she tells him.

CARLOS
Fremantle, Australia
1 October 2003

Carlos Sánchez is on the Fremantle docks, watching as the Australian they call Cactus carves part of the *Pescador*'s confiscated catch into thick fillets for the launch of his new diving and charter-boat business, 'Pirate Dives Down Under'. God knows what it'll taste like, Carlos thinks, after being frozen for so long. It's nearly one year since he arrived, under escort, in Fremantle. Tomorrow he will fly home, just in time to see his son turn one.

He watches as the ruddy-faced Australian arranges the white-fleshed fillets on a portable barbecue on the dock, with the impounded boat as a backdrop, for the occasion. The fish is seared quickly on both sides, and a woman called Connie is being kept busy dousing the cooked fish in lemon juice. Wafts of scorched seafood sail in the warm Fremantle air, whetting the appetites of the waiting media scrum.

Television cameras are filming a whole toothfish, the one they had kept for Migiliaro's wall trophy. It seems the Australian liked the boat-owner's idea and has had the two-metre specimen preserved and mounted onto a piece of polished jarrah. Carlos reads the words painted in gold lettering on the timber above the fish:

THE ILLEGAL FISHING VESSEL THE *PESCADOR*

APPREHENDED BY THE *AUSTRALIS*

OCTOBER 6, 2002

AFTER A TWENTY-DAY HOT PURSUIT ON THE SOUTHERN OCEAN.

— THE LONGEST SEA CHASE IN MARITIME HISTORY —

[SENIOR APPREHENDING CREW: CAPTAIN DAVE BATES,

MR HARRY PERDMAN AND MR JACK 'CACTUS' EVERETT]

Carlos has already answered a few questions for the media, at Cactus's request. The Australian paid him three hundred dollars just to turn up. Now it's Cactus's turn in front of the cameras.

'Accordin' to our young fisheries compliance officer,' Cactus says to one of the reporters within Carlos's hearing, 'she's probably thirty-five or forty years old and never swam more than twenty nautical miles from her subantarctic home. And now, she's clocked over eight thousand nautical miles, most of it in that boat's freezer,' Cactus points at the *Pescador* behind him, 'just so we could mount 'er on a piece of wood for you fellas to film!'

'So, have I got this right?' the female journalist asks. 'They were caught in Australian waters without authority, so the Australian government are within their rights to forfeit the catch and sink the boat. But because no one could prove that the crew were actually fishing at the time, they got off?'

'That's about the size of it, lovey,' Cactus says, his eyes on her tight skirt as she makes notes.

'What time is the boat being sunk?' another journalist asks, taking his mobile phone from his jacket pocket.

'Ten minutes or so,' Cactus replies. 'Get those cameras rollin'.'

When the news goes to air that night, Carlos Sánchez is back in the detention house. Just yesterday his passport had been returned, and he was offered a hotel room, but it seemed ridiculous to change his accommodation for just one night.

He sees a close-up of the *Pescador* on the screen and calls out to Manuel, who had opted not to join him at the docks, to come and see. Cactus is being interviewed and Carlos shakes his head when the Australian talks up his plans to use the *Pescador* as a dive site, the star attraction of his new business.

'It's such a waste!' Carlos says, as images of the *Pescador*, still afloat, fill the TV screen. Only a few hours ago, he had been there to watch her go down.

'It's not our problem any more,' Manuel says. 'You should just be pleased we got off. Eduardo must be looking out for us.'

Carlos tilts his head to the side as if briefly entertaining the possibility, but he doesn't take his eyes off the television.

'You were right not to admit anything.' Out of the corner of his eye he sees Manuel slowly nodding, and knows he'll be thanking his lucky stars that he also escaped charge over Dmitri's death. If the Uruguayan government hadn't believed the crew's claims that Manuel had shot the Russian in self-defence, the Spaniard could have been jailed for murder. 'I suspect young José's going to get what he deserves, though,' Carlos adds recalling how the Peruvian teenager had wept like a baby when he admitted to police that he had shot Roberto Cruz without provocation.

He runs his hand over Eduardo's logbook, which is resting on his lap. The Australian Federal Police gave it to him, just yesterday, after the trial, saying that it contained nothing of interest to them. Both men fix their eyes on the image of the *Pescador* on television as the countdown starts.

'Ten, nine, eight ...'

Carlos saw the boat go down before his eyes, heard her last sigh, yet it still doesn't seem real. He remembers the dank smell of the wheelhouse and can picture what it would be like to be looking out from the helm. How could they destroy the boat that served them so well, carrying them safely through the world's most treacherous seas? She even survived the ice, something she was not built for. The *Pescador* was just the sort of boat that he and Eduardo had hoped to own themselves one day.

'Three, two, one ...'

The explosion goes off midship, and tips the boat bow up, *Titanic*-style, before sinking her.

Manuel turns off the television and goes to bed without another word. Carlos opens Eduardo's logbook at the first page and starts to read. What seem like obscure, unrelated facts — about fish, the ocean, birds and whales — Eduardo has captured in his own voice, weaving them into his personal observations about the sea. He reads four pages of the neat, small print before closing his eyes.

'Let her sink.' Eduardo's voice invades the dream. 'She's cursed. She can take her bad luck with her. Spare the fish.' The logbook begins to slide off Carlos's lap, and he dreams that it is Eduardo falling overboard. Half awake, he reaches quickly for the book as if he is once more reaching for his friend. He holds it tight, as he wished he had held Eduardo, before letting the dream return and take hold. He thinks of the other lives lost: of Roberto Cruz on his way back to Spain for a home burial, and of Dmitri, who he could, so easily, have fed without regret to the sea. He sees a toothfish, old and pierced by hooks, picking up the Russian's bones — scavenged bare by bizarre life forms at the base of the ocean — and scattering them across the abyssal plains aided by deep-ocean currents. Very occasionally a toothfish will leave its subantarctic birthplace and travel between hemispheres. Carlos imagines such a fish carrying one of Dmitri's bones for thousands of nautical miles before dropping it somewhere north of the Equator. Eduardo re-enters the dream. This time he appears in the wheelhouse of the sunken *Pescador*, his new home. The first mate is happy in these waters off the west coast of Australia. They are warmer and more hospitable than those of the subantarctic, and he spends his time tending colourful reefs. When divers visit, they meet his ghost as it moves around the ship. He warns them against taking too many fish.

The logbook falls off Carlos's lap and onto the floor, waking him. It opens at a page he hasn't yet read. He picks it up and notices that the entries have been written in a different, more cursive, hand, but it is still recognisably Eduardo's writing. He reads words of love and longing. So, I was right, Carlos thinks, remembering the soulful expression on Eduardo's face when he interrupted him writing in his log. No wonder Eduardo had slammed the book shut. In addition to recording facts about the sea, the first mate had used the logbook to open his heart. Carlos finds himself smiling. When he had suggested that Eduardo had been composing love letters to Virginia, his friend had denied it.

Carlos feels guilty for invading his friend's privacy, but cannot prevent himself from reading on. This is a side of Eduardo that he rarely saw. It is as though his best friend is whispering in his ear.

He turns the page, the last page Eduardo had written on, and reads the entry:

She was so beautiful that day, more beautiful even
than when we first met. Her skin, softer than I
remember it when we were teenagers, her hair still like
silk. I'll never forget the way her dress, dotted with red
flowers, fell from her shoulders.

Carlos stops breathing.

He walks across to the photograph, now in a eucalypt frame, of Julia in that dress. How many times did he look at this picture taped to the wheelhouse wall with Eduardo by his side? How could he not have realised what had been going on? His mind flies back in time to the beach at La Paloma. To the holidays they all spent there together. It had started then. In the photograph he sees the warmth — the love — in his wife's eyes. He takes the picture out of its frame and turns it over. *'For Julia.'* It is the same handwriting that Eduardo reserved for his most personal logbook entries. Carlos takes hold of the printout, also framed, of little Eduardo with his bent ear. Perhaps part of him has known all along.

The feeling that rises inside him he can't define. If it is betrayal, it hurts less than he imagined. If it is anger, he is not sure who to punish. His best friend is dead and Julia has suffered enough. Whatever has happened between them is over. And, Carlos knows, it can't be undone.

He decides, at that moment, never to think of this again. He will not mention it to another living soul. Not even to

Julia. Eduardo had always hoped for a son to carry on the fishing tradition when he was gone. That boy needs a father.

Carlos takes a long breath as vast as the ocean.

When he is back home in Montevideo next week, he will let Migiliaro know that he has kept all his original correspondences telling him where to fish, including the owner's explicit order to input false data into the vessel monitoring system when fishing in the waters off Heard Island. He will tell him that unless he agrees to certain conditions he will send the information to the authorities in both Australia and Uruguay. Uruguayan Fisheries would then be obliged, under international law, to cancel all of Migiliaro's fishing permits. The conditions, Carlos will insist, are that he be given a good boat, a licence to fish and money in the bank, US$250,000, half of which he will give to Virginia.

Carlos's eyes fall again on Eduardo's logbook as if he is seeing into the soul of the first mate himself. He promises to fish legally, within the limits, just as Eduardo had dreamed of fishing. And, if there is still a toothfish fishery in two decades' time, he promises to give the little boy at home in Julia's arms the option of continuing in his father's footsteps. Perhaps then Eduardo will stop haunting his dreams.

Epilogue

While all characters and incidents described in this novel are fictitious, a chase of a Uruguayan-flagged longliner by an unarmed Australian patrol vessel did occur in 2003. The Uruguayan vessel suspected of illegally fishing Patagonian toothfish in the waters around Australia's Heard Island was the *Viarsa 1*. The Australian civil patrol vessel was the *Southern Supporter*. The chase that ensued was the longest in maritime history, covering almost four thousand nautical miles. The vessels encountered ten-metre waves, eighty-knot winds and wind-chill temperatures as low as minus twenty degrees Celsius.

Unlike the fictional *Pescador*, the *Viarsa 1* did not display its flag state at the time of arrest. It did, however, respond to radio requests from the *Southern Supporter* to identify itself. Believing the *Viarsa 1* to be in breach of the *Fisheries Management Act 1991*, the fisheries officer on board the *Southern Supporter* ordered the *Viarsa 1* to proceed to Fremantle. When that order was not observed, the *Southern Supporter* initiated the 'hot pursuit'. Fifteen days into the pursuit, the crew of the *Viarsa 1* raised the Uruguayan flag, advising that they had been arrested by Uruguayan authorities ordered home to Montevideo to be investigated by their flag state. The mid-Atlantic boarding on 28 August 2003 was assisted by a South African icebreaker deployed from Marion Island, and a UK patrol vessel dispatched from the Falkland Islands. The *Viarsa 1* was then escorted back to Fremantle, where Western Australia's Department of Fisheries invited tenders for the catch of Patagonian toothfish.

Vessel Monitoring System (VMS) records provided to the Australian Government by the Uruguayan Government for the week leading up to the first sighting show the vessel being three thousand nautical miles from its alleged location.

The *Viarsa 1*'s Uruguayan master and four senior crew members were held in a Fremantle merchant seamen's hostel for two years awaiting the outcome of legal hearings. In November 2005, a Perth District Court jury acquitted the men, from Uruguay, Spain and Chile, on all counts. The *Viarsa 1* has since been wrecked in India.

Australian Associated Press (AAP) reported that the Uruguayan master would retire from fishing to be with his family once he returned home.

Australia is now patrolling the Southern Ocean with a vessel armed with twin deck-mounted machine guns. The vessel will also carry an armed Customs boarding party. It is encouraging the implementation of a catch-documentation scheme to make it more difficult to sell illegal, unreported or unregulated catches.

A Coalition of Legal Toothfish Operators (COLTO) was formed in 2003, appealing for any information on toothfish pirates. It has received many calls.

Acknowledgments

My thanks to the following for assistance with this novel: Sophie Hamley, for her enthusiasm and insight; Jo Butler, for her sensitive and considered editing; Peter Bishop and Linda Funnell for the wonderful opportunity that is the Varuna HarperCollins Awards for Manuscript Development; the Macquarie Group Foundation for the LongLines Program; Arts Tasmania; the Tasmanian Writers' Centre and Rosie Dub and Janice Bird, for their early comments on the manuscript.

And for their expertise in matters relating to illegal fishing, the toothfish fishery, fisheries science, seamanship, maritime electronics, the United Nations International Law of the Sea, naval operations and medicine, my thanks to: Martin Exel and David Carter (Austral Fisheries Pty Ltd); Darby Ross; Graham Robertson, Dick Williams and Steve Nicol (Australian Antarctic Division); Keith Sainsbury, Matt Sherlock, Don McKenzie and Al Graham (CSIRO Marine and Atmospheric Research); Marcus Haward (University of Tasmania, School of Government); Commander Andrew McCrindell (Royal Australian Navy); and Scott Wilson (general practitioner). For information on Uruguay and Spanish language, thanks to Hermes Morales Grosskopf,

Victoria Villar Vidal and Mauricio Duarte. For information on Russian language, thanks to Helen Kaminskaya. Any errors are my own.

Various sources were used to draw information for the novel. They include: *Mysteries of the Deep,* edited by Joseph J. Thorndike, Jr; *Ocean Enough and Time* by James Gorman; *Antarctica: An Encyclopedia from Abbott Ice Shelf to Zooplankton,* edited by Mary Trewby; 'Extinction, survival or recovery of large predatory fishes' in the *Philosophical Transactions of the Royal Society Series B* in 2005 by Ransom Myers and Boris Worm; 'Rapid Worldwide Depletion of Predatory Fish Communities' in *Nature* 423 in 2003 by Ransom Myers and Boris Worm; COLTO and TRAFFIC websites; *'South America on a Shoestring',* Lonely Planet Guide, and 'Viarsa captain praises justice system', Australian Associated Press, 7 November 2005; 'Report of Members' Activities in the Convention Area: Australia 2002-03 (CCAMLR)', <www.ccamlr.org/pu/E/e_pubs/ma/02-03/australia.pdf.>

Personal thanks to my family, particularly my parents Susan and Robert Bleakley, and friends. Heartfelt thanks, of course, to my husband, Craig Johnson, for his unwavering support and belief in this book, and to my children for their inspiration and patience.

Celebrating New Writing

THE HARPERCOLLINS VARUNA AWARDS FOR MANUSCRIPT DEVELOPMENT

The HarperCollins Varuna Awards for Manuscript Development has been a successful and productive program since 2000 in developing manuscripts of fiction and narrative non-fiction.

The program provides five new or emerging writers each year with the experience of working closely with a senior in-house editor from HarperCollins Publishers on the development of a manuscript at Varuna, the Writers' House in the Blue Mountains of New South Wales. The awards aim to give practical assistance to writers to bring their work to publication.

Many books have resulted from the program since its inception in 2000. One of the writers from that year, Ian Townsend, was selected on the basis of a thriller he was writing. At a certain point, he realised that this book was a practice book, and that he was ready for the real thing. With the support of his editor, he worked on a new idea that became the novel *Affection*. *Affection* was longlisted for the 2007 Dublin IMPAC literary award, and shortlisted for the 2006 Commonwealth Writers' Prize for Best First Book, the Foundation of Australian Literary Studies' Colin Roderick

Award for the best Australian book of 2005, and the 2005 Vance Palmer Prize for Fiction in the Victorian Premier's Literary Awards. His new novel, *The Devil's Eye*, was published by HarperCollins Publishers in 2008.

Other recent HarperCollins Varuna Awards publications include Pip Newling's memoir *Knockabout Girl*, Mark O'Flynn's novel *Grass Dogs*, and Kim Huynh's memoir *Where the Sea Takes Us*. In addition to *Pescador's Wake*, in 2009 Siew Siang Tay's sensitive and subtle exploration of the world of a mail-order bride, *Handpicked*, will be released.

For more information visit:

www.varuna.com.au/harpercollinspathways.html